PETER PANZERFAUST

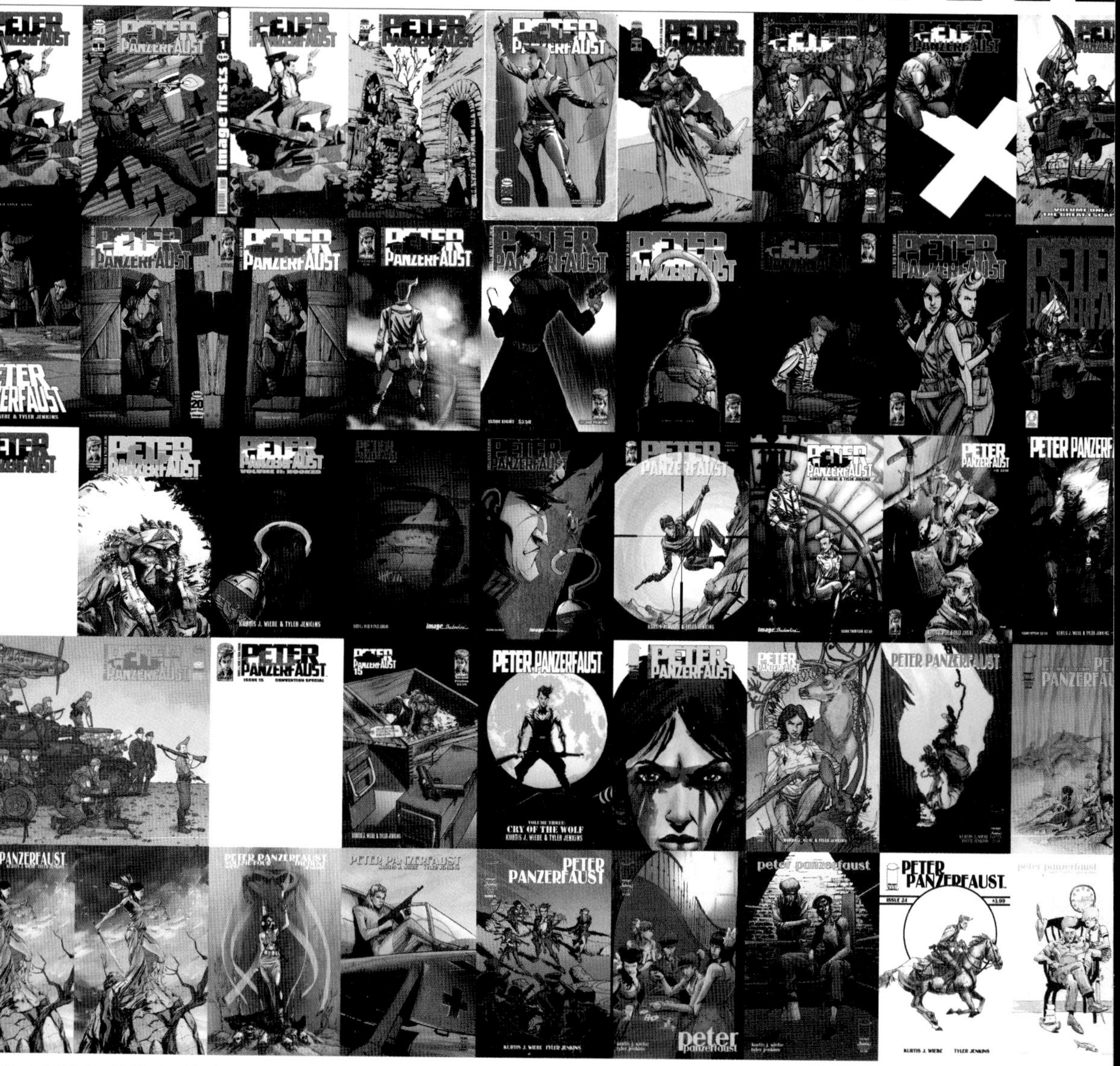
PETER PANZERFAUST
image firsts
KURTIS J. WIEBE & TYLER JENKINS
ISSUE 15 CONVENTION SPECIAL
VOLUME THREE: CRY OF THE WOLF
KURTIS J. WIEBE & TYLER JENKINS
peter panzerfaust
ISSUE 24
$3.99
KURTIS J. WIEBE TYLER JENKINS

VOL. 5: ON 'TIL MORNING

image® COMICS PRESENTS

KURTIS J. WIEBE
WRITER

TYLER JENKINS
ILLUSTRATOR,
COLORS issues 24-25

ROC UPCHURCH
issue 21 cover A

MICHAEL AVON OEMING
issue 21 cover B

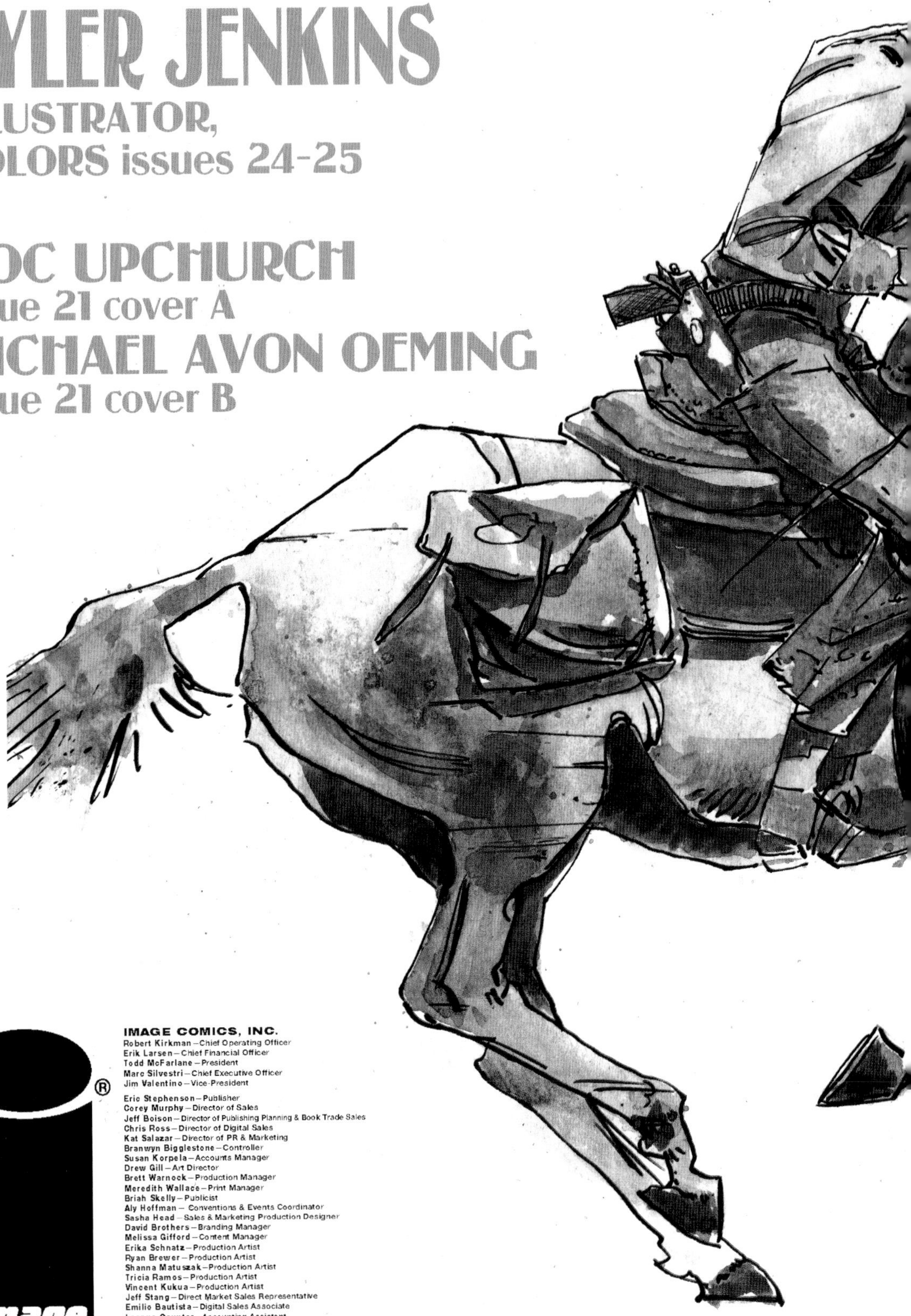

IMAGE COMICS, INC.
Robert Kirkman—Chief Operating Officer
Erik Larsen—Chief Financial Officer
Todd McFarlane—President
Marc Silvestri—Chief Executive Officer
Jim Valentino—Vice-President

Eric Stephenson—Publisher
Corey Murphy—Director of Sales
Jeff Boison—Director of Publishing Planning & Book Trade Sales
Chris Ross—Director of Digital Sales
Kat Salazar—Director of PR & Marketing
Branwyn Bigglestone—Controller
Susan Korpela—Accounts Manager
Drew Gill—Art Director
Brett Warnock—Production Manager
Meredith Wallace—Print Manager
Briah Skelly—Publicist
Aly Hoffman— Conventions & Events Coordinator
Sasha Head—Sales & Marketing Production Designer
David Brothers—Branding Manager
Melissa Gifford—Content Manager
Erika Schnatz—Production Artist
Ryan Brewer—Production Artist
Shanna Matuszak—Production Artist
Tricia Ramos—Production Artist
Vincent Kukua—Production Artist
Jeff Stang—Direct Market Sales Representative
Emilio Bautista—Digital Sales Associate
Leanna Caunter—Accounting Assistant
Chloe Ramos-Peterson—Library Market Sales Representative
IMAGECOMICS.COM

ED BRISSON
LETTERS

KELLY FITZPATRICK
COLORS issues 21-23

HILARY JENKINS
ADDITIONAL COLORS issue 25

LAURA TAVISHATI
EDITS

MARC LOMBARDI
COMMUNICATIONS

JIM VALENTINO
PUBLISHER/BOOK DESIGN

A
Shadowline®
PRODUCTION

First Printing. March 2017.

ISBN: 978-1-5343-0110-8

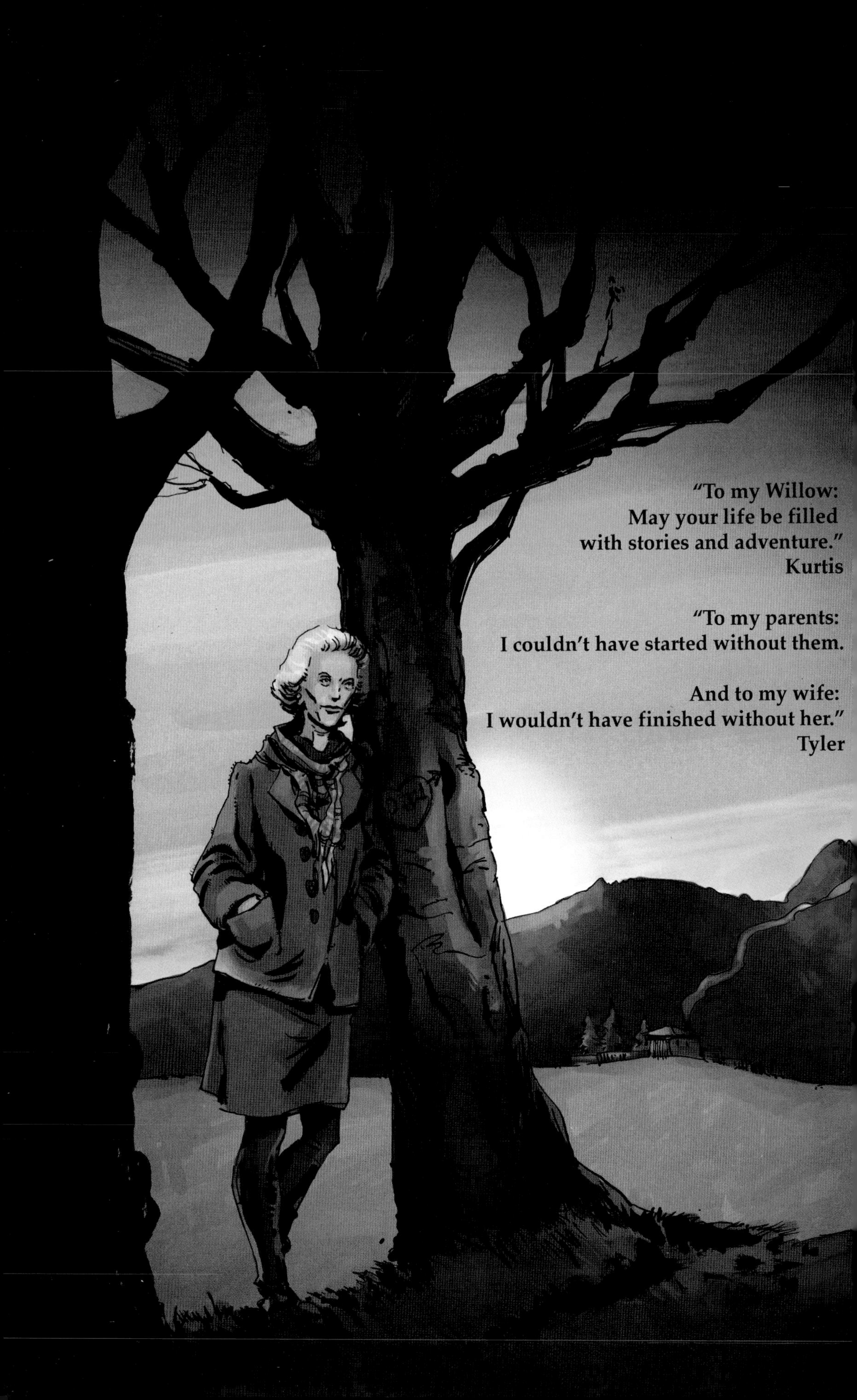

"To my Willow:
May your life be filled
with stories and adventure."
Kurtis

"To my parents:
I couldn't have started without them.

And to my wife:
I wouldn't have finished without her."
Tyler

CHAPTER TWENTY-ONE

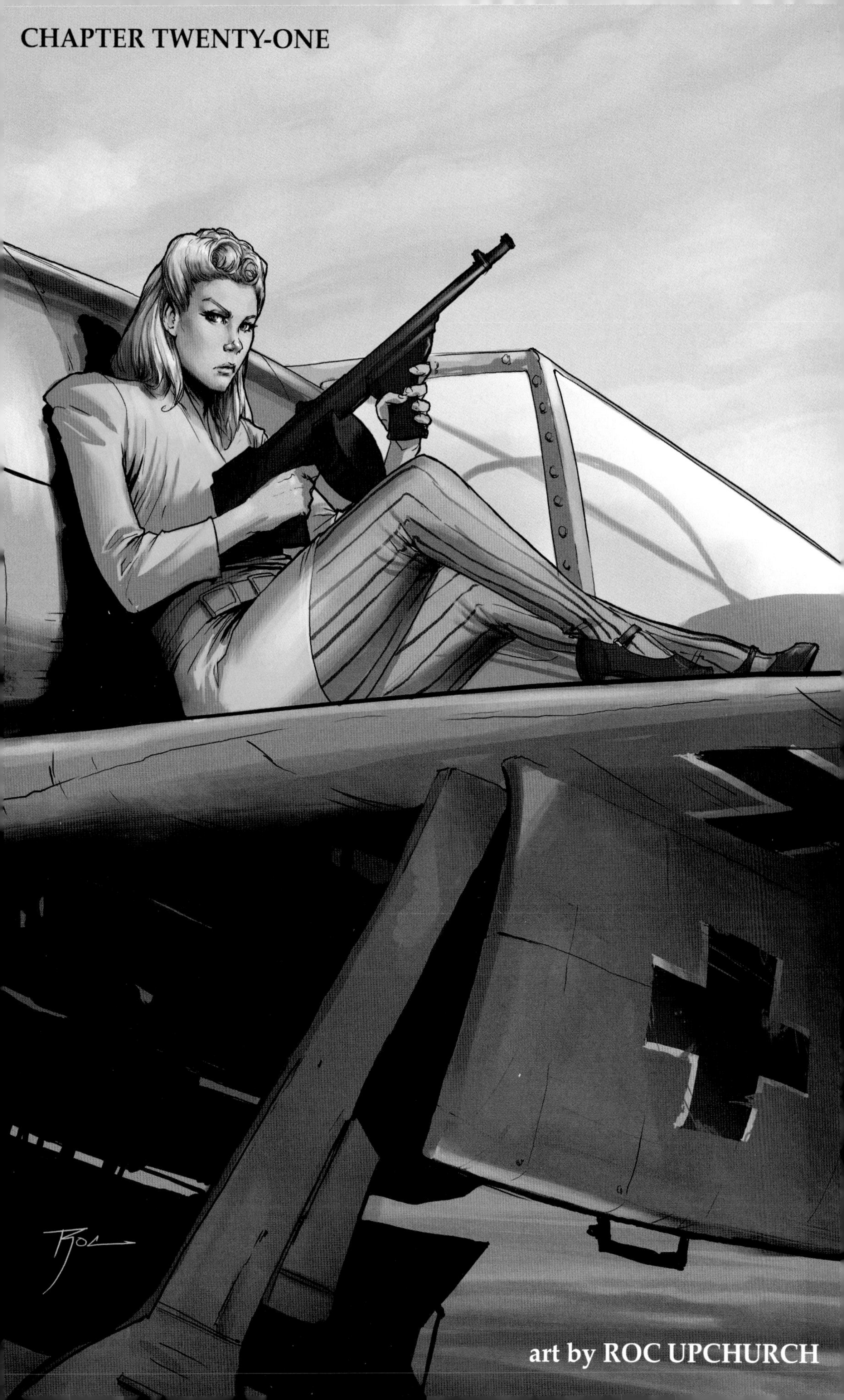

art by ROC UPCHURCH

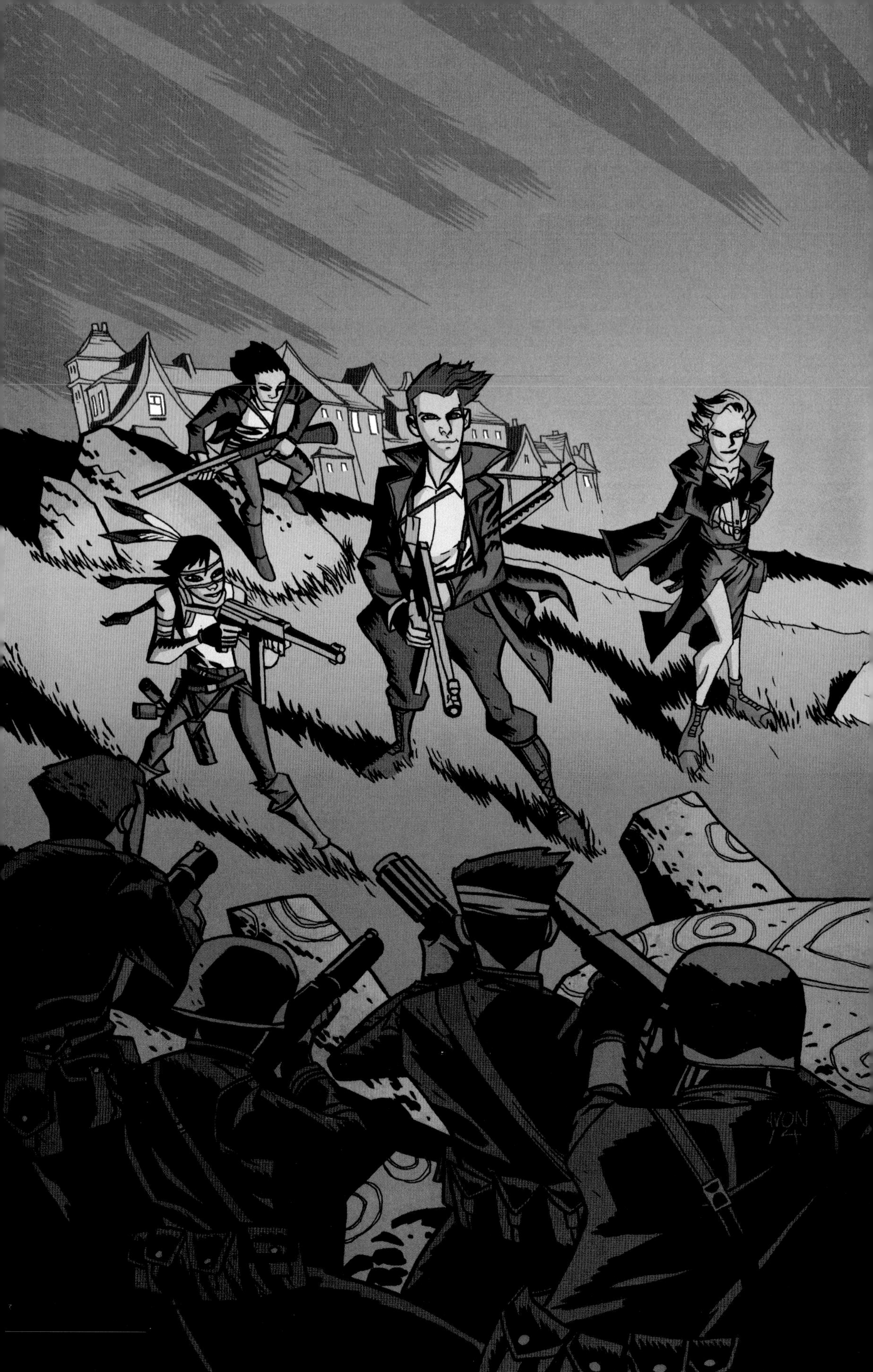

ISSUE 21 Alternate cover art by MICHAEL AVON OEMING

THE USUAL, MAURICE?

YES, PLEASE.

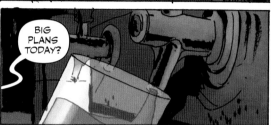

BIG PLANS TODAY?

JUST THE DAILY ADVENTURE. COUNTING DAYS BY THE PINT.

HAH! SOUNDS LIKE MY IDEAL RETIREMENT.

MIND IF I JOIN YOU?

MON DIEU.

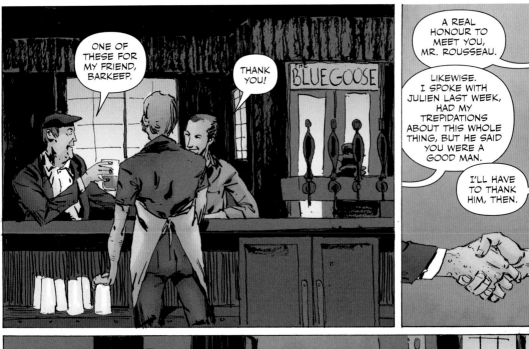

ONE OF THESE FOR MY FRIEND, BARKEEP.

THANK YOU!

THE BLUE GOOSE

A REAL HONOUR TO MEET YOU, MR. ROUSSEAU.

LIKEWISE. I SPOKE WITH JULIEN LAST WEEK, HAD MY TREPIDATIONS ABOUT THIS WHOLE THING, BUT HE SAID YOU WERE A GOOD MAN.

I'LL HAVE TO THANK HIM, THEN.

SO, YOU'RE LOOKING FOR STORIES ABOUT PETER.

THAT'S PART OF IT, YES. AT LEAST, THAT WAS THE ORIGINAL INTENT WHEN I SET OUT ON THIS JOURNEY. I THINK IN A LOT OF WAYS IT'S BECOME SOMETHING ELSE.

OH?

IN SEARCHING FOR PETER, I'VE UNCOVERED SO MUCH MORE.

HE'S PART OF A MUCH BIGGER STORY, A STORY I COULD NEVER HAVE IMAGINED.

YOU'RE BEING DRAMATIC, NOW.

WHY DO YOU SAY THAT?

IT'S A STORY, AS ANY OTHER, EXPERIENCED BY THOUSANDS OF PEOPLE LIVING IN THAT TIME.

THE HARD PART WASN'T SURVIVING THE WAR, IT WAS FIGURING OUT WHAT TO DO WITH THE TIME AFTER IT.

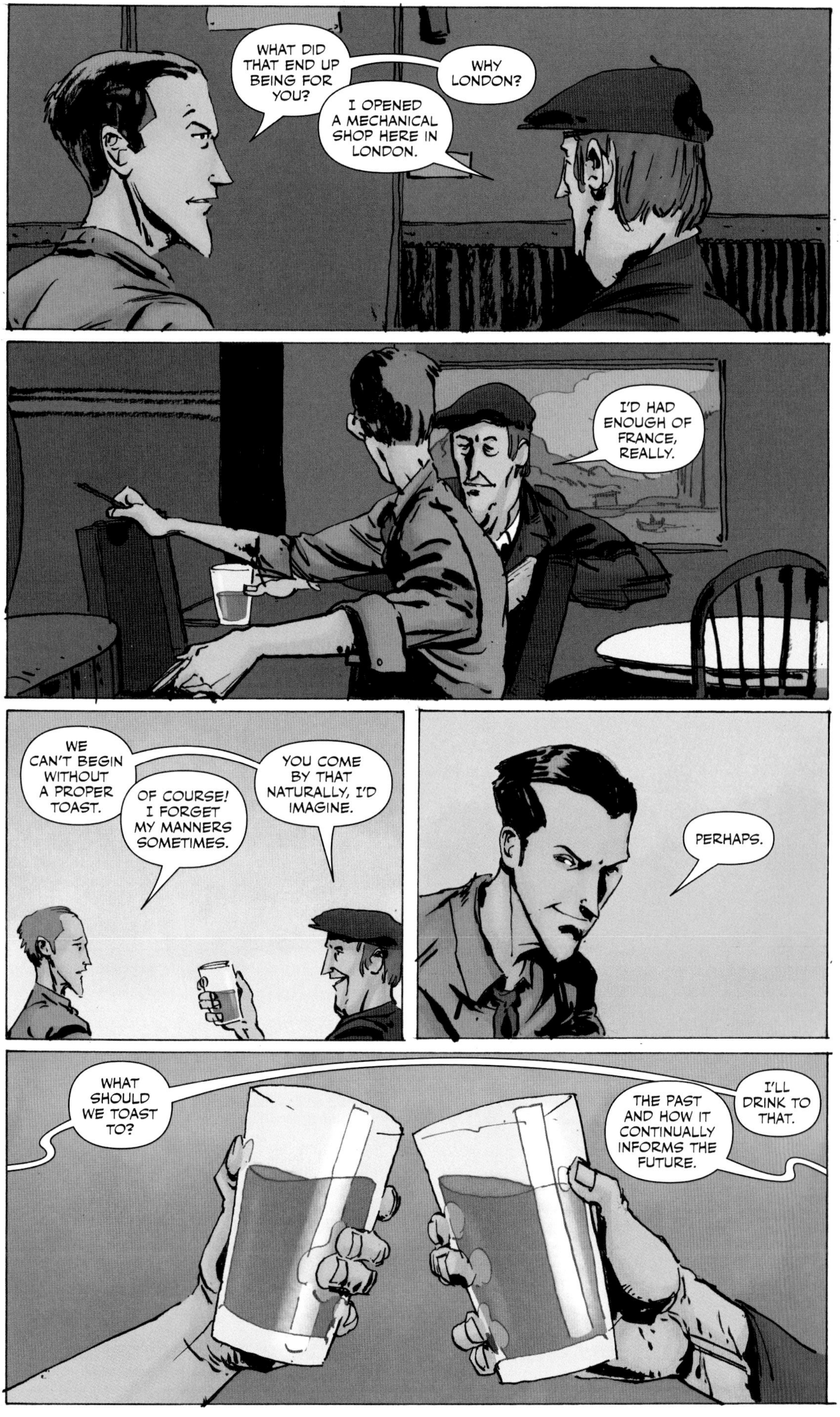
WHAT DID THAT END UP BEING FOR YOU?
I OPENED A MECHANICAL SHOP HERE IN LONDON.
WHY LONDON?
I'D HAD ENOUGH OF FRANCE, REALLY.
WE CAN'T BEGIN WITHOUT A PROPER TOAST.
OF COURSE! I FORGET MY MANNERS SOMETIMES.
YOU COME BY THAT NATURALLY, I'D IMAGINE.
PERHAPS.
WHAT SHOULD WE TOAST TO?
THE PAST AND HOW IT CONTINUALLY INFORMS THE FUTURE.
I'LL DRINK TO THAT.

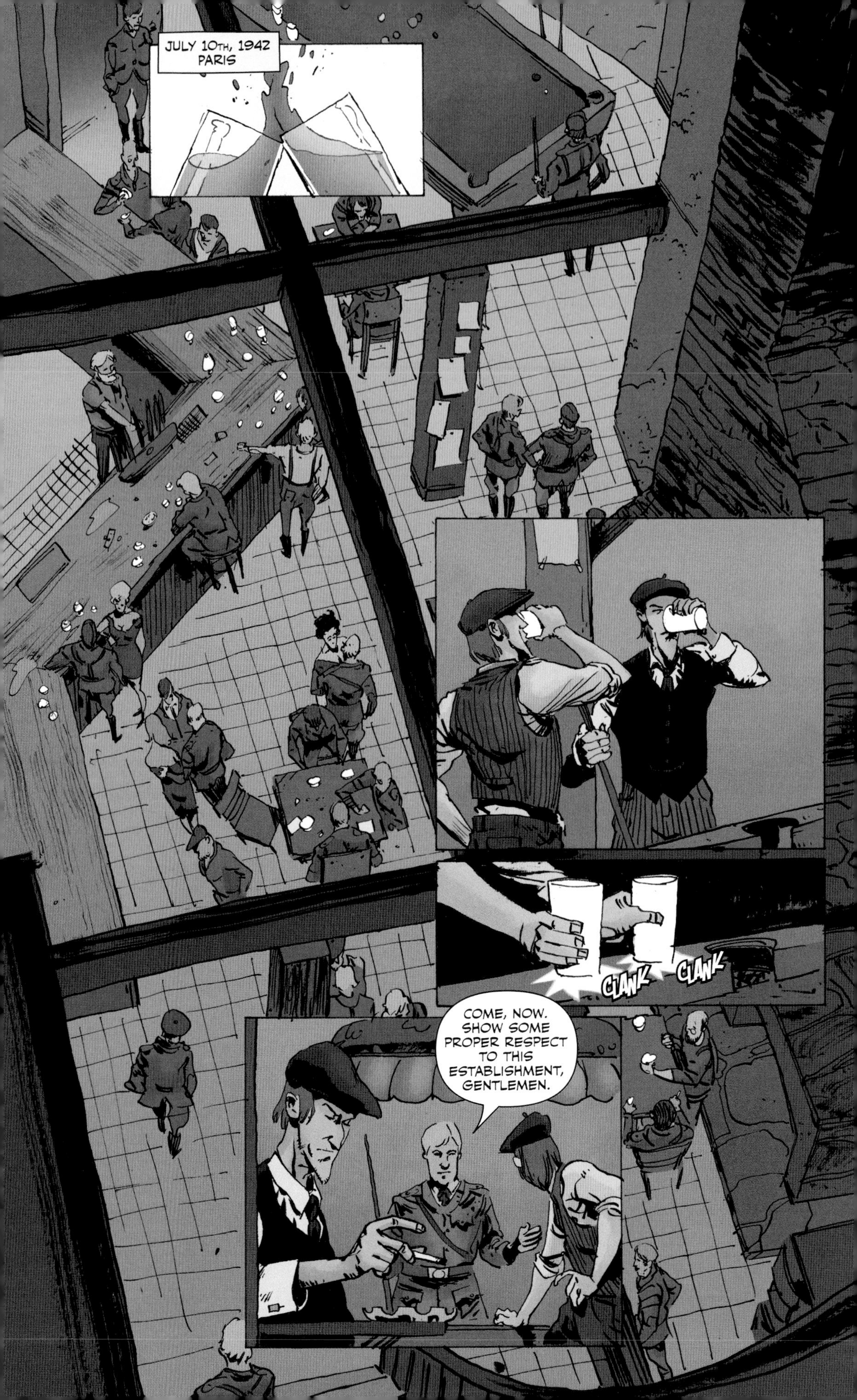
JULY 10TH, 1942
PARIS
CLANK
CLANK
COME, NOW. SHOW SOME PROPER RESPECT TO THIS ESTABLISHMENT, GENTLEMEN.

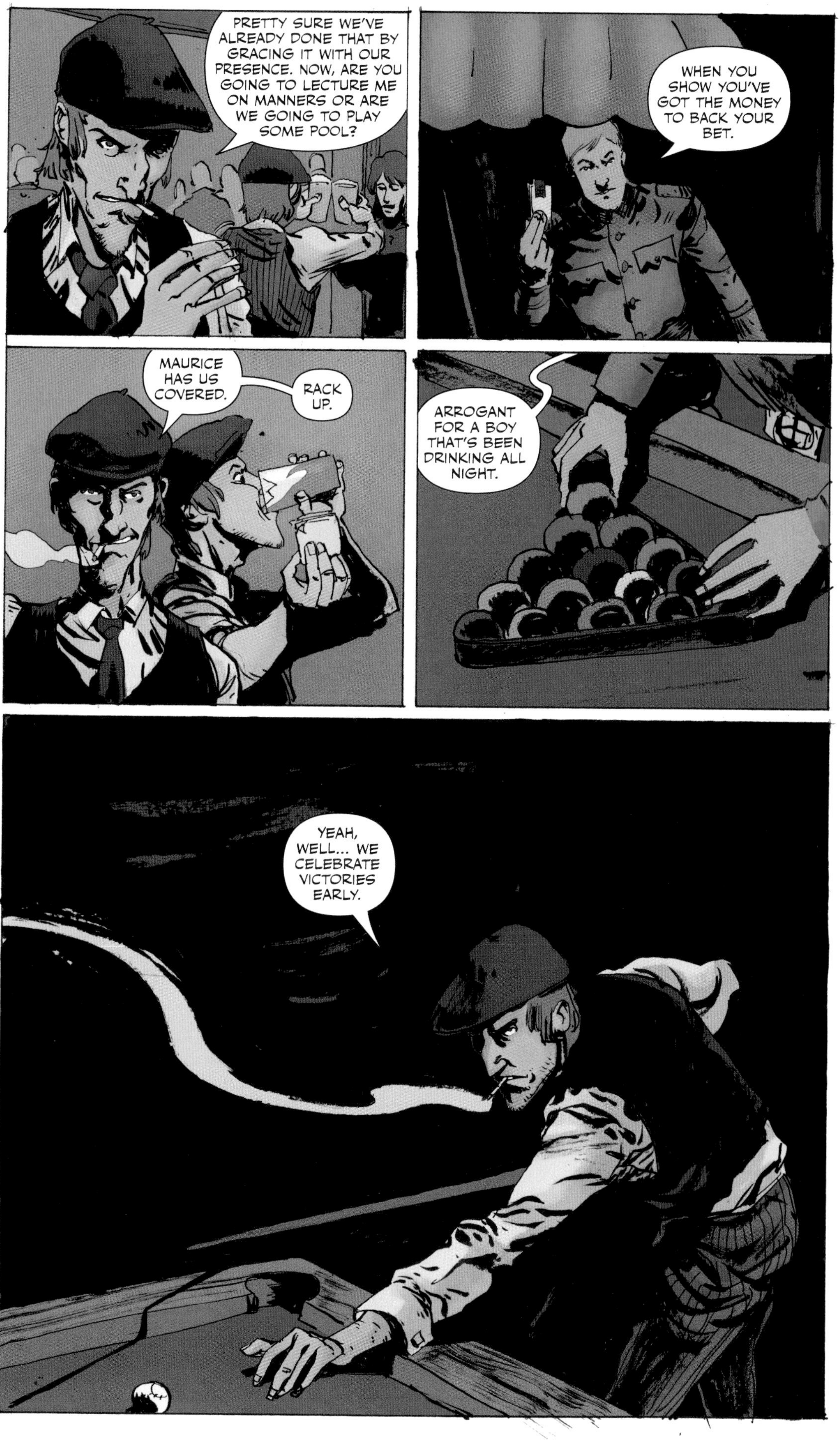
PRETTY SURE WE'VE ALREADY DONE THAT BY GRACING IT WITH OUR PRESENCE. NOW, ARE YOU GOING TO LECTURE ME ON MANNERS OR ARE WE GOING TO PLAY SOME POOL?
WHEN YOU SHOW YOU'VE GOT THE MONEY TO BACK YOUR BET.
MAURICE HAS US COVERED.
RACK UP.
ARROGANT FOR A BOY THAT'S BEEN DRINKING ALL NIGHT.
YEAH, WELL... WE CELEBRATE VICTORIES EARLY.

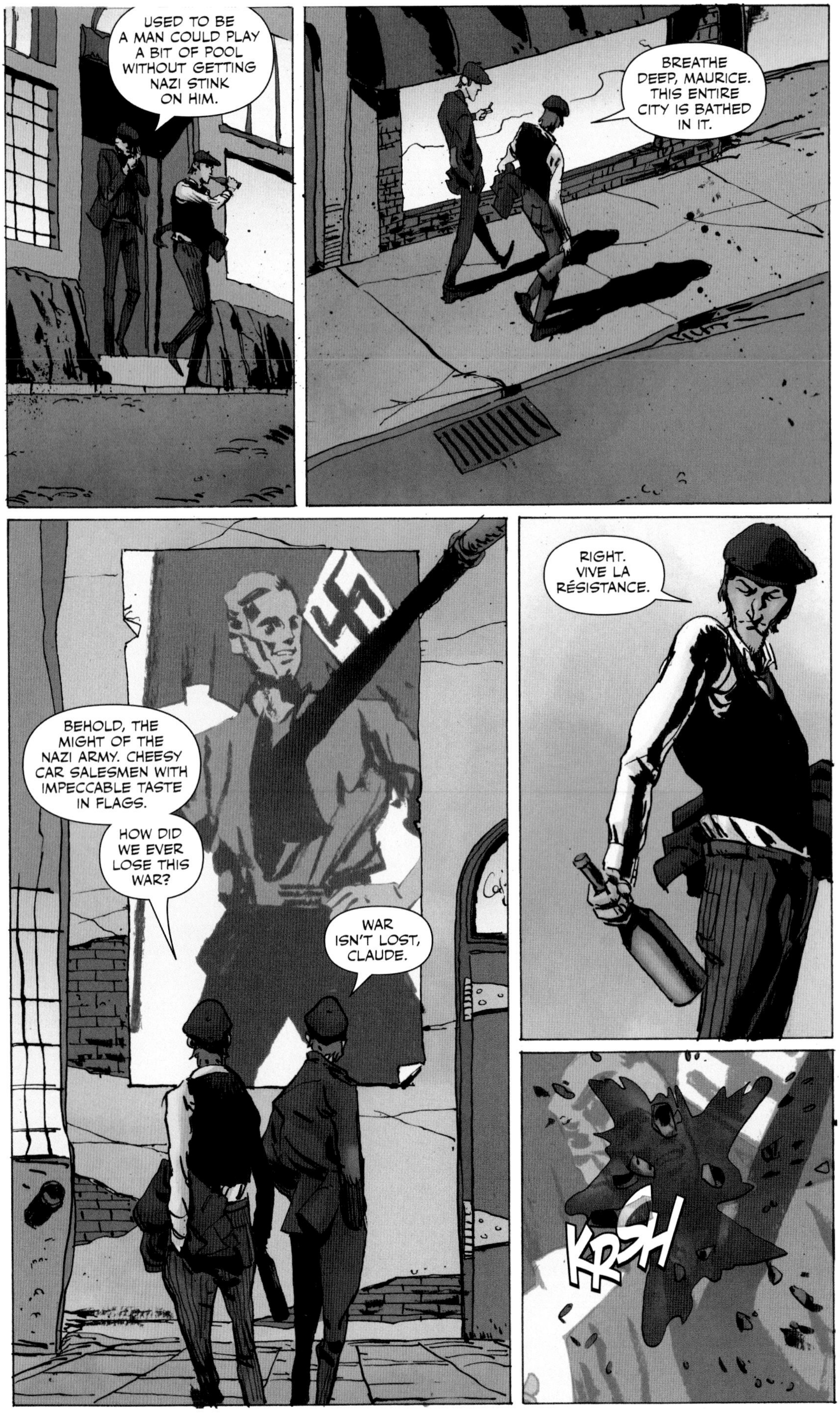
USED TO BE A MAN COULD PLAY A BIT OF POOL WITHOUT GETTING NAZI STINK ON HIM.
BREATHE DEEP, MAURICE. THIS ENTIRE CITY IS BATHED IN IT.
BEHOLD, THE MIGHT OF THE NAZI ARMY. CHEESY CAR SALESMEN WITH IMPECCABLE TASTE IN FLAGS.
HOW DID WE EVER LOSE THIS WAR?
WAR ISN'T LOST, CLAUDE.
RIGHT. VIVE LA RÉSISTANCE.
KRSH

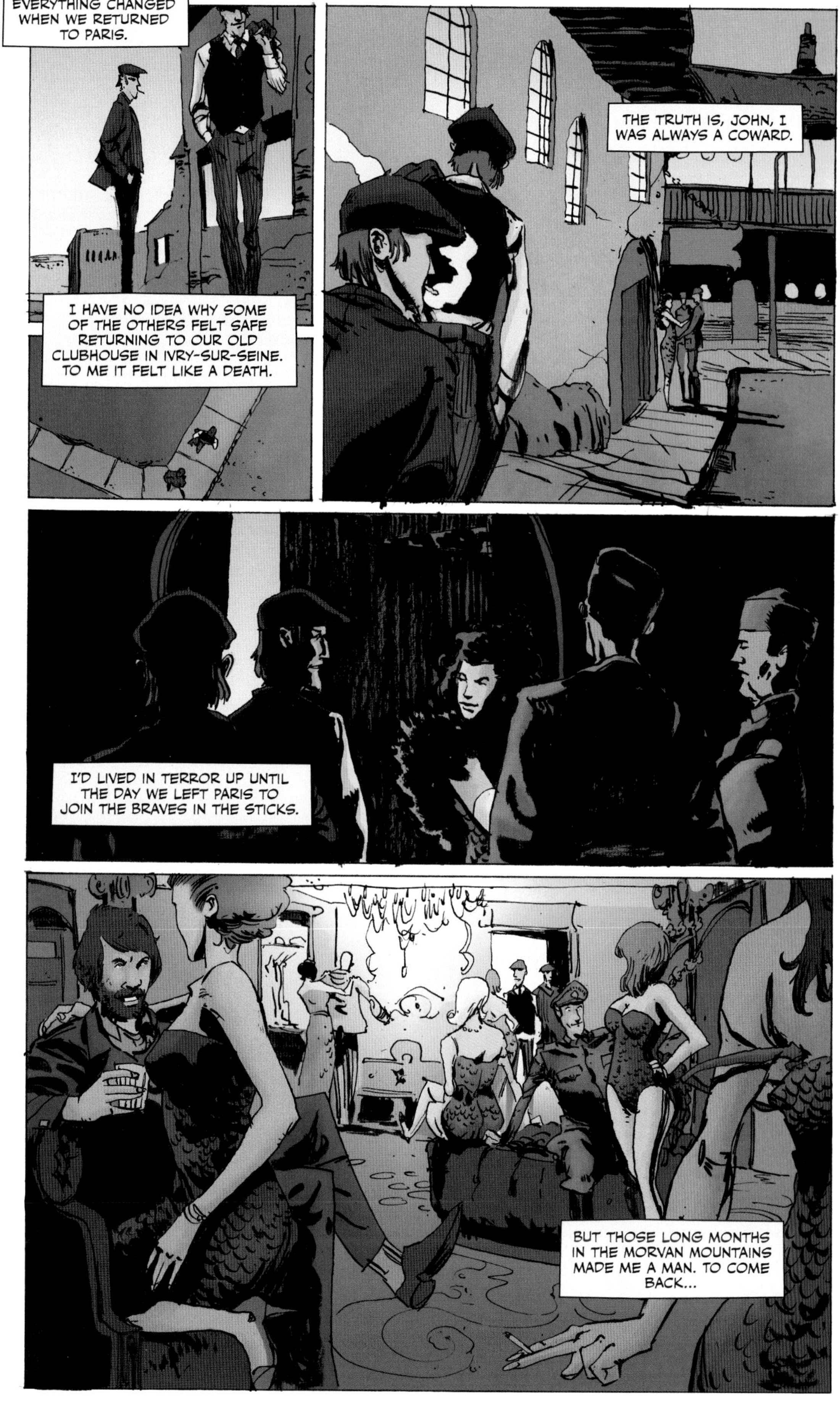

EVERYTHING CHANGED WHEN WE RETURNED TO PARIS.
I HAVE NO IDEA WHY SOME OF THE OTHERS FELT SAFE RETURNING TO OUR OLD CLUBHOUSE IN IVRY-SUR-SEINE. TO ME IT FELT LIKE A DEATH.
THE TRUTH IS, JOHN, I WAS ALWAYS A COWARD.
I'D LIVED IN TERROR UP UNTIL THE DAY WE LEFT PARIS TO JOIN THE BRAVES IN THE STICKS.
BUT THOSE LONG MONTHS IN THE MORVAN MOUNTAINS MADE ME A MAN. TO COME BACK...

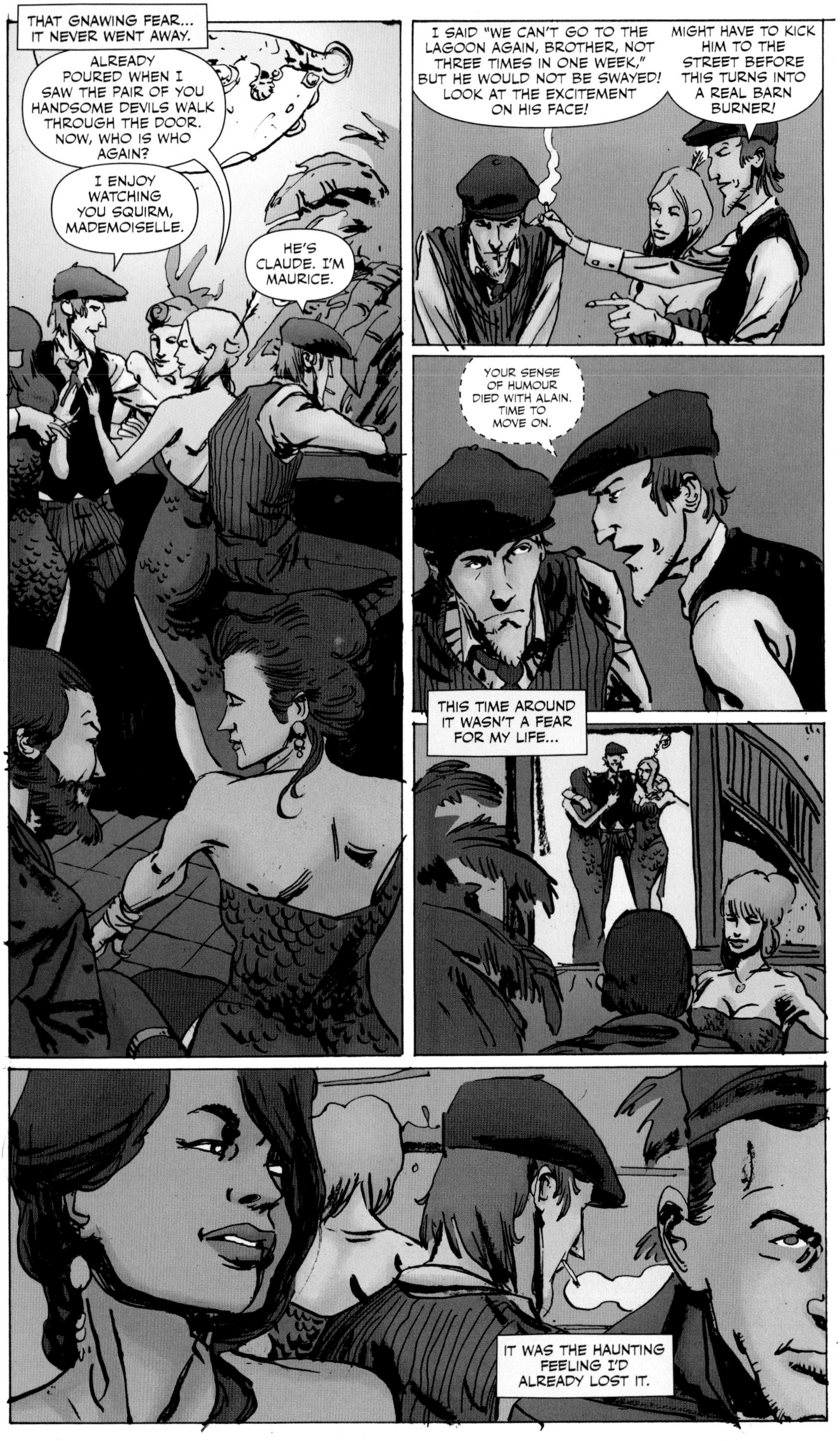

THAT GNAWING FEAR... IT NEVER WENT AWAY.
ALREADY POURED WHEN I SAW THE PAIR OF YOU HANDSOME DEVILS WALK THROUGH THE DOOR. NOW, WHO IS WHO AGAIN?
I ENJOY WATCHING YOU SQUIRM, MADEMOISELLE.
HE'S CLAUDE. I'M MAURICE.
I SAID "WE CAN'T GO TO THE LAGOON AGAIN, BROTHER, NOT THREE TIMES IN ONE WEEK," BUT HE WOULD NOT BE SWAYED! LOOK AT THE EXCITEMENT ON HIS FACE!
MIGHT HAVE TO KICK HIM TO THE STREET BEFORE THIS TURNS INTO A REAL BARN BURNER!
YOUR SENSE OF HUMOUR DIED WITH ALAIN. TIME TO MOVE ON.
THIS TIME AROUND IT WASN'T A FEAR FOR MY LIFE...
IT WAS THE HAUNTING FEELING I'D ALREADY LOST IT.

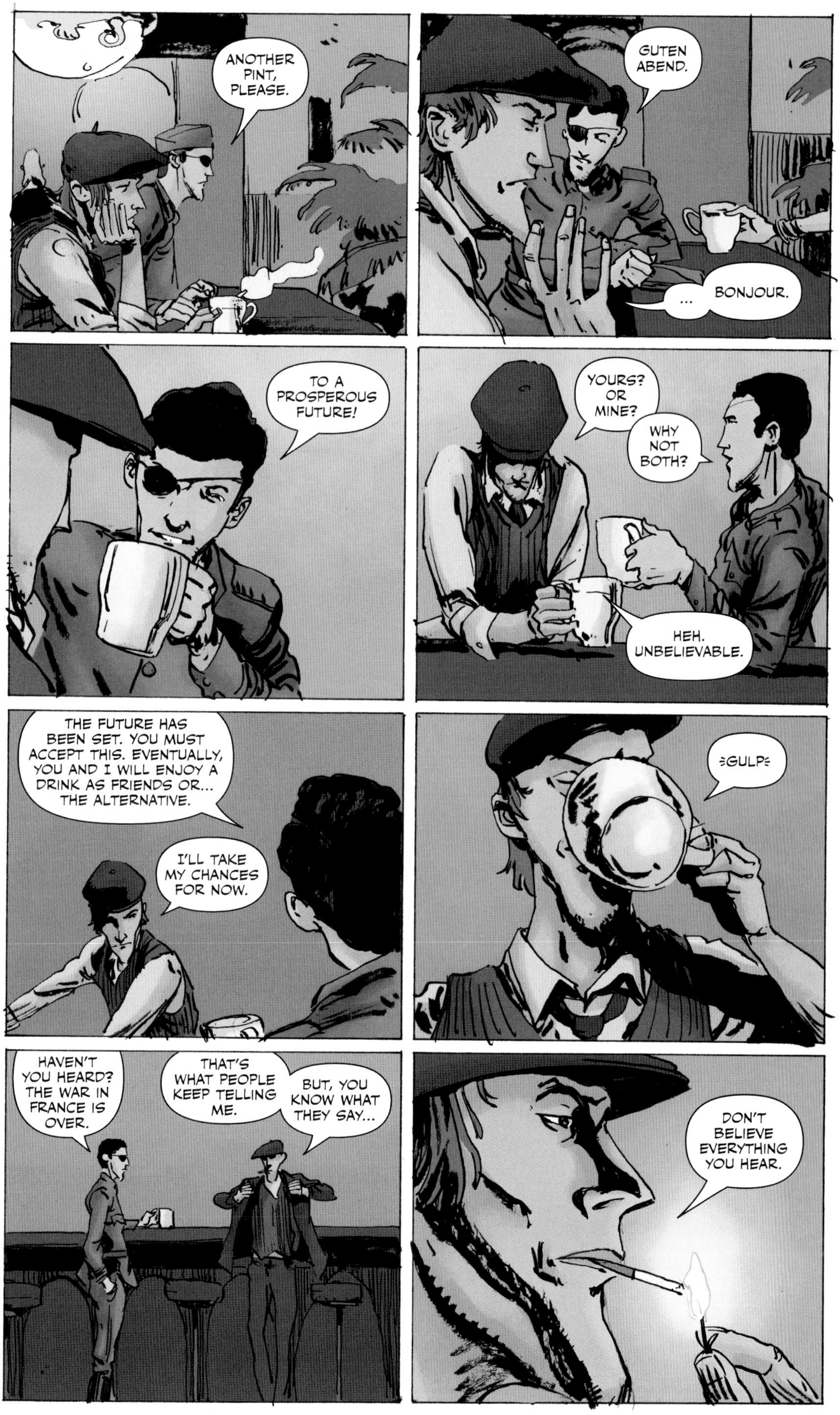
ANOTHER PINT, PLEASE.
GUTEN ABEND.
...
BONJOUR.
TO A PROSPEROUS FUTURE!
YOURS? OR MINE?
WHY NOT BOTH?
HEH. UNBELIEVABLE.
THE FUTURE HAS BEEN SET. YOU MUST ACCEPT THIS. EVENTUALLY, YOU AND I WILL ENJOY A DRINK AS FRIENDS OR... THE ALTERNATIVE.
I'LL TAKE MY CHANCES FOR NOW.
GULP
HAVEN'T YOU HEARD? THE WAR IN FRANCE IS OVER.
THAT'S WHAT PEOPLE KEEP TELLING ME.
BUT, YOU KNOW WHAT THEY SAY...
DON'T BELIEVE EVERYTHING YOU HEAR.

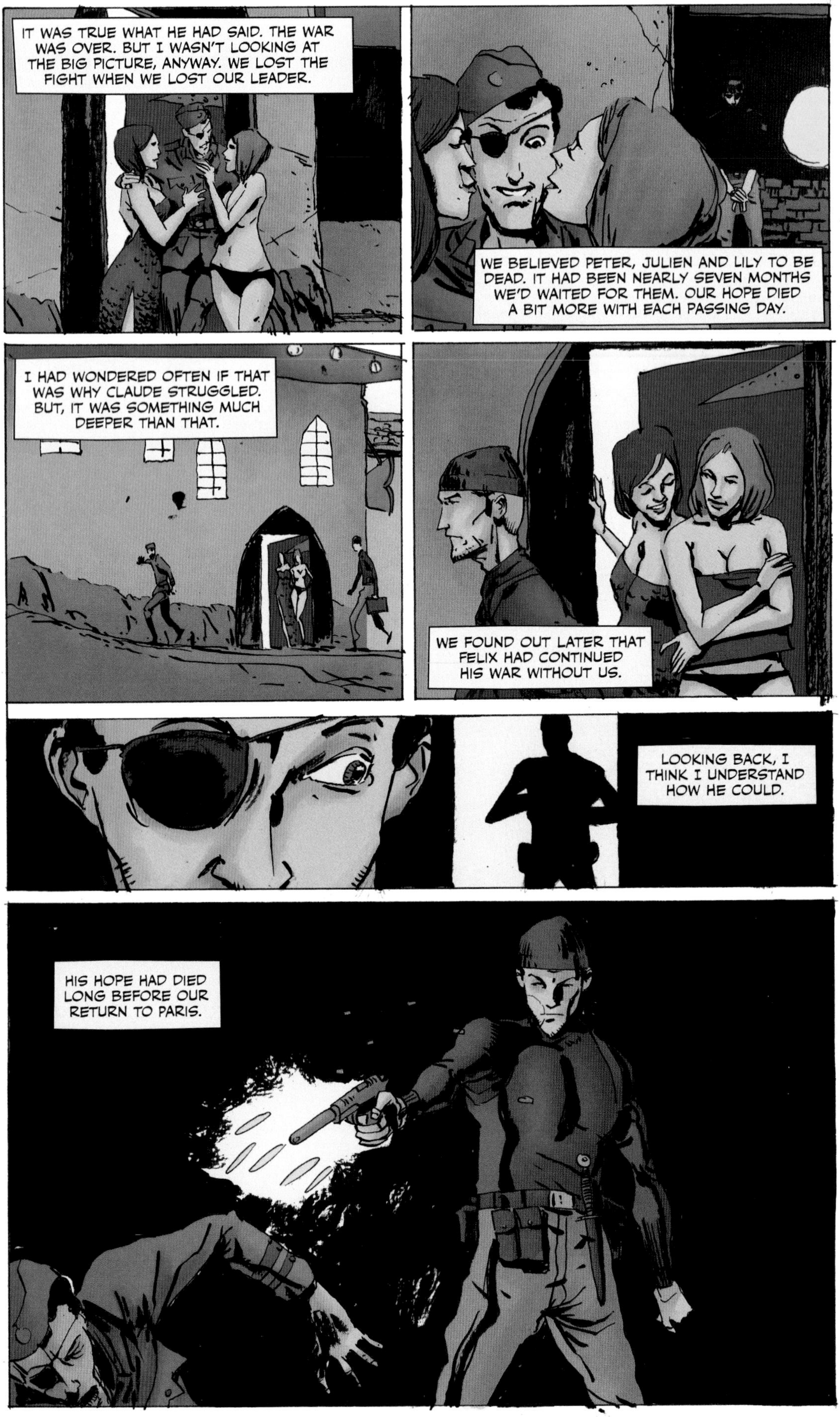
IT WAS TRUE WHAT HE HAD SAID. THE WAR WAS OVER. BUT I WASN'T LOOKING AT THE BIG PICTURE, ANYWAY. WE LOST THE FIGHT WHEN WE LOST OUR LEADER.
WE BELIEVED PETER, JULIEN AND LILY TO BE DEAD. IT HAD BEEN NEARLY SEVEN MONTHS WE'D WAITED FOR THEM. OUR HOPE DIED A BIT MORE WITH EACH PASSING DAY.
I HAD WONDERED OFTEN IF THAT WAS WHY CLAUDE STRUGGLED. BUT, IT WAS SOMETHING MUCH DEEPER THAN THAT.
WE FOUND OUT LATER THAT FELIX HAD CONTINUED HIS WAR WITHOUT US.
LOOKING BACK, I THINK I UNDERSTAND HOW HE COULD.
HIS HOPE HAD DIED LONG BEFORE OUR RETURN TO PARIS.

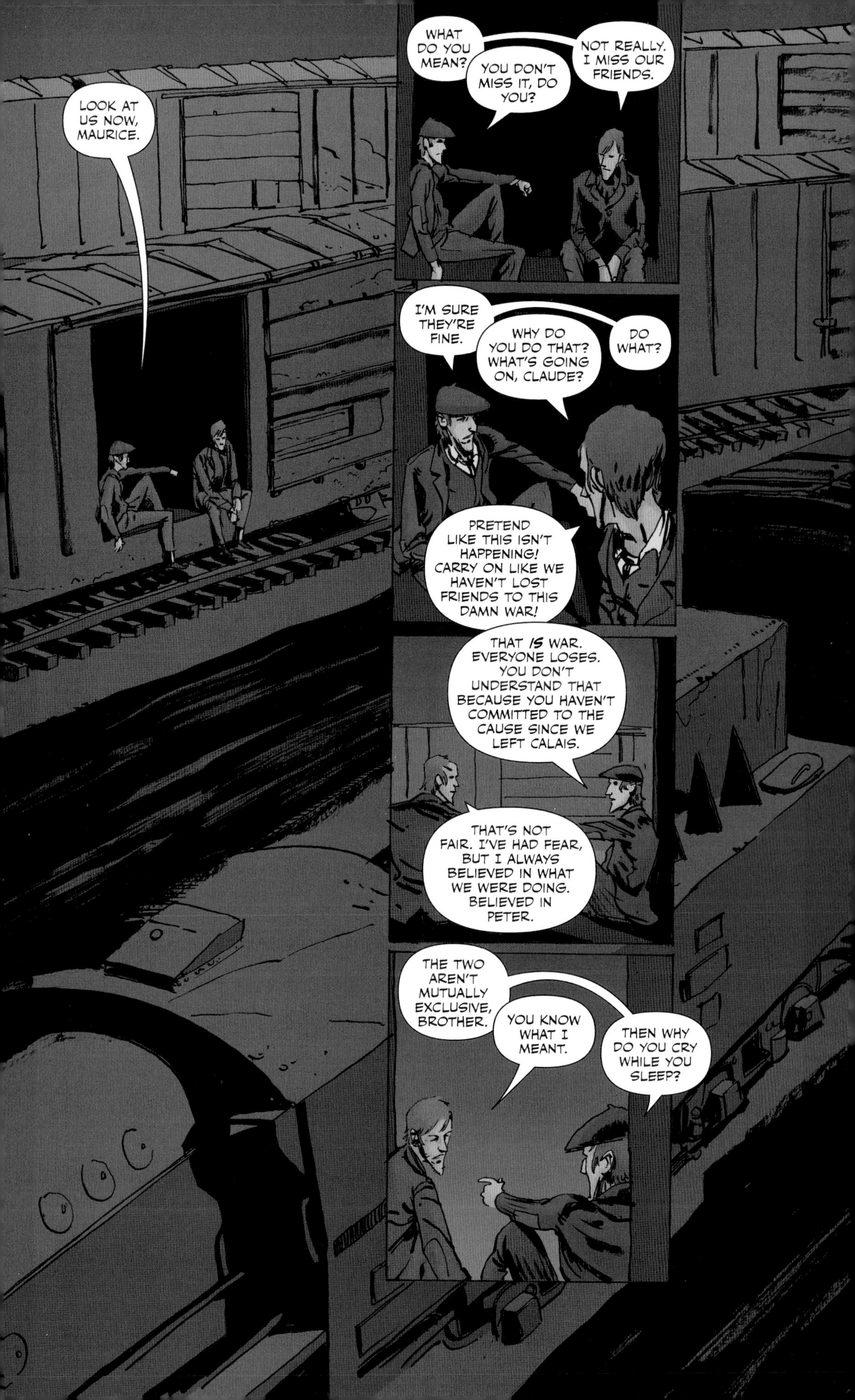
LOOK AT US NOW, MAURICE.
WHAT DO YOU MEAN?
YOU DON'T MISS IT, DO YOU?
NOT REALLY. I MISS OUR FRIENDS.
I'M SURE THEY'RE FINE.
WHY DO YOU DO THAT? WHAT'S GOING ON, CLAUDE?
DO WHAT?
PRETEND LIKE THIS ISN'T HAPPENING! CARRY ON LIKE WE HAVEN'T LOST FRIENDS TO THIS DAMN WAR!
THAT *IS* WAR. EVERYONE LOSES. YOU DON'T UNDERSTAND THAT BECAUSE YOU HAVEN'T COMMITTED TO THE CAUSE SINCE WE LEFT CALAIS.
THAT'S NOT FAIR. I'VE HAD FEAR, BUT I ALWAYS BELIEVED IN WHAT WE WERE DOING. BELIEVED IN PETER.
THE TWO AREN'T MUTUALLY EXCLUSIVE, BROTHER.
YOU KNOW WHAT I MEANT.
THEN WHY DO YOU CRY WHILE YOU SLEEP?

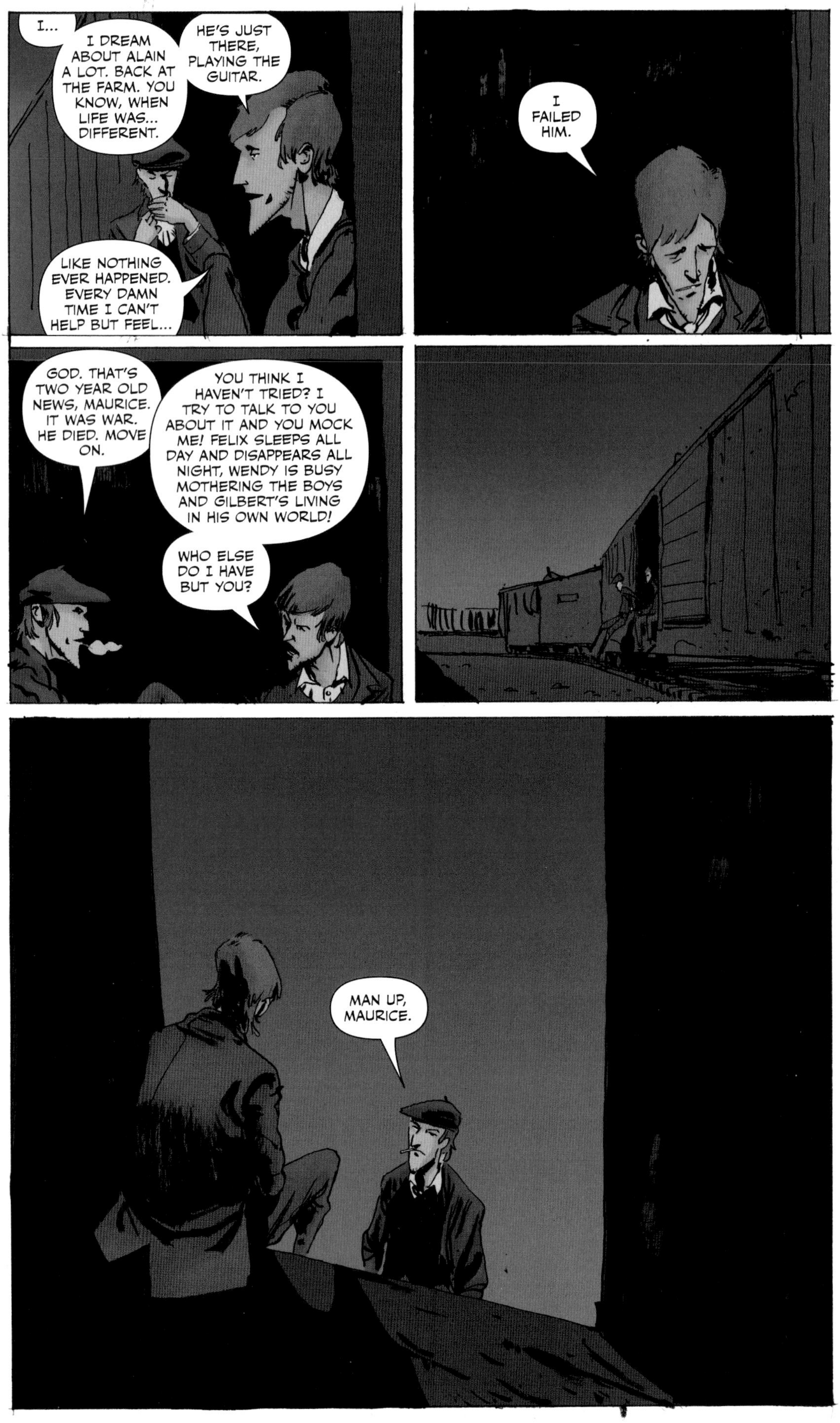
I...
I DREAM ABOUT ALAIN A LOT. BACK AT THE FARM. YOU KNOW, WHEN LIFE WAS... DIFFERENT.
HE'S JUST THERE, PLAYING THE GUITAR.
LIKE NOTHING EVER HAPPENED. EVERY DAMN TIME I CAN'T HELP BUT FEEL...
I FAILED HIM.
GOD. THAT'S TWO YEAR OLD NEWS, MAURICE. IT WAS WAR. HE DIED. MOVE ON.
YOU THINK I HAVEN'T TRIED? I TRY TO TALK TO YOU ABOUT IT AND YOU MOCK ME! FELIX SLEEPS ALL DAY AND DISAPPEARS ALL NIGHT, WENDY IS BUSY MOTHERING THE BOYS AND GILBERT'S LIVING IN HIS OWN WORLD!
WHO ELSE DO I HAVE BUT YOU?
MAN UP, MAURICE.

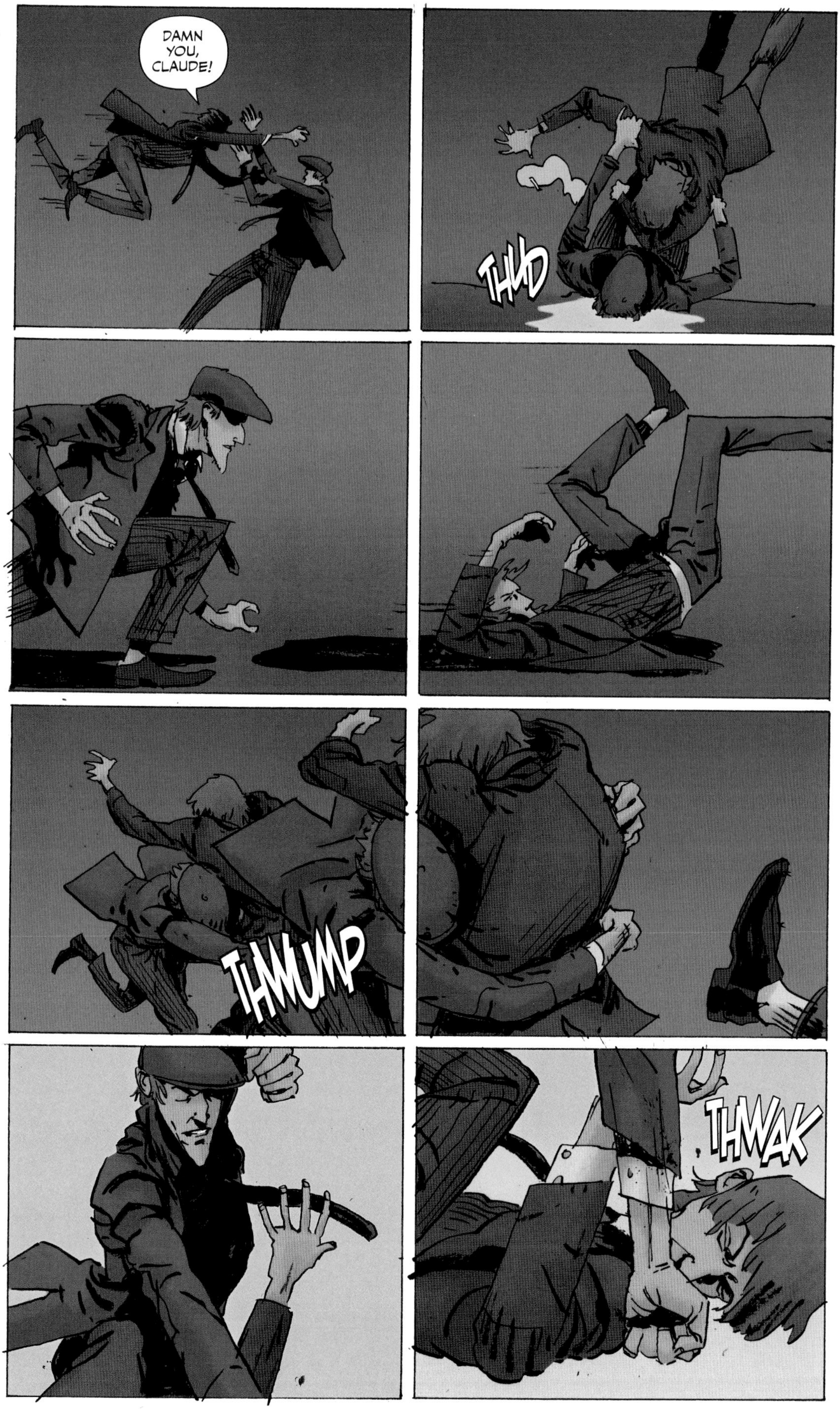
DAMN YOU, CLAUDE!
THUD
THWUMP
THWAK

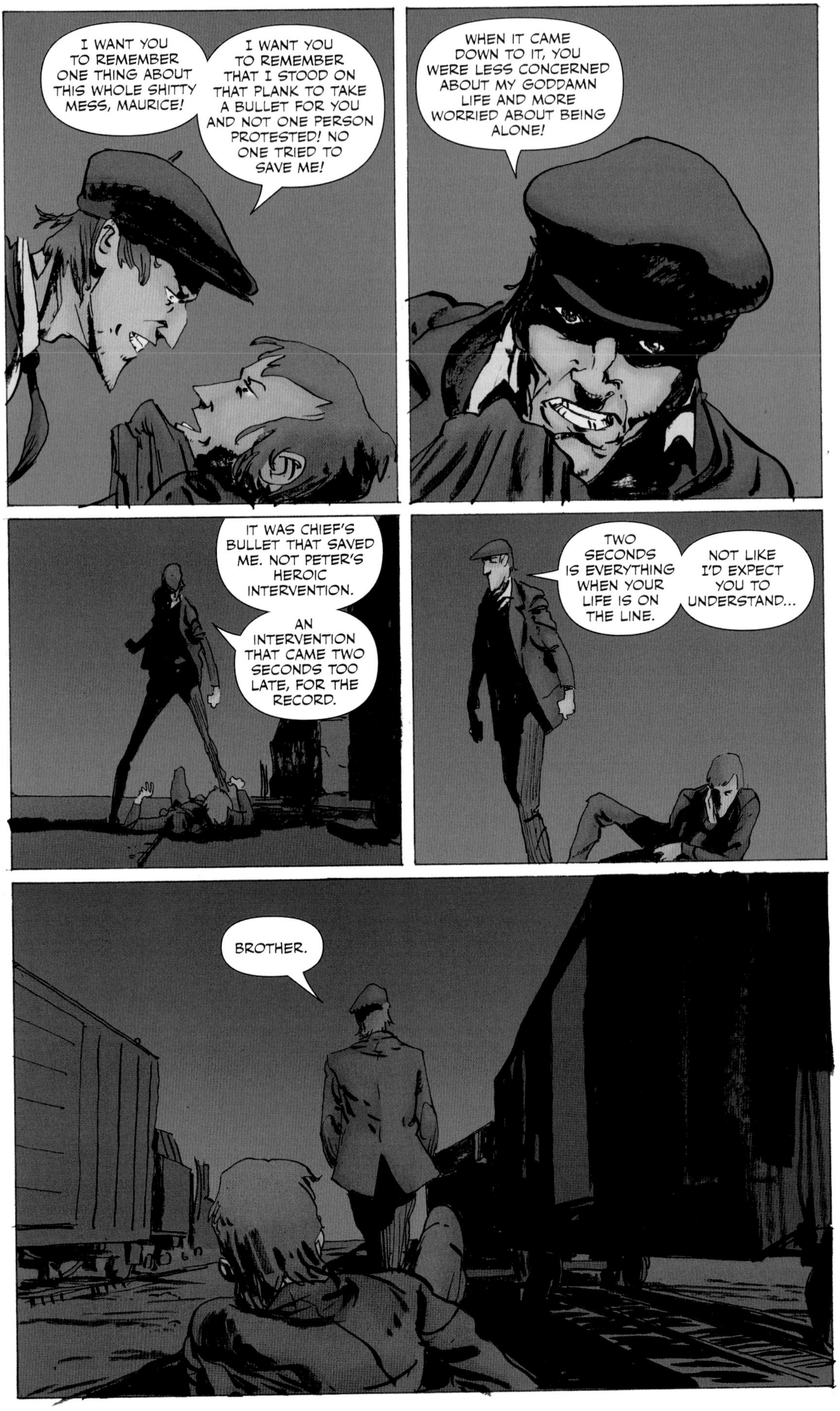
I WANT YOU TO REMEMBER ONE THING ABOUT THIS WHOLE SHITTY MESS, MAURICE!
I WANT YOU TO REMEMBER THAT I STOOD ON THAT PLANK TO TAKE A BULLET FOR YOU AND NOT ONE PERSON PROTESTED! NO ONE TRIED TO SAVE ME!
WHEN IT CAME DOWN TO IT, YOU WERE LESS CONCERNED ABOUT MY GODDAMN LIFE AND MORE WORRIED ABOUT BEING ALONE!
IT WAS CHIEF'S BULLET THAT SAVED ME. NOT PETER'S HEROIC INTERVENTION.
AN INTERVENTION THAT CAME TWO SECONDS TOO LATE, FOR THE RECORD.
TWO SECONDS IS EVERYTHING WHEN YOUR LIFE IS ON THE LINE.
NOT LIKE I'D EXPECT YOU TO UNDERSTAND...
BROTHER.

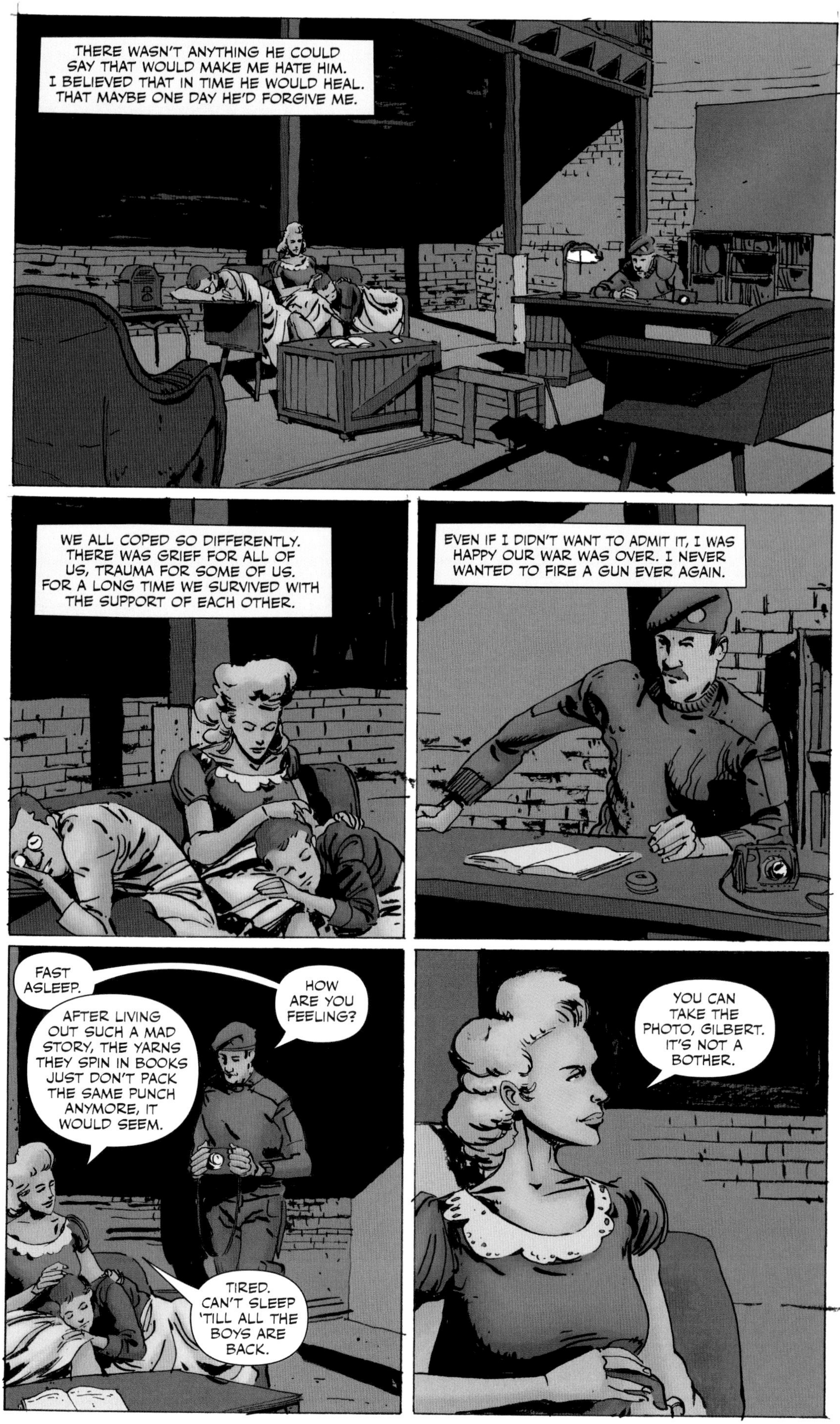
THERE WASN'T ANYTHING HE COULD SAY THAT WOULD MAKE ME HATE HIM. I BELIEVED THAT IN TIME HE WOULD HEAL. THAT MAYBE ONE DAY HE'D FORGIVE ME.
WE ALL COPED SO DIFFERENTLY. THERE WAS GRIEF FOR ALL OF US, TRAUMA FOR SOME OF US. FOR A LONG TIME WE SURVIVED WITH THE SUPPORT OF EACH OTHER.
EVEN IF I DIDN'T WANT TO ADMIT IT, I WAS HAPPY OUR WAR WAS OVER. I NEVER WANTED TO FIRE A GUN EVER AGAIN.
FAST ASLEEP.
HOW ARE YOU FEELING?
AFTER LIVING OUT SUCH A MAD STORY, THE YARNS THEY SPIN IN BOOKS JUST DON'T PACK THE SAME PUNCH ANYMORE, IT WOULD SEEM.
TIRED. CAN'T SLEEP 'TILL ALL THE BOYS ARE BACK.
YOU CAN TAKE THE PHOTO, GILBERT. IT'S NOT A BOTHER.

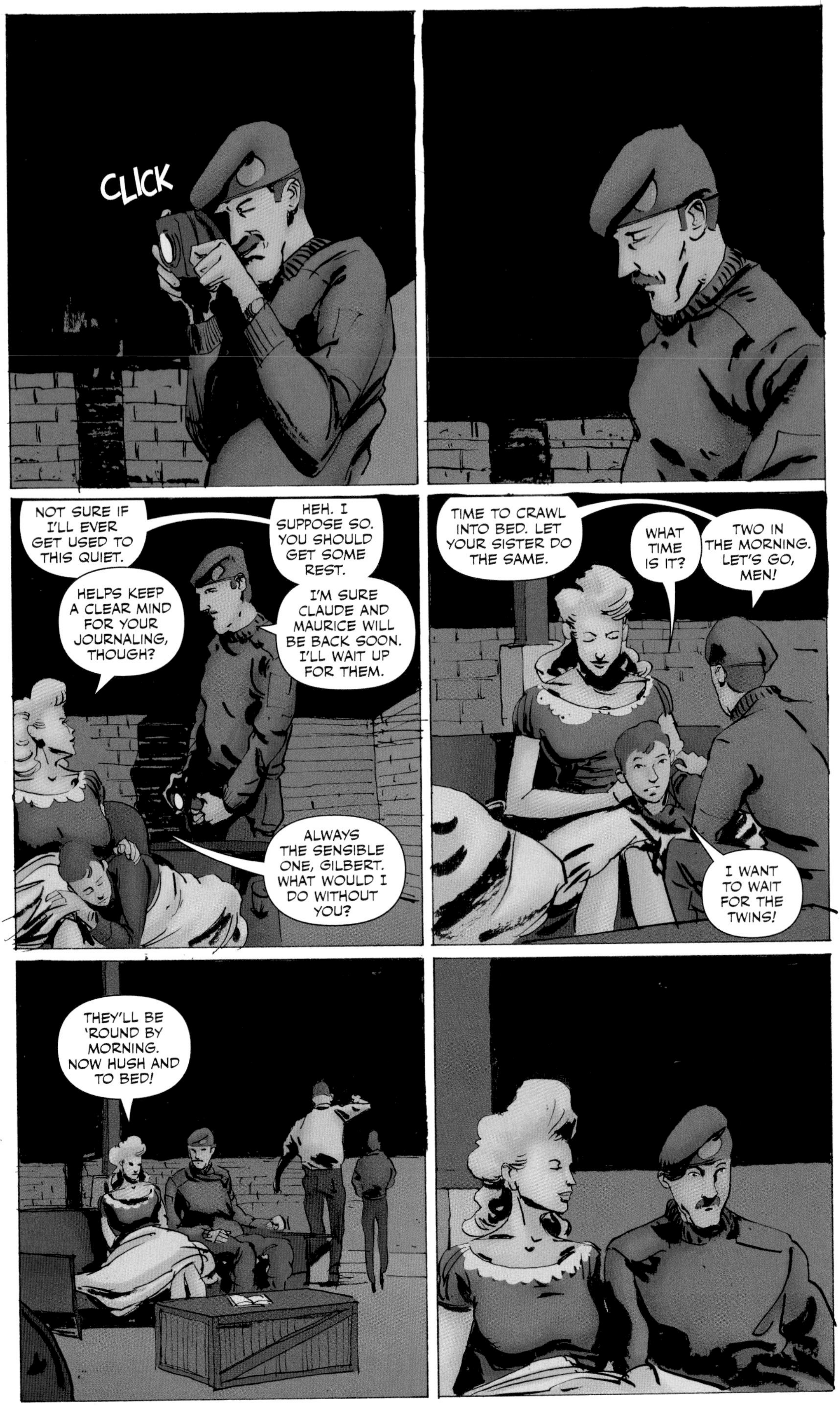
CLICK
NOT SURE IF I'LL EVER GET USED TO THIS QUIET.
HEH. I SUPPOSE SO. YOU SHOULD GET SOME REST.
HELPS KEEP A CLEAR MIND FOR YOUR JOURNALING, THOUGH?
I'M SURE CLAUDE AND MAURICE WILL BE BACK SOON. I'LL WAIT UP FOR THEM.
ALWAYS THE SENSIBLE ONE, GILBERT. WHAT WOULD I DO WITHOUT YOU?
TIME TO CRAWL INTO BED. LET YOUR SISTER DO THE SAME.
WHAT TIME IS IT?
TWO IN THE MORNING. LET'S GO, MEN!
I WANT TO WAIT FOR THE TWINS!
THEY'LL BE 'ROUND BY MORNING. NOW HUSH AND TO BED!

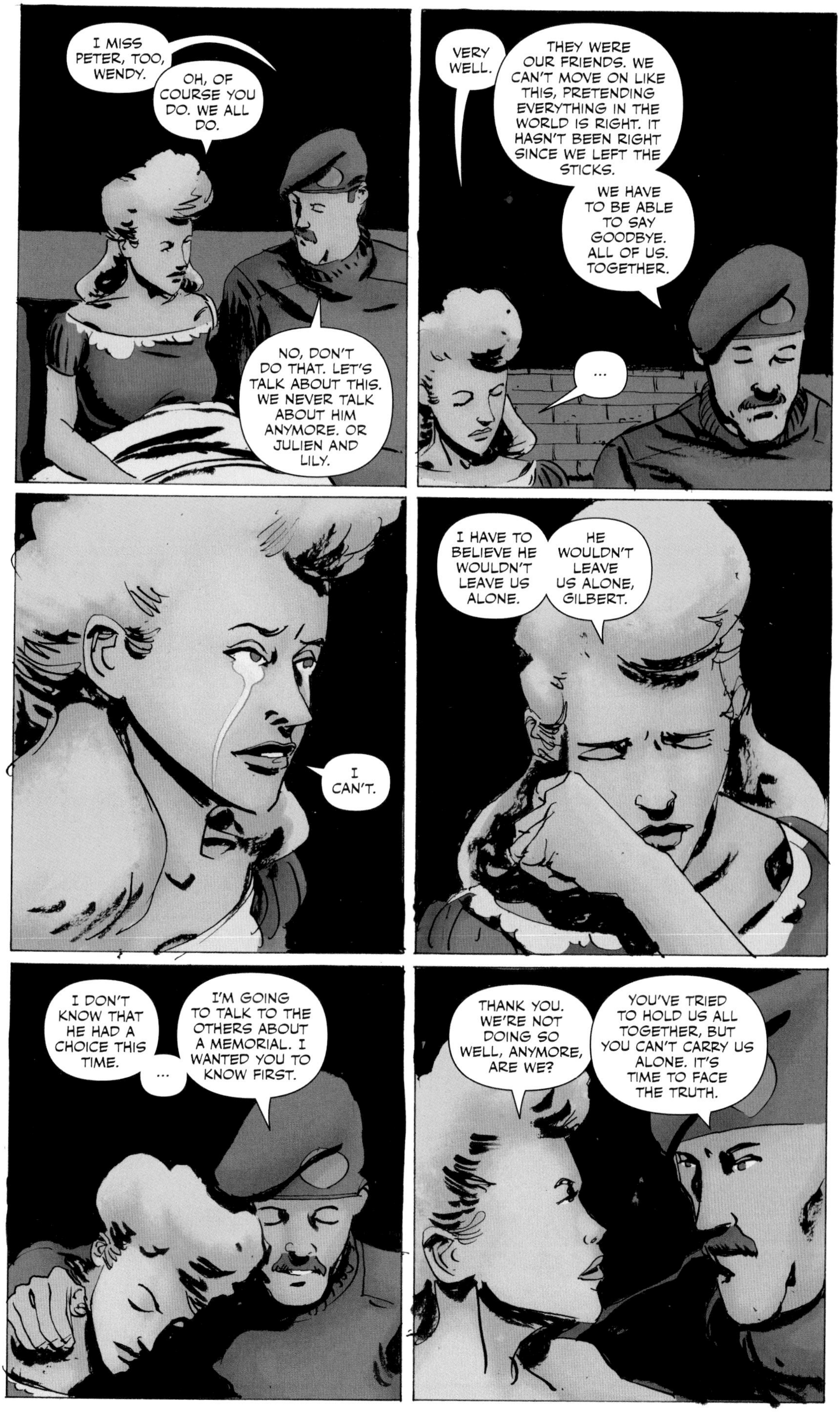
I MISS PETER, TOO, WENDY.
OH, OF COURSE YOU DO. WE ALL DO.
NO, DON'T DO THAT. LET'S TALK ABOUT THIS. WE NEVER TALK ABOUT HIM ANYMORE. OR JULIEN AND LILY.
VERY WELL.
THEY WERE OUR FRIENDS. WE CAN'T MOVE ON LIKE THIS, PRETENDING EVERYTHING IN THE WORLD IS RIGHT. IT HASN'T BEEN RIGHT SINCE WE LEFT THE STICKS.
WE HAVE TO BE ABLE TO SAY GOODBYE. ALL OF US. TOGETHER.
...
I CAN'T.
I HAVE TO BELIEVE HE WOULDN'T LEAVE US ALONE.
HE WOULDN'T LEAVE US ALONE, GILBERT.
I DON'T KNOW THAT HE HAD A CHOICE THIS TIME.
...
I'M GOING TO TALK TO THE OTHERS ABOUT A MEMORIAL. I WANTED YOU TO KNOW FIRST.
THANK YOU. WE'RE NOT DOING SO WELL, ANYMORE, ARE WE?
YOU'VE TRIED TO HOLD US ALL TOGETHER, BUT YOU CAN'T CARRY US ALONE. IT'S TIME TO FACE THE TRUTH.

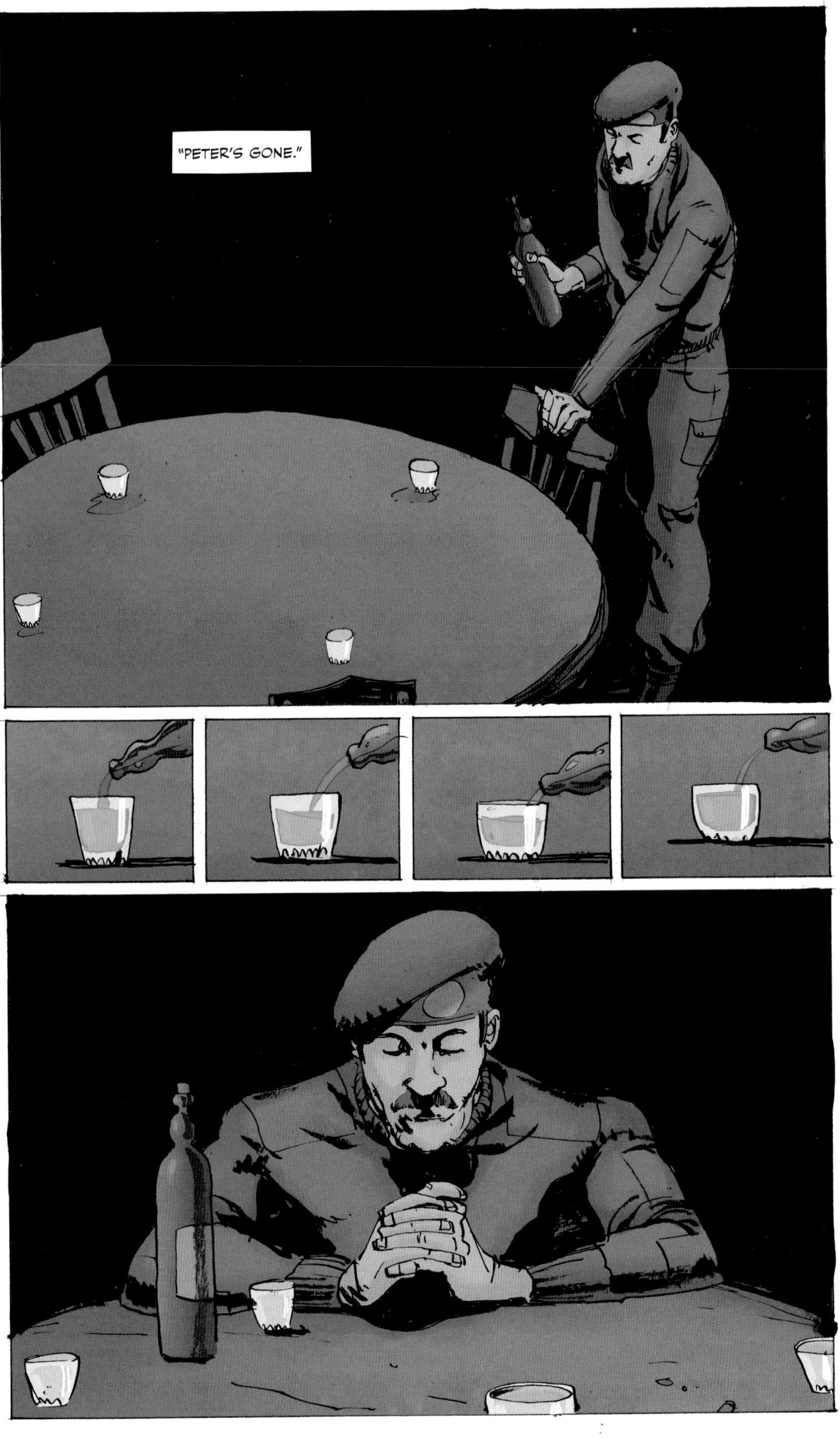
"PETER'S GONE."

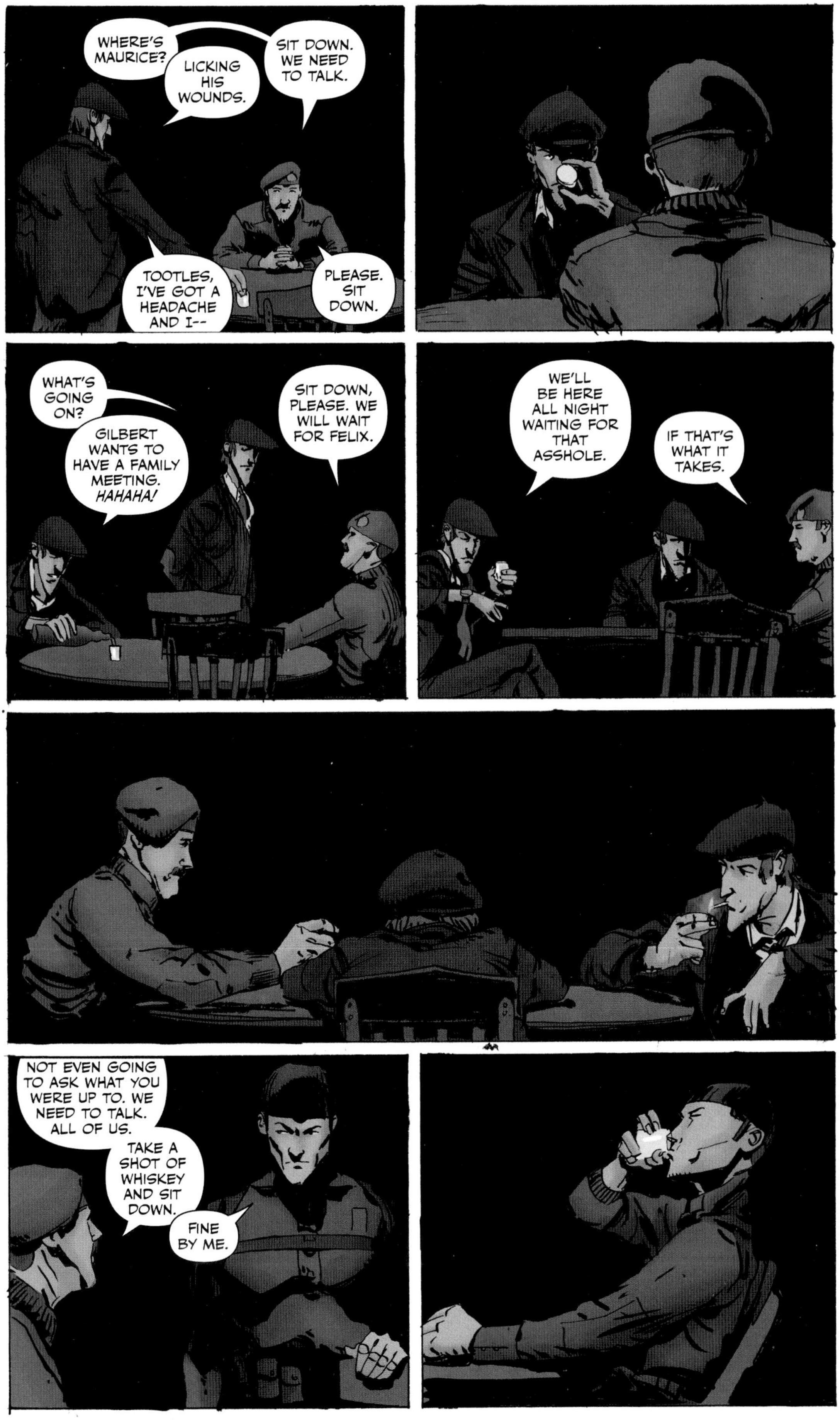
WHERE'S MAURICE?
LICKING HIS WOUNDS.
SIT DOWN. WE NEED TO TALK.
TOOTLES, I'VE GOT A HEADACHE AND I--
PLEASE. SIT DOWN.
WHAT'S GOING ON?
GILBERT WANTS TO HAVE A FAMILY MEETING. *HAHAHA!*
SIT DOWN, PLEASE. WE WILL WAIT FOR FELIX.
WE'LL BE HERE ALL NIGHT WAITING FOR THAT ASSHOLE.
IF THAT'S WHAT IT TAKES.
NOT EVEN GOING TO ASK WHAT YOU WERE UP TO. WE NEED TO TALK. ALL OF US.
TAKE A SHOT OF WHISKEY AND SIT DOWN.
FINE BY ME.

PETER'S DEAD.

WHAT?

HOW DO YOU KNOW?

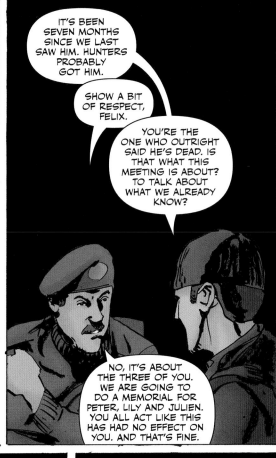

IT'S BEEN SEVEN MONTHS SINCE WE LAST SAW HIM. HUNTERS PROBABLY GOT HIM.

SHOW A BIT OF RESPECT, FELIX.

YOU'RE THE ONE WHO OUTRIGHT SAID HE'S DEAD. IS THAT WHAT THIS MEETING IS ABOUT? TO TALK ABOUT WHAT WE ALREADY KNOW?

NO, IT'S ABOUT THE THREE OF YOU. WE ARE GOING TO DO A MEMORIAL FOR PETER, LILY AND JULIEN. YOU ALL ACT LIKE THIS HAS HAD NO EFFECT ON YOU. AND THAT'S FINE.

SOME OF US ARE GRIEVING. WE NEED TO LET GO.

THIS PROVES MY POINT. ONCE WE SAY OUR GOODBYES, I WANT YOU TO DO THE SAME AND LEAVE.

WENDY STAYS UP WAITING ON ALL OF YOU AND I DOUBT YOU'VE NOTICED OR EVEN CARE. SHE'S IN NO CONDITION TO HAVE YOU WEIGHING ON HER MIND. YOU'RE CANCER.

THAT'S WHAT I'VE BEEN SAYING ALL ALONG.

SHUT YOUR MOUTH, CLAUDE!

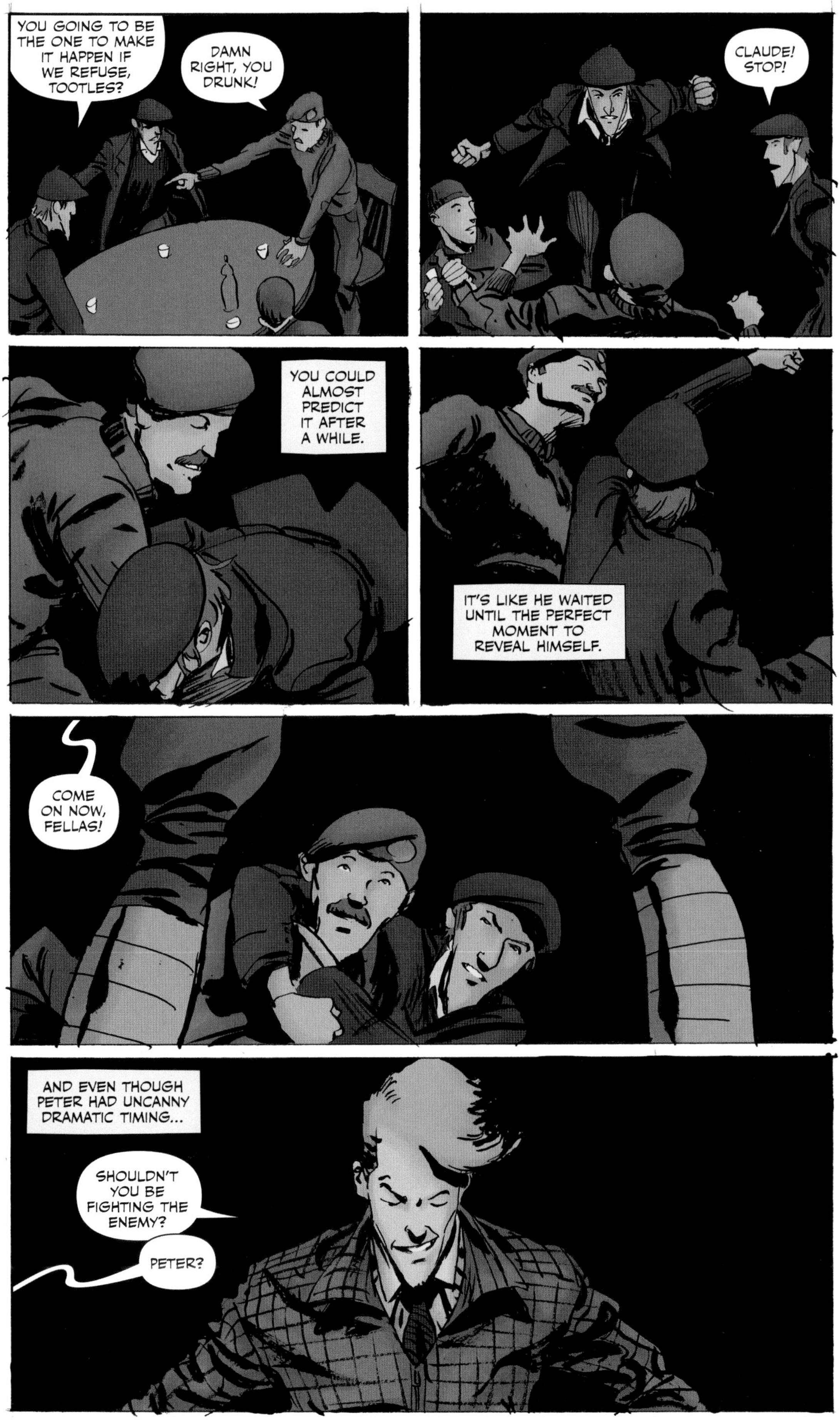
YOU GOING TO BE THE ONE TO MAKE IT HAPPEN IF WE REFUSE, TOOTLES?
DAMN RIGHT, YOU DRUNK!
CLAUDE! STOP!
YOU COULD ALMOST PREDICT IT AFTER A WHILE.
IT'S LIKE HE WAITED UNTIL THE PERFECT MOMENT TO REVEAL HIMSELF.
COME ON NOW, FELLAS!
AND EVEN THOUGH PETER HAD UNCANNY DRAMATIC TIMING...
SHOULDN'T YOU BE FIGHTING THE ENEMY?
PETER?

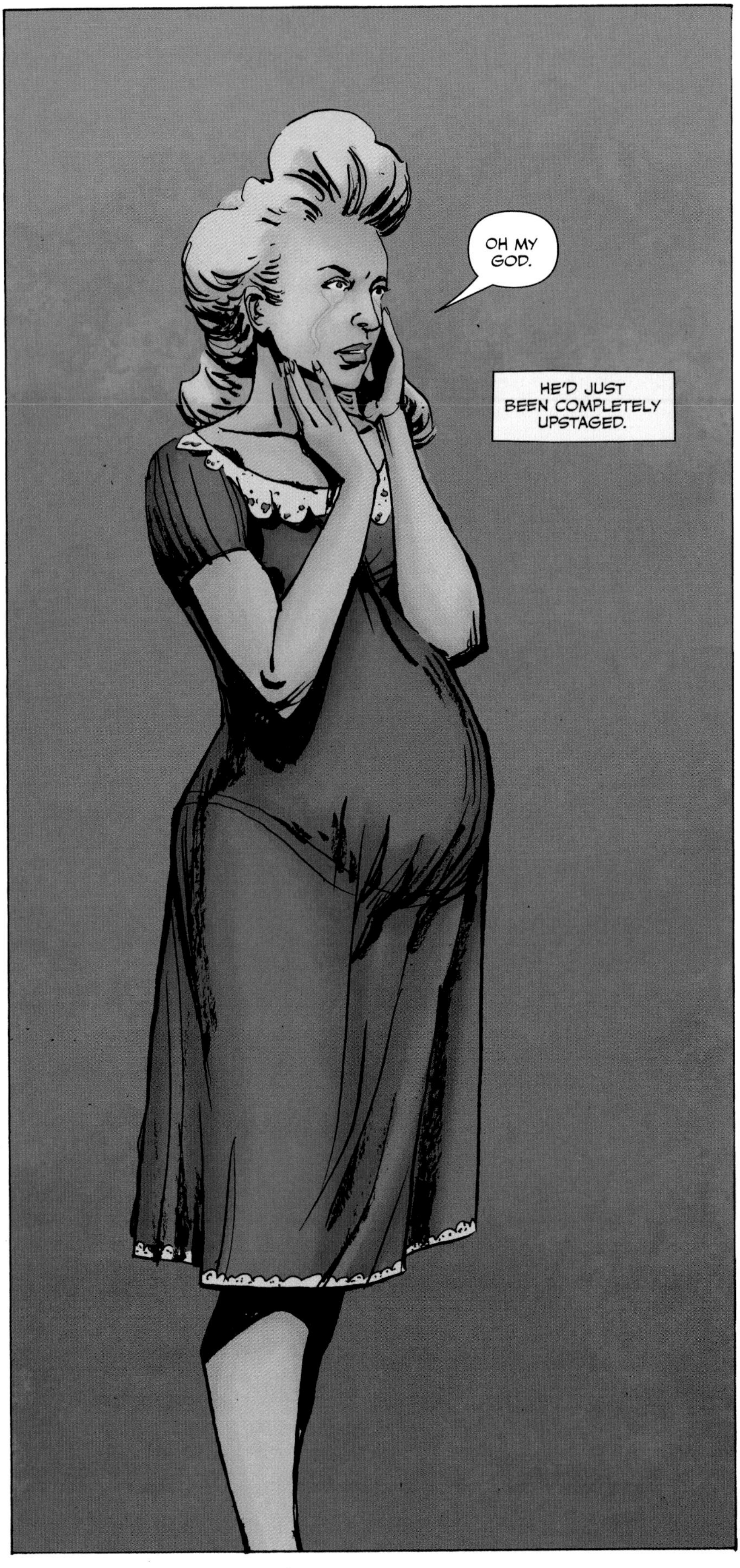
OH MY GOD.
HE'D JUST BEEN COMPLETELY UPSTAGED.

CHAPTER TWENTY-TWO

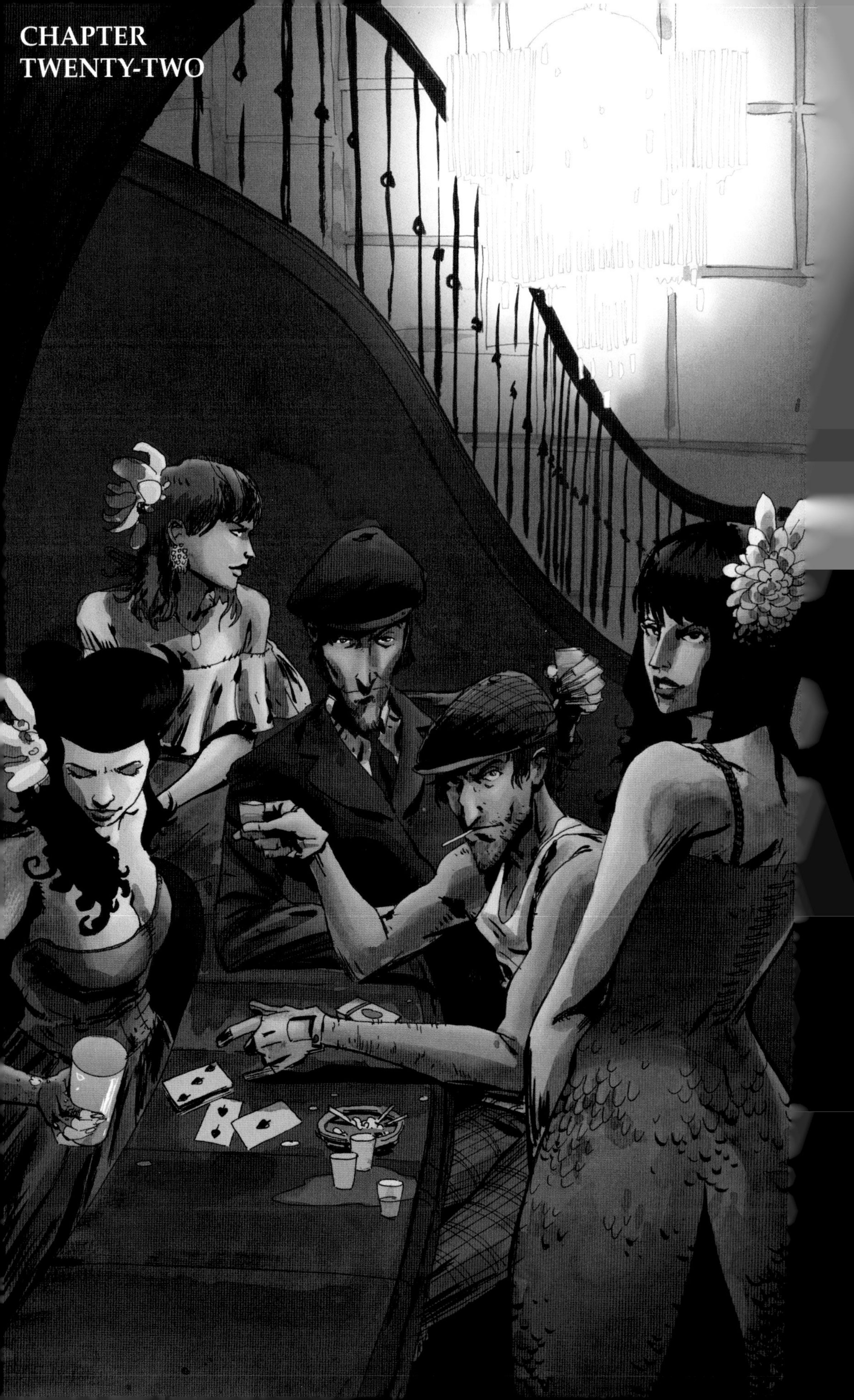

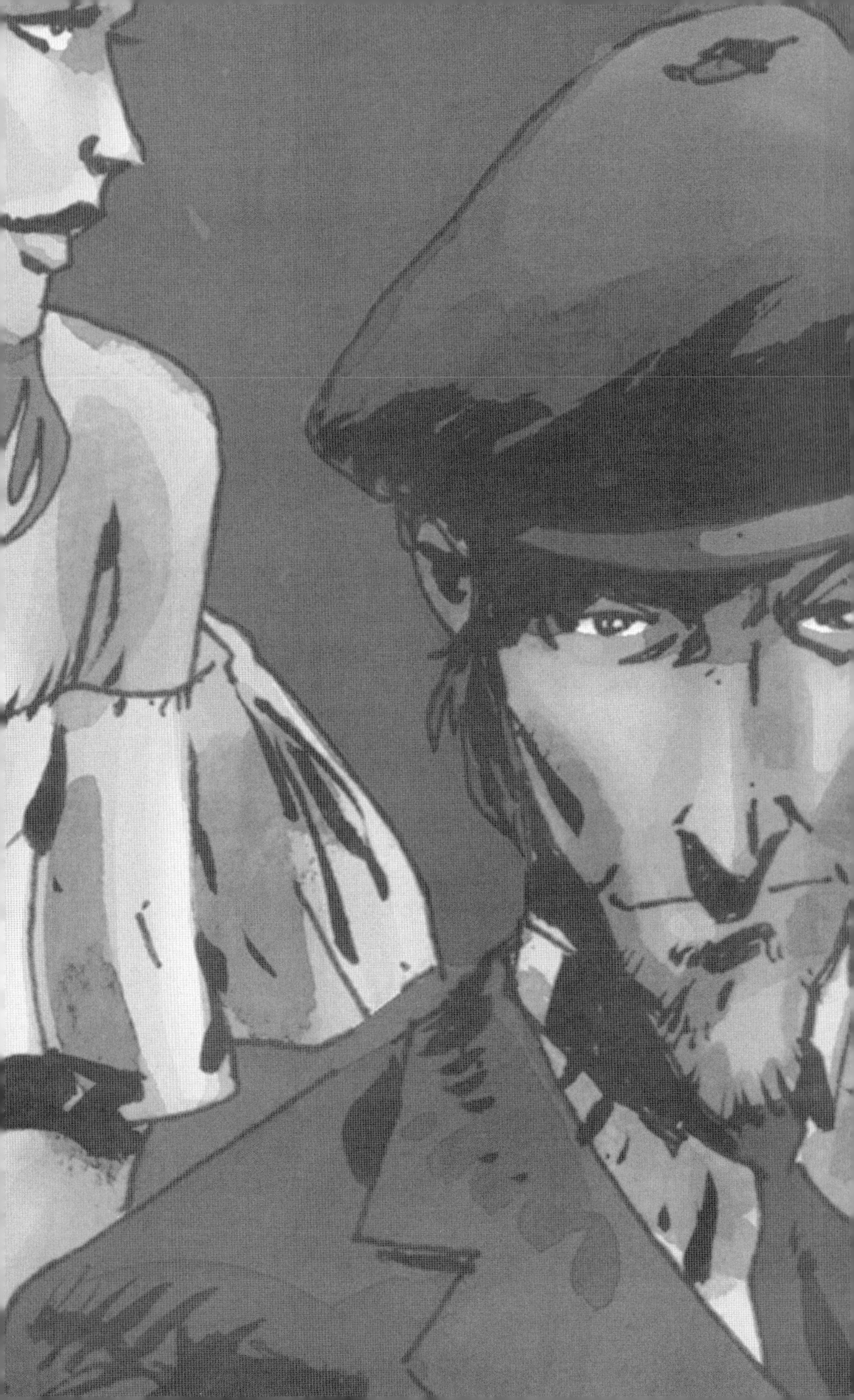

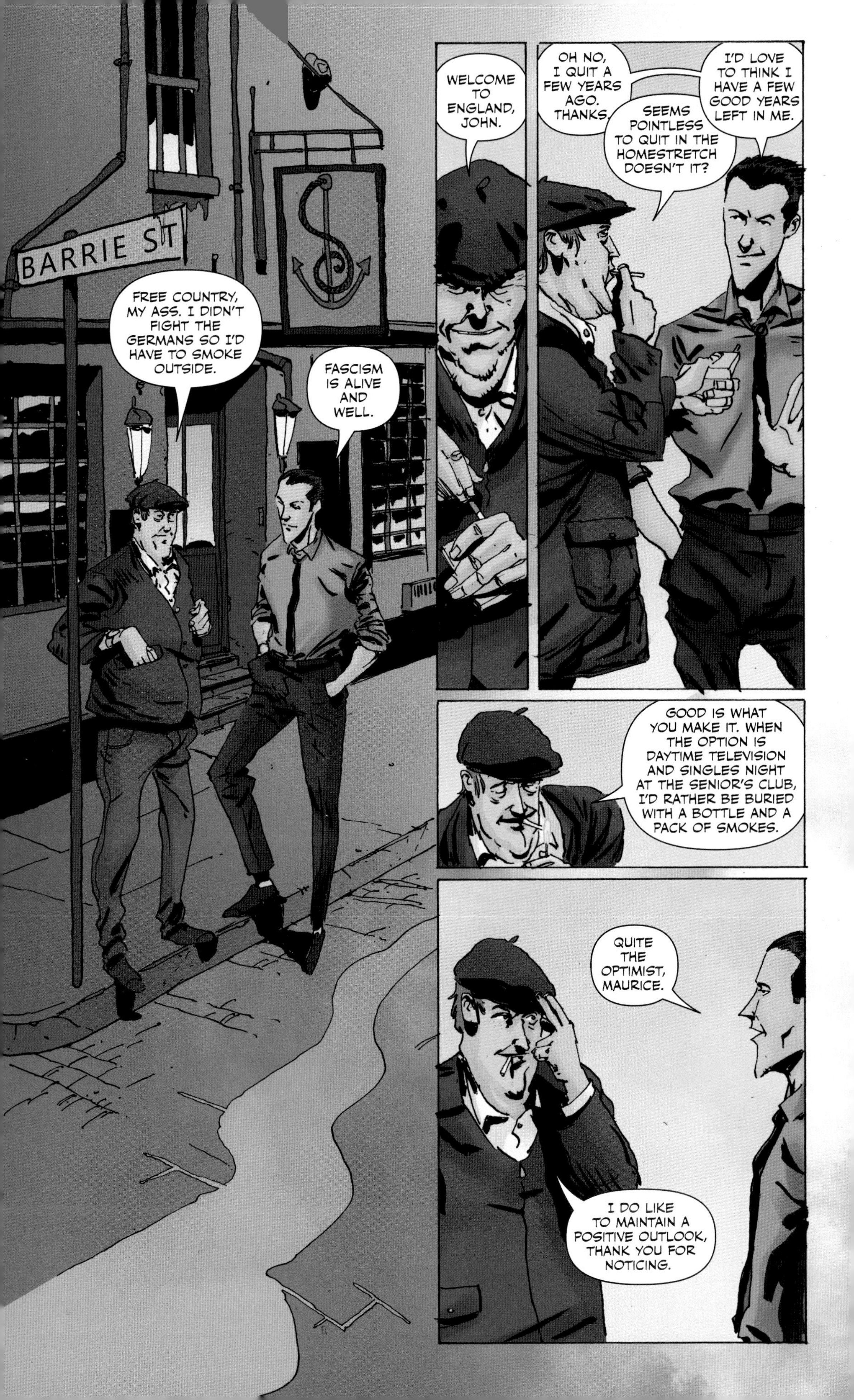
BARRIE ST
FREE COUNTRY, MY ASS. I DIDN'T FIGHT THE GERMANS SO I'D HAVE TO SMOKE OUTSIDE.
FASCISM IS ALIVE AND WELL.
WELCOME TO ENGLAND, JOHN.
OH NO, I QUIT A FEW YEARS AGO. THANKS.
I'D LOVE TO THINK I HAVE A FEW GOOD YEARS LEFT IN ME.
SEEMS POINTLESS TO QUIT IN THE HOMESTRETCH DOESN'T IT?
GOOD IS WHAT YOU MAKE IT. WHEN THE OPTION IS DAYTIME TELEVISION AND SINGLES NIGHT AT THE SENIOR'S CLUB, I'D RATHER BE BURIED WITH A BOTTLE AND A PACK OF SMOKES.
QUITE THE OPTIMIST, MAURICE.
I DO LIKE TO MAINTAIN A POSITIVE OUTLOOK, THANK YOU FOR NOTICING.

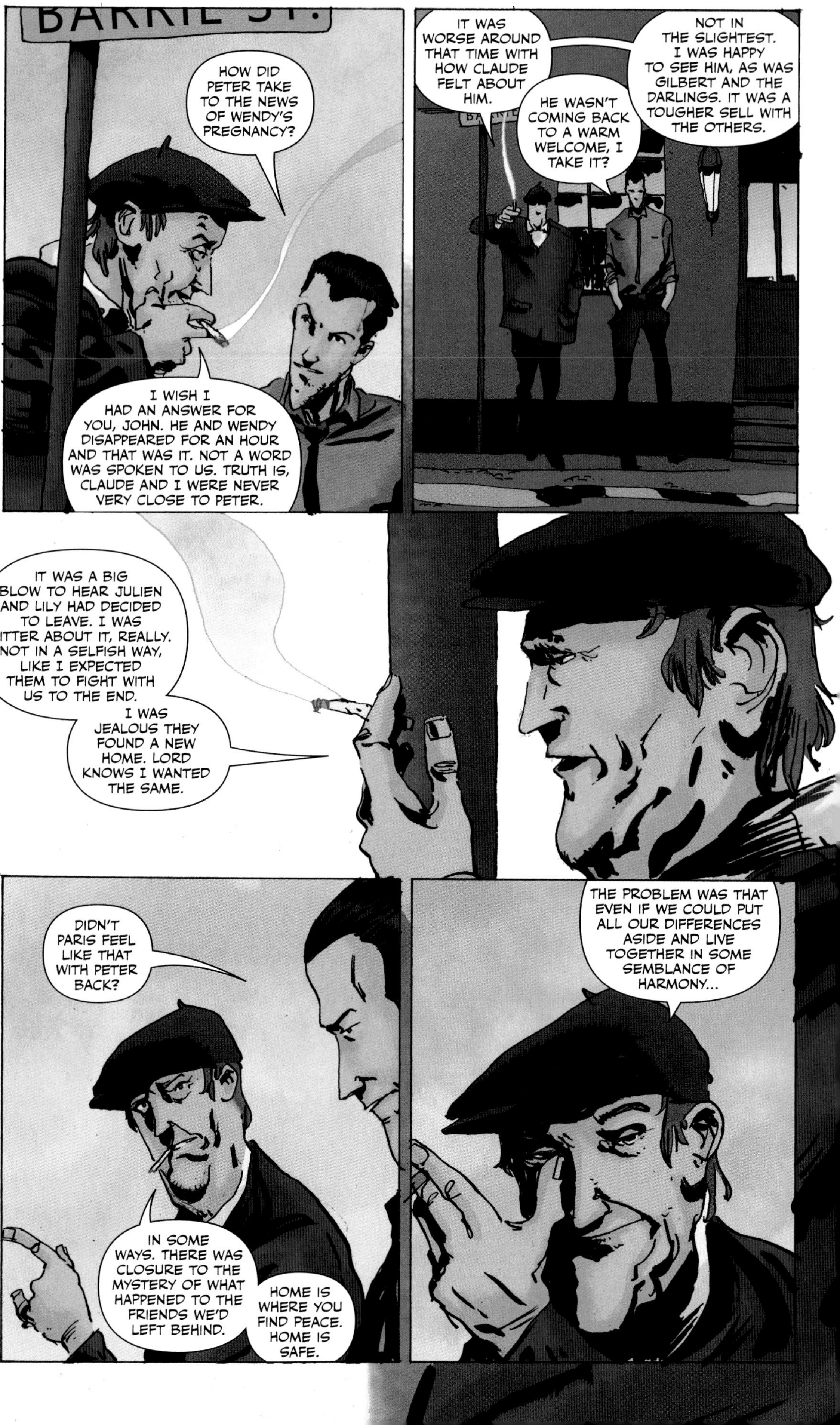
BARRIE ST.
HOW DID PETER TAKE TO THE NEWS OF WENDY'S PREGNANCY?
I WISH I HAD AN ANSWER FOR YOU, JOHN. HE AND WENDY DISAPPEARED FOR AN HOUR AND THAT WAS IT. NOT A WORD WAS SPOKEN TO US. TRUTH IS, CLAUDE AND I WERE NEVER VERY CLOSE TO PETER.
HE WASN'T COMING BACK TO A WARM WELCOME, I TAKE IT?
NOT IN THE SLIGHTEST. I WAS HAPPY TO SEE HIM, AS WAS GILBERT AND THE DARLINGS. IT WAS A TOUGHER SELL WITH THE OTHERS.
IT WAS WORSE AROUND THAT TIME WITH HOW CLAUDE FELT ABOUT HIM.
IT WAS A BIG BLOW TO HEAR JULIEN AND LILY HAD DECIDED TO LEAVE. I WAS BITTER ABOUT IT, REALLY. NOT IN A SELFISH WAY, LIKE I EXPECTED THEM TO FIGHT WITH US TO THE END.
I WAS JEALOUS THEY FOUND A NEW HOME. LORD KNOWS I WANTED THE SAME.
DIDN'T PARIS FEEL LIKE THAT WITH PETER BACK?
IN SOME WAYS. THERE WAS CLOSURE TO THE MYSTERY OF WHAT HAPPENED TO THE FRIENDS WE'D LEFT BEHIND.
HOME IS WHERE YOU FIND PEACE. HOME IS SAFE.
THE PROBLEM WAS THAT EVEN IF WE COULD PUT ALL OUR DIFFERENCES ASIDE AND LIVE TOGETHER IN SOME SEMBLANCE OF HARMONY...

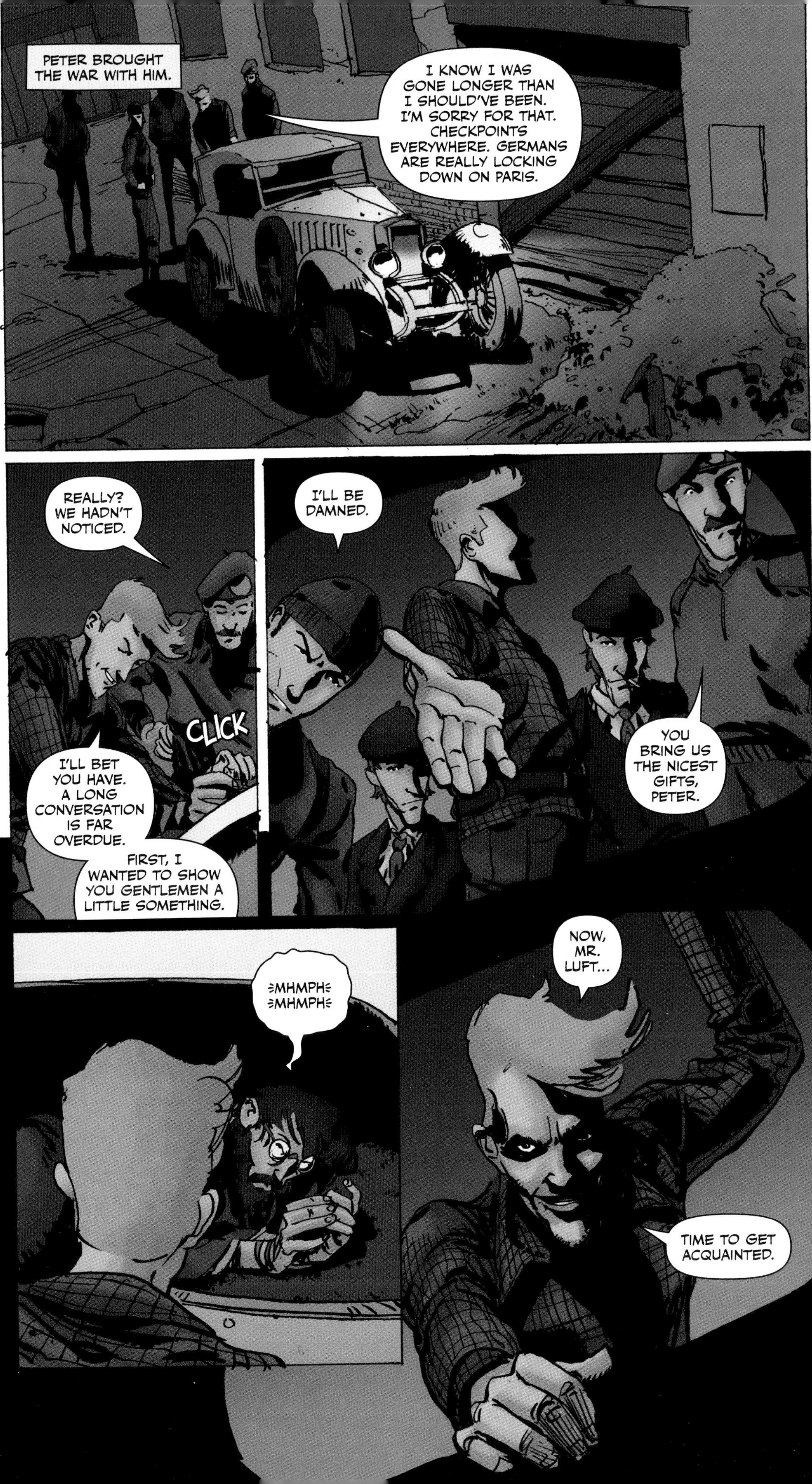

PETER BROUGHT THE WAR WITH HIM.
I KNOW I WAS GONE LONGER THAN I SHOULD'VE BEEN. I'M SORRY FOR THAT. CHECKPOINTS EVERYWHERE. GERMANS ARE REALLY LOCKING DOWN ON PARIS.
REALLY? WE HADN'T NOTICED.
CLICK
I'LL BET YOU HAVE. A LONG CONVERSATION IS FAR OVERDUE.
FIRST, I WANTED TO SHOW YOU GENTLEMEN A LITTLE SOMETHING.
I'LL BE DAMNED.
YOU BRING US THE NICEST GIFTS, PETER.
MHMPH MHMPH
NOW, MR. LUFT...
TIME TO GET ACQUAINTED.

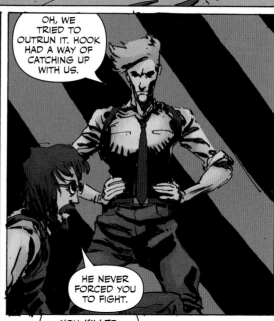

OH, WE TRIED TO OUTRUN IT. HOOK HAD A WAY OF CATCHING UP WITH US.

HE NEVER FORCED YOU TO FIGHT.

YOU'VE HAD MONTHS TO THINK ABOUT THIS SCENE, LUFT. HAVE YOU PRACTICED A SPEECH? READY TO SPILL EVERYTHING YOU KNOW?

THIS IS MORBID. YOU'RE JUST BOYS. WHY ARE YOU PLAYING AT WAR?

YOU *KILLED* ALAIN AND THEN EXPECTED US NOT TO AVENGE HIM?

I WASN'T THERE. I DIDN'T KNOW OF YOUR LOSS.

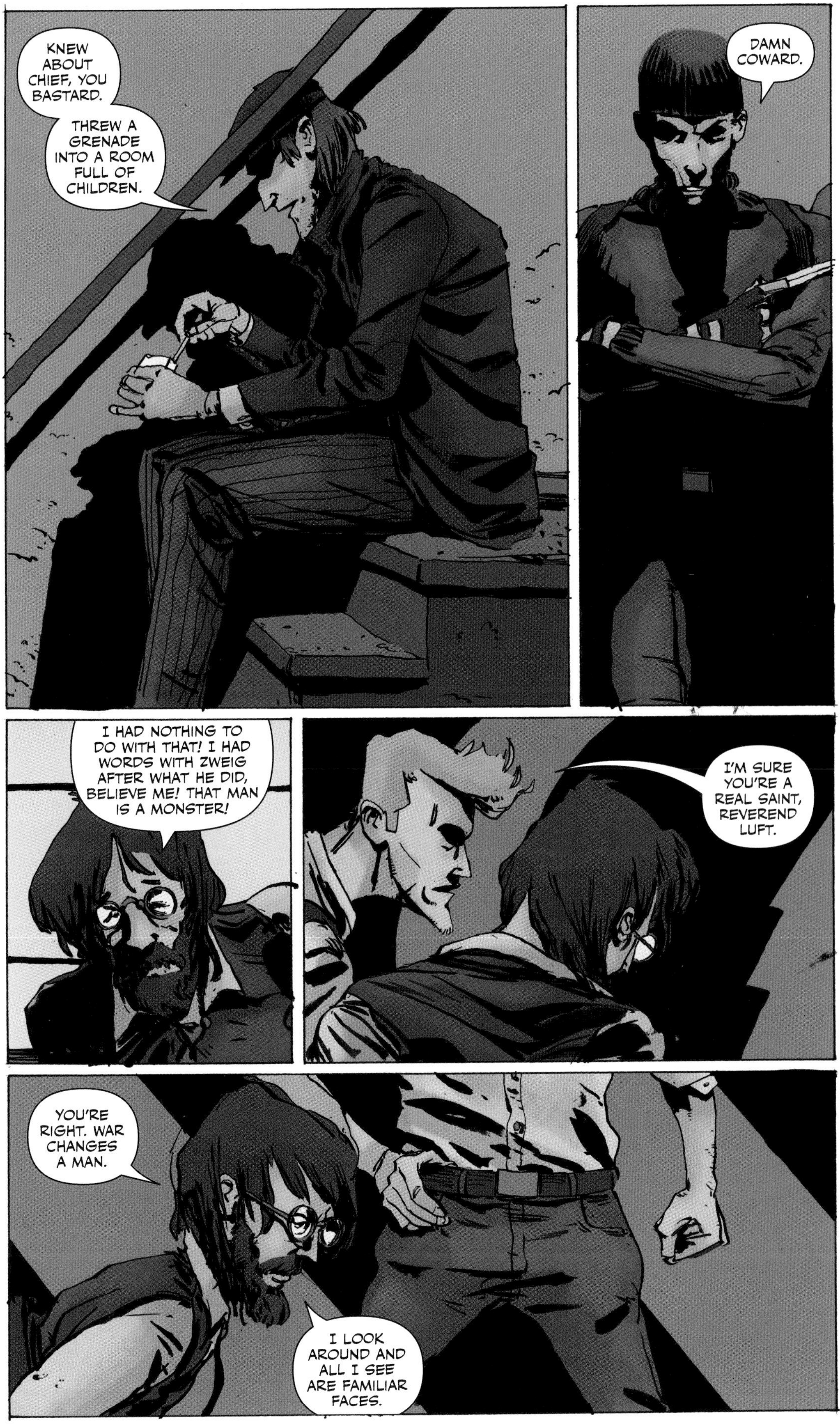
KNEW ABOUT CHIEF, YOU BASTARD.
THREW A GRENADE INTO A ROOM FULL OF CHILDREN.
DAMN COWARD.
I HAD NOTHING TO DO WITH THAT! I HAD WORDS WITH ZWEIG AFTER WHAT HE DID, BELIEVE ME! THAT MAN IS A MONSTER!
I'M SURE YOU'RE A REAL SAINT, REVEREND LUFT.
YOU'RE RIGHT. WAR CHANGES A MAN.
I LOOK AROUND AND ALL I SEE ARE FAMILIAR FACES.

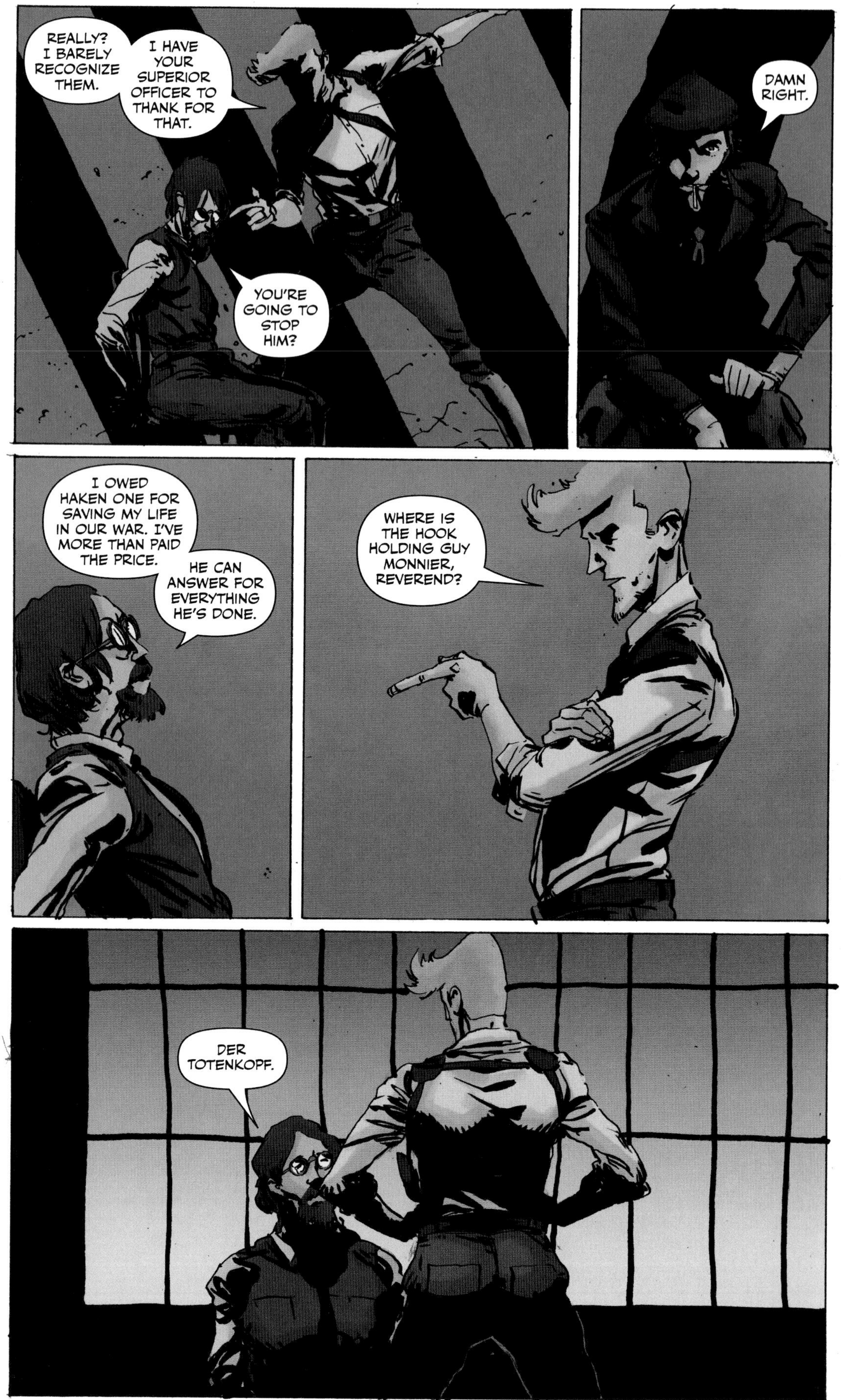
REALLY? I BARELY RECOGNIZE THEM.
I HAVE YOUR SUPERIOR OFFICER TO THANK FOR THAT.
YOU'RE GOING TO STOP HIM?
DAMN RIGHT.
I OWED HAKEN ONE FOR SAVING MY LIFE IN OUR WAR. I'VE MORE THAN PAID THE PRICE.
HE CAN ANSWER FOR EVERYTHING HE'S DONE.
WHERE IS THE HOOK HOLDING GUY MONNIER, REVEREND?
DER TOTENKOPF.

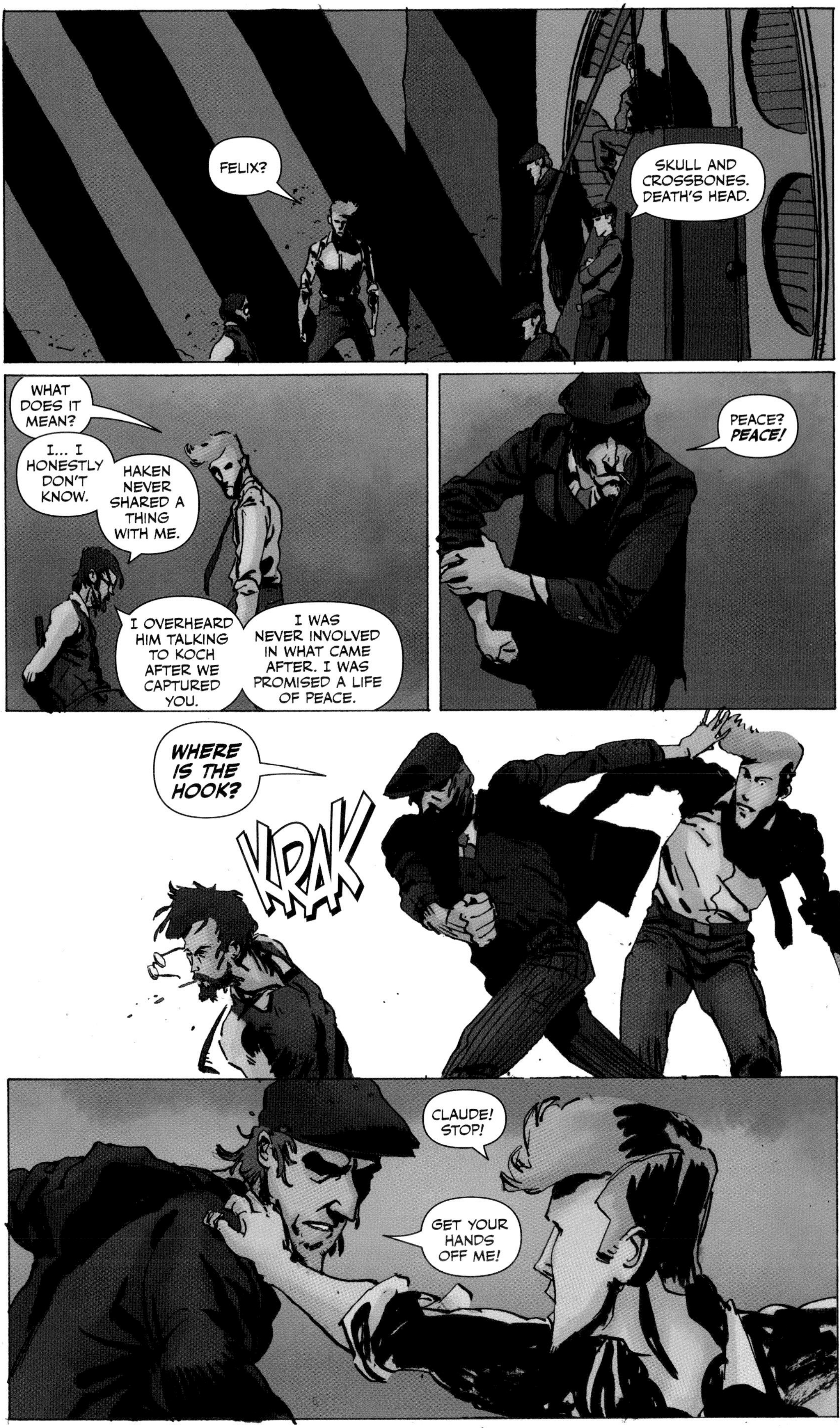
FELIX?
SKULL AND CROSSBONES. DEATH'S HEAD.
WHAT DOES IT MEAN?
I... I HONESTLY DON'T KNOW.
HAKEN NEVER SHARED A THING WITH ME.
I OVERHEARD HIM TALKING TO KOCH AFTER WE CAPTURED YOU.
I WAS NEVER INVOLVED IN WHAT CAME AFTER. I WAS PROMISED A LIFE OF PEACE.
PEACE? PEACE!
WHERE IS THE HOOK?
KRAK
CLAUDE! STOP!
GET YOUR HANDS OFF ME!

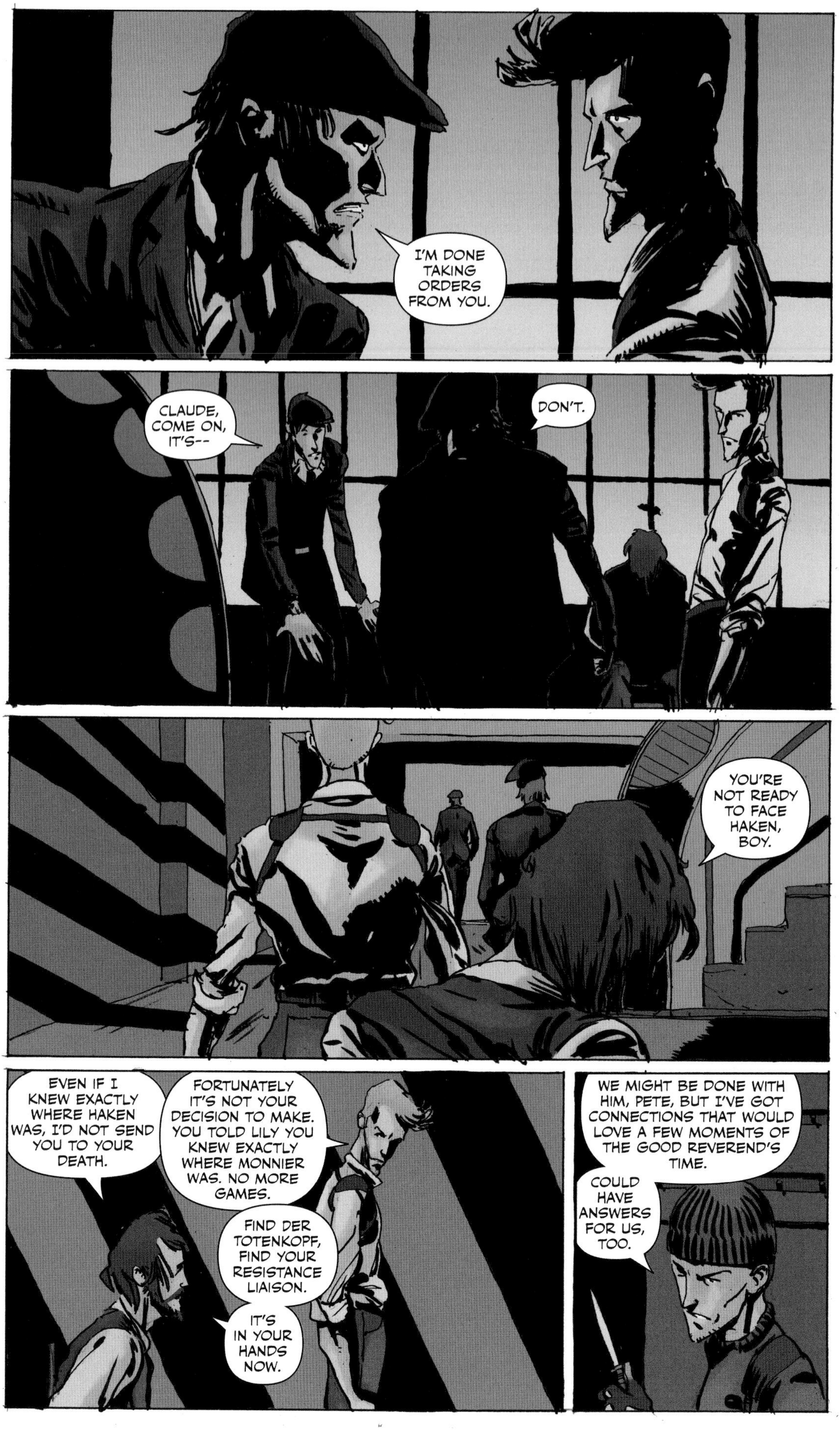
I'M DONE TAKING ORDERS FROM YOU.
CLAUDE, COME ON, IT'S--
DON'T.
YOU'RE NOT READY TO FACE HAKEN, BOY.
EVEN IF I KNEW EXACTLY WHERE HAKEN WAS, I'D NOT SEND YOU TO YOUR DEATH.
FORTUNATELY IT'S NOT YOUR DECISION TO MAKE. YOU TOLD LILY YOU KNEW EXACTLY WHERE MONNIER WAS. NO MORE GAMES.
FIND DER TOTENKOPF, FIND YOUR RESISTANCE LIAISON.
IT'S IN YOUR HANDS NOW.
WE MIGHT BE DONE WITH HIM, PETE, BUT I'VE GOT CONNECTIONS THAT WOULD LOVE A FEW MOMENTS OF THE GOOD REVEREND'S TIME.
COULD HAVE ANSWERS FOR US, TOO.

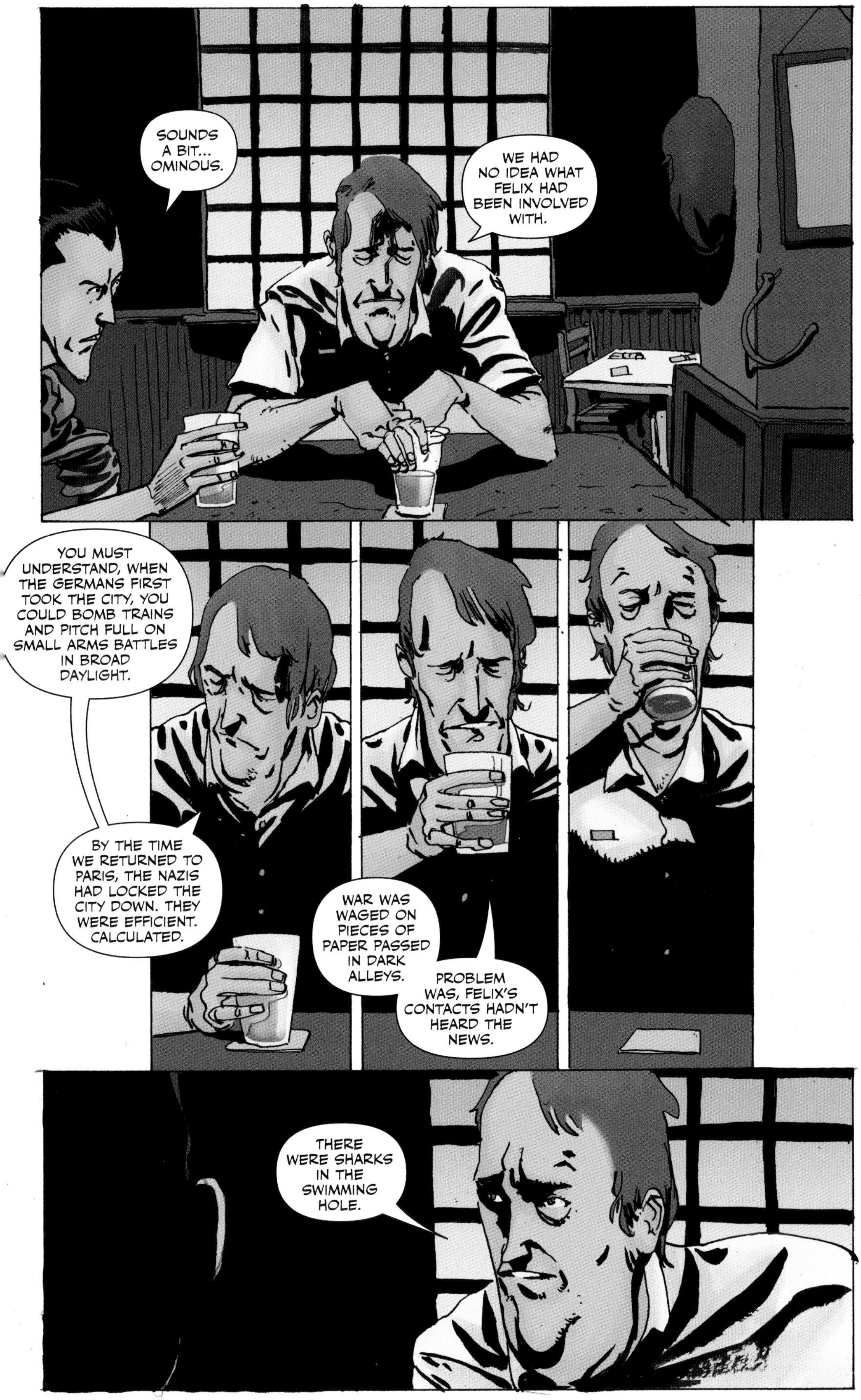
SOUNDS A BIT... OMINOUS.
WE HAD NO IDEA WHAT FELIX HAD BEEN INVOLVED WITH.
YOU MUST UNDERSTAND, WHEN THE GERMANS FIRST TOOK THE CITY, YOU COULD BOMB TRAINS AND PITCH FULL ON SMALL ARMS BATTLES IN BROAD DAYLIGHT.
BY THE TIME WE RETURNED TO PARIS, THE NAZIS HAD LOCKED THE CITY DOWN. THEY WERE EFFICIENT. CALCULATED.
WAR WAS WAGED ON PIECES OF PAPER PASSED IN DARK ALLEYS.
PROBLEM WAS, FELIX'S CONTACTS HADN'T HEARD THE NEWS.
THERE WERE SHARKS IN THE SWIMMING HOLE.

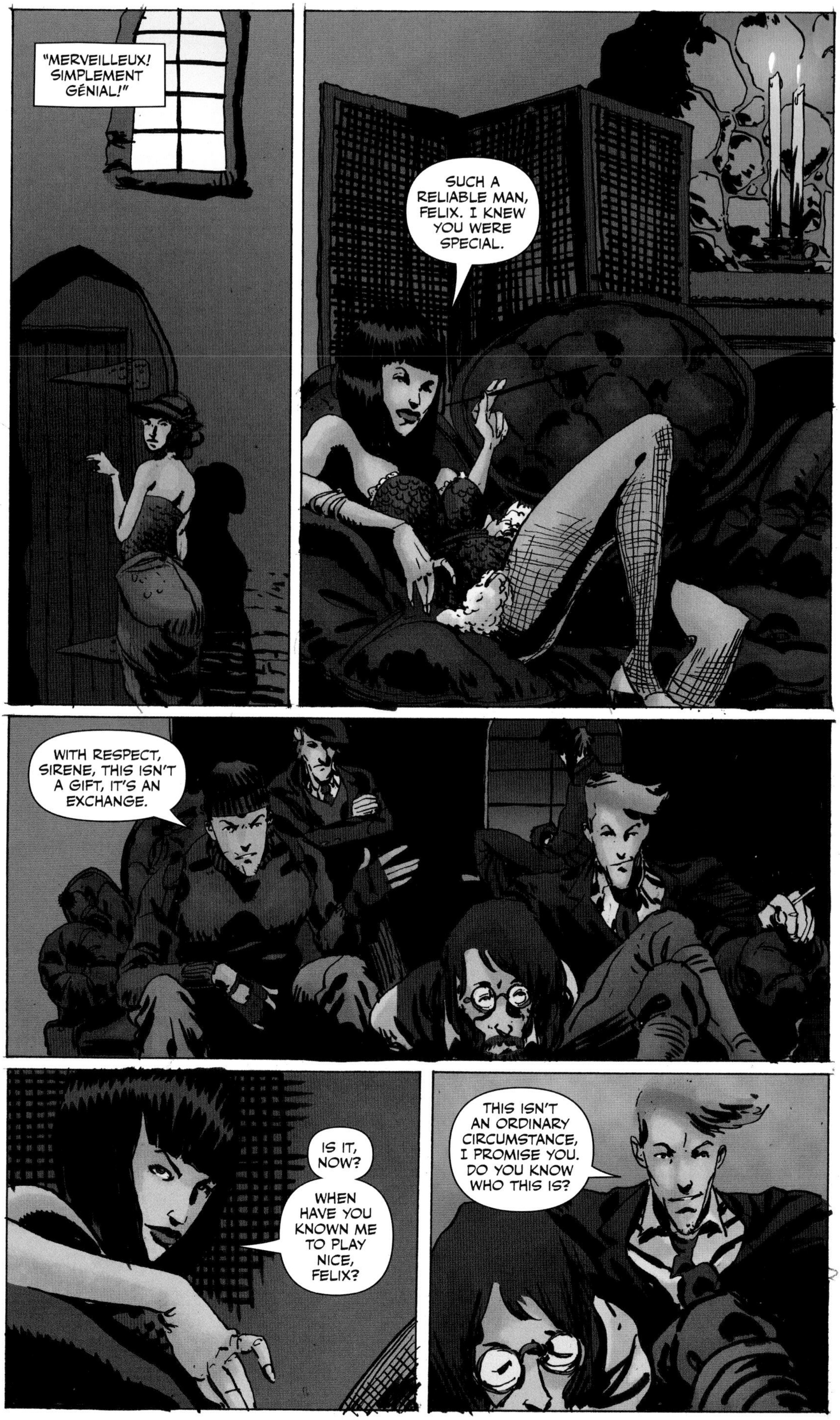
"MERVEILLEUX! SIMPLEMENT GÉNIAL!"
SUCH A RELIABLE MAN, FELIX. I KNEW YOU WERE SPECIAL.
WITH RESPECT, SIRENE, THIS ISN'T A GIFT, IT'S AN EXCHANGE.
IS IT, NOW?
WHEN HAVE YOU KNOWN ME TO PLAY NICE, FELIX?
THIS ISN'T AN ORDINARY CIRCUMSTANCE, I PROMISE YOU. DO YOU KNOW WHO THIS IS?

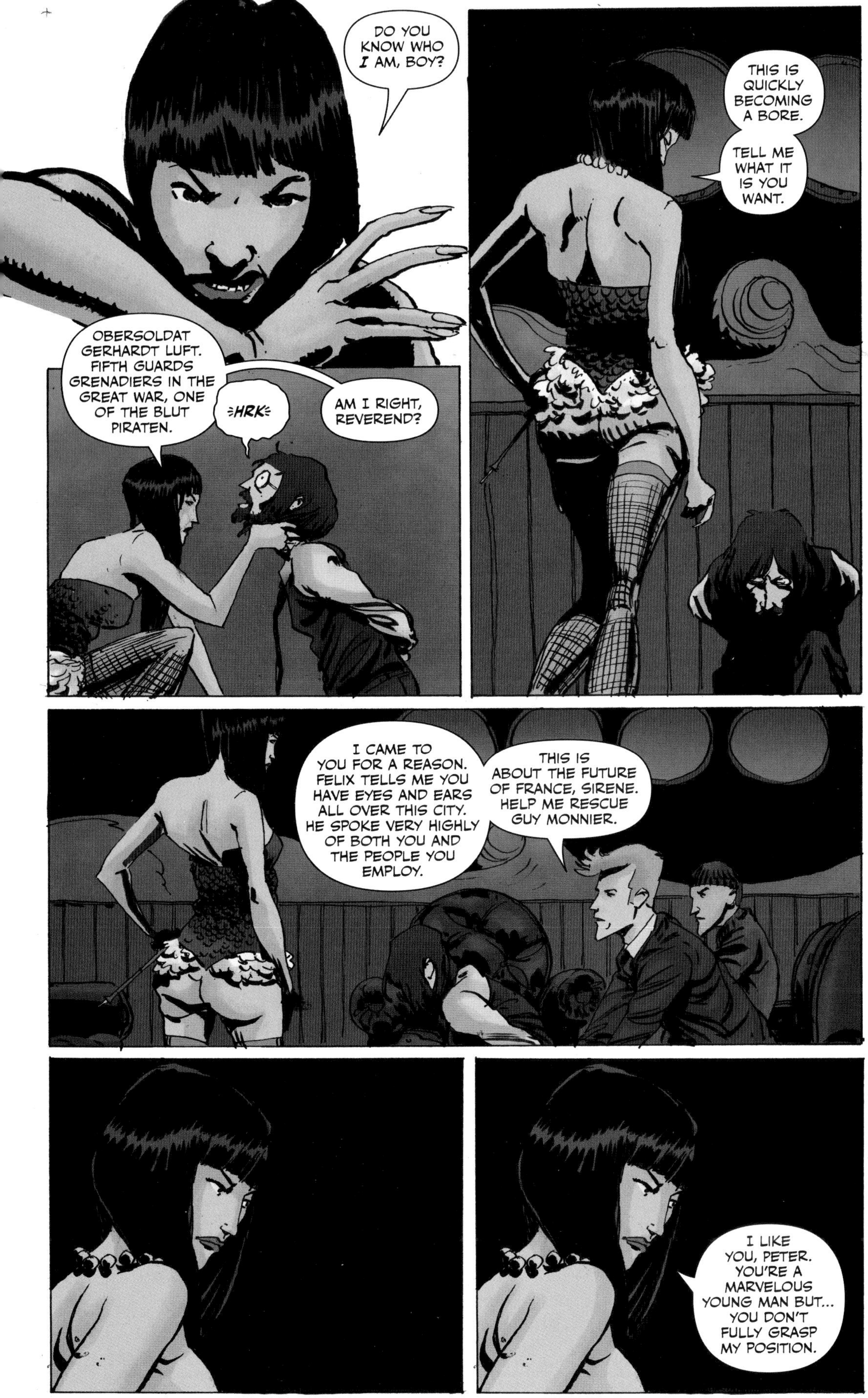

DO YOU KNOW WHO I AM, BOY?
THIS IS QUICKLY BECOMING A BORE.
TELL ME WHAT IT IS YOU WANT.
OBERSOLDAT GERHARDT LUFT. FIFTH GUARDS GRENADIERS IN THE GREAT WAR, ONE OF THE BLUT PIRATEN.
HRK
AM I RIGHT, REVEREND?
I CAME TO YOU FOR A REASON. FELIX TELLS ME YOU HAVE EYES AND EARS ALL OVER THIS CITY. HE SPOKE VERY HIGHLY OF BOTH YOU AND THE PEOPLE YOU EMPLOY.
THIS IS ABOUT THE FUTURE OF FRANCE, SIRENE. HELP ME RESCUE GUY MONNIER.
I LIKE YOU, PETER. YOU'RE A MARVELOUS YOUNG MAN BUT... YOU DON'T FULLY GRASP MY POSITION.

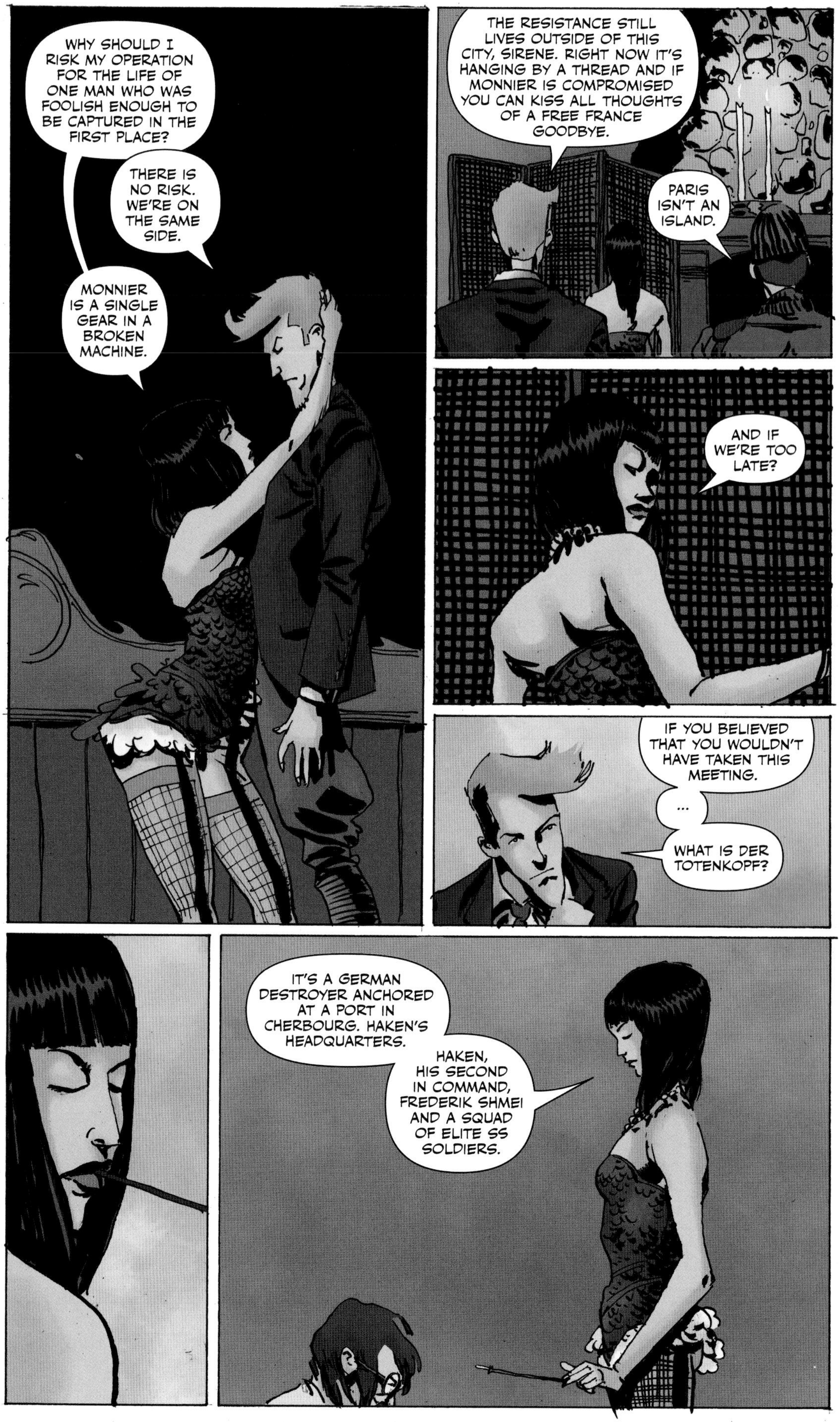
WHY SHOULD I RISK MY OPERATION FOR THE LIFE OF ONE MAN WHO WAS FOOLISH ENOUGH TO BE CAPTURED IN THE FIRST PLACE?
THERE IS NO RISK. WE'RE ON THE SAME SIDE.
MONNIER IS A SINGLE GEAR IN A BROKEN MACHINE.
THE RESISTANCE STILL LIVES OUTSIDE OF THIS CITY, SIRENE. RIGHT NOW IT'S HANGING BY A THREAD AND IF MONNIER IS COMPROMISED YOU CAN KISS ALL THOUGHTS OF A FREE FRANCE GOODBYE.
PARIS ISN'T AN ISLAND.
AND IF WE'RE TOO LATE?
IF YOU BELIEVED THAT YOU WOULDN'T HAVE TAKEN THIS MEETING.
...
WHAT IS DER TOTENKOPF?
IT'S A GERMAN DESTROYER ANCHORED AT A PORT IN CHERBOURG. HAKEN'S HEADQUARTERS.
HAKEN, HIS SECOND IN COMMAND, FREDERIK SHMEI AND A SQUAD OF ELITE SS SOLDIERS.

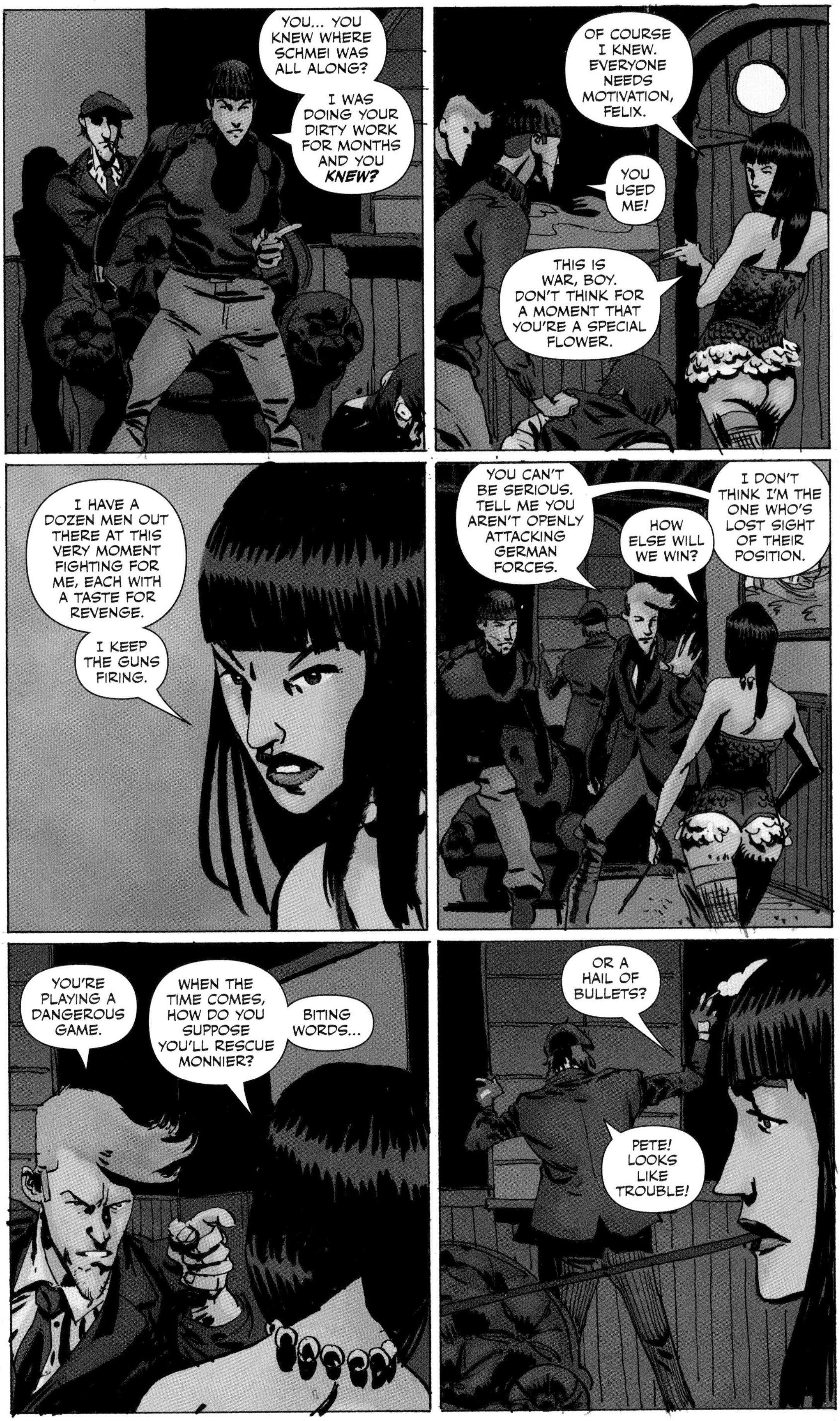

YOU... YOU KNEW WHERE SCHMEI WAS ALL ALONG?
I WAS DOING YOUR DIRTY WORK FOR MONTHS AND YOU *KNEW?*
OF COURSE I KNEW. EVERYONE NEEDS MOTIVATION, FELIX.
YOU USED ME!
THIS IS WAR, BOY. DON'T THINK FOR A MOMENT THAT YOU'RE A SPECIAL FLOWER.
I HAVE A DOZEN MEN OUT THERE AT THIS VERY MOMENT FIGHTING FOR ME, EACH WITH A TASTE FOR REVENGE.
I KEEP THE GUNS FIRING.
YOU CAN'T BE SERIOUS. TELL ME YOU AREN'T OPENLY ATTACKING GERMAN FORCES.
HOW ELSE WILL WE WIN?
I DON'T THINK I'M THE ONE WHO'S LOST SIGHT OF THEIR POSITION.
YOU'RE PLAYING A DANGEROUS GAME.
WHEN THE TIME COMES, HOW DO YOU SUPPOSE YOU'LL RESCUE MONNIER?
BITING WORDS...
OR A HAIL OF BULLETS?
PETE! LOOKS LIKE TROUBLE!

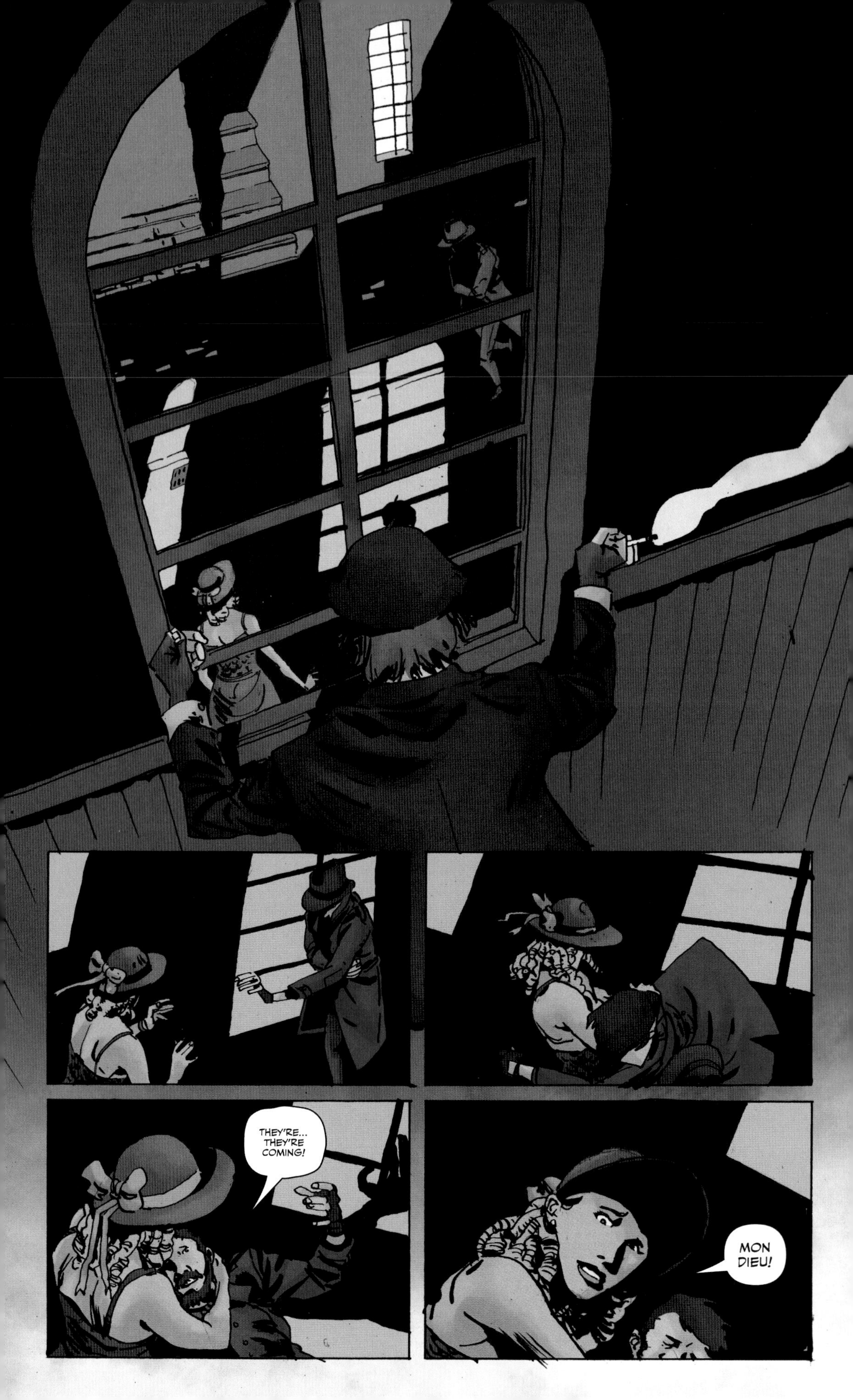
THEY'RE... THEY'RE COMING!
MON DIEU!

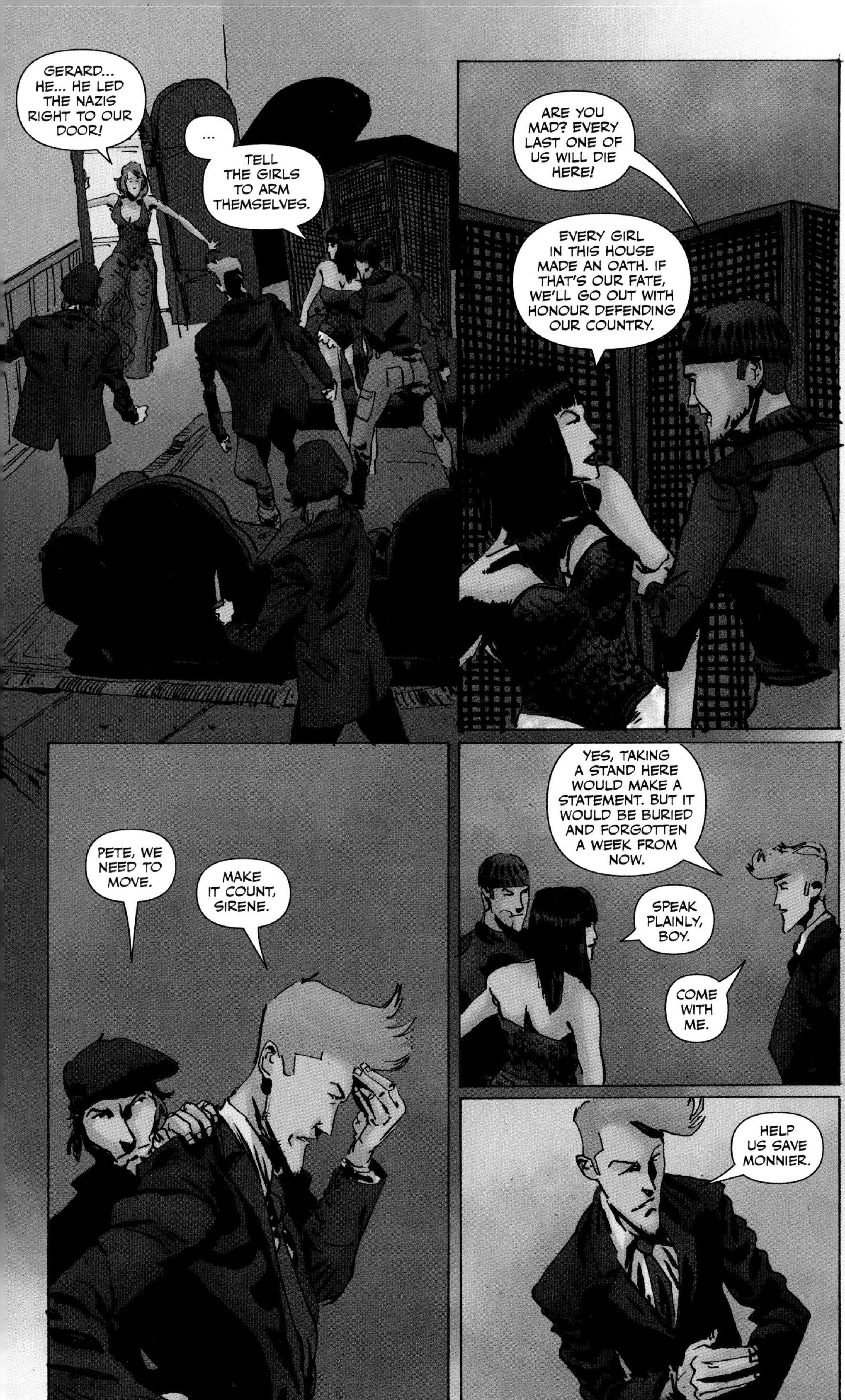
GERARD... HE... HE LED THE NAZIS RIGHT TO OUR DOOR!
...
TELL THE GIRLS TO ARM THEMSELVES.
ARE YOU MAD? EVERY LAST ONE OF US WILL DIE HERE!
EVERY GIRL IN THIS HOUSE MADE AN OATH. IF THAT'S OUR FATE, WE'LL GO OUT WITH HONOUR DEFENDING OUR COUNTRY.
PETE, WE NEED TO MOVE.
MAKE IT COUNT, SIRENE.
YES, TAKING A STAND HERE WOULD MAKE A STATEMENT. BUT IT WOULD BE BURIED AND FORGOTTEN A WEEK FROM NOW.
SPEAK PLAINLY, BOY.
COME WITH ME.
HELP US SAVE MONNIER.

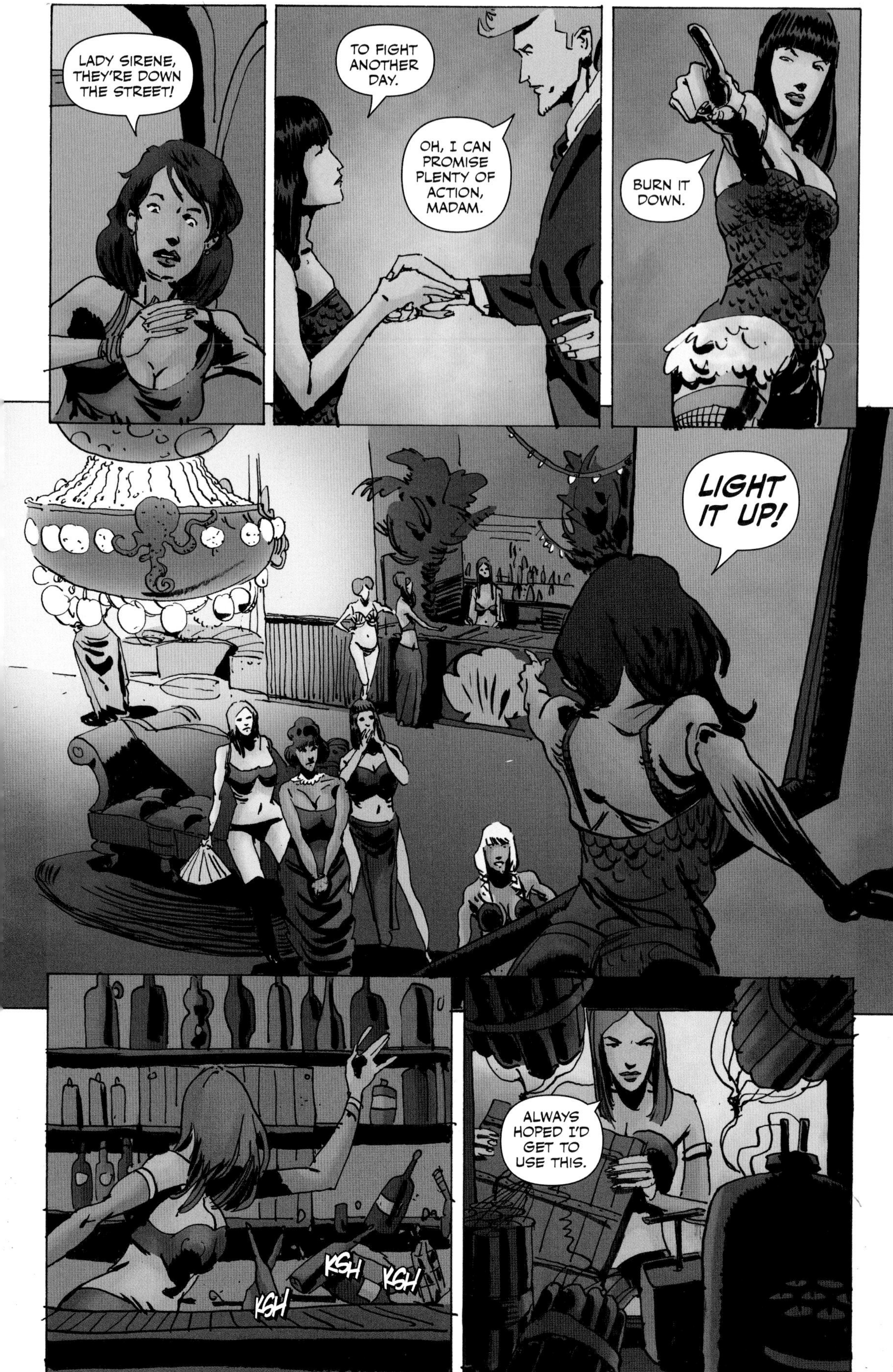
LADY SIRENE, THEY'RE DOWN THE STREET!
TO FIGHT ANOTHER DAY.
OH, I CAN PROMISE PLENTY OF ACTION, MADAM.
BURN IT DOWN.
LIGHT IT UP!
KSH
KSH
KSH
ALWAYS HOPED I'D GET TO USE THIS.

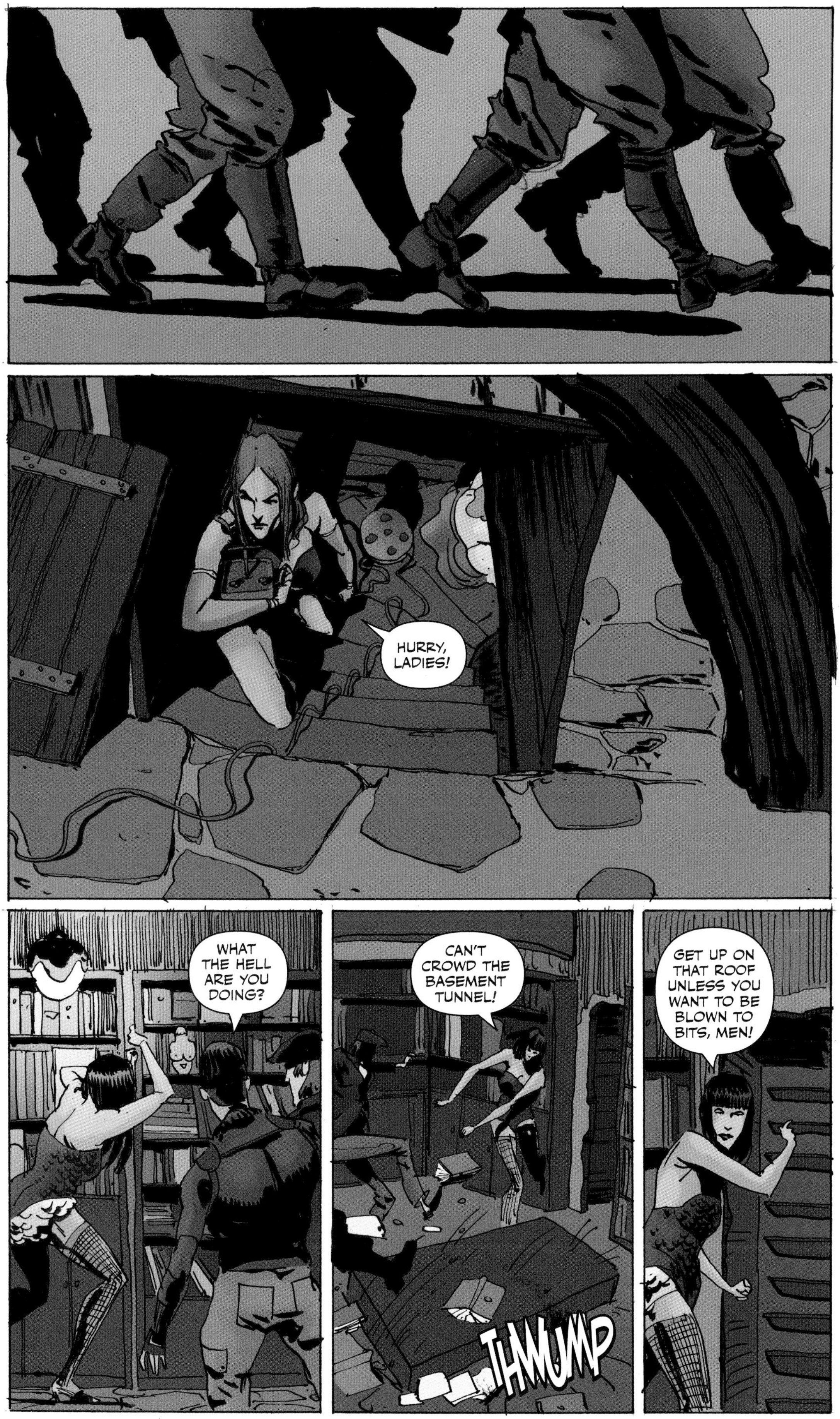
HURRY, LADIES!
WHAT THE HELL ARE YOU DOING?
CAN'T CROWD THE BASEMENT TUNNEL!
THMUMP
GET UP ON THAT ROOF UNLESS YOU WANT TO BE BLOWN TO BITS, MEN!

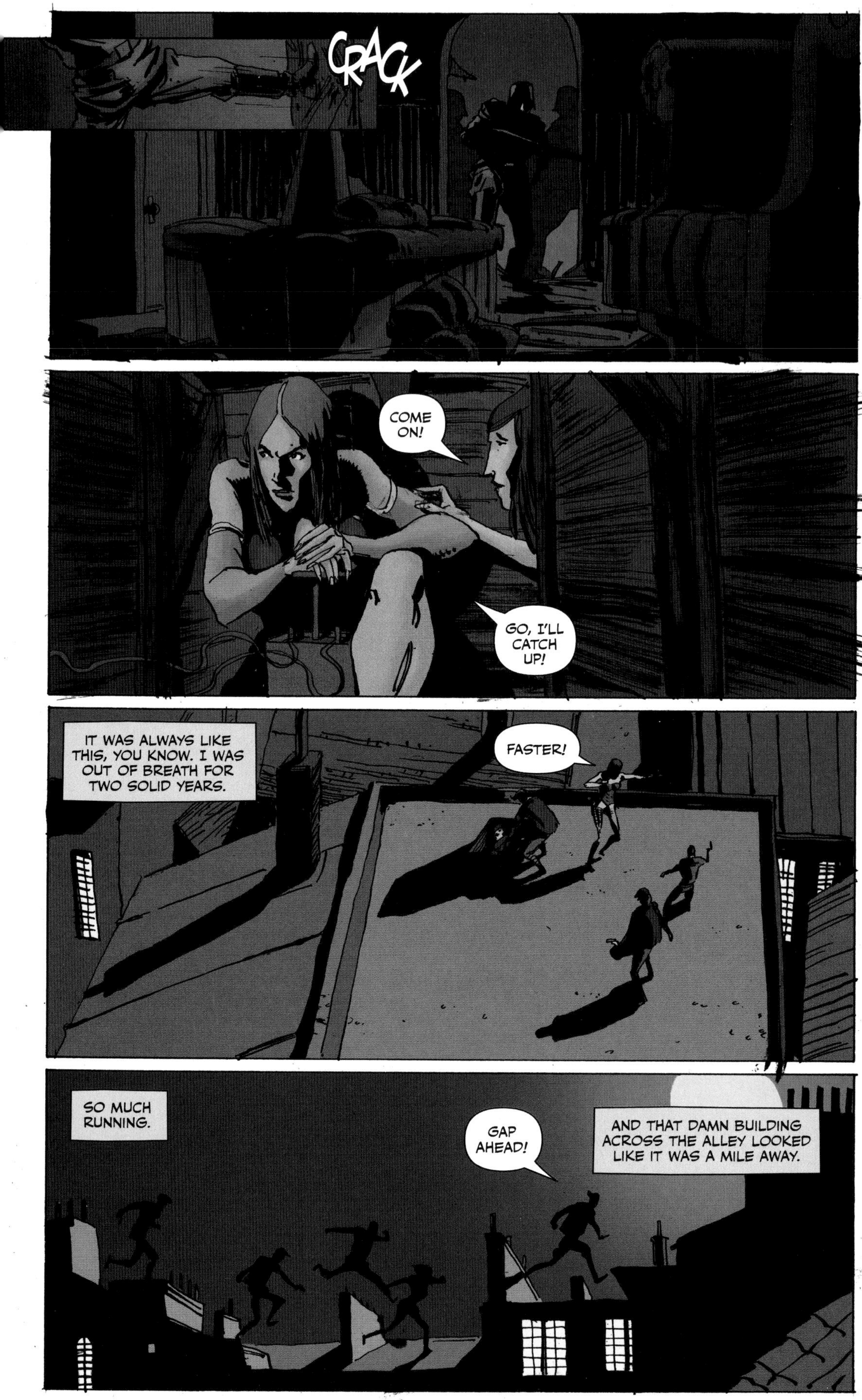
CRACK
COME ON!
GO, I'LL CATCH UP!
IT WAS ALWAYS LIKE THIS, YOU KNOW. I WAS OUT OF BREATH FOR TWO SOLID YEARS.
FASTER!
SO MUCH RUNNING.
GAP AHEAD!
AND THAT DAMN BUILDING ACROSS THE ALLEY LOOKED LIKE IT WAS A MILE AWAY.

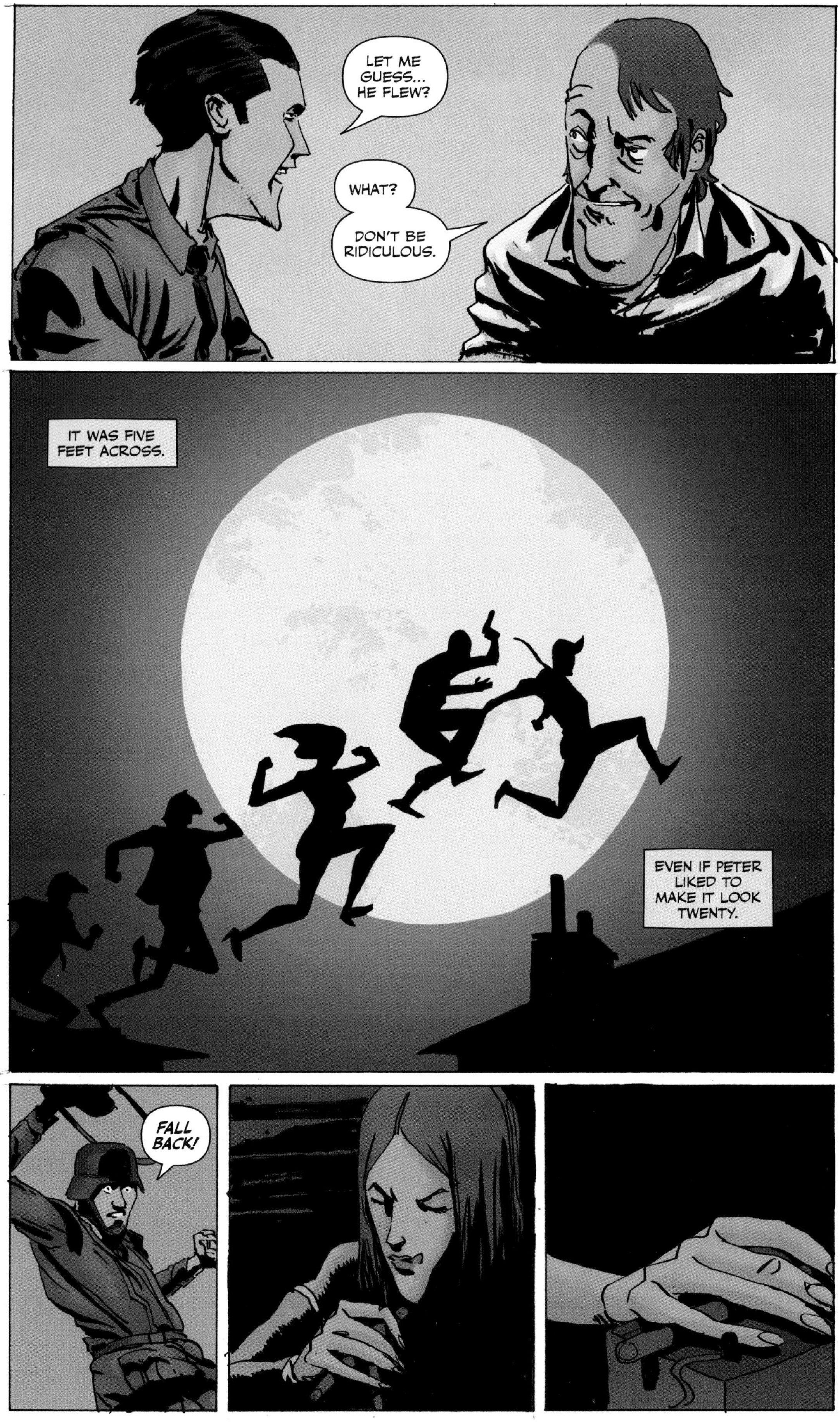
LET ME GUESS... HE FLEW?
WHAT?
DON'T BE RIDICULOUS.
IT WAS FIVE FEET ACROSS.
EVEN IF PETER LIKED TO MAKE IT LOOK TWENTY.
FALL BACK!

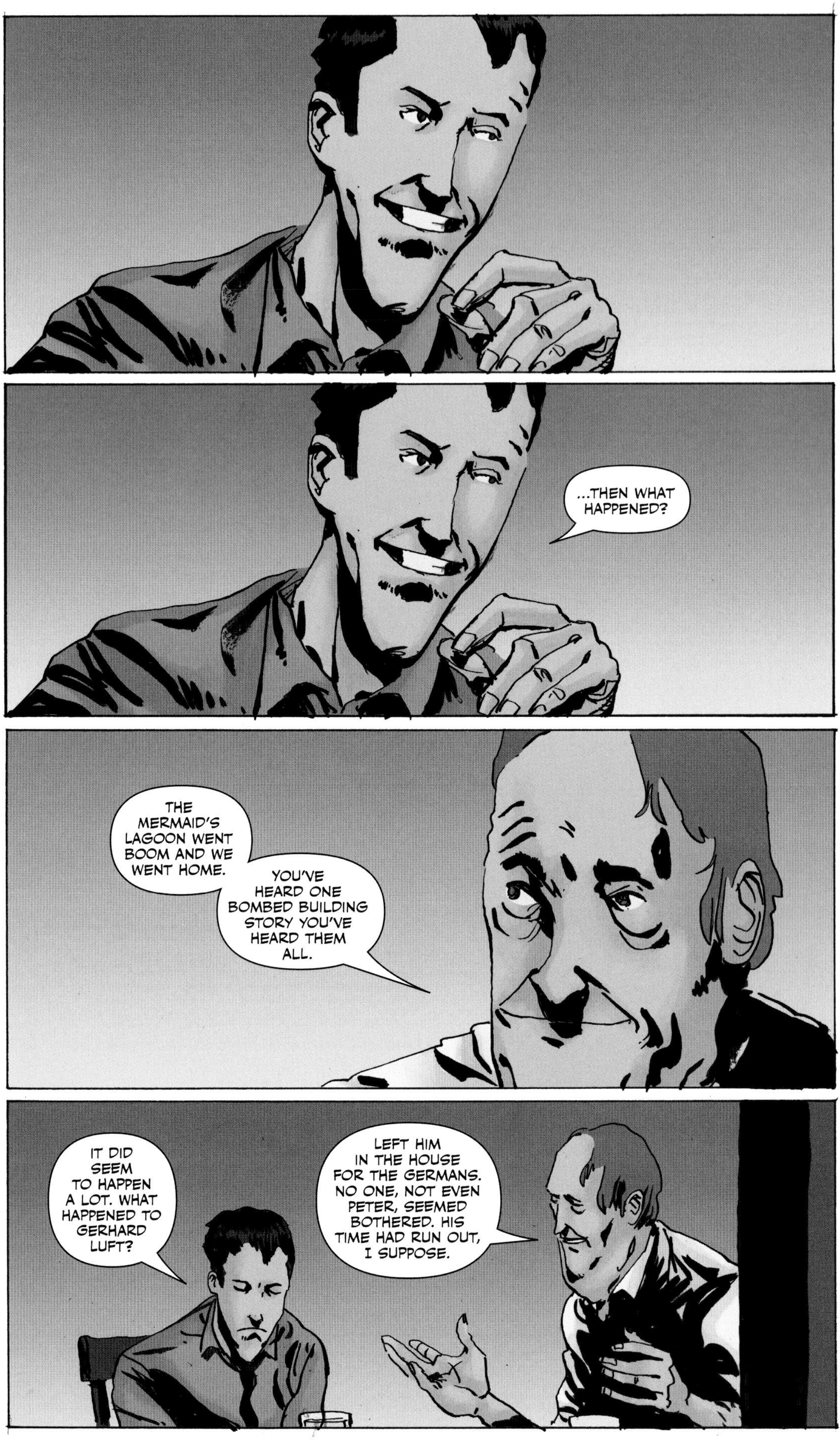
...THEN WHAT HAPPENED?
THE MERMAID'S LAGOON WENT BOOM AND WE WENT HOME.
YOU'VE HEARD ONE BOMBED BUILDING STORY YOU'VE HEARD THEM ALL.
IT DID SEEM TO HAPPEN A LOT. WHAT HAPPENED TO GERHARD LUFT?
LEFT HIM IN THE HOUSE FOR THE GERMANS. NO ONE, NOT EVEN PETER, SEEMED BOTHERED. HIS TIME HAD RUN OUT, I SUPPOSE.

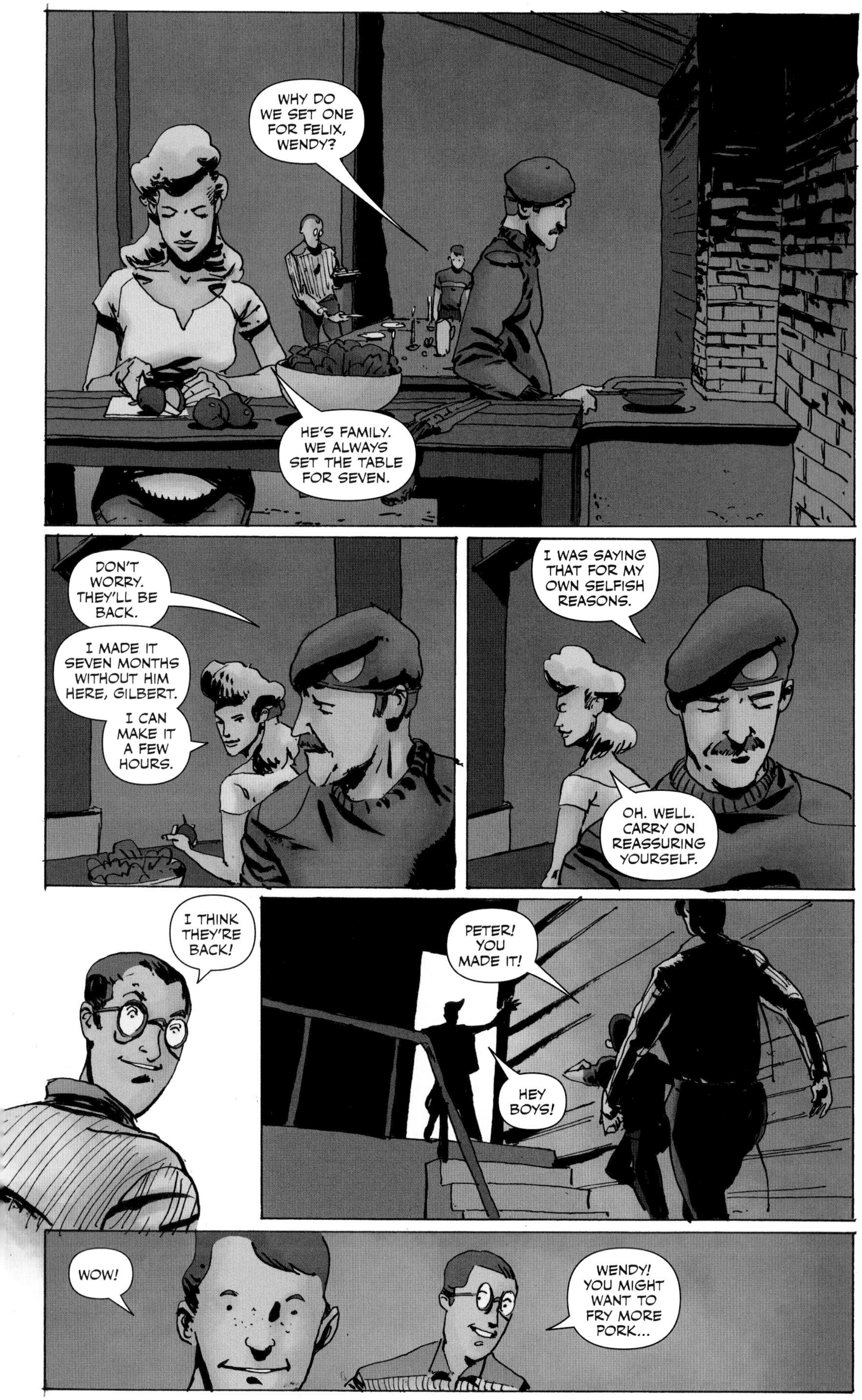
WHY DO WE SET ONE FOR FELIX, WENDY?
HE'S FAMILY. WE ALWAYS SET THE TABLE FOR SEVEN.
DON'T WORRY. THEY'LL BE BACK.
I MADE IT SEVEN MONTHS WITHOUT HIM HERE, GILBERT.
I CAN MAKE IT A FEW HOURS.
I WAS SAYING THAT FOR MY OWN SELFISH REASONS.
OH. WELL. CARRY ON REASSURING YOURSELF.
I THINK THEY'RE BACK!
PETER! YOU MADE IT!
HEY BOYS!
WOW!
WENDY! YOU MIGHT WANT TO FRY MORE PORK...

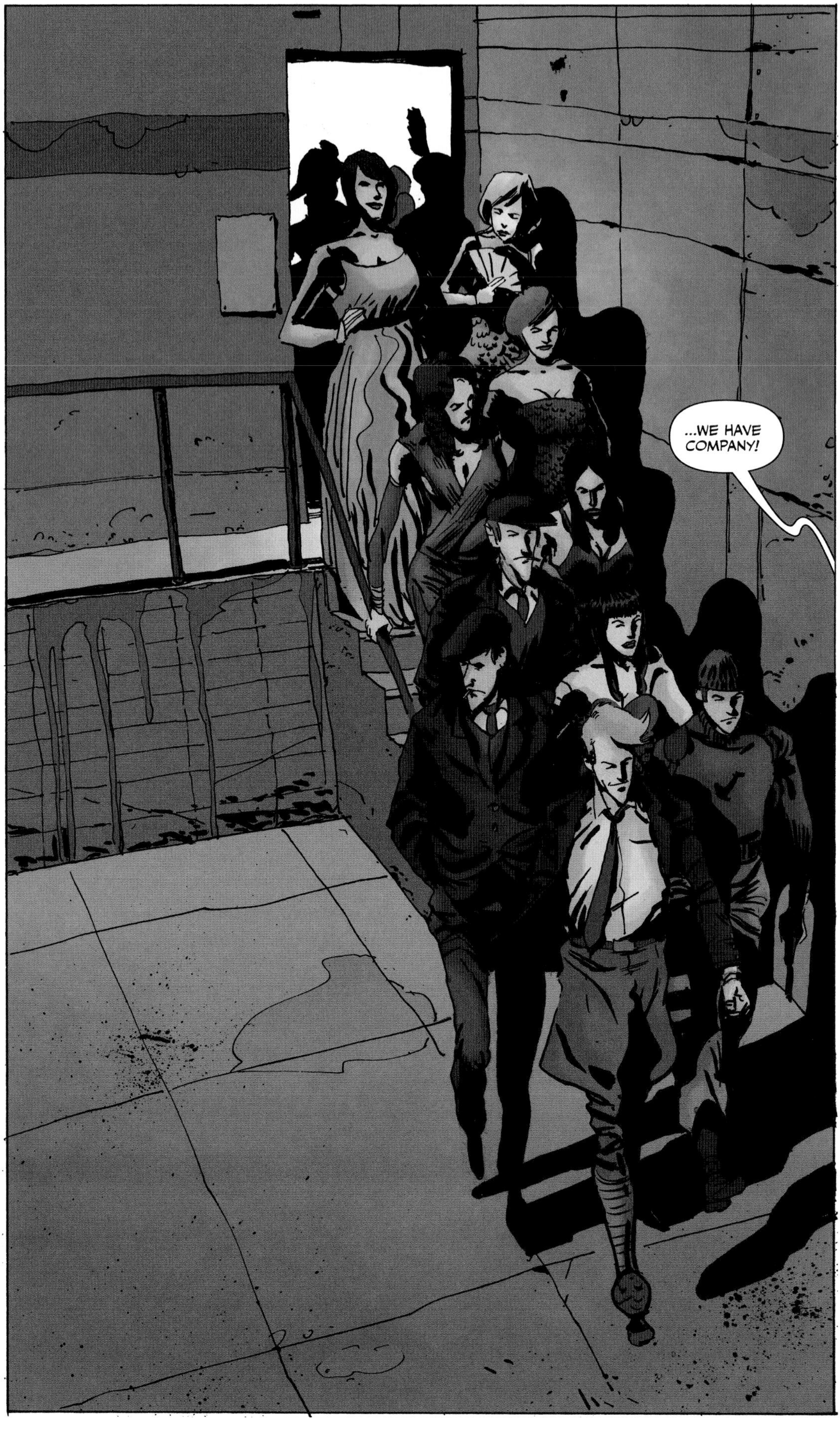
...WE HAVE COMPANY!

CHAPTER TWENTY-THREE

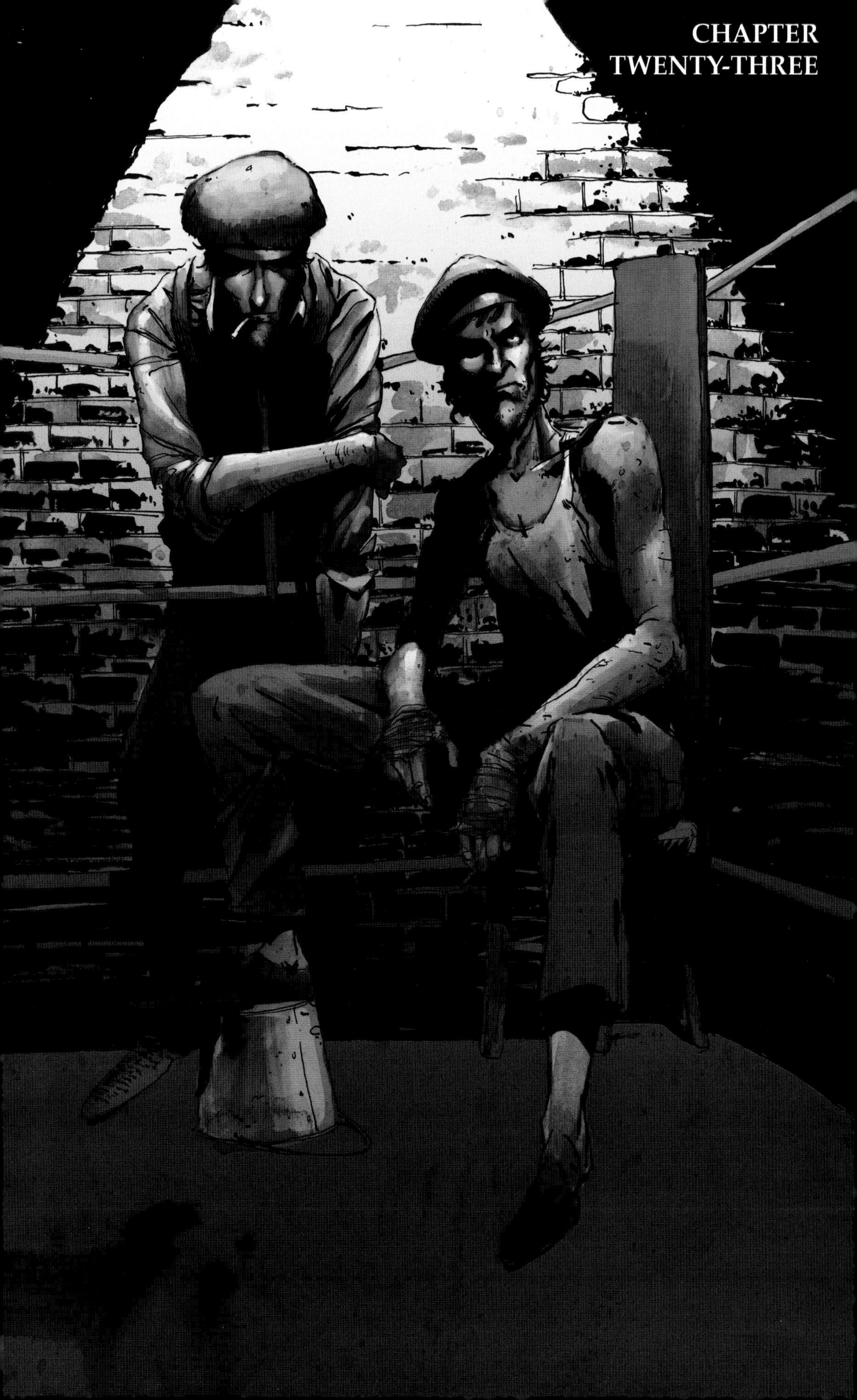

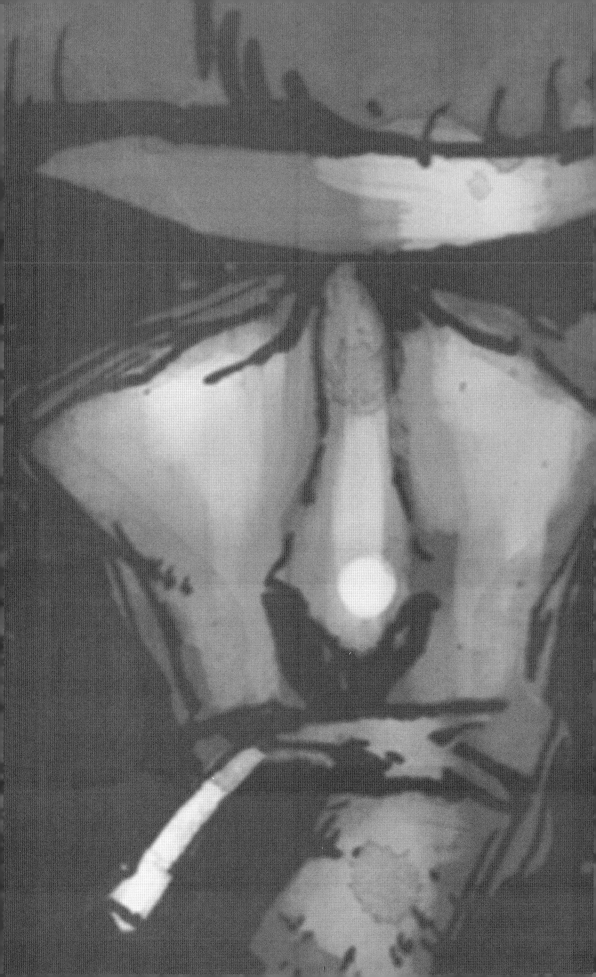

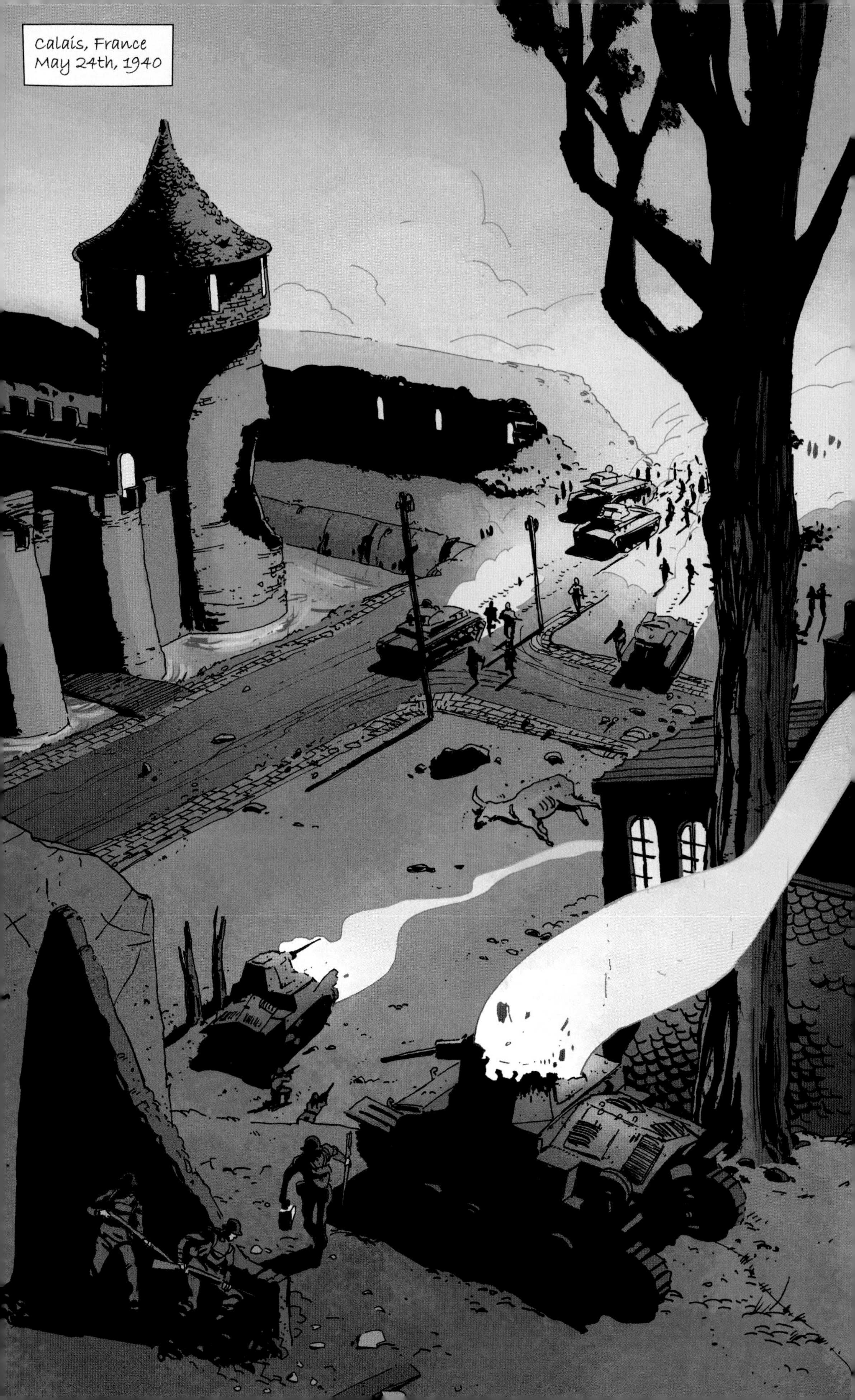
Calais, France
May 24th, 1940

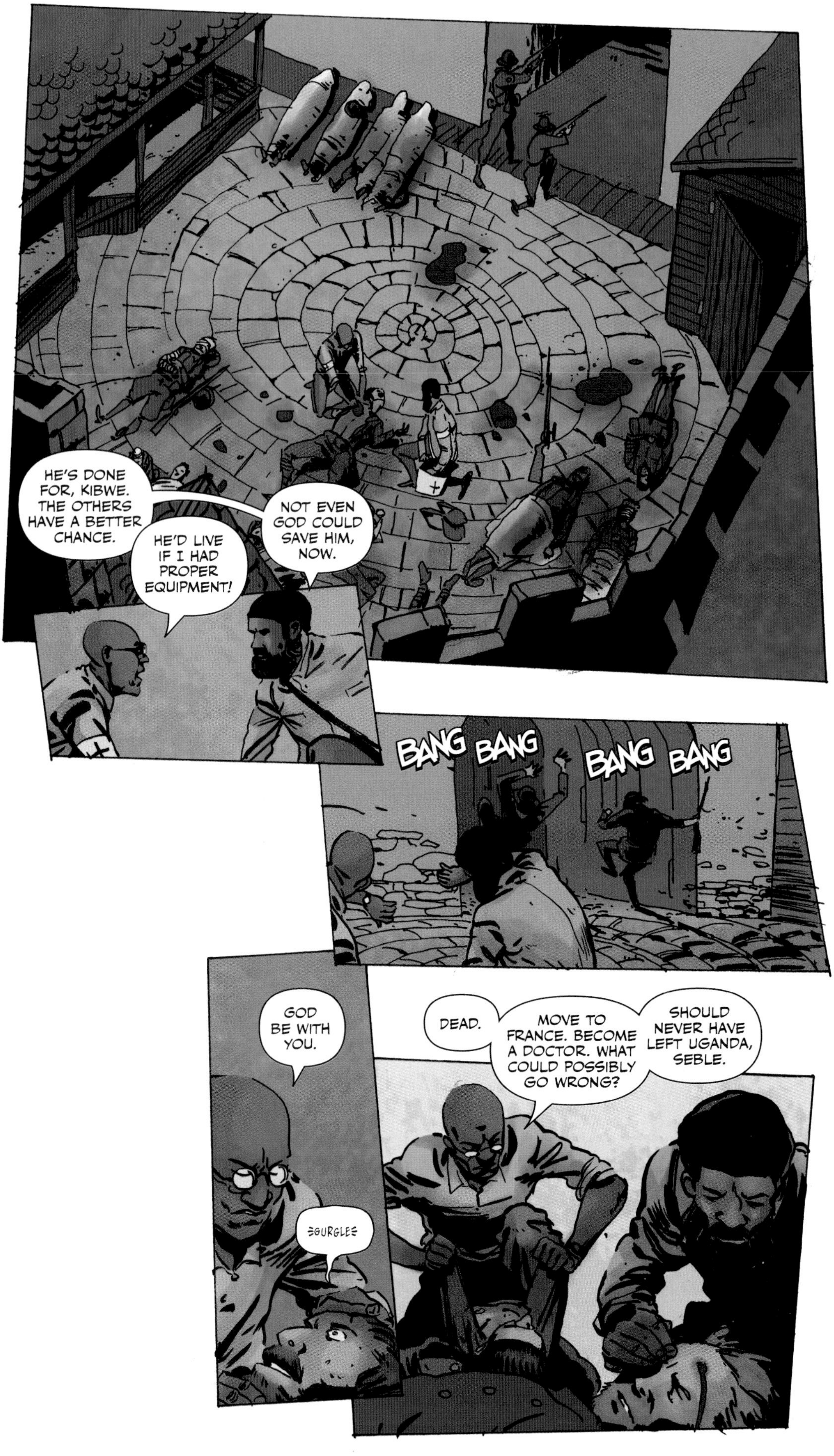
HE'S DONE FOR, KIBWE. THE OTHERS HAVE A BETTER CHANCE.
HE'D LIVE IF I HAD PROPER EQUIPMENT!
NOT EVEN GOD COULD SAVE HIM, NOW.
BANG BANG BANG BANG
GOD BE WITH YOU.
=GURGLE=
DEAD.
MOVE TO FRANCE. BECOME A DOCTOR. WHAT COULD POSSIBLY GO WRONG?
SHOULD NEVER HAVE LEFT UGANDA, SEBLE.

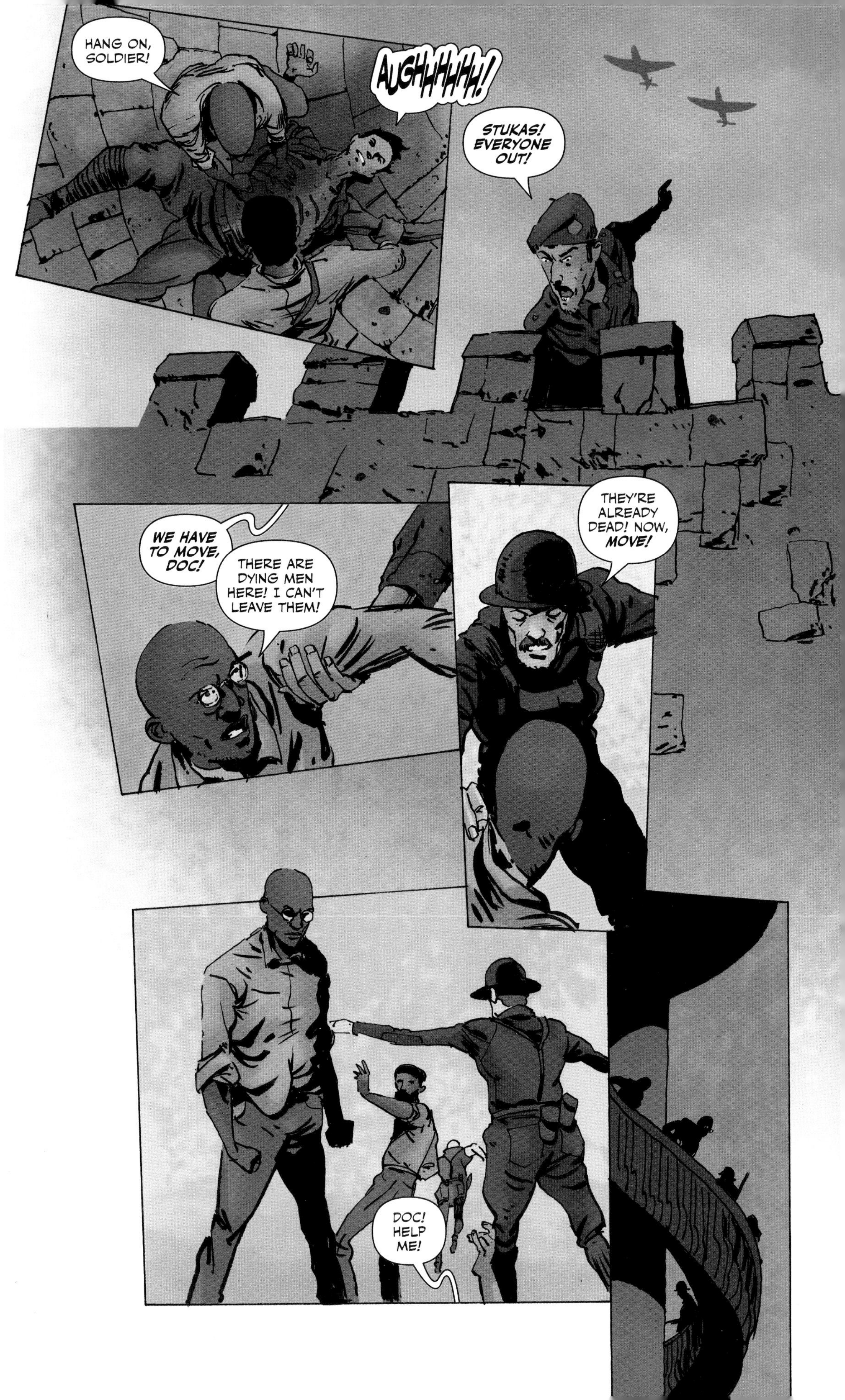
HANG ON, SOLDIER!
AUGHHHHHH!
STUKAS! EVERYONE OUT!
WE HAVE TO MOVE, DOC!
THERE ARE DYING MEN HERE! I CAN'T LEAVE THEM!
THEY'RE ALREADY DEAD! NOW, MOVE!
DOC! HELP ME!

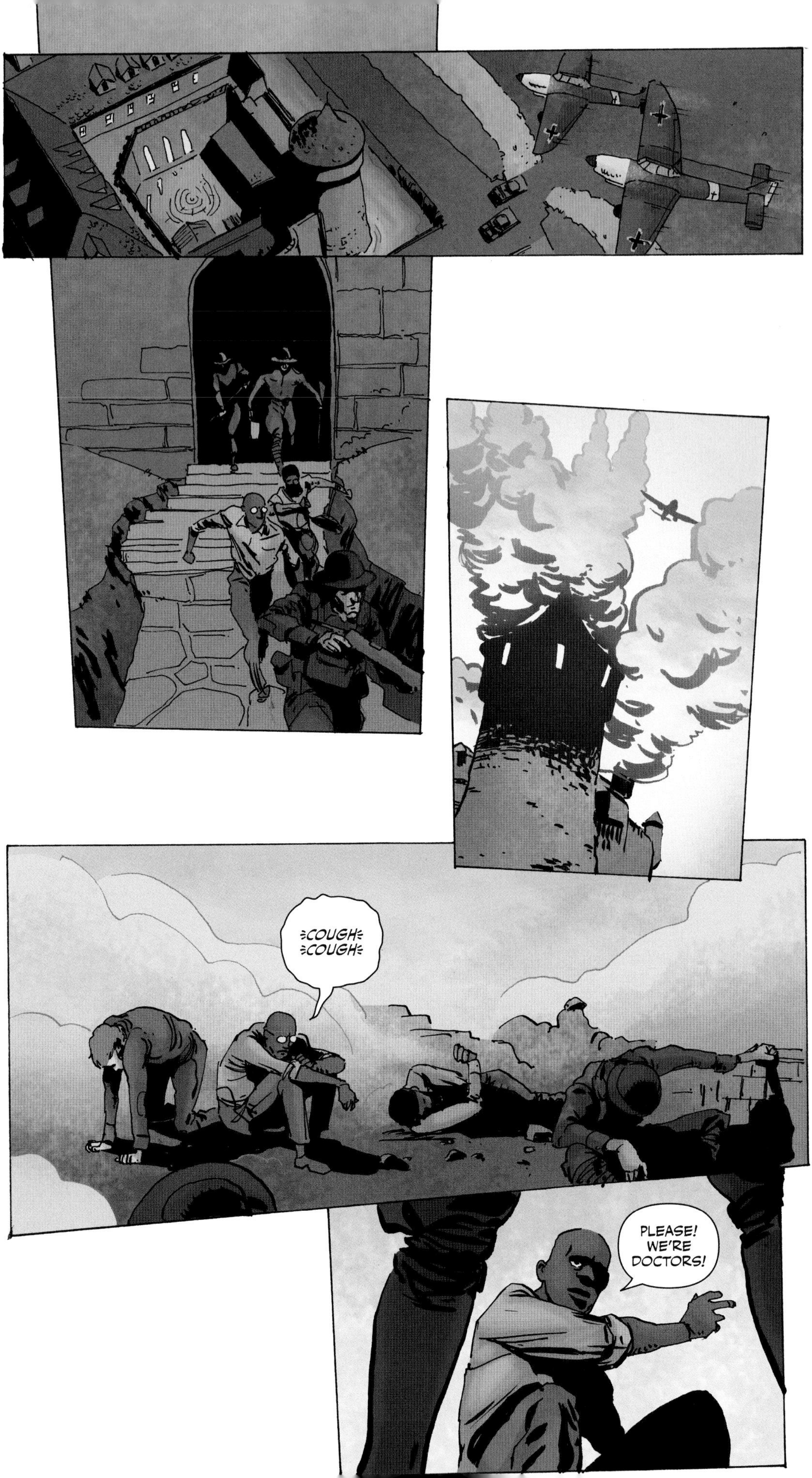
COUGH COUGH
PLEASE! WE'RE DOCTORS!

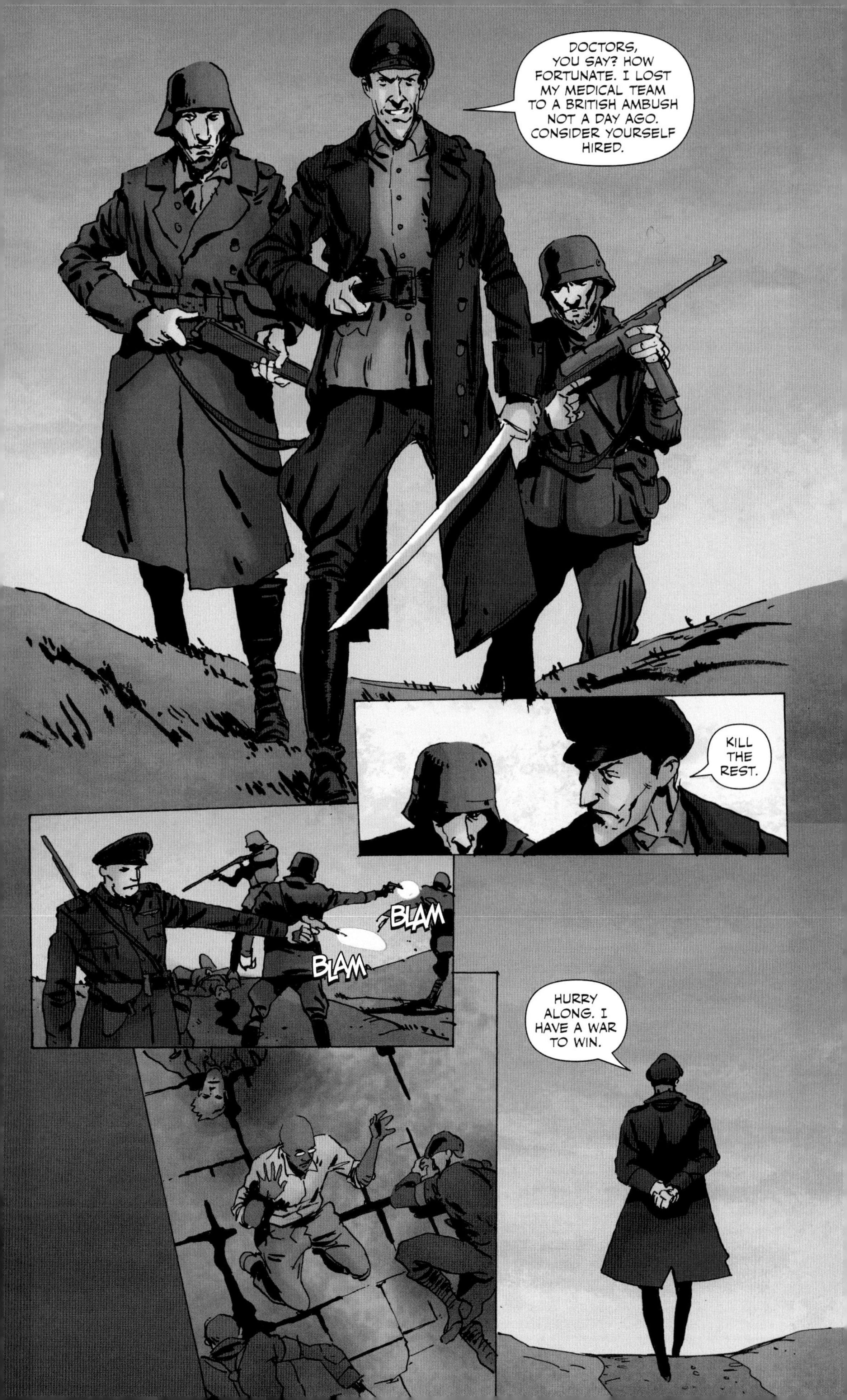
DOCTORS, YOU SAY? HOW FORTUNATE. I LOST MY MEDICAL TEAM TO A BRITISH AMBUSH NOT A DAY AGO. CONSIDER YOURSELF HIRED.
KILL THE REST.
BLAM
BLAM
HURRY ALONG. I HAVE A WAR TO WIN.

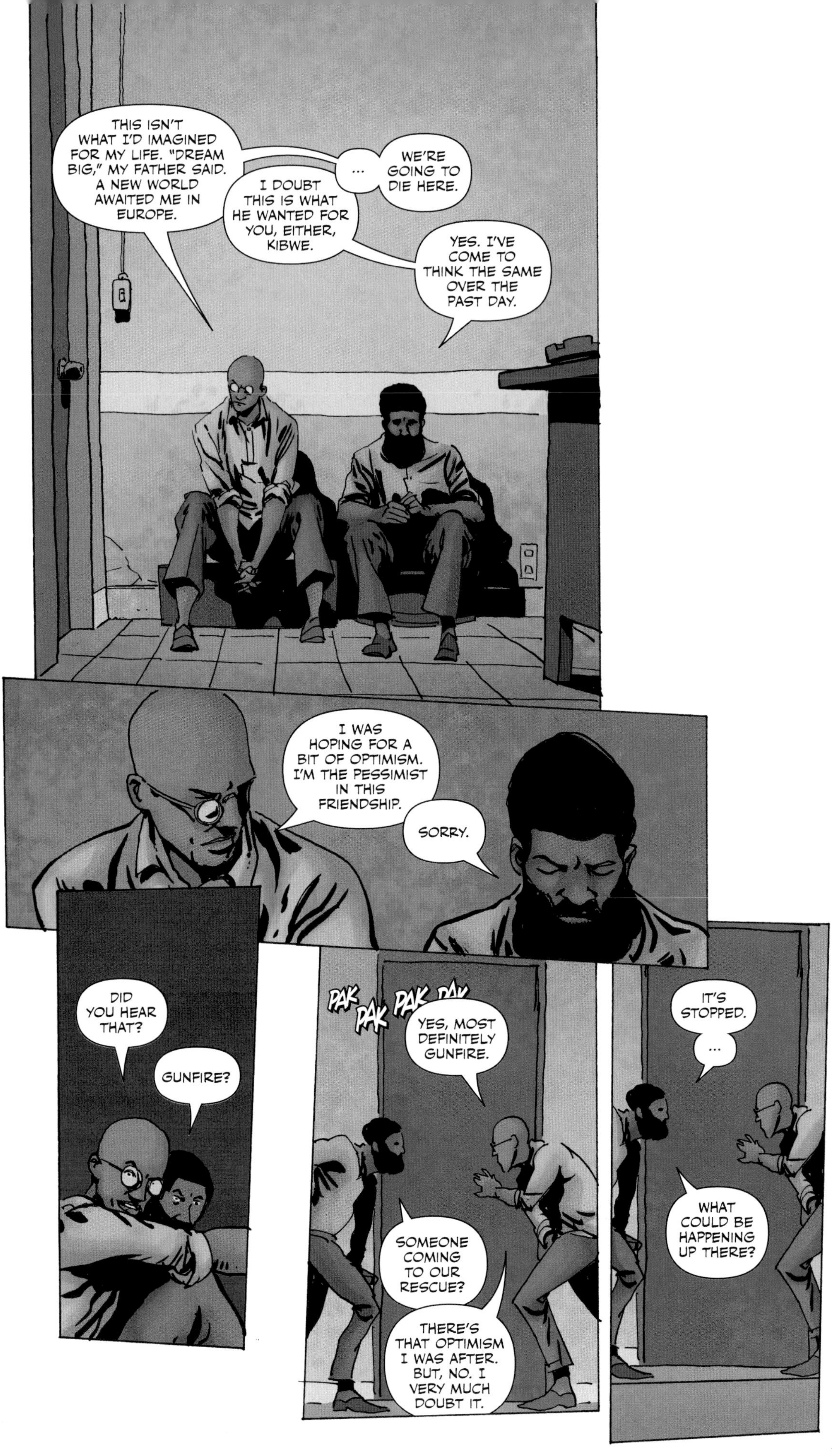
THIS ISN'T WHAT I'D IMAGINED FOR MY LIFE. "DREAM BIG," MY FATHER SAID. A NEW WORLD AWAITED ME IN EUROPE.
...
WE'RE GOING TO DIE HERE.
I DOUBT THIS IS WHAT HE WANTED FOR YOU, EITHER, KIBWE.
YES. I'VE COME TO THINK THE SAME OVER THE PAST DAY.
I WAS HOPING FOR A BIT OF OPTIMISM. I'M THE PESSIMIST IN THIS FRIENDSHIP.
SORRY.
DID YOU HEAR THAT?
GUNFIRE?
PAK PAK PAK
YES, MOST DEFINITELY GUNFIRE.
SOMEONE COMING TO OUR RESCUE?
THERE'S THAT OPTIMISM I WAS AFTER. BUT, NO. I VERY MUCH DOUBT IT.
IT'S STOPPED.
...
WHAT COULD BE HAPPENING UP THERE?

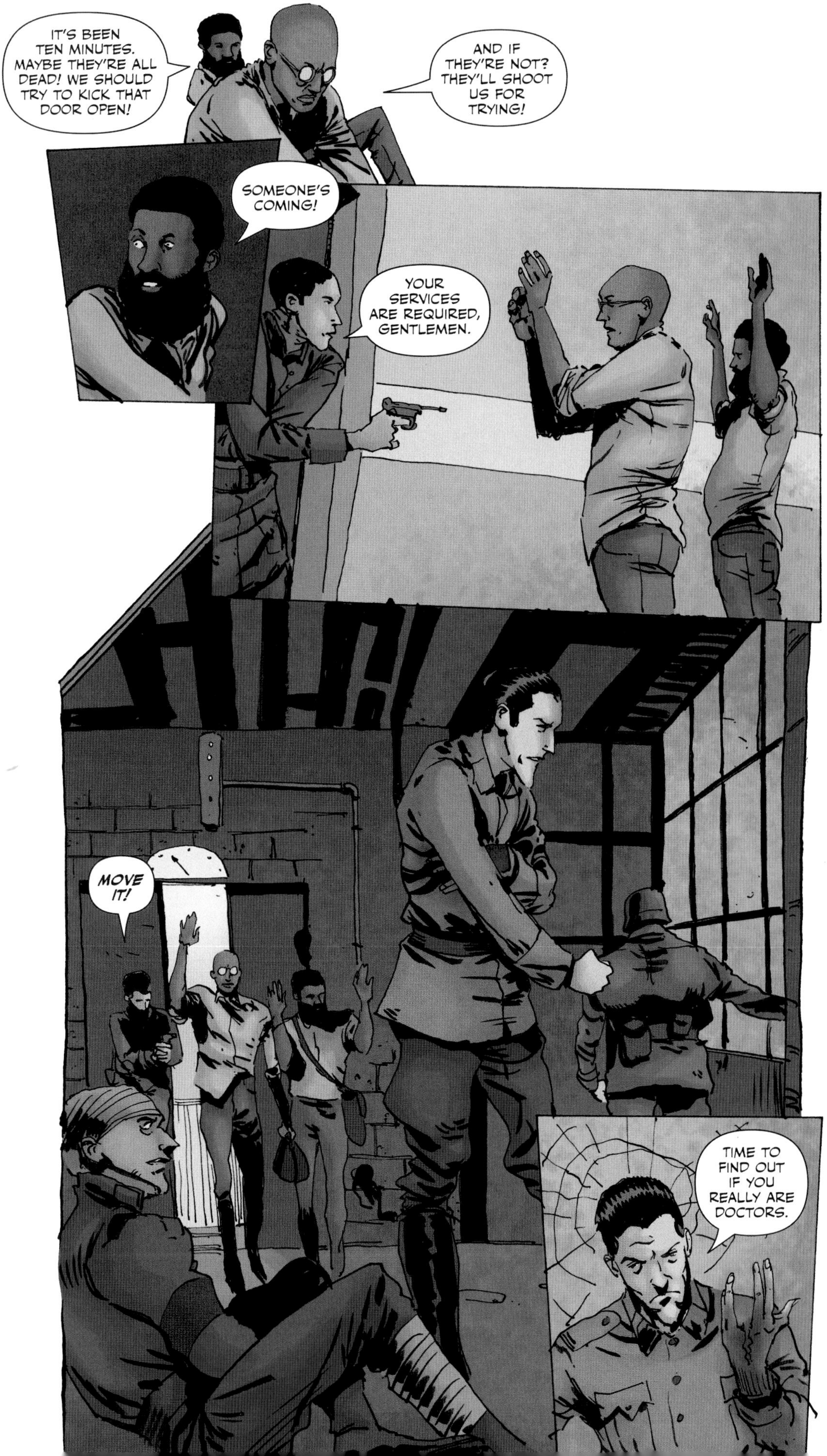
IT'S BEEN TEN MINUTES. MAYBE THEY'RE ALL DEAD! WE SHOULD TRY TO KICK THAT DOOR OPEN!
AND IF THEY'RE NOT? THEY'LL SHOOT US FOR TRYING!
SOMEONE'S COMING!
YOUR SERVICES ARE REQUIRED, GENTLEMEN.
MOVE IT!
TIME TO FIND OUT IF YOU REALLY ARE DOCTORS.

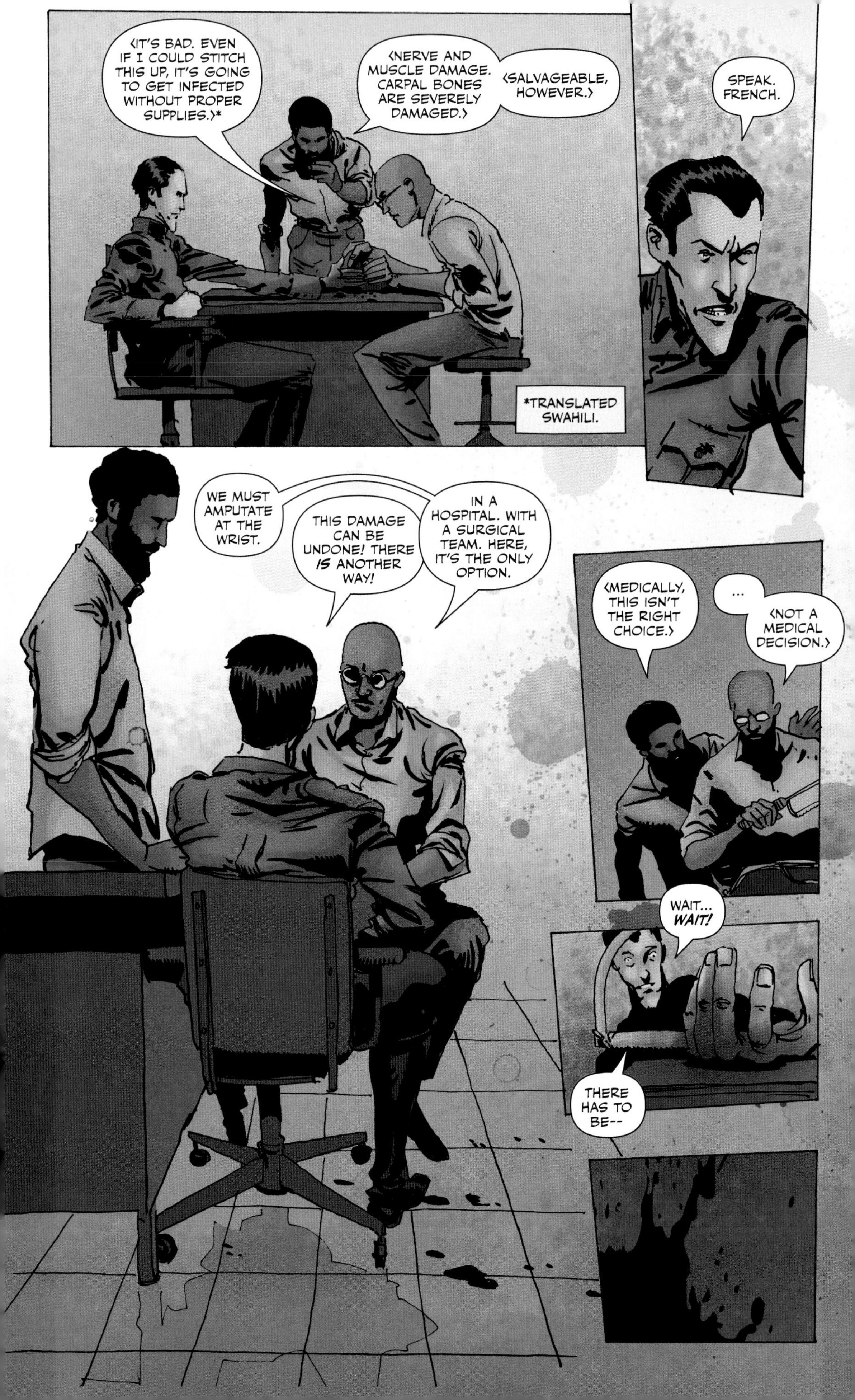

<IT'S BAD. EVEN IF I COULD STITCH THIS UP, IT'S GOING TO GET INFECTED WITHOUT PROPER SUPPLIES.>*
<NERVE AND MUSCLE DAMAGE. CARPAL BONES ARE SEVERELY DAMAGED.>
<SALVAGEABLE, HOWEVER.>
*TRANSLATED SWAHILI.
SPEAK. FRENCH.
WE MUST AMPUTATE AT THE WRIST.
IN A HOSPITAL. WITH A SURGICAL TEAM. HERE, IT'S THE ONLY OPTION.
THIS DAMAGE CAN BE UNDONE! THERE *IS* ANOTHER WAY!
<MEDICALLY, THIS ISN'T THE RIGHT CHOICE.>
...
<NOT A MEDICAL DECISION.>
WAIT... ***WAIT!***
THERE HAS TO BE--

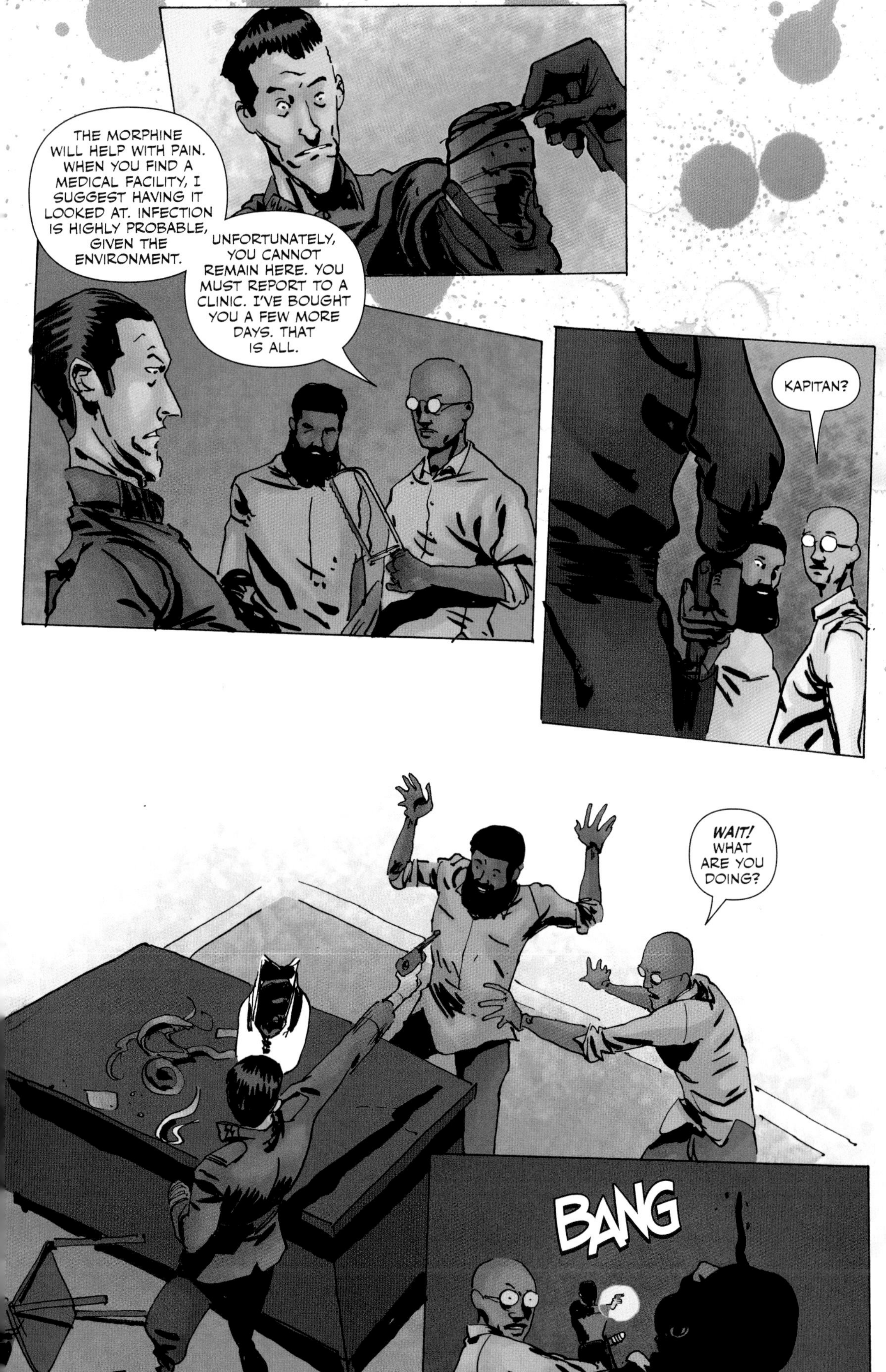
THE MORPHINE WILL HELP WITH PAIN. WHEN YOU FIND A MEDICAL FACILITY, I SUGGEST HAVING IT LOOKED AT. INFECTION IS HIGHLY PROBABLE, GIVEN THE ENVIRONMENT.
UNFORTUNATELY, YOU CANNOT REMAIN HERE. YOU MUST REPORT TO A CLINIC. I'VE BOUGHT YOU A FEW MORE DAYS. THAT IS ALL.
KAPITAN?
WAIT! WHAT ARE YOU DOING?
BANG

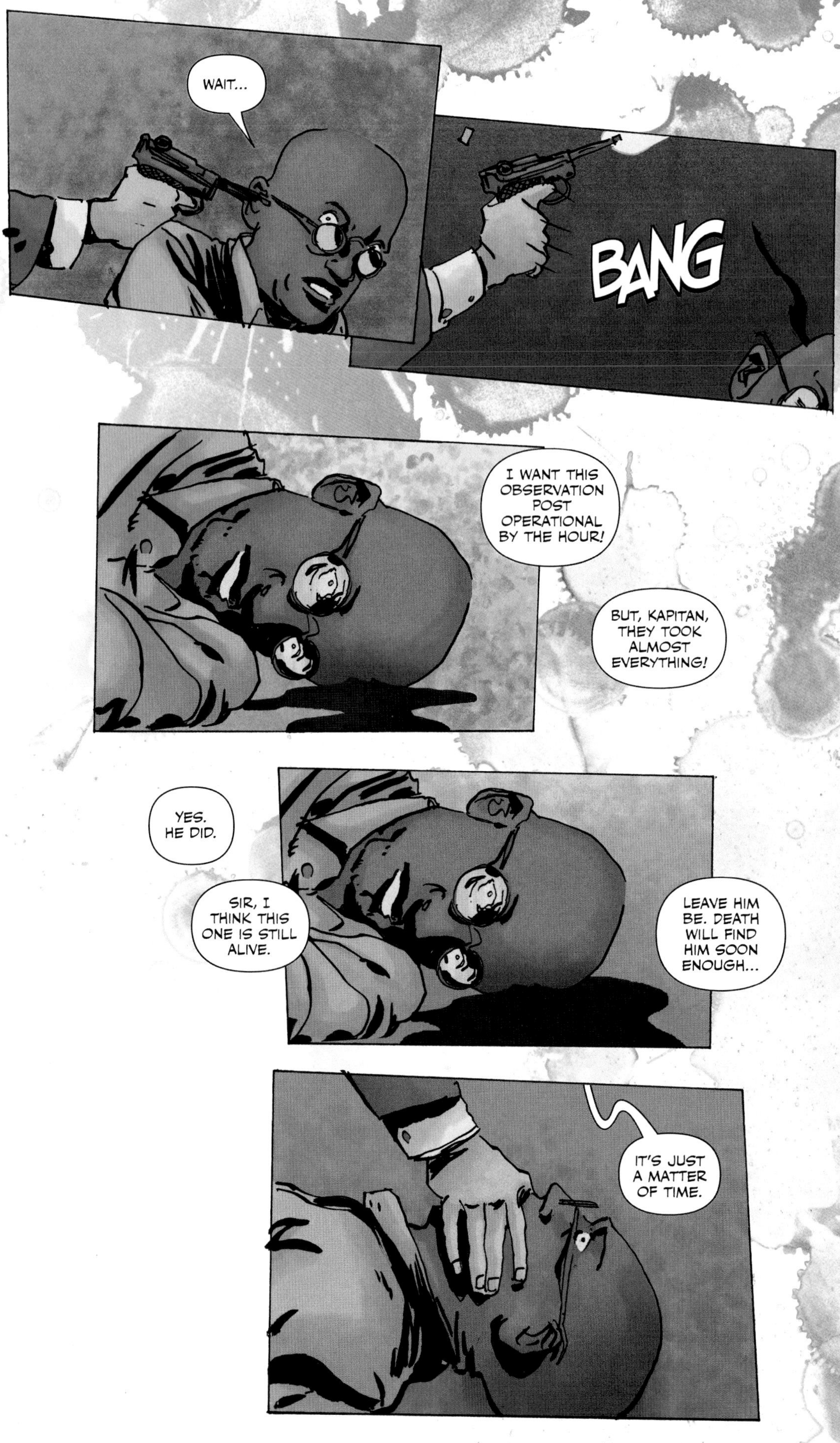
WAIT...
BANG
I WANT THIS OBSERVATION POST OPERATIONAL BY THE HOUR!
BUT, KAPITAN, THEY TOOK ALMOST EVERYTHING!
YES. HE DID.
SIR, I THINK THIS ONE IS STILL ALIVE.
LEAVE HIM BE. DEATH WILL FIND HIM SOON ENOUGH...
IT'S JUST A MATTER OF TIME.

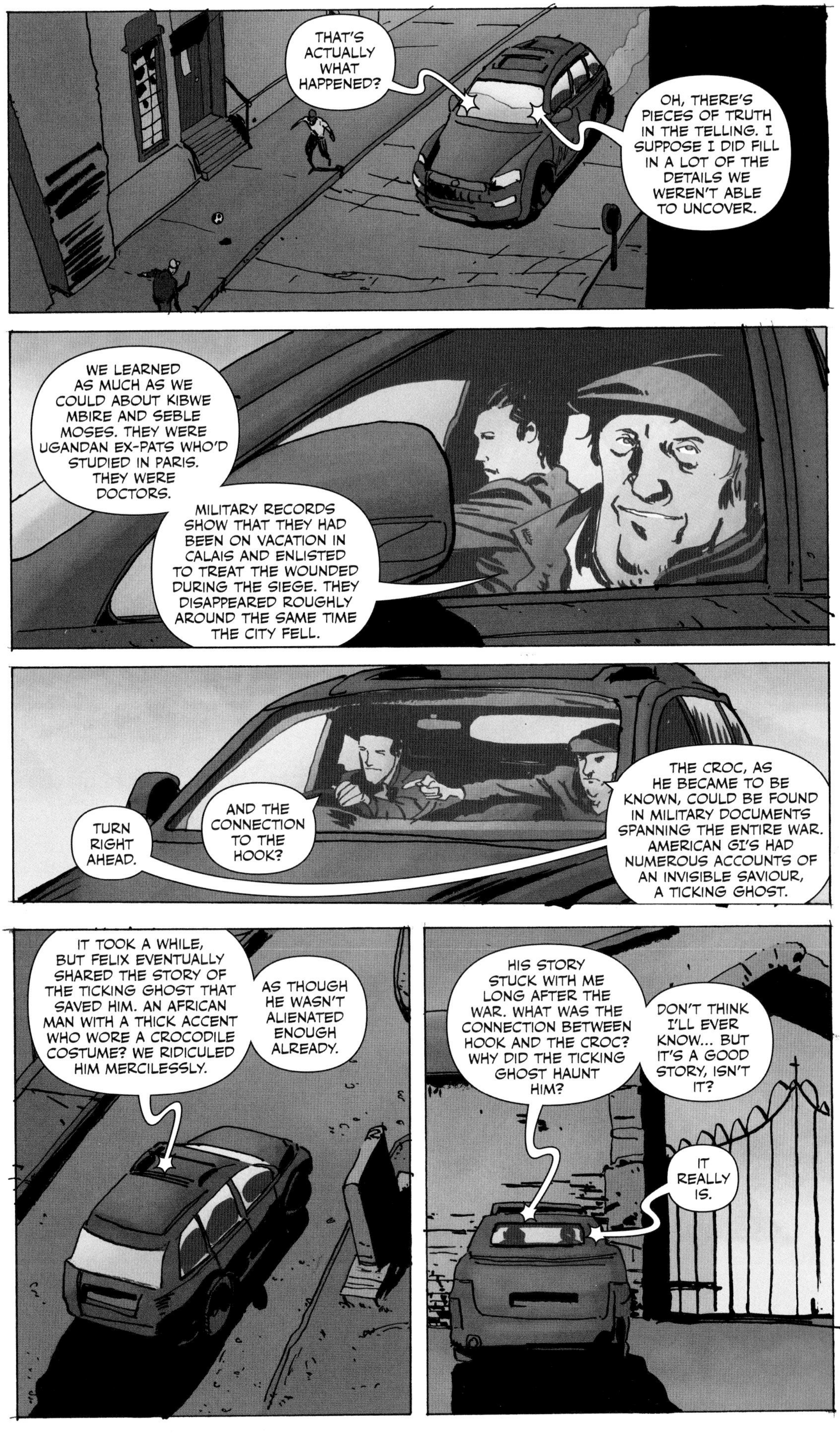
THAT'S ACTUALLY WHAT HAPPENED?
OH, THERE'S PIECES OF TRUTH IN THE TELLING. I SUPPOSE I DID FILL IN A LOT OF THE DETAILS WE WEREN'T ABLE TO UNCOVER.
WE LEARNED AS MUCH AS WE COULD ABOUT KIBWE MBIRE AND SEBLE MOSES. THEY WERE UGANDAN EX-PATS WHO'D STUDIED IN PARIS. THEY WERE DOCTORS.
MILITARY RECORDS SHOW THAT THEY HAD BEEN ON VACATION IN CALAIS AND ENLISTED TO TREAT THE WOUNDED DURING THE SIEGE. THEY DISAPPEARED ROUGHLY AROUND THE SAME TIME THE CITY FELL.
AND THE CONNECTION TO THE HOOK?
THE CROC, AS HE BECAME TO BE KNOWN, COULD BE FOUND IN MILITARY DOCUMENTS SPANNING THE ENTIRE WAR. AMERICAN GI'S HAD NUMEROUS ACCOUNTS OF AN INVISIBLE SAVIOUR, A TICKING GHOST.
TURN RIGHT AHEAD.
IT TOOK A WHILE, BUT FELIX EVENTUALLY SHARED THE STORY OF THE TICKING GHOST THAT SAVED HIM. AN AFRICAN MAN WITH A THICK ACCENT WHO WORE A CROCODILE COSTUME? WE RIDICULED HIM MERCILESSLY.
AS THOUGH HE WASN'T ALIENATED ENOUGH ALREADY.
HIS STORY STUCK WITH ME LONG AFTER THE WAR. WHAT WAS THE CONNECTION BETWEEN HOOK AND THE CROC? WHY DID THE TICKING GHOST HAUNT HIM?
DON'T THINK I'LL EVER KNOW... BUT IT'S A GOOD STORY, ISN'T IT?
IT REALLY IS.

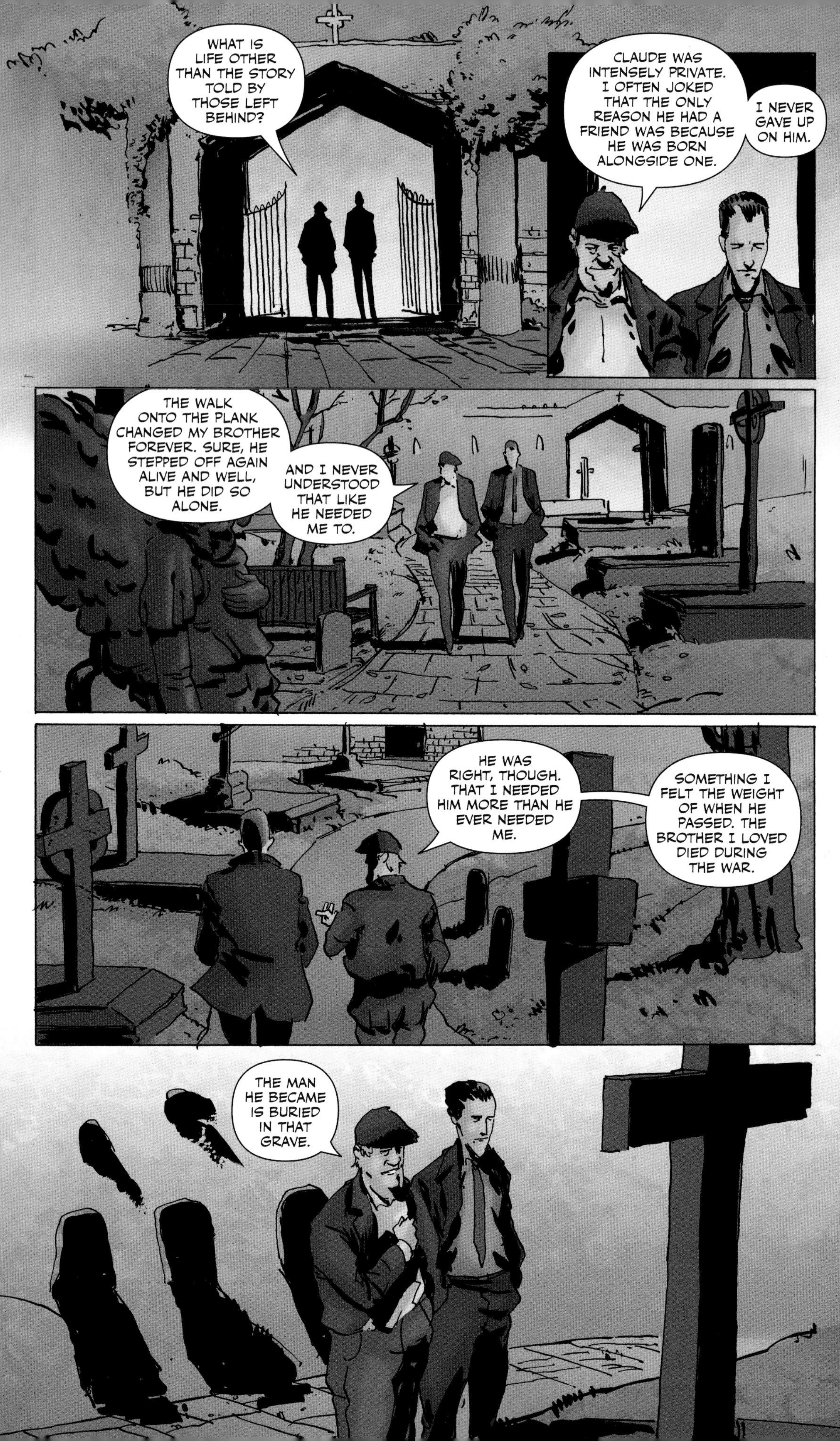
WHAT IS LIFE OTHER THAN THE STORY TOLD BY THOSE LEFT BEHIND?
CLAUDE WAS INTENSELY PRIVATE. I OFTEN JOKED THAT THE ONLY REASON HE HAD A FRIEND WAS BECAUSE HE WAS BORN ALONGSIDE ONE.
I NEVER GAVE UP ON HIM.
THE WALK ONTO THE PLANK CHANGED MY BROTHER FOREVER. SURE, HE STEPPED OFF AGAIN ALIVE AND WELL, BUT HE DID SO ALONE.
AND I NEVER UNDERSTOOD THAT LIKE HE NEEDED ME TO.
HE WAS RIGHT, THOUGH. THAT I NEEDED HIM MORE THAN HE EVER NEEDED ME.
SOMETHING I FELT THE WEIGHT OF WHEN HE PASSED. THE BROTHER I LOVED DIED DURING THE WAR.
THE MAN HE BECAME IS BURIED IN THAT GRAVE.

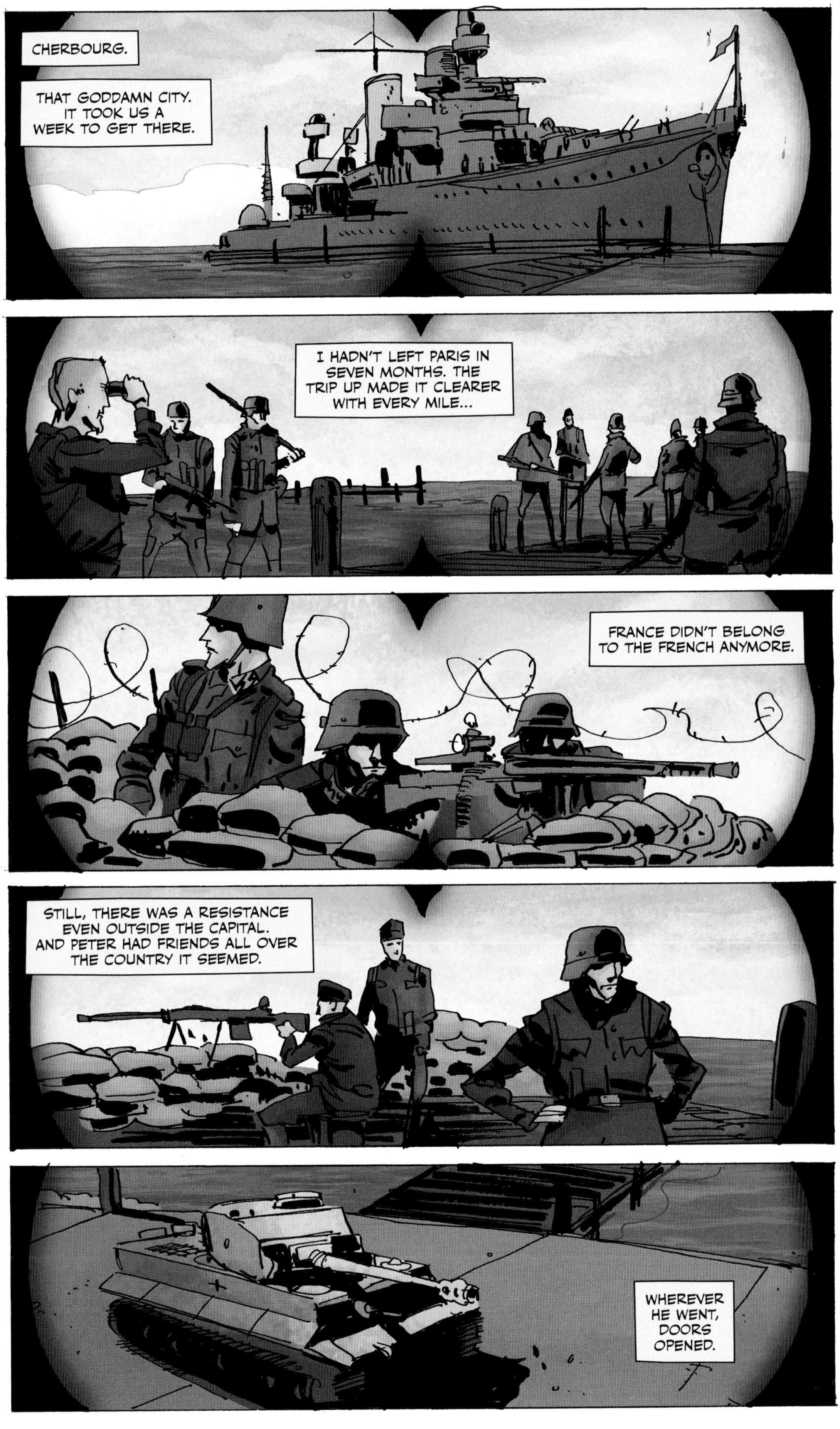
CHERBOURG.
THAT GODDAMN CITY. IT TOOK US A WEEK TO GET THERE.
I HADN'T LEFT PARIS IN SEVEN MONTHS. THE TRIP UP MADE IT CLEARER WITH EVERY MILE...
FRANCE DIDN'T BELONG TO THE FRENCH ANYMORE.
STILL, THERE WAS A RESISTANCE EVEN OUTSIDE THE CAPITAL. AND PETER HAD FRIENDS ALL OVER THE COUNTRY IT SEEMED.
WHEREVER HE WENT, DOORS OPENED.

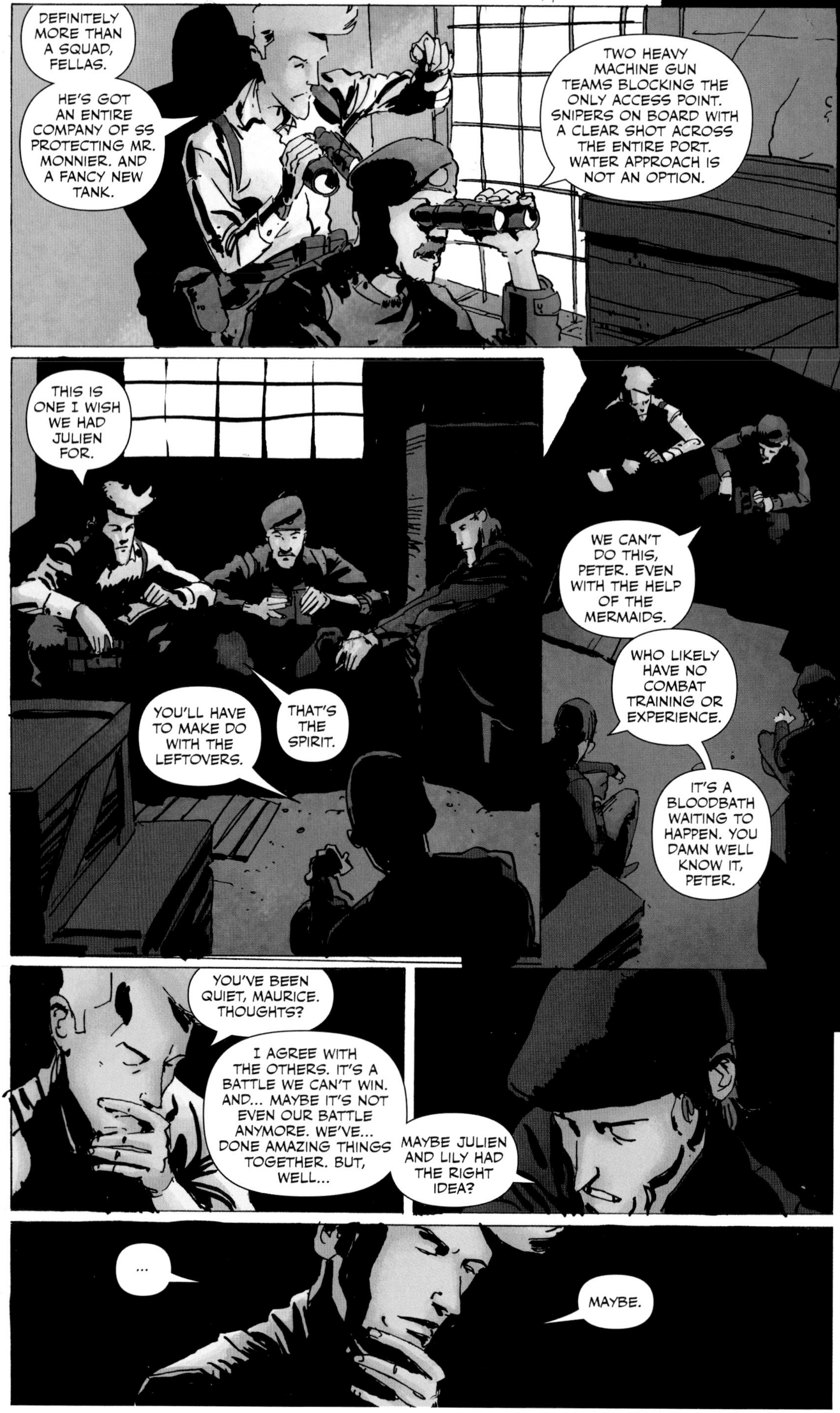
DEFINITELY MORE THAN A SQUAD, FELLAS.
HE'S GOT AN ENTIRE COMPANY OF SS PROTECTING MR. MONNIER. AND A FANCY NEW TANK.
TWO HEAVY MACHINE GUN TEAMS BLOCKING THE ONLY ACCESS POINT. SNIPERS ON BOARD WITH A CLEAR SHOT ACROSS THE ENTIRE PORT. WATER APPROACH IS NOT AN OPTION.
THIS IS ONE I WISH WE HAD JULIEN FOR.
YOU'LL HAVE TO MAKE DO WITH THE LEFTOVERS.
THAT'S THE SPIRIT.
WE CAN'T DO THIS, PETER. EVEN WITH THE HELP OF THE MERMAIDS.
WHO LIKELY HAVE NO COMBAT TRAINING OR EXPERIENCE.
IT'S A BLOODBATH WAITING TO HAPPEN. YOU DAMN WELL KNOW IT, PETER.
YOU'VE BEEN QUIET, MAURICE. THOUGHTS?
I AGREE WITH THE OTHERS. IT'S A BATTLE WE CAN'T WIN. AND... MAYBE IT'S NOT EVEN OUR BATTLE ANYMORE. WE'VE... DONE AMAZING THINGS TOGETHER. BUT, WELL...
MAYBE JULIEN AND LILY HAD THE RIGHT IDEA?
...
MAYBE.

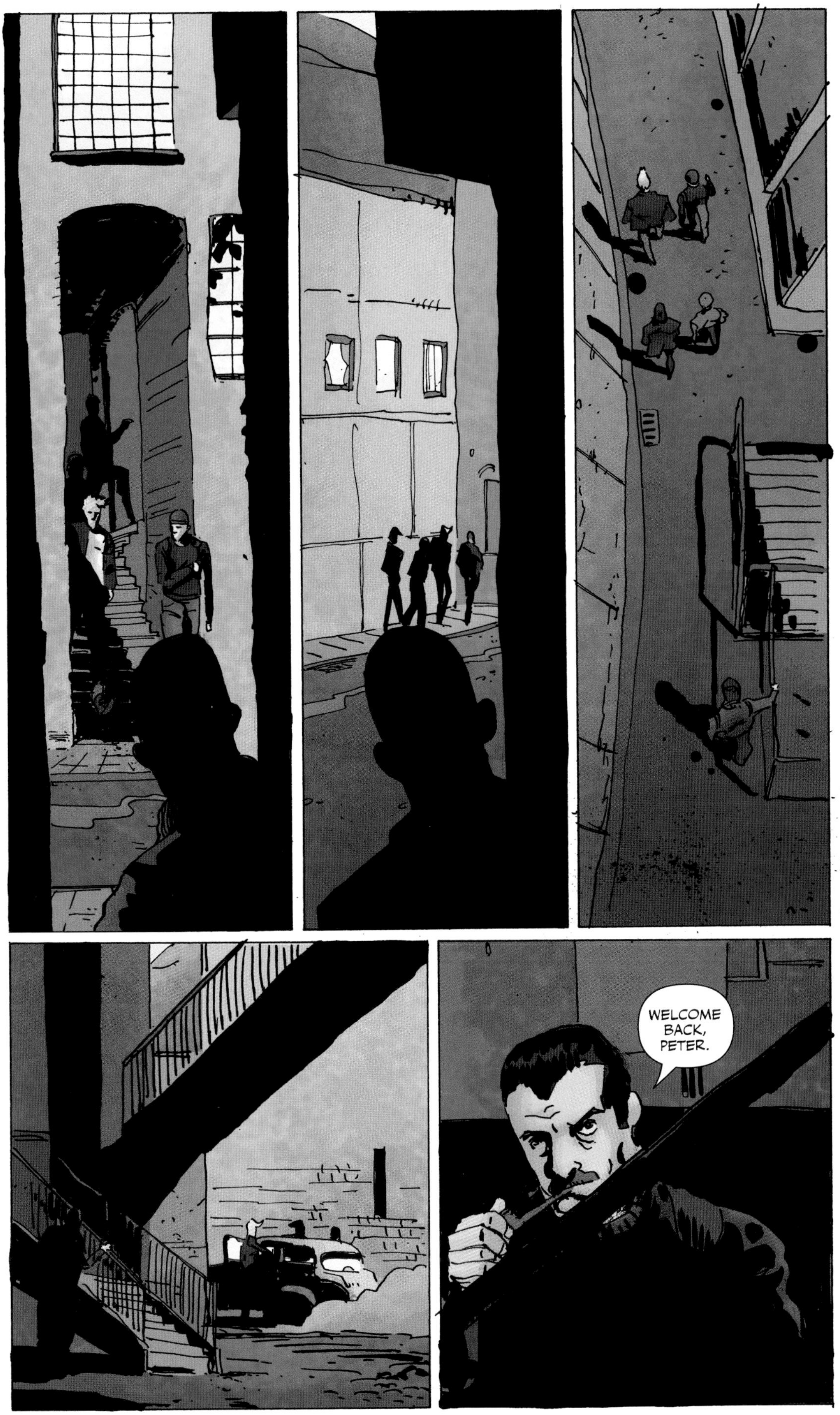
WELCOME BACK, PETER.

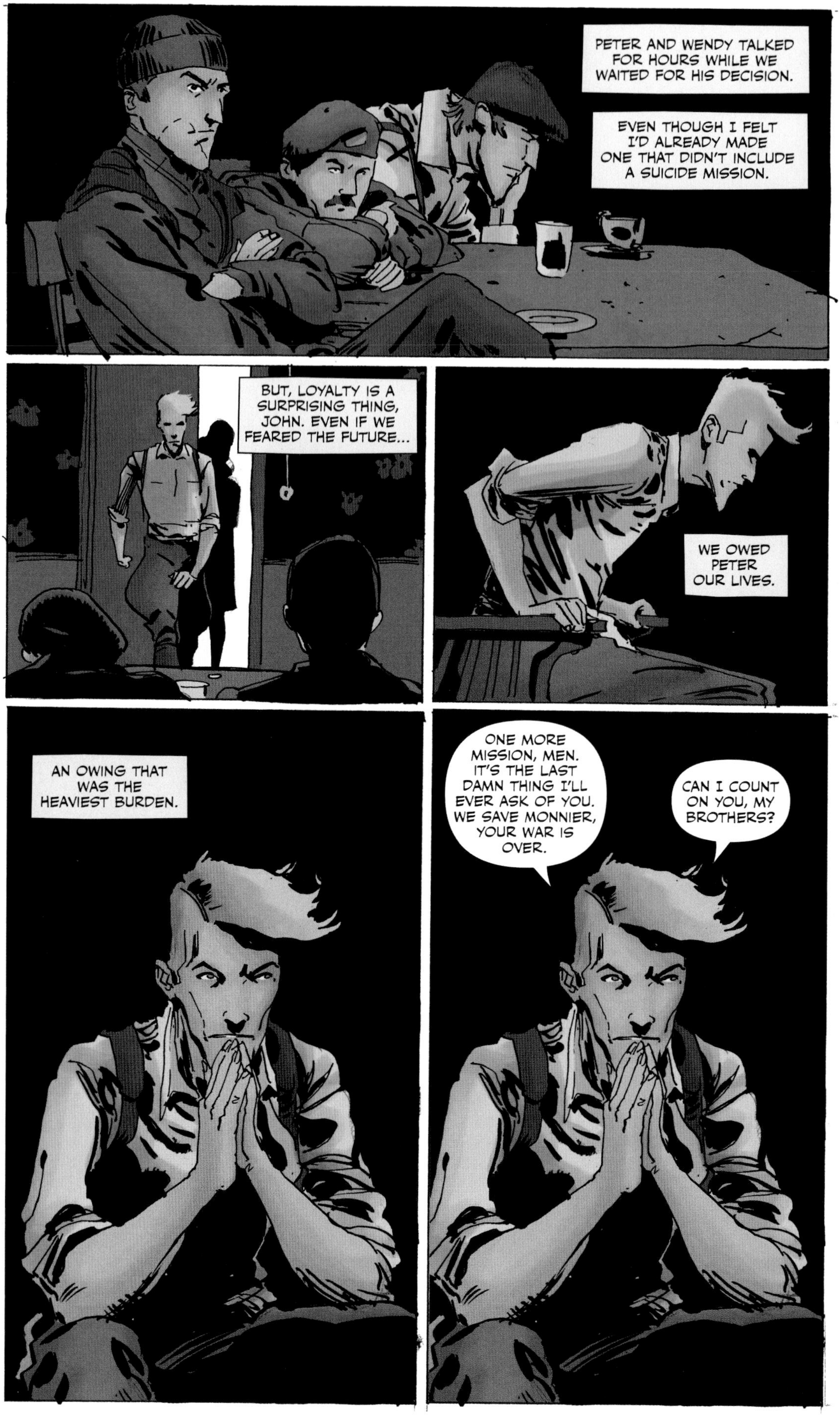
PETER AND WENDY TALKED FOR HOURS WHILE WE WAITED FOR HIS DECISION.
EVEN THOUGH I FELT I'D ALREADY MADE ONE THAT DIDN'T INCLUDE A SUICIDE MISSION.
BUT, LOYALTY IS A SURPRISING THING, JOHN. EVEN IF WE FEARED THE FUTURE...
WE OWED PETER OUR LIVES.
AN OWING THAT WAS THE HEAVIEST BURDEN.
ONE MORE MISSION, MEN. IT'S THE LAST DAMN THING I'LL EVER ASK OF YOU. WE SAVE MONNIER, YOUR WAR IS OVER.
CAN I COUNT ON YOU, MY BROTHERS?

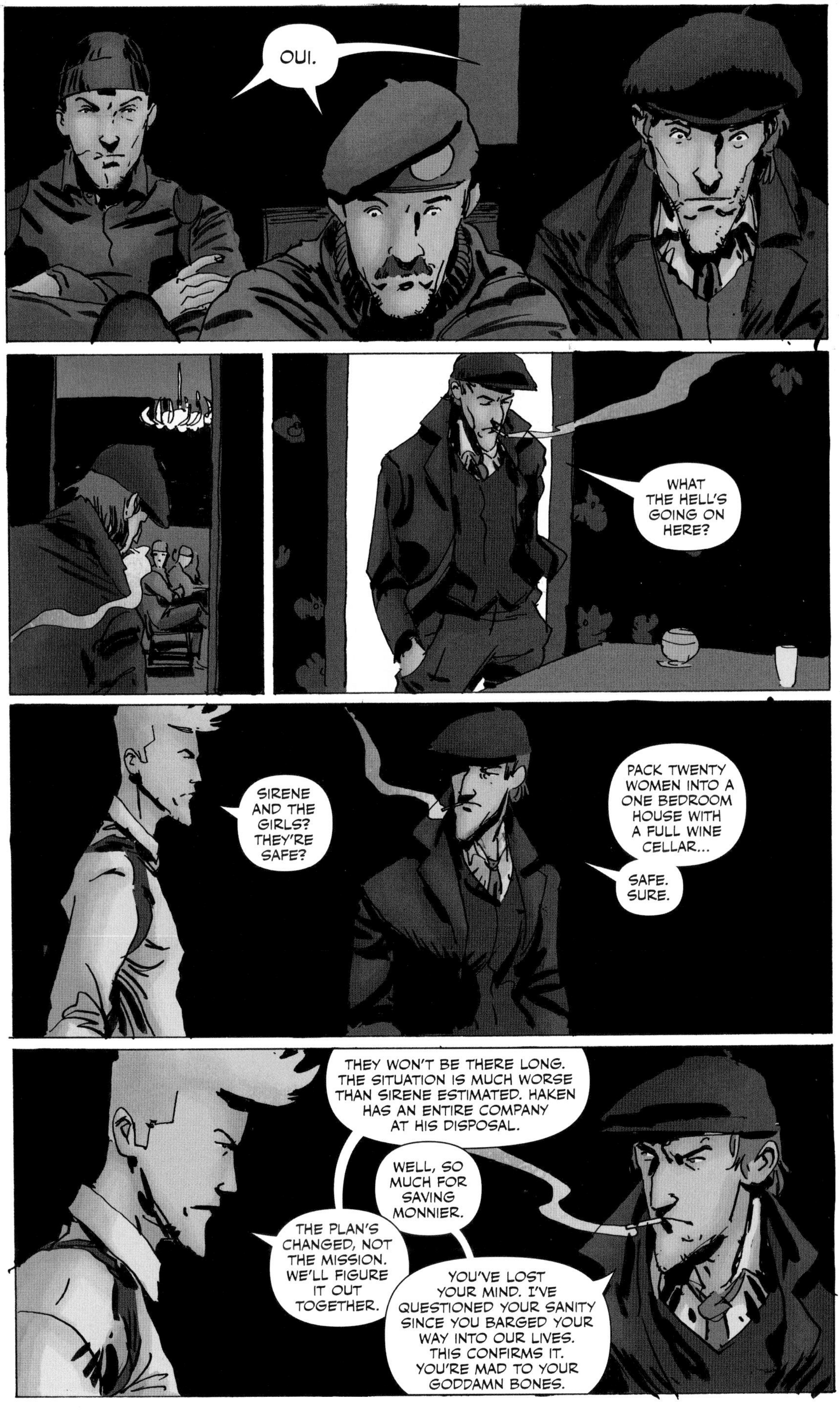
OUI.
WHAT THE HELL'S GOING ON HERE?
SIRENE AND THE GIRLS? THEY'RE SAFE?
PACK TWENTY WOMEN INTO A ONE BEDROOM HOUSE WITH A FULL WINE CELLAR...
SAFE. SURE.
THEY WON'T BE THERE LONG. THE SITUATION IS MUCH WORSE THAN SIRENE ESTIMATED. HAKEN HAS AN ENTIRE COMPANY AT HIS DISPOSAL.
WELL, SO MUCH FOR SAVING MONNIER.
THE PLAN'S CHANGED, NOT THE MISSION. WE'LL FIGURE IT OUT TOGETHER.
YOU'VE LOST YOUR MIND. I'VE QUESTIONED YOUR SANITY SINCE YOU BARGED YOUR WAY INTO OUR LIVES. THIS CONFIRMS IT. YOU'RE MAD TO YOUR GODDAMN BONES.

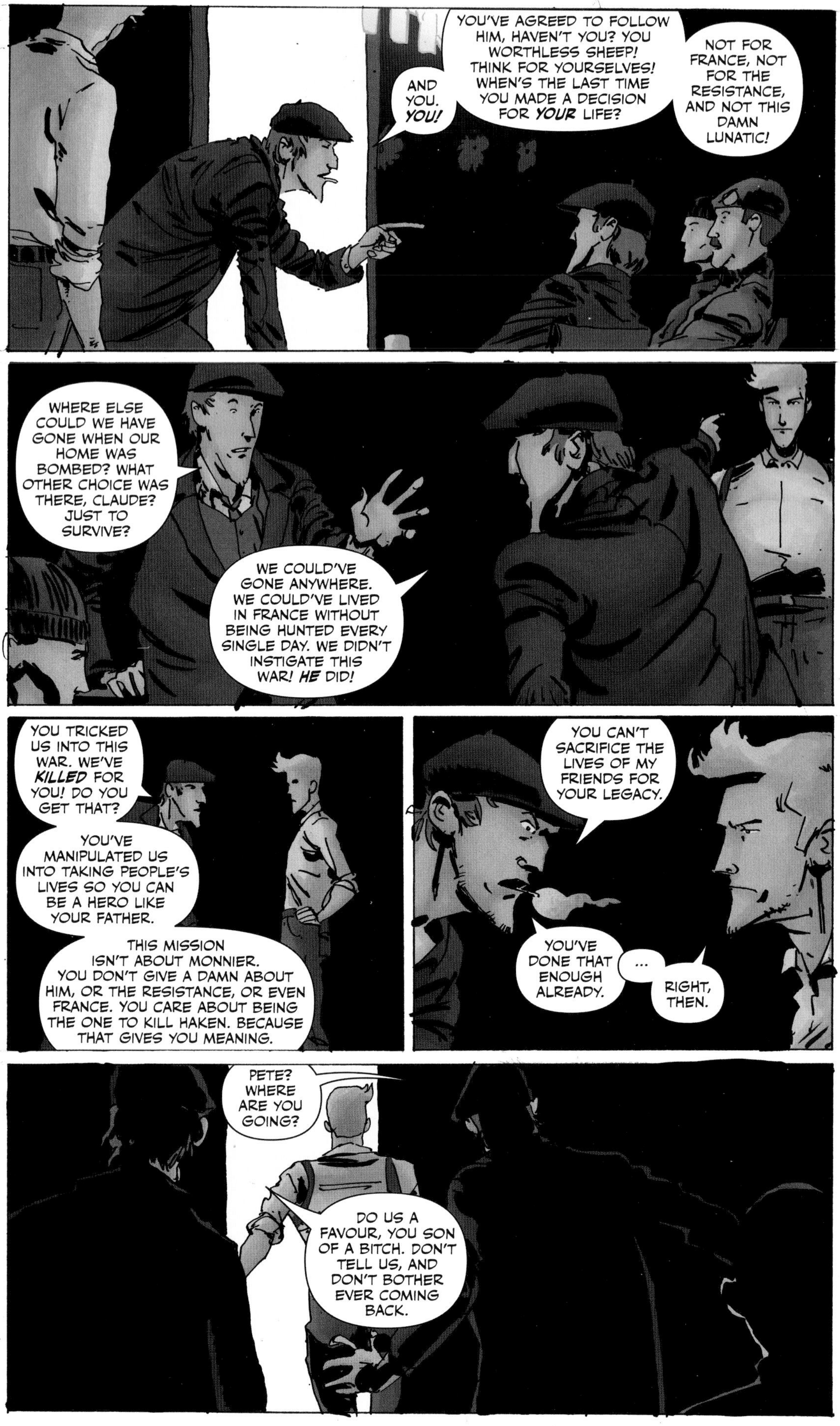
AND YOU. YOU!
YOU'VE AGREED TO FOLLOW HIM, HAVEN'T YOU? YOU WORTHLESS SHEEP! THINK FOR YOURSELVES! WHEN'S THE LAST TIME YOU MADE A DECISION FOR YOUR LIFE?
NOT FOR FRANCE, NOT FOR THE RESISTANCE, AND NOT THIS DAMN LUNATIC!
WHERE ELSE COULD WE HAVE GONE WHEN OUR HOME WAS BOMBED? WHAT OTHER CHOICE WAS THERE, CLAUDE? JUST TO SURVIVE?
WE COULD'VE GONE ANYWHERE. WE COULD'VE LIVED IN FRANCE WITHOUT BEING HUNTED EVERY SINGLE DAY. WE DIDN'T INSTIGATE THIS WAR! HE DID!
YOU TRICKED US INTO THIS WAR. WE'VE KILLED FOR YOU! DO YOU GET THAT?
YOU'VE MANIPULATED US INTO TAKING PEOPLE'S LIVES SO YOU CAN BE A HERO LIKE YOUR FATHER.
THIS MISSION ISN'T ABOUT MONNIER. YOU DON'T GIVE A DAMN ABOUT HIM, OR THE RESISTANCE, OR EVEN FRANCE. YOU CARE ABOUT BEING THE ONE TO KILL HAKEN. BECAUSE THAT GIVES YOU MEANING.
YOU CAN'T SACRIFICE THE LIVES OF MY FRIENDS FOR YOUR LEGACY.
YOU'VE DONE THAT ENOUGH ALREADY.
...
RIGHT, THEN.
PETE? WHERE ARE YOU GOING?
DO US A FAVOUR, YOU SON OF A BITCH. DON'T TELL US, AND DON'T BOTHER EVER COMING BACK.

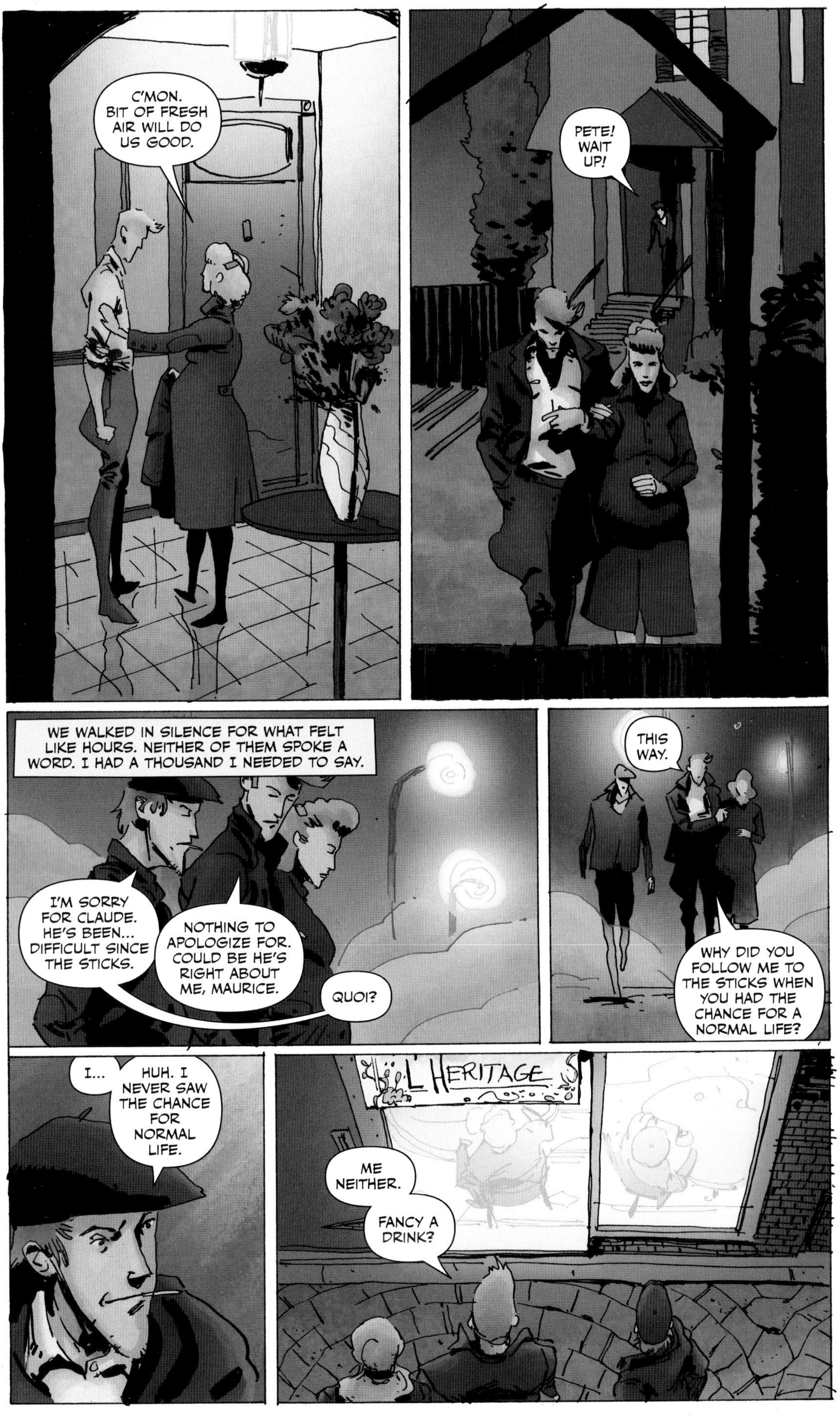
C'MON. BIT OF FRESH AIR WILL DO US GOOD.
PETE! WAIT UP!
WE WALKED IN SILENCE FOR WHAT FELT LIKE HOURS. NEITHER OF THEM SPOKE A WORD. I HAD A THOUSAND I NEEDED TO SAY.
I'M SORRY FOR CLAUDE. HE'S BEEN... DIFFICULT SINCE THE STICKS.
NOTHING TO APOLOGIZE FOR. COULD BE HE'S RIGHT ABOUT ME, MAURICE.
QUOI?
THIS WAY.
WHY DID YOU FOLLOW ME TO THE STICKS WHEN YOU HAD THE CHANCE FOR A NORMAL LIFE?
I...
HUH. I NEVER SAW THE CHANCE FOR NORMAL LIFE.
L'HERITAGE
ME NEITHER.
FANCY A DRINK?

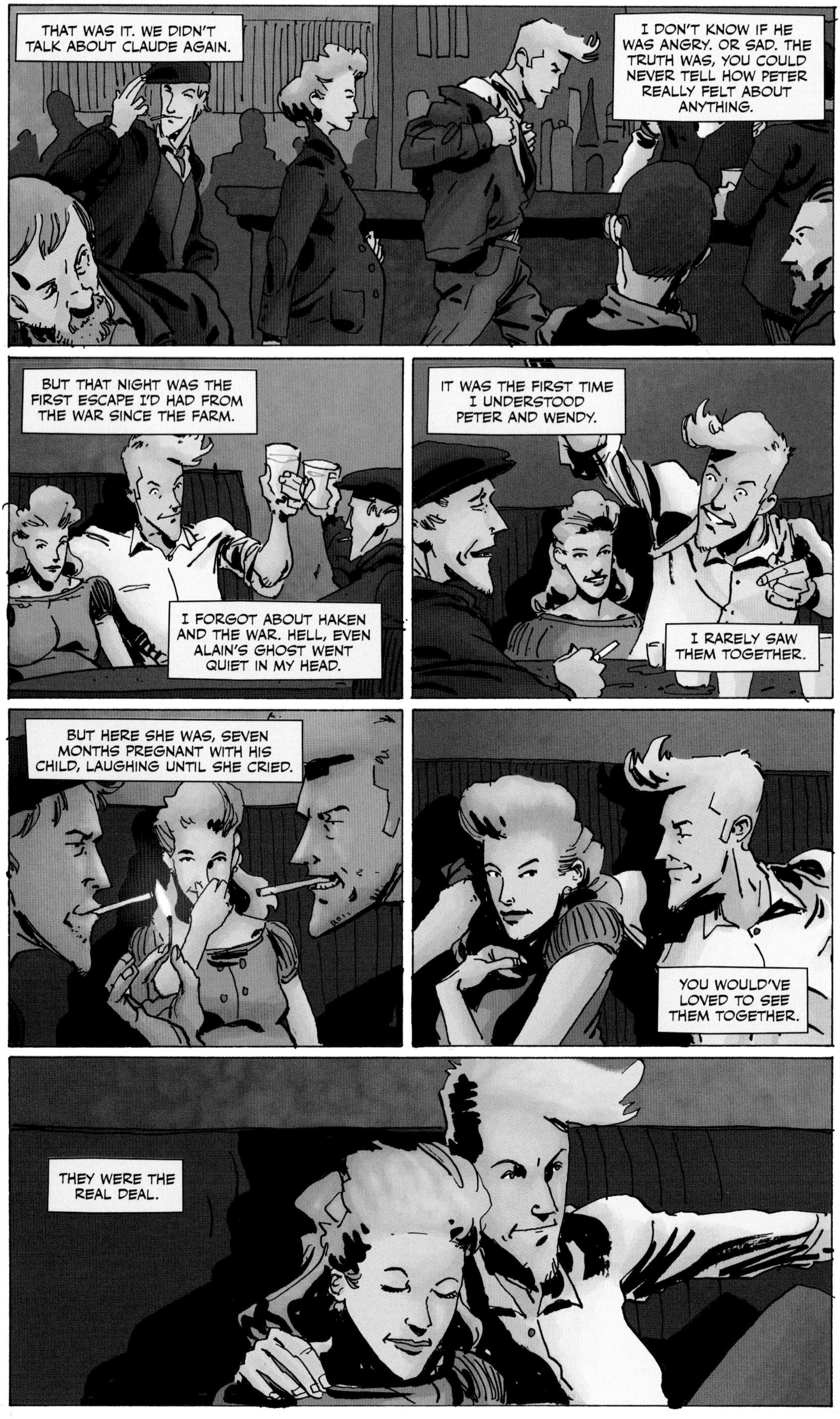
THAT WAS IT. WE DIDN'T TALK ABOUT CLAUDE AGAIN.
I DON'T KNOW IF HE WAS ANGRY. OR SAD. THE TRUTH WAS, YOU COULD NEVER TELL HOW PETER REALLY FELT ABOUT ANYTHING.
BUT THAT NIGHT WAS THE FIRST ESCAPE I'D HAD FROM THE WAR SINCE THE FARM.
I FORGOT ABOUT HAKEN AND THE WAR. HELL, EVEN ALAIN'S GHOST WENT QUIET IN MY HEAD.
IT WAS THE FIRST TIME I UNDERSTOOD PETER AND WENDY.
I RARELY SAW THEM TOGETHER.
BUT HERE SHE WAS, SEVEN MONTHS PREGNANT WITH HIS CHILD, LAUGHING UNTIL SHE CRIED.
YOU WOULD'VE LOVED TO SEE THEM TOGETHER.
THEY WERE THE REAL DEAL.

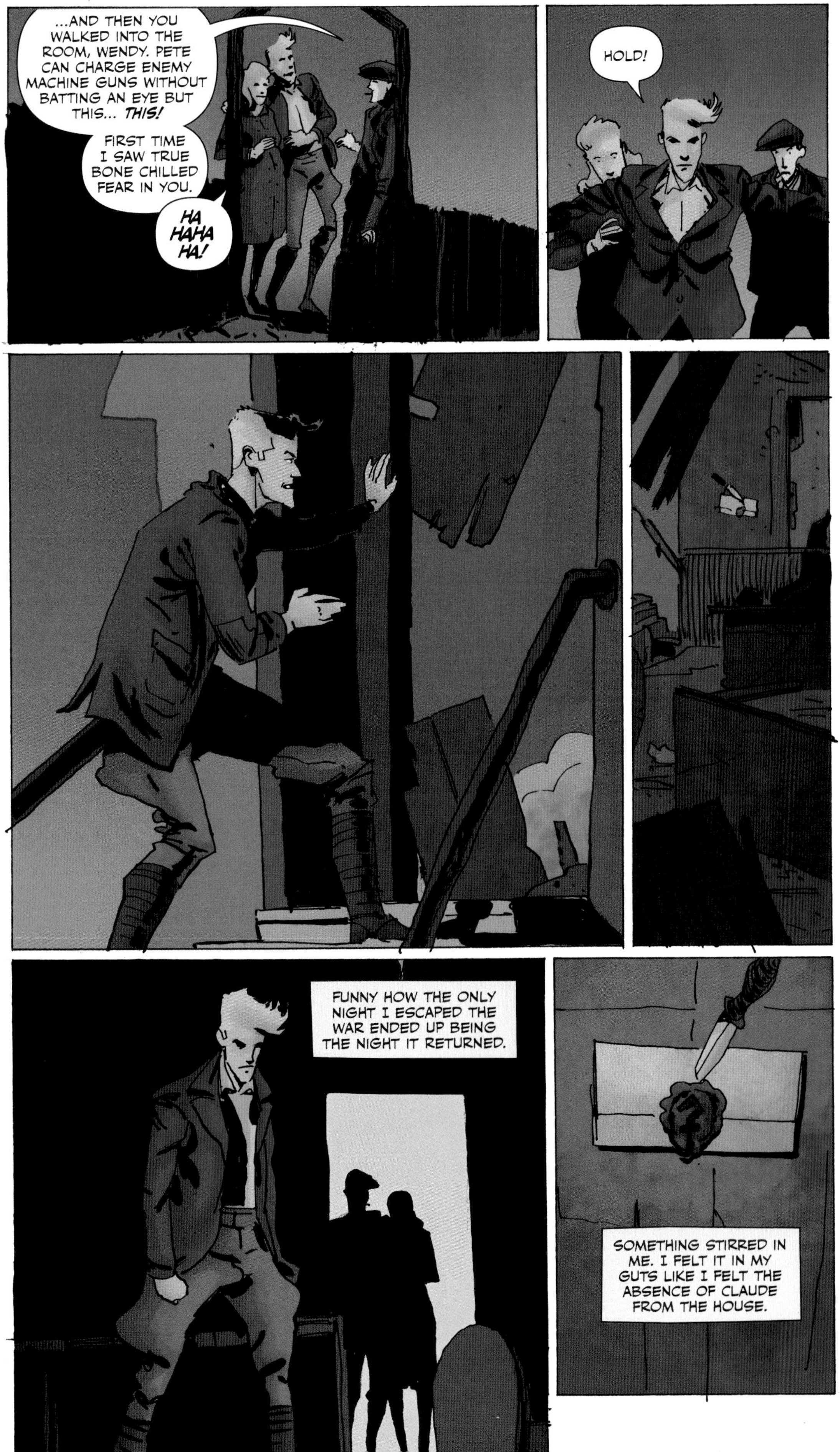
...AND THEN YOU WALKED INTO THE ROOM, WENDY. PETE CAN CHARGE ENEMY MACHINE GUNS WITHOUT BATTING AN EYE BUT THIS... THIS!
FIRST TIME I SAW TRUE BONE CHILLED FEAR IN YOU.
HA HAHA HA!
HOLD!
FUNNY HOW THE ONLY NIGHT I ESCAPED THE WAR ENDED UP BEING THE NIGHT IT RETURNED.
SOMETHING STIRRED IN ME. I FELT IT IN MY GUTS LIKE I FELT THE ABSENCE OF CLAUDE FROM THE HOUSE.

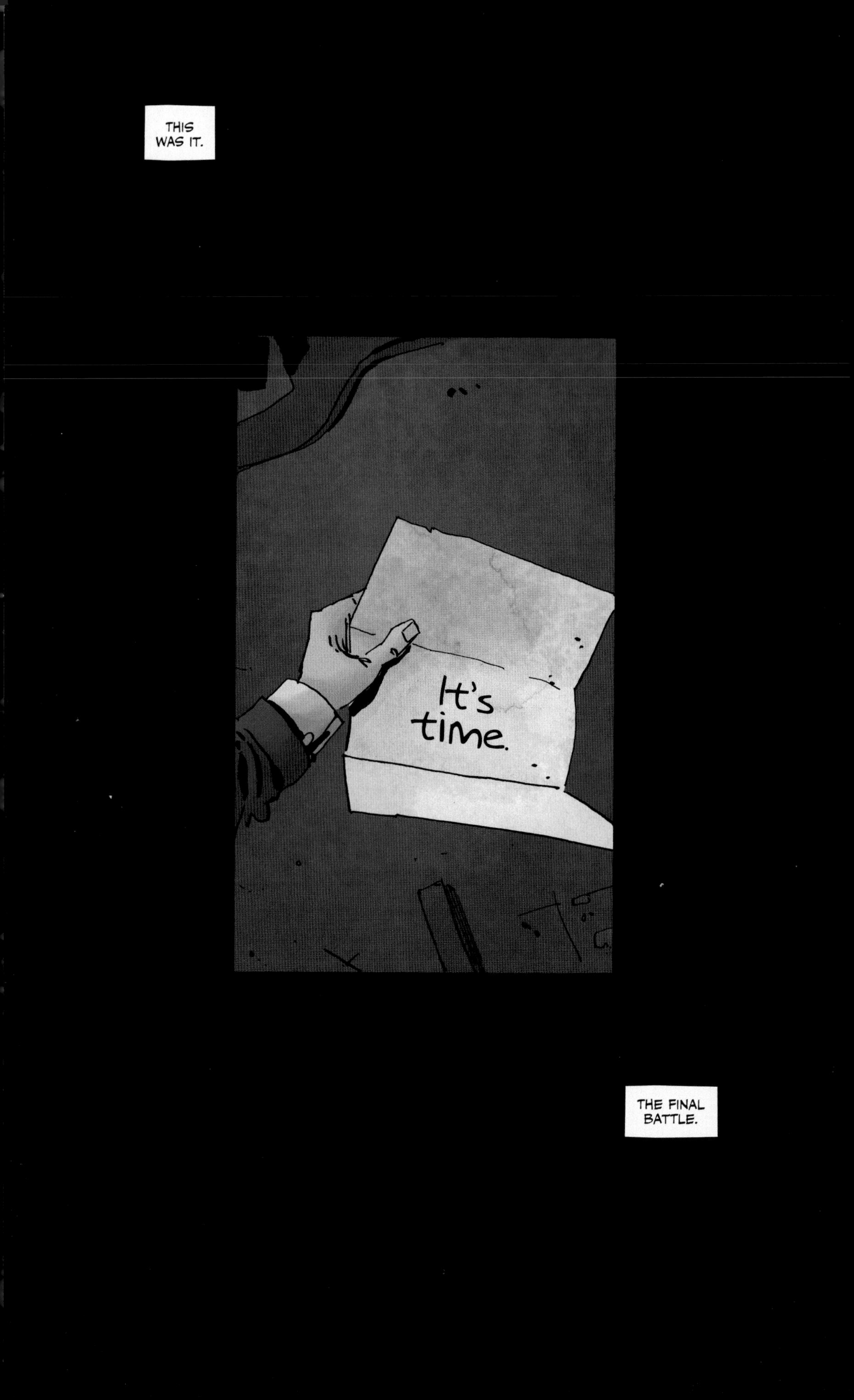
THIS WAS IT.
It's time.
THE FINAL BATTLE.

CHAPTER TWENTY-FOUR

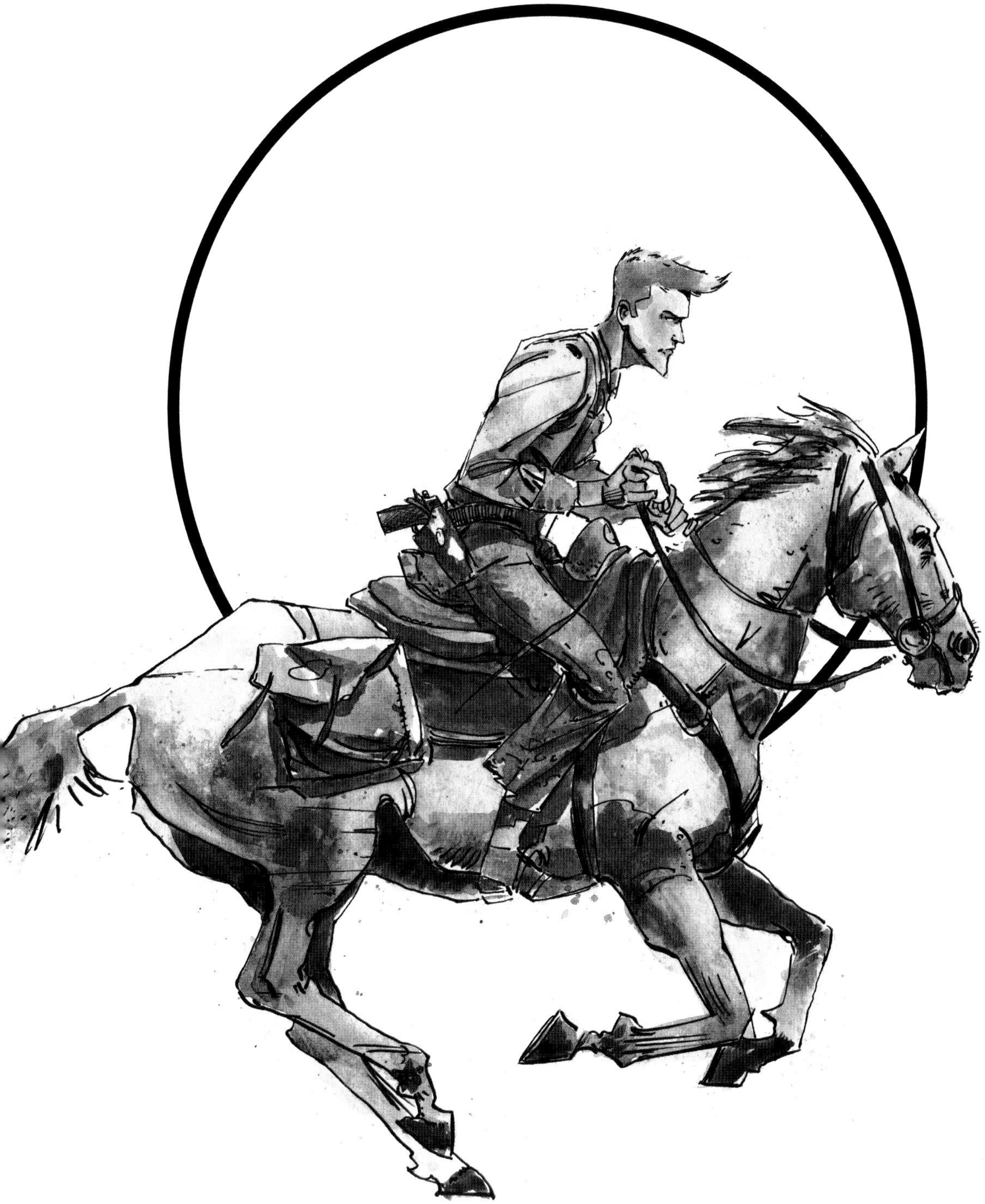

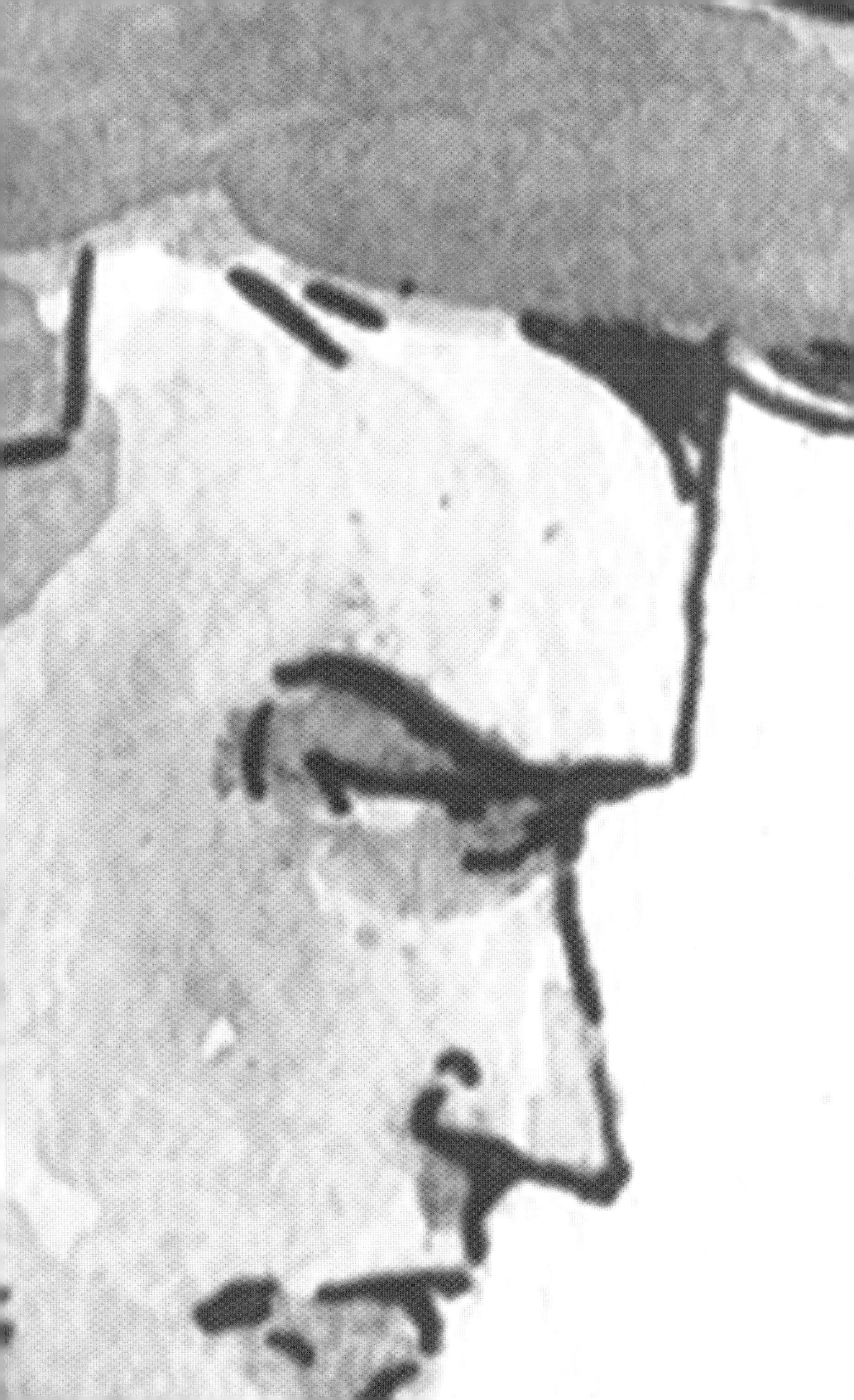

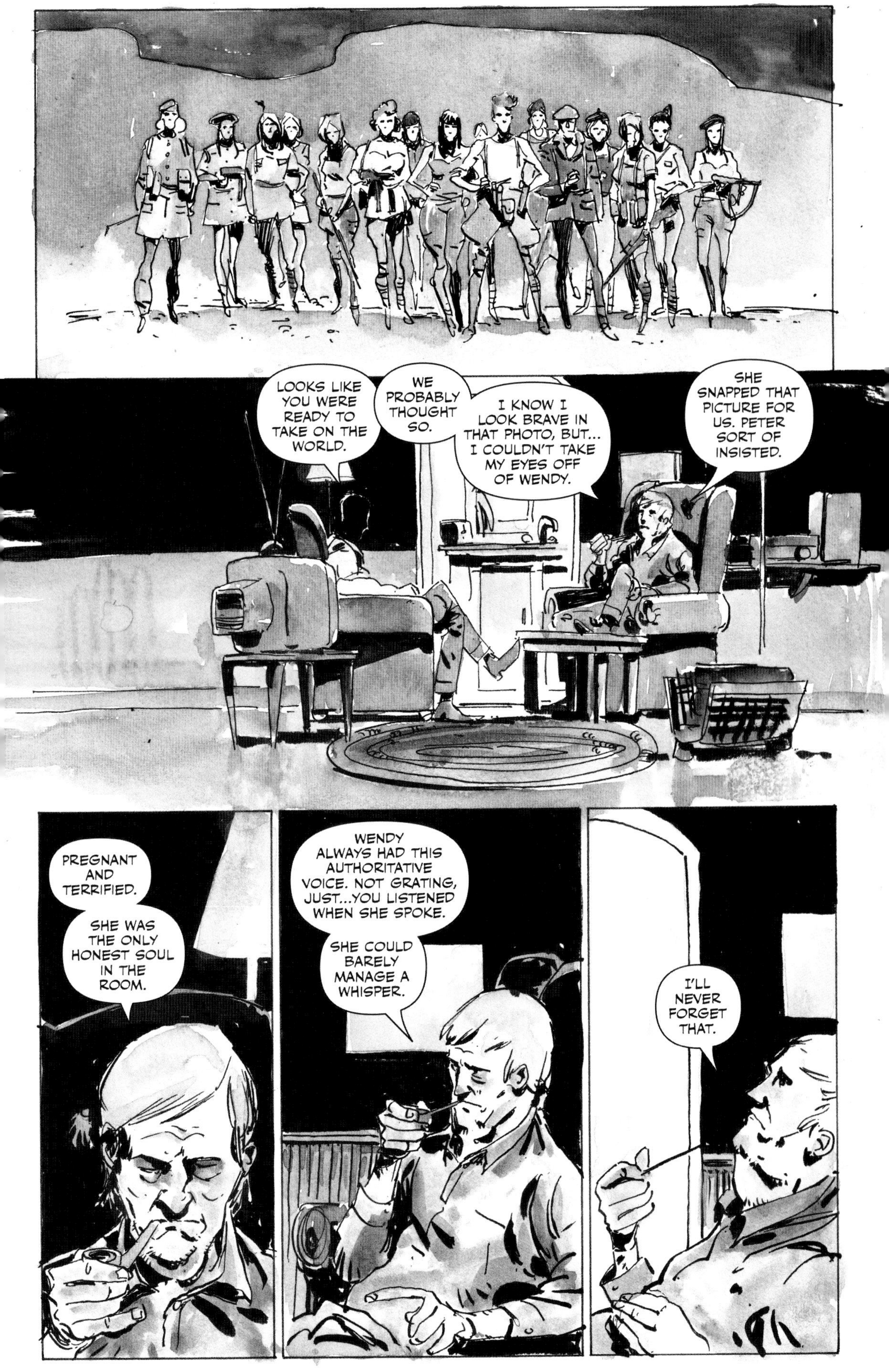
LOOKS LIKE YOU WERE READY TO TAKE ON THE WORLD.
WE PROBABLY THOUGHT SO.
I KNOW I LOOK BRAVE IN THAT PHOTO, BUT... I COULDN'T TAKE MY EYES OFF OF WENDY.
SHE SNAPPED THAT PICTURE FOR US. PETER SORT OF INSISTED.
PREGNANT AND TERRIFIED.
SHE WAS THE ONLY HONEST SOUL IN THE ROOM.
WENDY ALWAYS HAD THIS AUTHORITATIVE VOICE. NOT GRATING, JUST...YOU LISTENED WHEN SHE SPOKE.
SHE COULD BARELY MANAGE A WHISPER.
I'LL NEVER FORGET THAT.

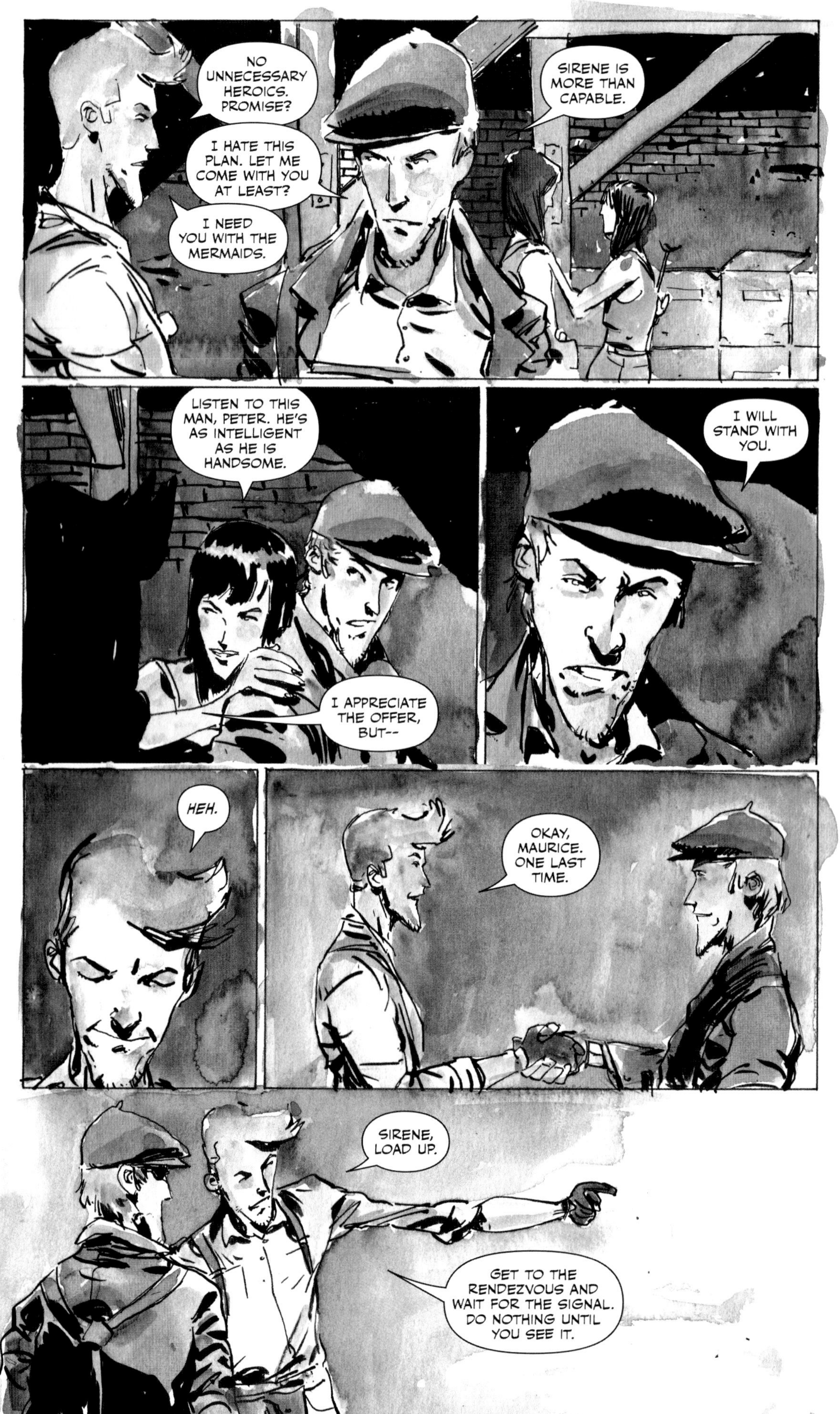
NO UNNECESSARY HEROICS. PROMISE?
I HATE THIS PLAN. LET ME COME WITH YOU AT LEAST?
I NEED YOU WITH THE MERMAIDS.
SIRENE IS MORE THAN CAPABLE.
LISTEN TO THIS MAN, PETER. HE'S AS INTELLIGENT AS HE IS HANDSOME.
I APPRECIATE THE OFFER, BUT--
I WILL STAND WITH YOU.
HEH.
OKAY, MAURICE. ONE LAST TIME.
SIRENE, LOAD UP.
GET TO THE RENDEZVOUS AND WAIT FOR THE SIGNAL. DO NOTHING UNTIL YOU SEE IT.

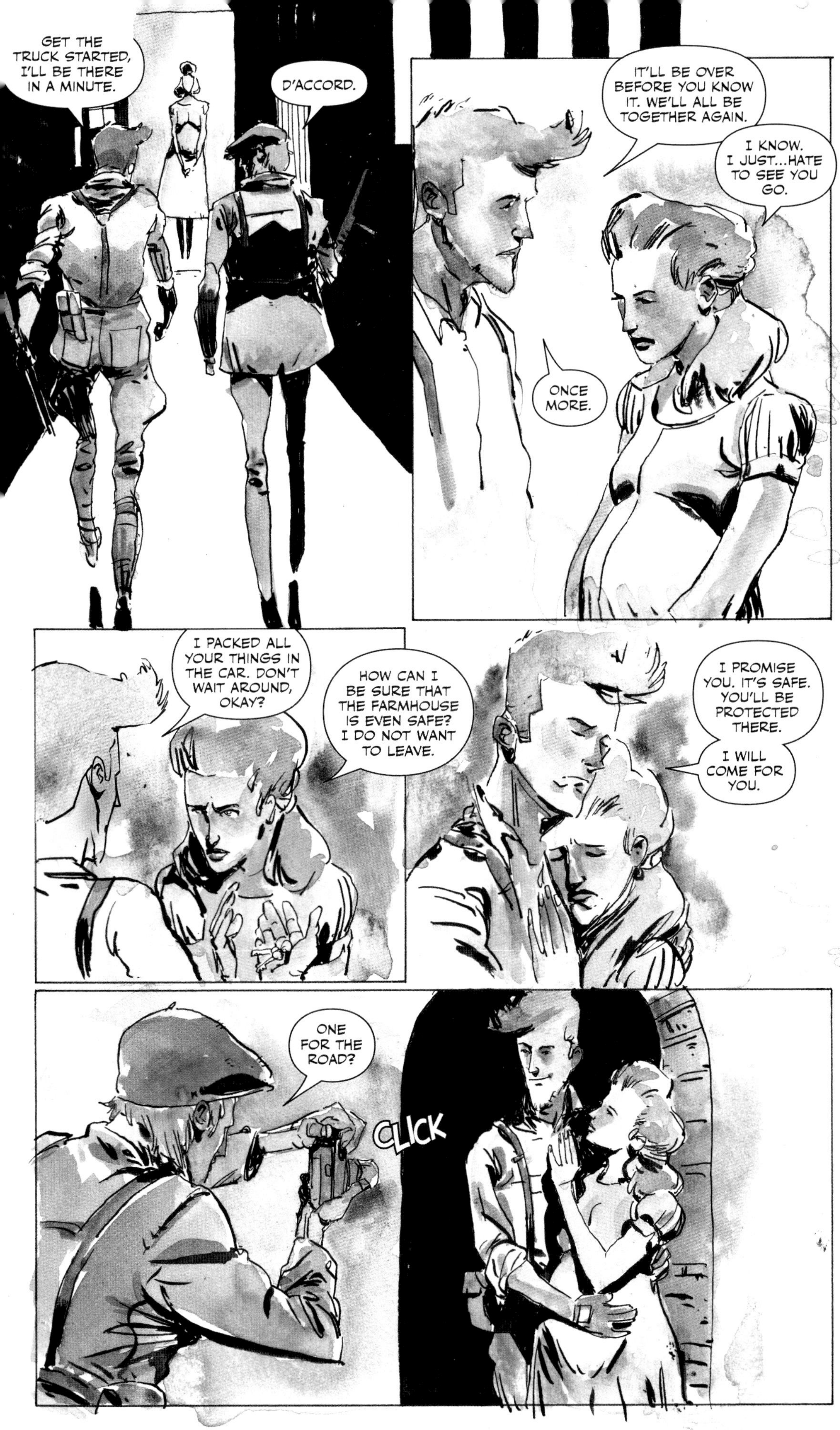
GET THE TRUCK STARTED, I'LL BE THERE IN A MINUTE.
D'ACCORD.
IT'LL BE OVER BEFORE YOU KNOW IT. WE'LL ALL BE TOGETHER AGAIN.
I KNOW. I JUST...HATE TO SEE YOU GO.
ONCE MORE.
I PACKED ALL YOUR THINGS IN THE CAR. DON'T WAIT AROUND, OKAY?
HOW CAN I BE SURE THAT THE FARMHOUSE IS EVEN SAFE? I DO NOT WANT TO LEAVE.
I PROMISE YOU. IT'S SAFE. YOU'LL BE PROTECTED THERE.
I WILL COME FOR YOU.
ONE FOR THE ROAD?
CLICK

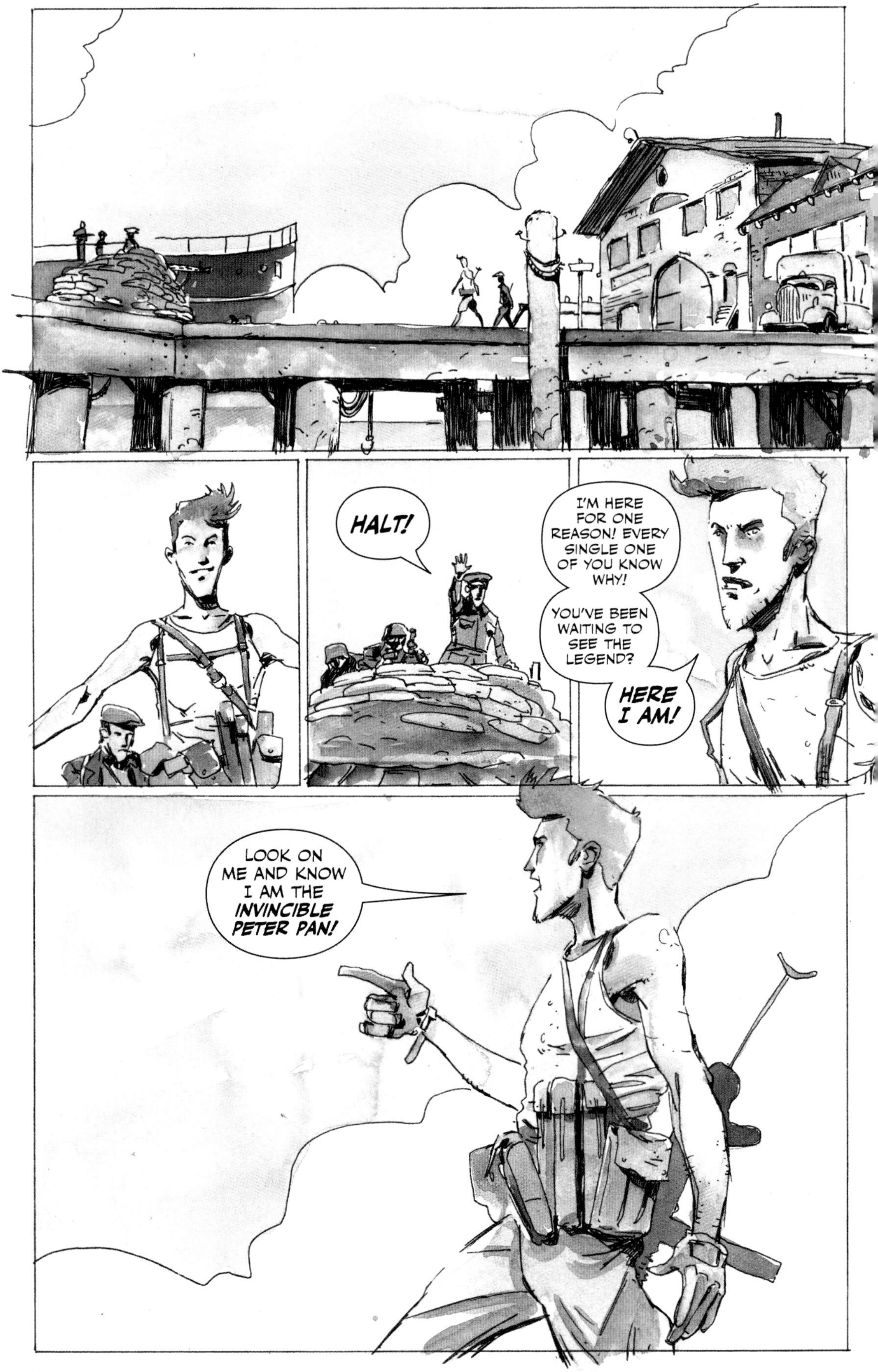
HALT!
I'M HERE FOR ONE REASON! EVERY SINGLE ONE OF YOU KNOW WHY!
YOU'VE BEEN WAITING TO SEE THE LEGEND?
HERE I AM!
LOOK ON ME AND KNOW I AM THE INVINCIBLE PETER PAN!

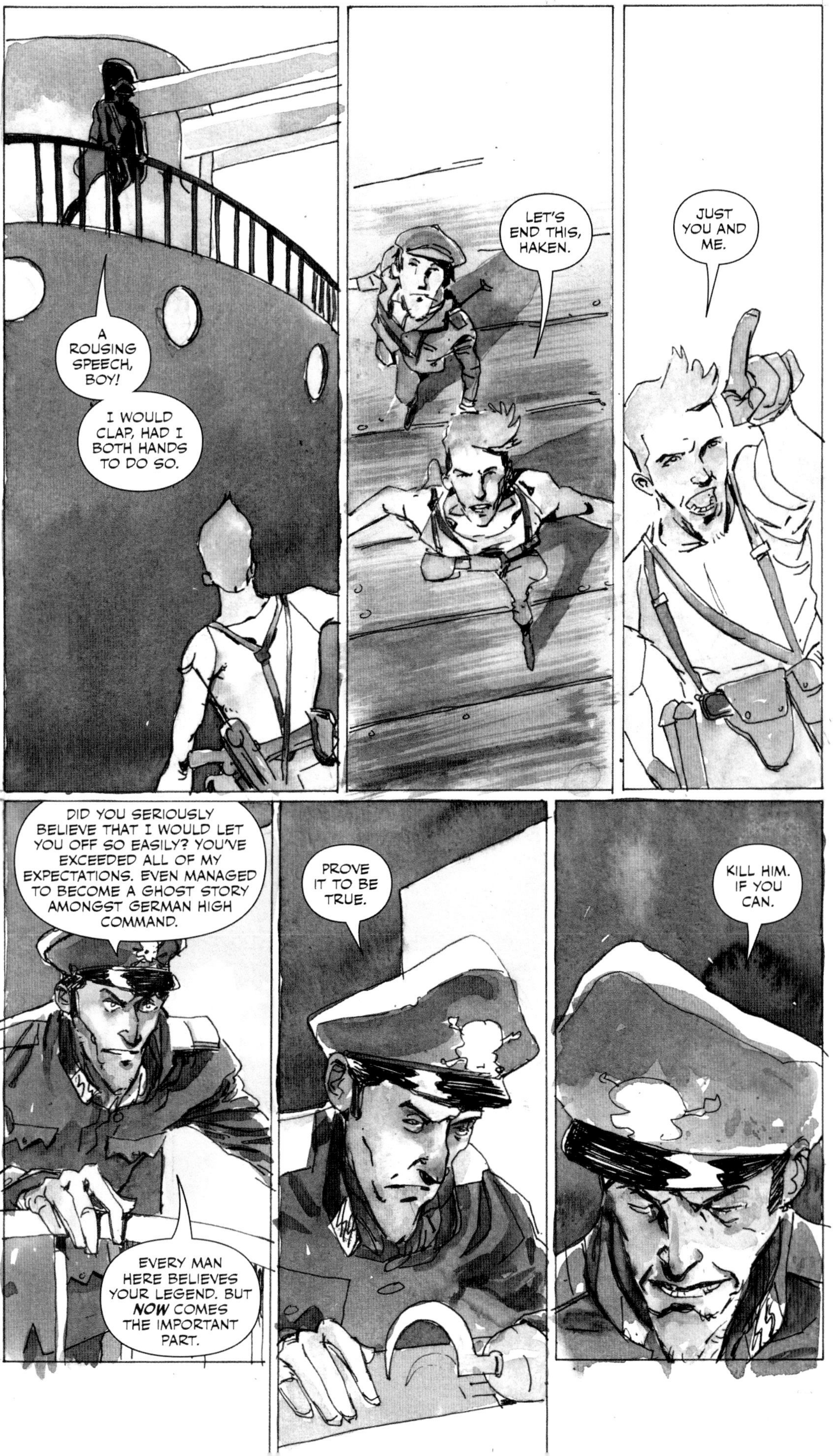
A ROUSING SPEECH, BOY!
I WOULD CLAP, HAD I BOTH HANDS TO DO SO.
LET'S END THIS, HAKEN.
JUST YOU AND ME.
DID YOU SERIOUSLY BELIEVE THAT I WOULD LET YOU OFF SO EASILY? YOU'VE EXCEEDED ALL OF MY EXPECTATIONS. EVEN MANAGED TO BECOME A GHOST STORY AMONGST GERMAN HIGH COMMAND.
EVERY MAN HERE BELIEVES YOUR LEGEND. BUT *NOW* COMES THE IMPORTANT PART.
PROVE IT TO BE TRUE.
KILL HIM. IF YOU CAN.

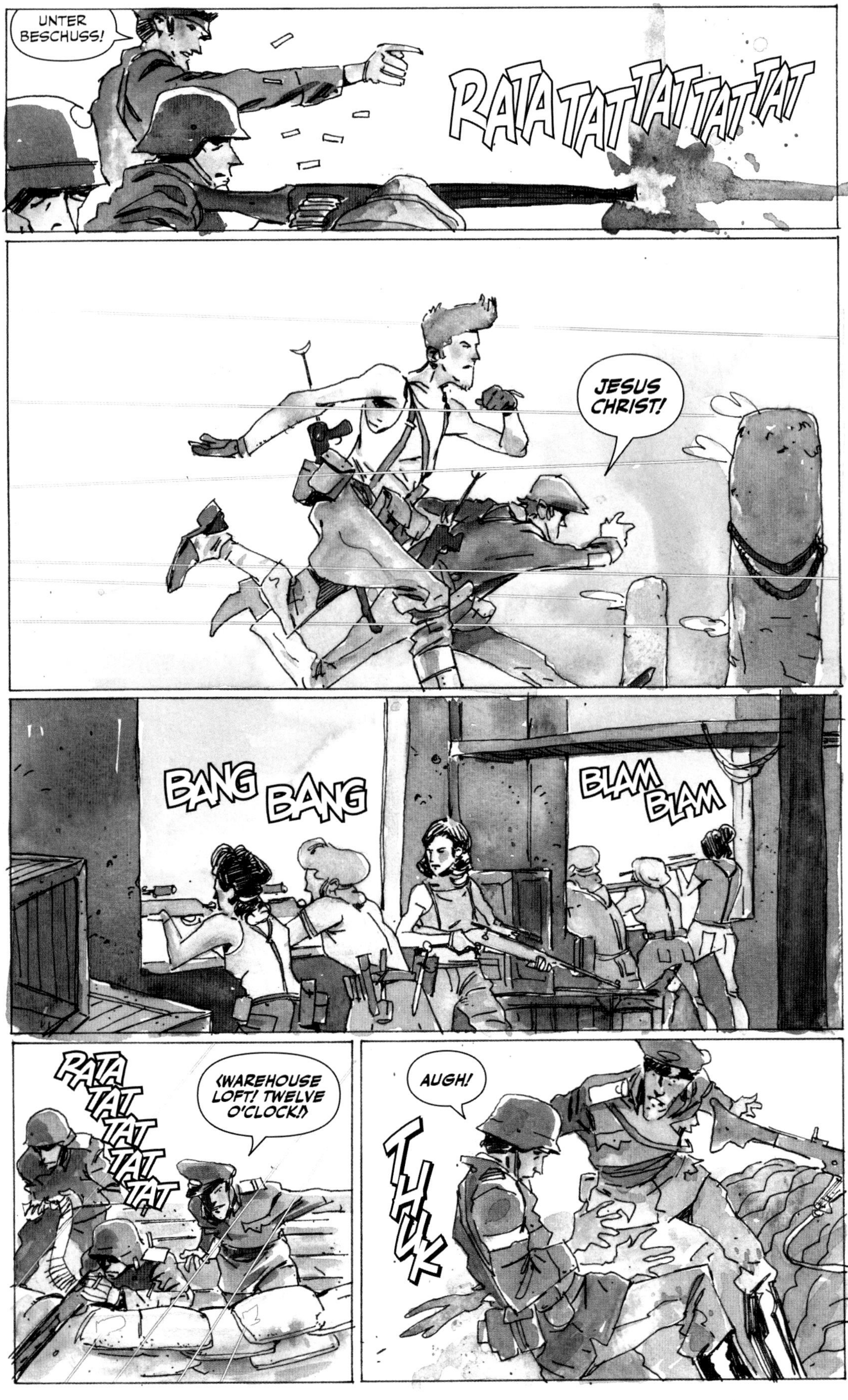
UNTER BESCHUSS!
RATATATTATTATTAT
JESUS CHRIST!
BANG BANG
BLAM BLAM
RATATATTATTATTAT
‹WAREHOUSE LOFT! TWELVE O'CLOCK!›
AUGH!
THUK

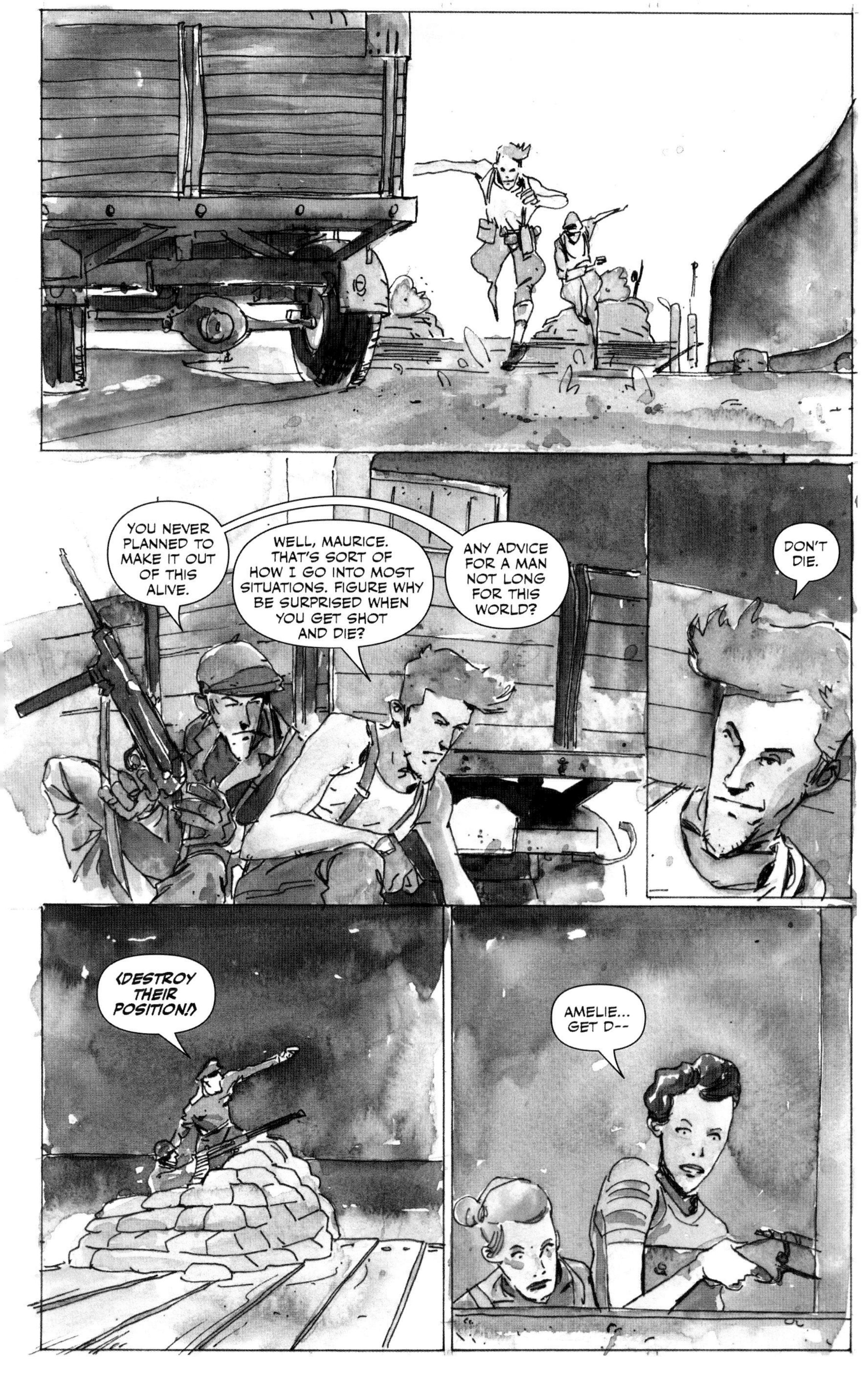
YOU NEVER PLANNED TO MAKE IT OUT OF THIS ALIVE.
WELL, MAURICE. THAT'S SORT OF HOW I GO INTO MOST SITUATIONS. FIGURE WHY BE SURPRISED WHEN YOU GET SHOT AND DIE?
ANY ADVICE FOR A MAN NOT LONG FOR THIS WORLD?
DON'T DIE.
<DESTROY THEIR POSITION!>
AMELIE... GET D--

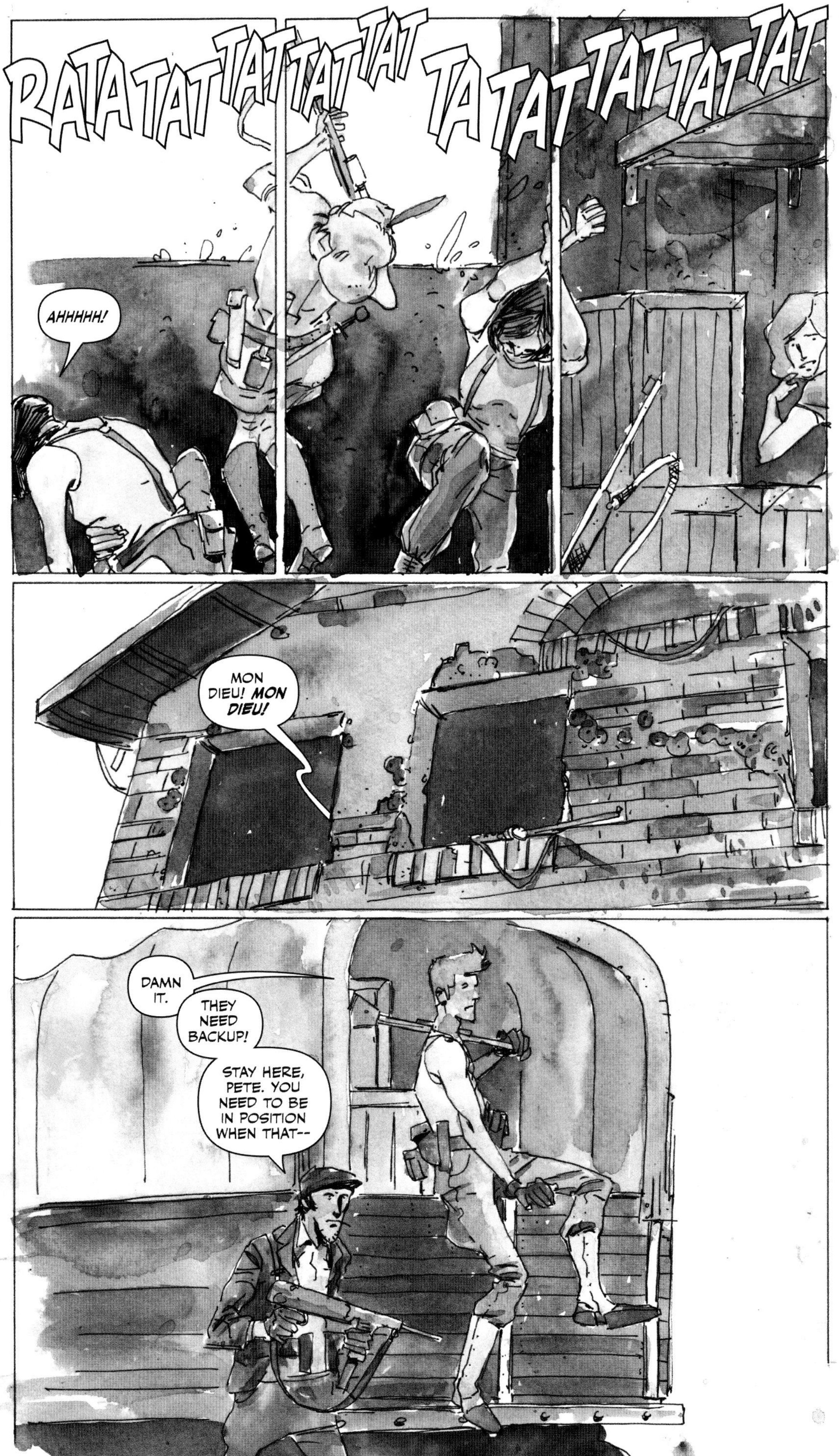
RATATATTATTATTAT TATATTATTATTAT
AHHHHH!
MON DIEU! MON DIEU!
DAMN IT.
THEY NEED BACKUP!
STAY HERE, PETE. YOU NEED TO BE IN POSITION WHEN THAT--

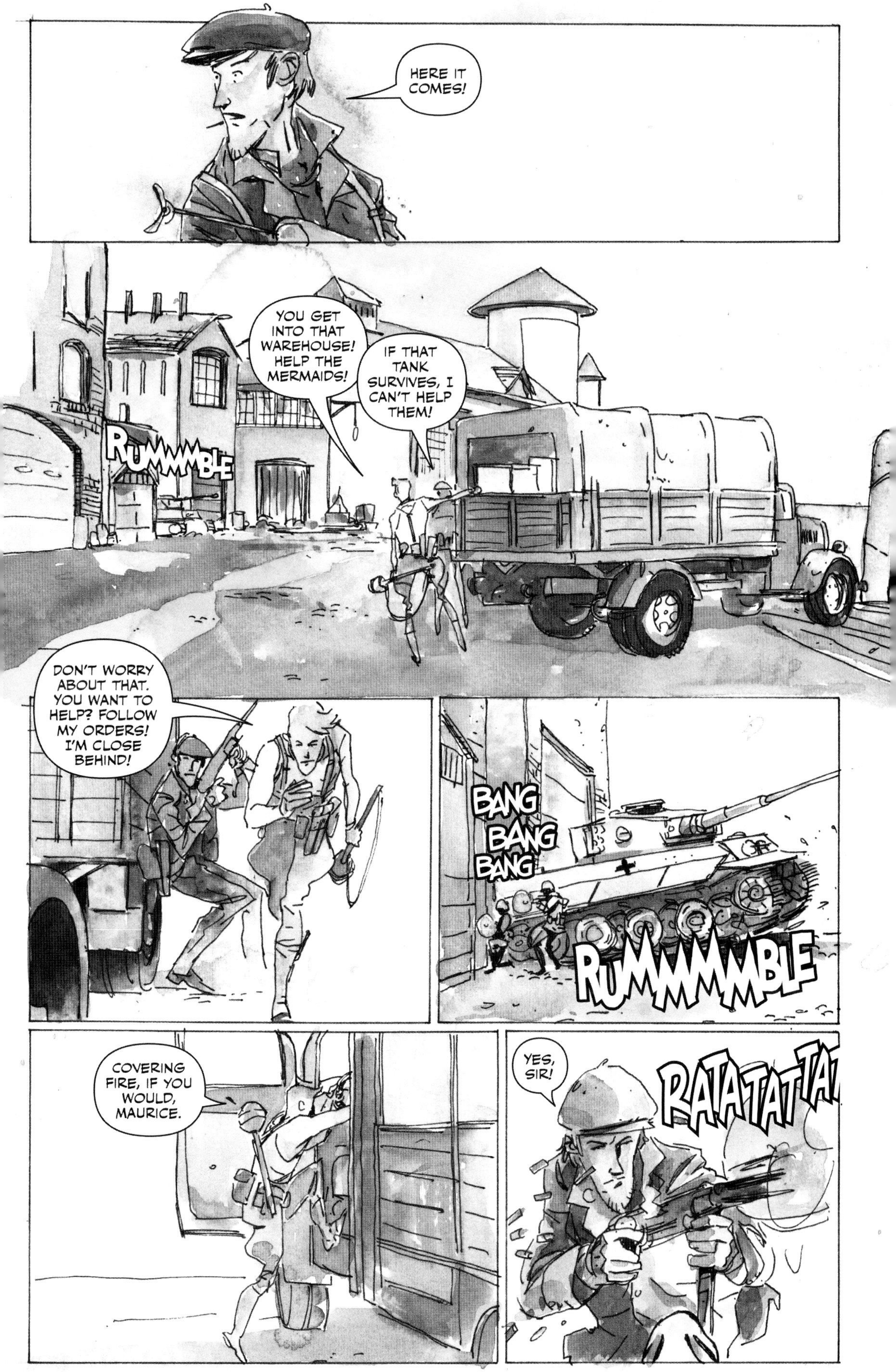
HERE IT COMES!
YOU GET INTO THAT WAREHOUSE! HELP THE MERMAIDS!
IF THAT TANK SURVIVES, I CAN'T HELP THEM!
RUMMMBLE
DON'T WORRY ABOUT THAT. YOU WANT TO HELP? FOLLOW MY ORDERS! I'M CLOSE BEHIND!
BANG
BANG
BANG
RUMMMMMBLE
COVERING FIRE, IF YOU WOULD, MAURICE.
YES, SIR!
RATATATTAT

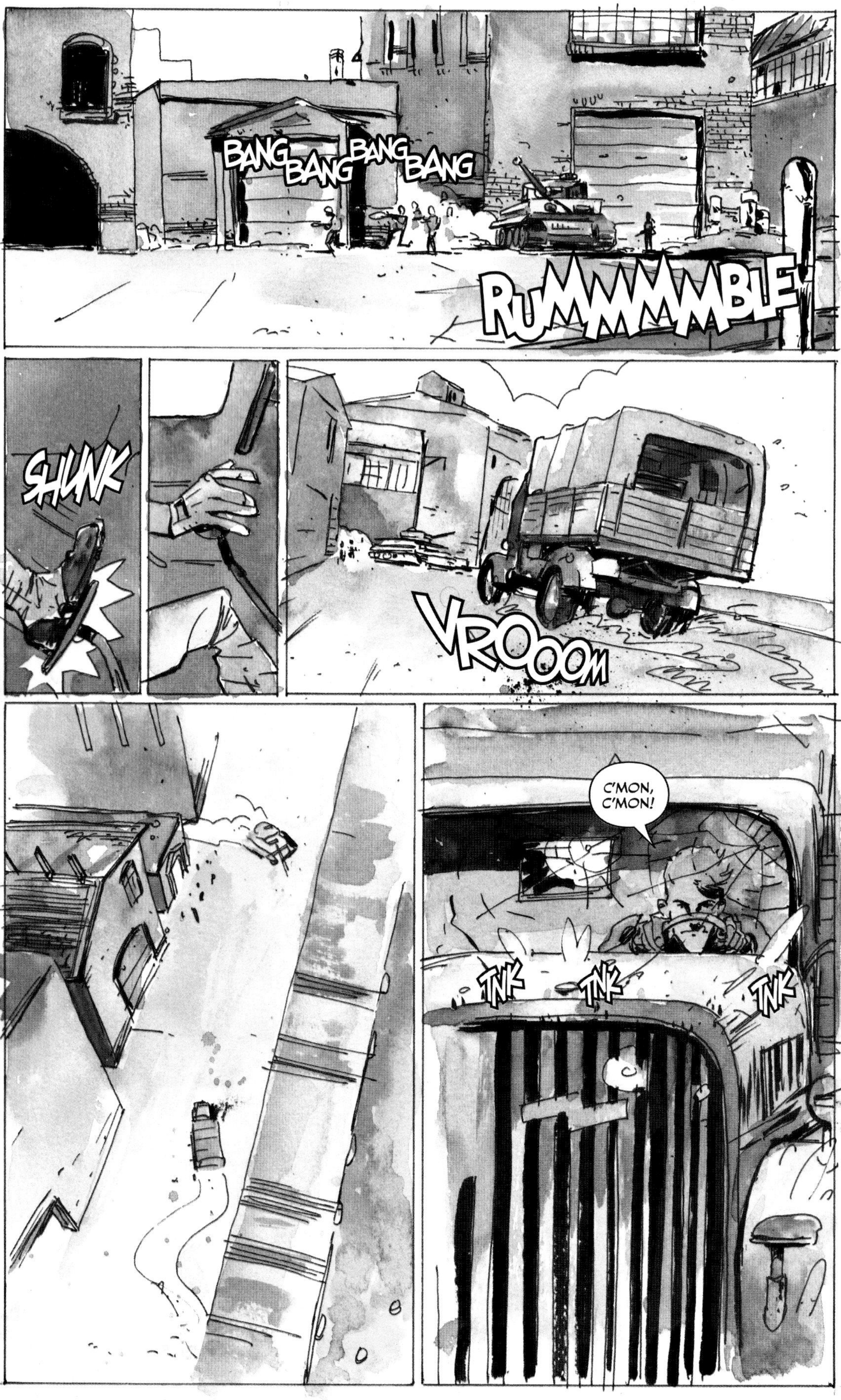
BANG BANG BANG BANG
RUMMMMBLE
SHUNK
VROOOM
C'MON, C'MON!
TNK
TNK
TNK

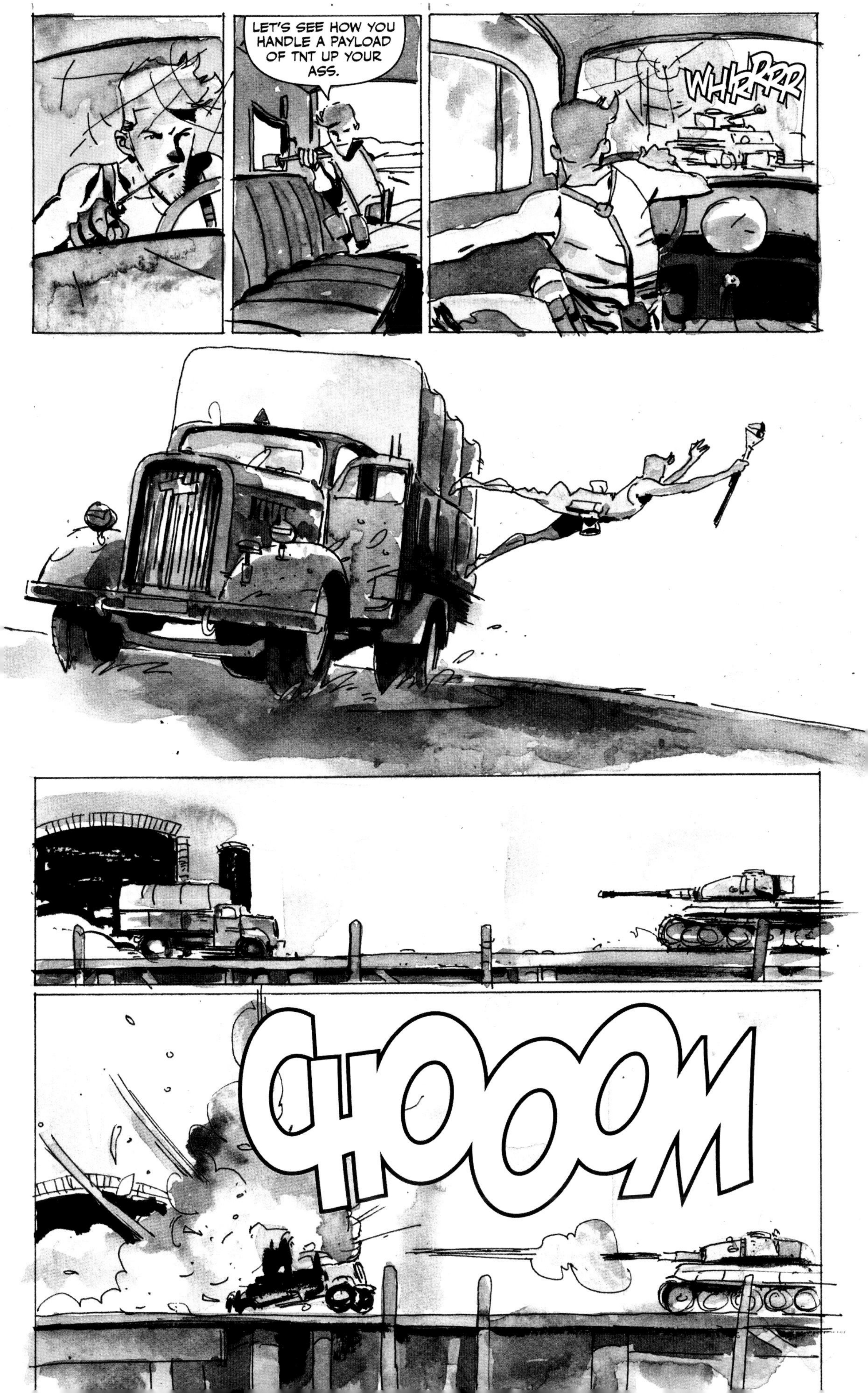
LET'S SEE HOW YOU HANDLE A PAYLOAD OF TNT UP YOUR ASS.
WHIRRRR
CHOOOM

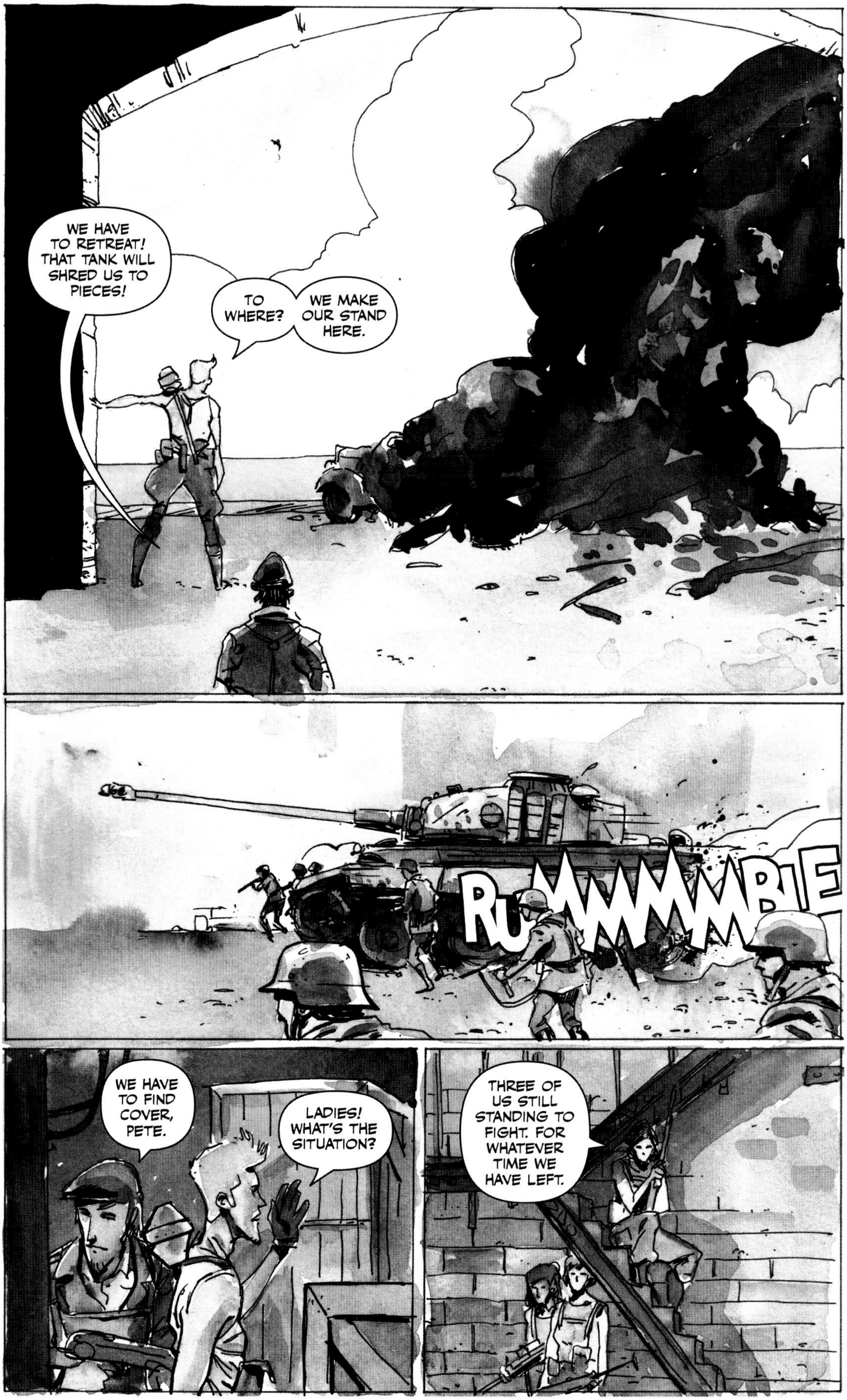
WE HAVE TO RETREAT! THAT TANK WILL SHRED US TO PIECES!
TO WHERE?
WE MAKE OUR STAND HERE.
RUMMMMMBLE
WE HAVE TO FIND COVER, PETE.
LADIES! WHAT'S THE SITUATION?
THREE OF US STILL STANDING TO FIGHT. FOR WHATEVER TIME WE HAVE LEFT.

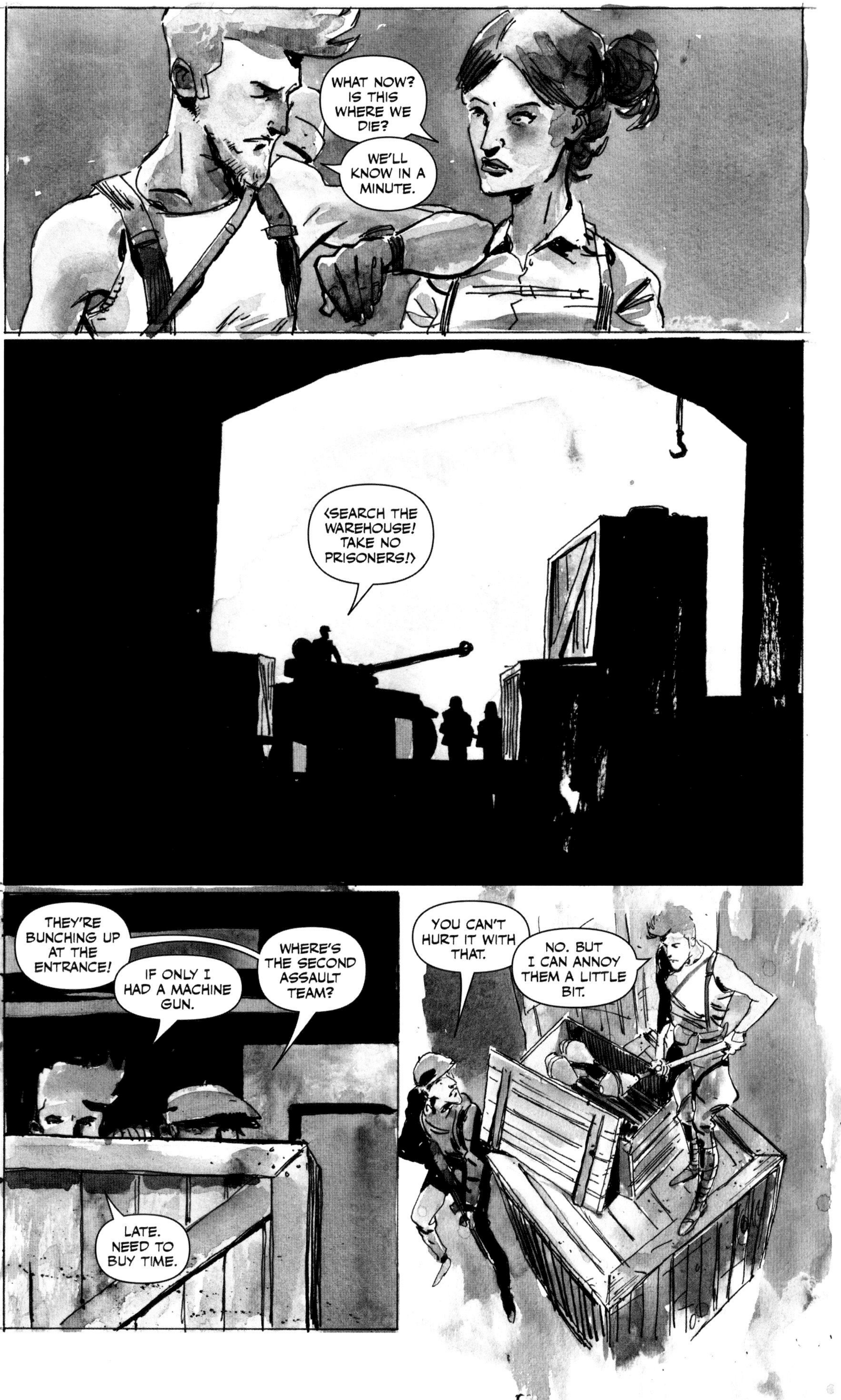
WHAT NOW? IS THIS WHERE WE DIE?
WE'LL KNOW IN A MINUTE.
‹SEARCH THE WAREHOUSE! TAKE NO PRISONERS!›
THEY'RE BUNCHING UP AT THE ENTRANCE!
WHERE'S THE SECOND ASSAULT TEAM?
IF ONLY I HAD A MACHINE GUN.
LATE. NEED TO BUY TIME.
YOU CAN'T HURT IT WITH THAT.
NO. BUT I CAN ANNOY THEM A LITTLE BIT.

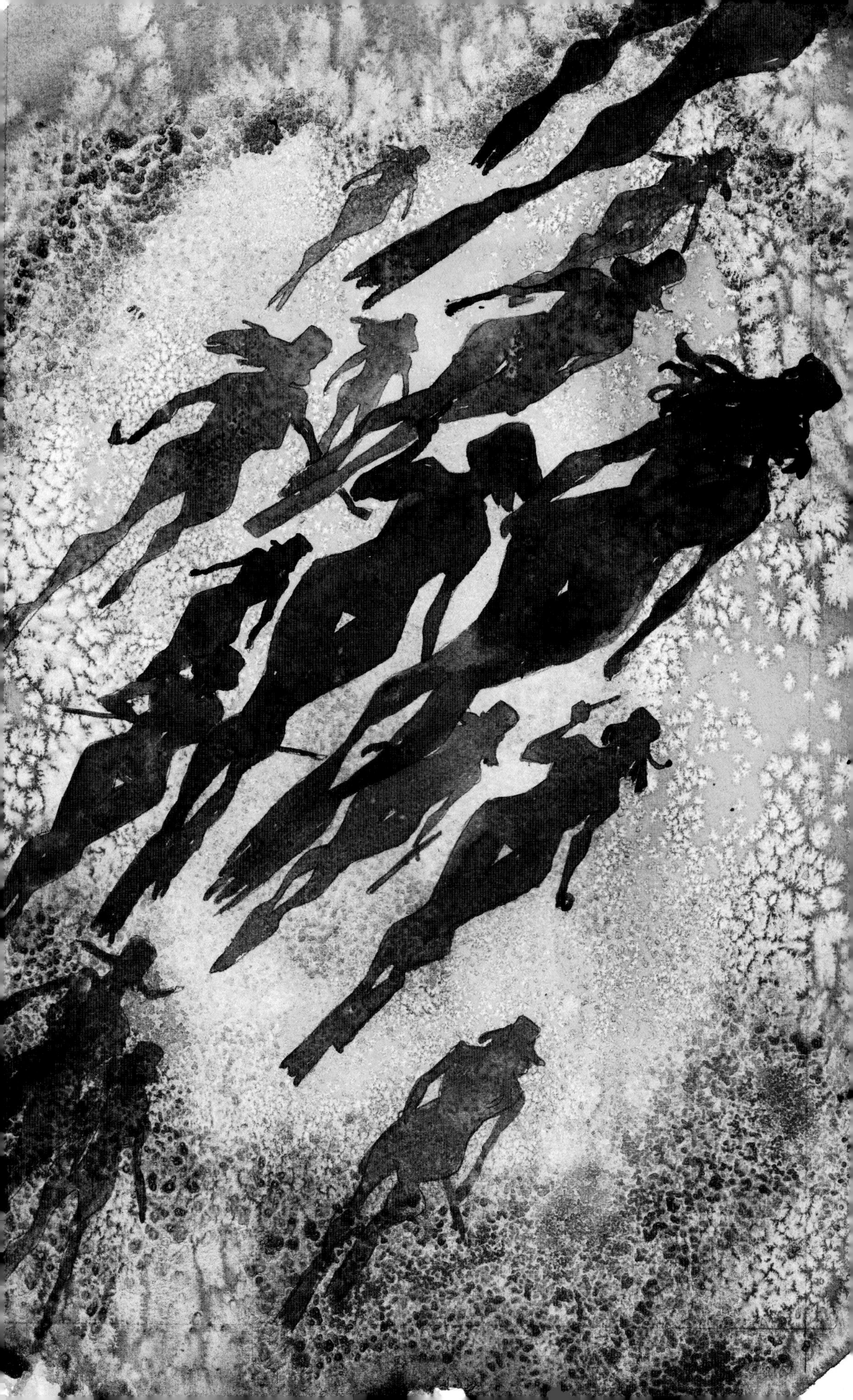

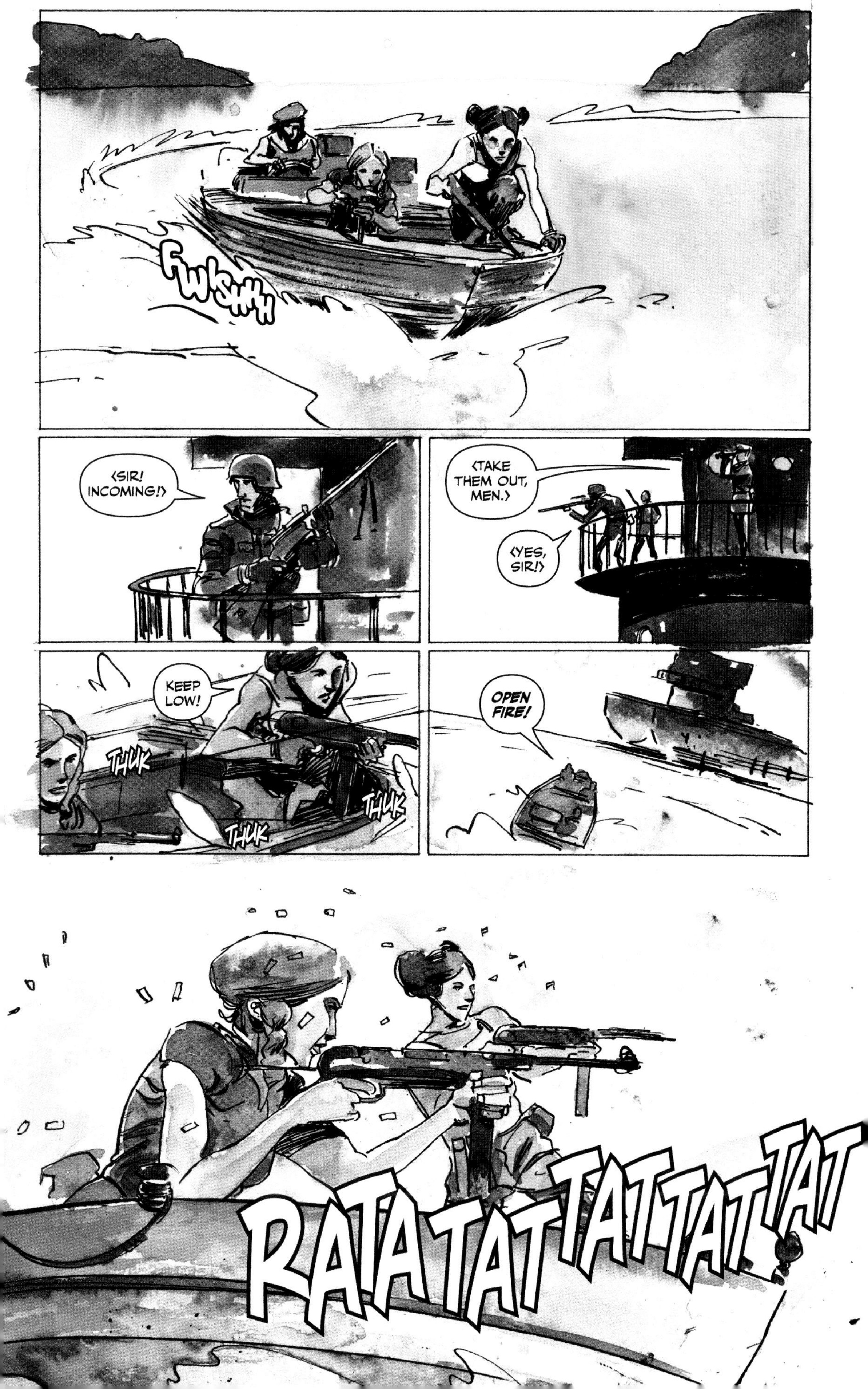
FWISHHH
‹SIR! INCOMING!›
‹TAKE THEM OUT, MEN.›
‹YES, SIR!›
KEEP LOW!
THUK
THUK
THUK
OPEN FIRE!
RATATAT TAT TAT TAT

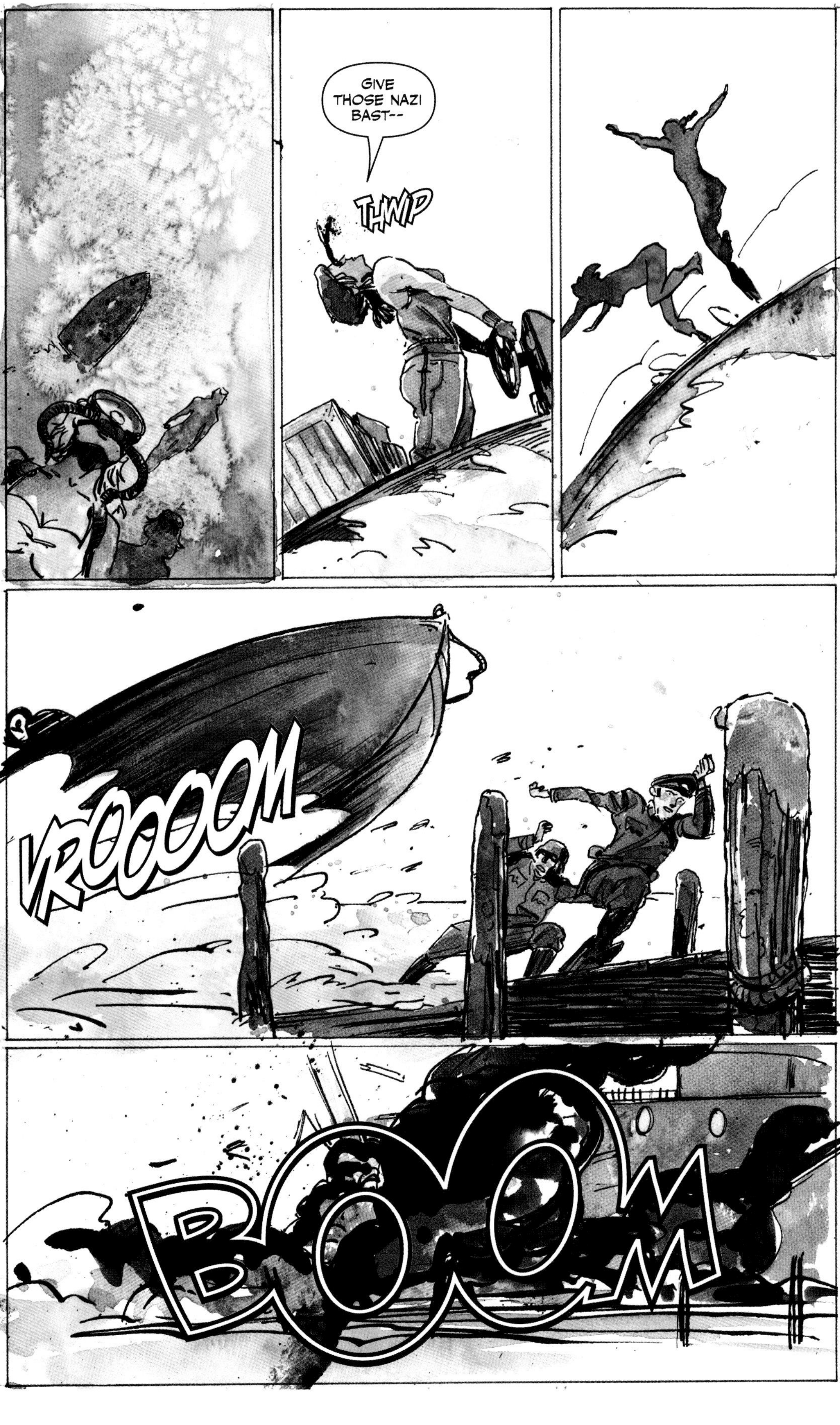
GIVE THOSE NAZI BAST--
THWIP
VROOOOM
BOOOM

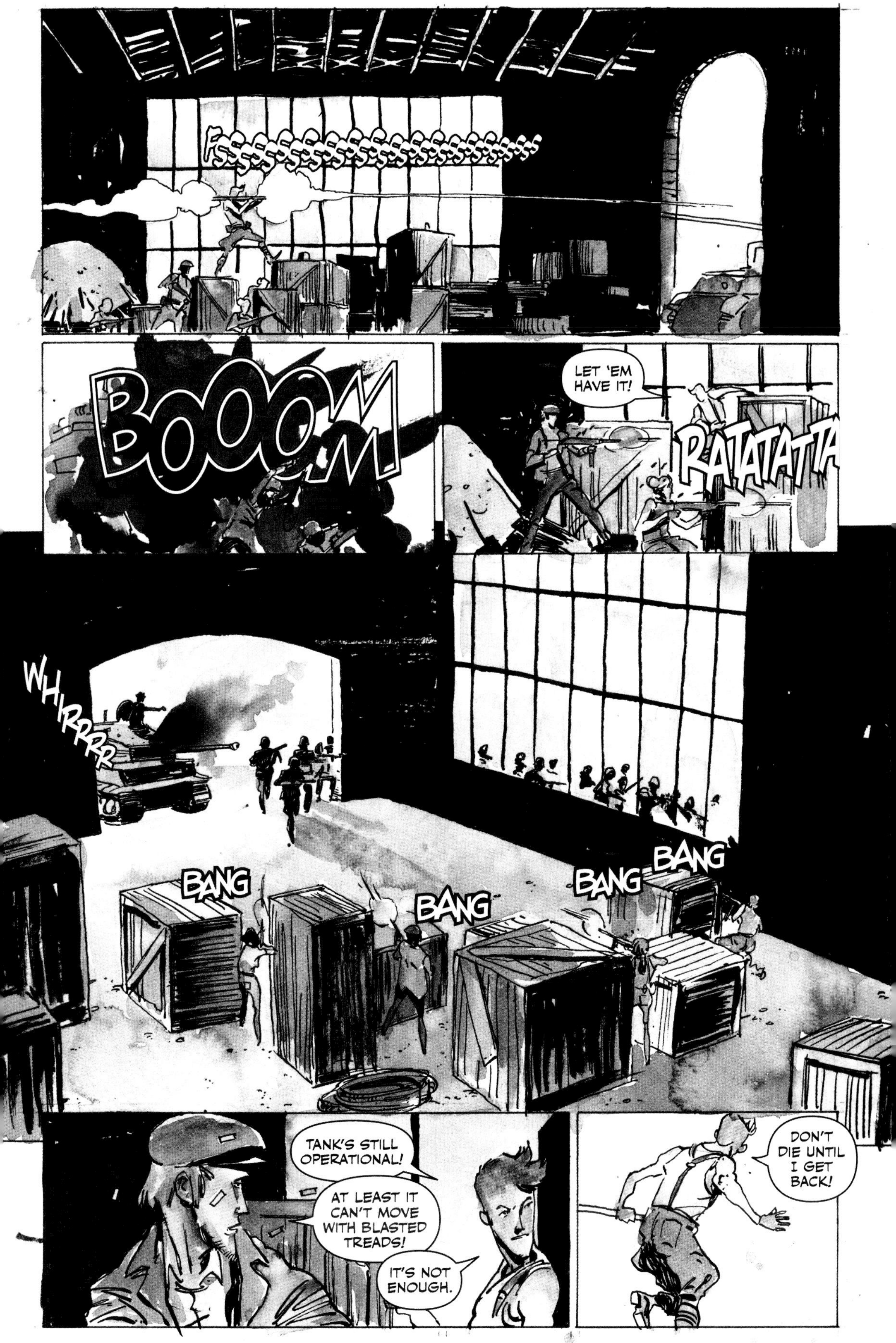
FSSSSSSSSSSSSSSSSSSSSSSSSSSSSS
BOOOM
LET 'EM HAVE IT!
RATATATTA
WHIRRRRR
BANG
BANG
BANG
BANG
TANK'S STILL OPERATIONAL!
AT LEAST IT CAN'T MOVE WITH BLASTED TREADS!
IT'S NOT ENOUGH.
DON'T DIE UNTIL I GET BACK!

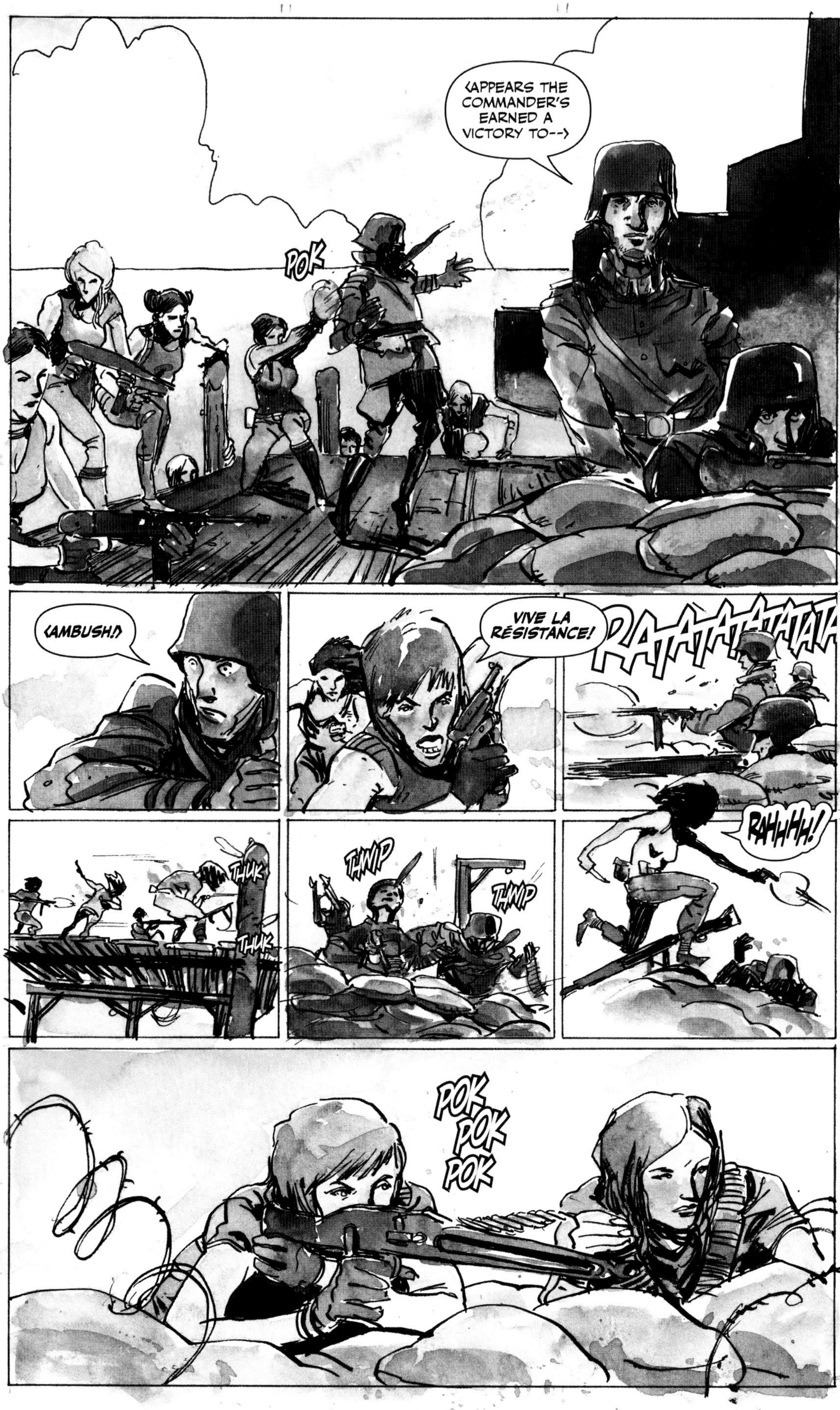
‹APPEARS THE COMMANDER'S EARNED A VICTORY TO--›
POK
‹AMBUSH!›
VIVE LA RÉSISTANCE!
RATATATATATATA
THUK
THUK
THWIP
THWIP
RAHHHH!
POK
POK
POK

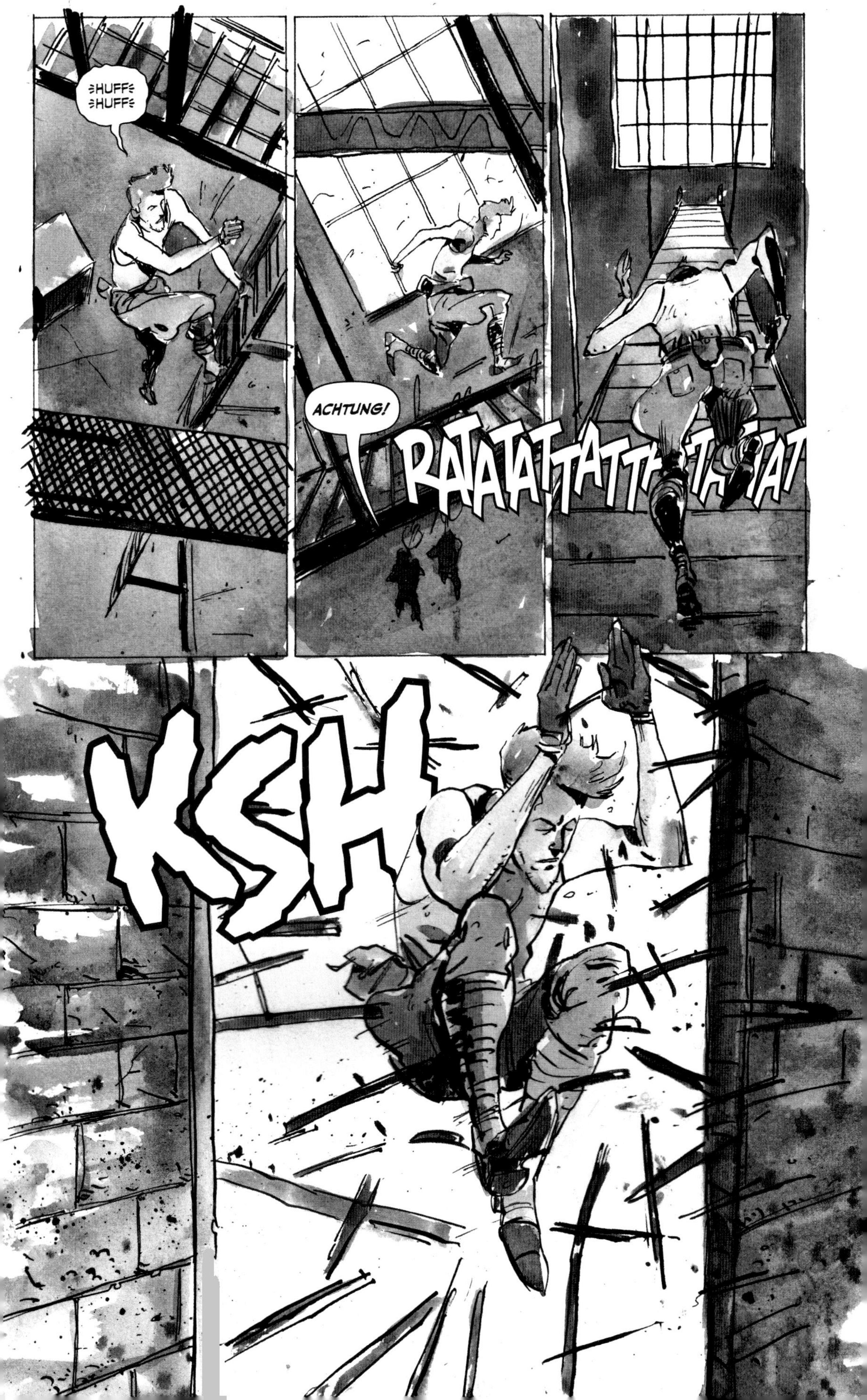

HUFF HUFF
ACHTUNG!
RATATATTATTATATAT
KSH

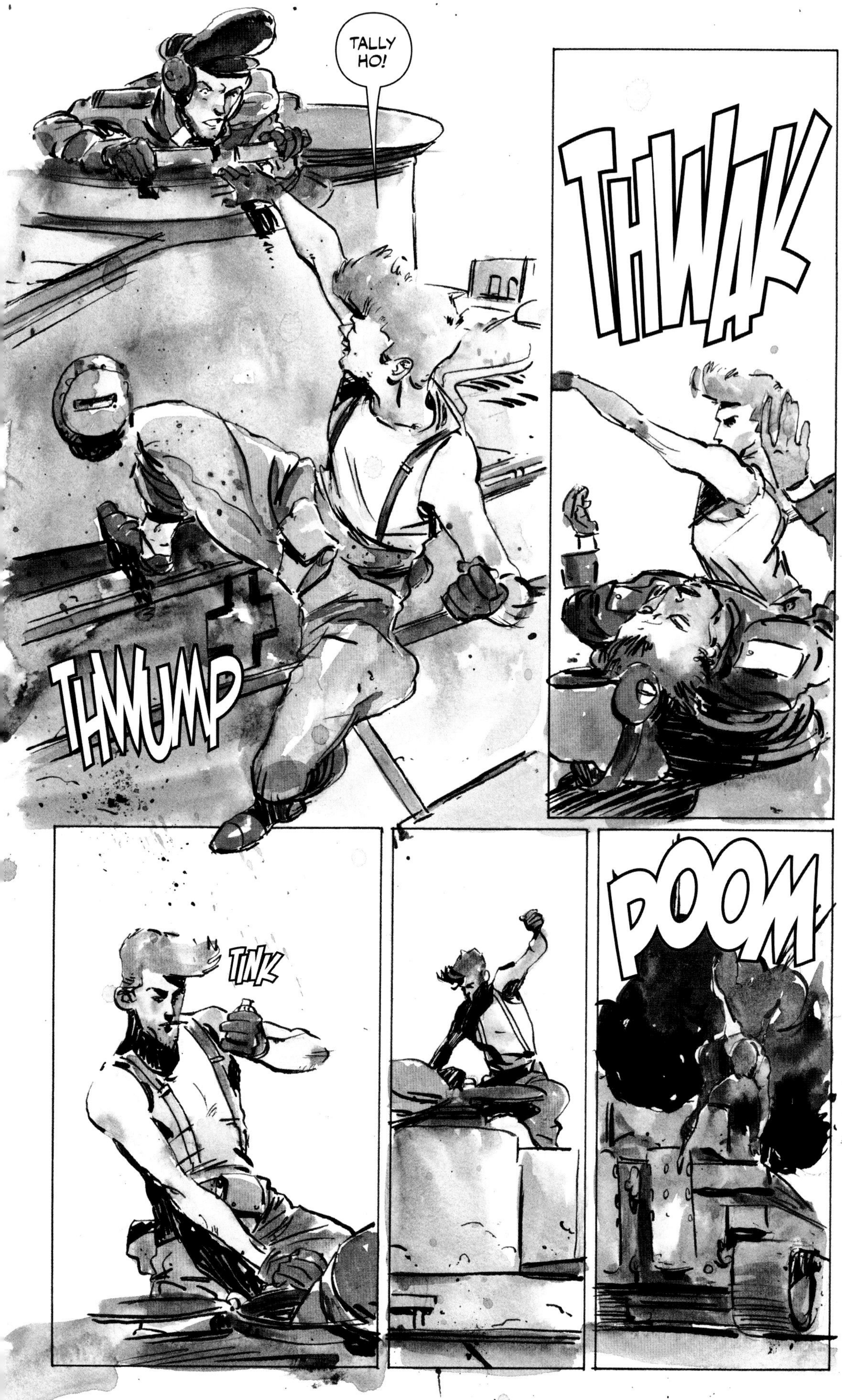
TALLY HO!
THWUMP
THWAK
TINK
POOM

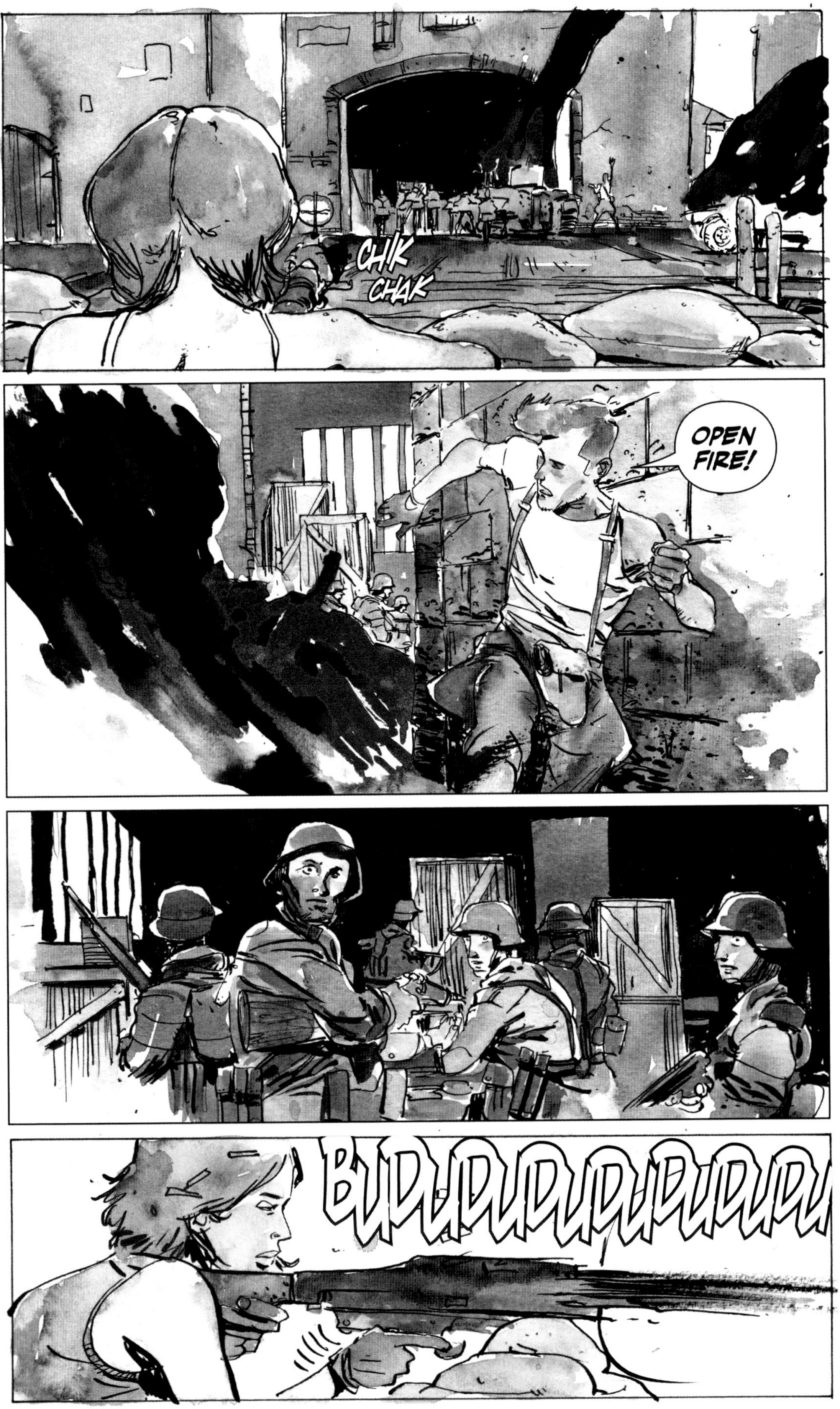
CHIK
CHAK
OPEN FIRE!
BUDUDUDUDUDUDUDU

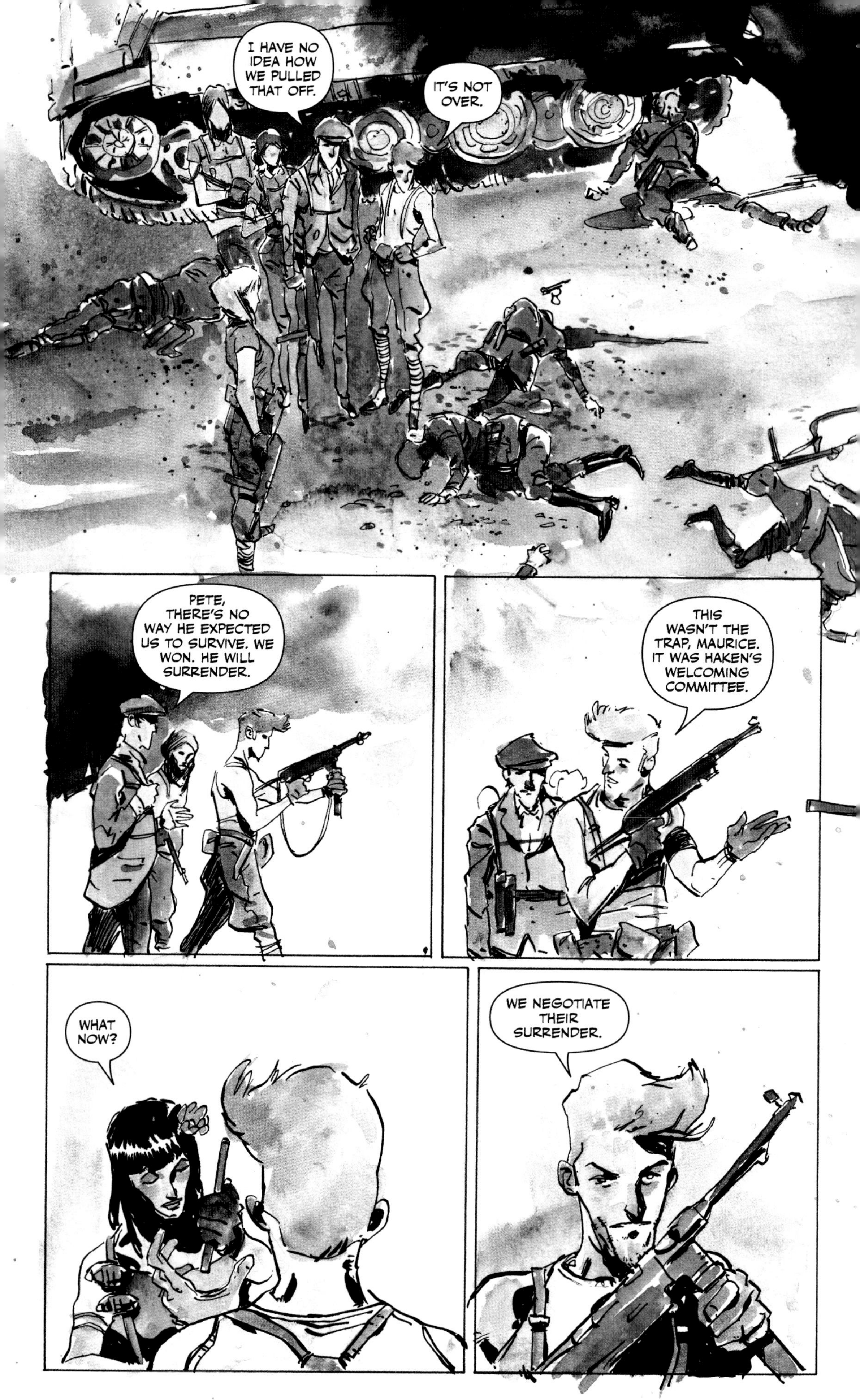

I HAVE NO IDEA HOW WE PULLED THAT OFF.
IT'S NOT OVER.
PETE, THERE'S NO WAY HE EXPECTED US TO SURVIVE. WE WON. HE WILL SURRENDER.
THIS WASN'T THE TRAP, MAURICE. IT WAS HAKEN'S WELCOMING COMMITTEE.
WHAT NOW?
WE NEGOTIATE THEIR SURRENDER.

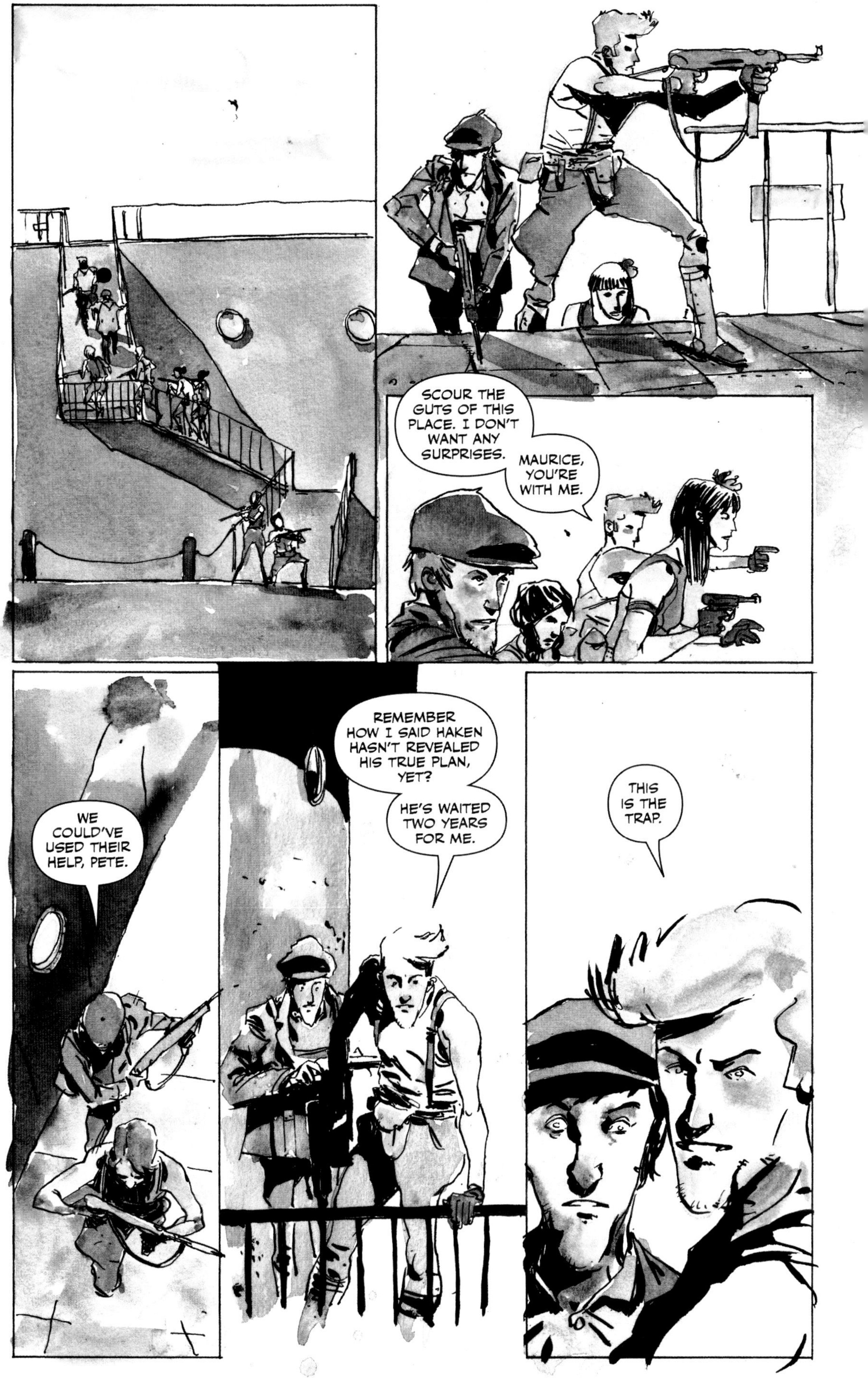
SCOUR THE GUTS OF THIS PLACE. I DON'T WANT ANY SURPRISES.
MAURICE, YOU'RE WITH ME.
WE COULD'VE USED THEIR HELP, PETE.
REMEMBER HOW I SAID HAKEN HASN'T REVEALED HIS TRUE PLAN, YET?
HE'S WAITED TWO YEARS FOR ME.
THIS IS THE TRAP.

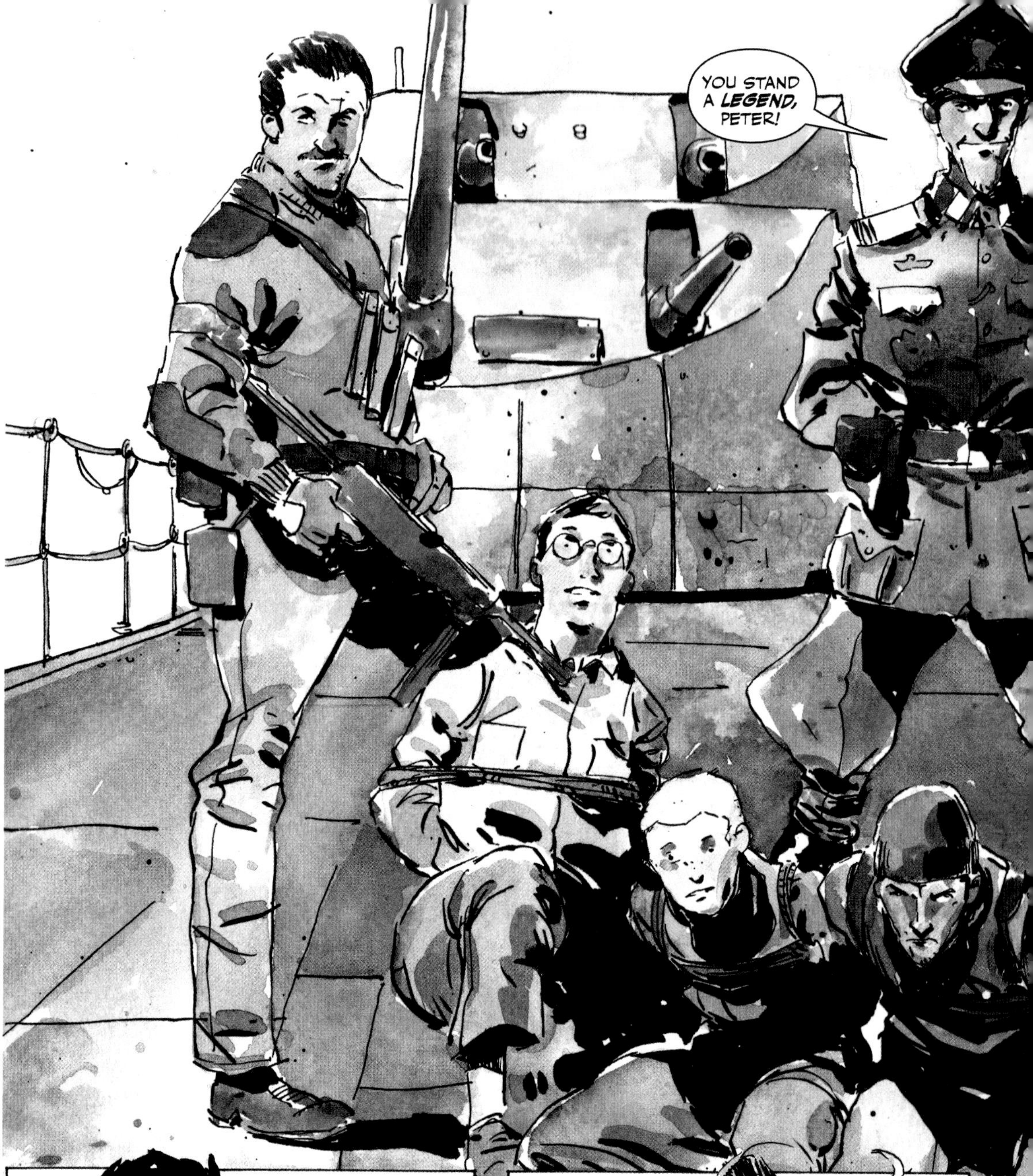
YOU STAND A LEGEND, PETER!

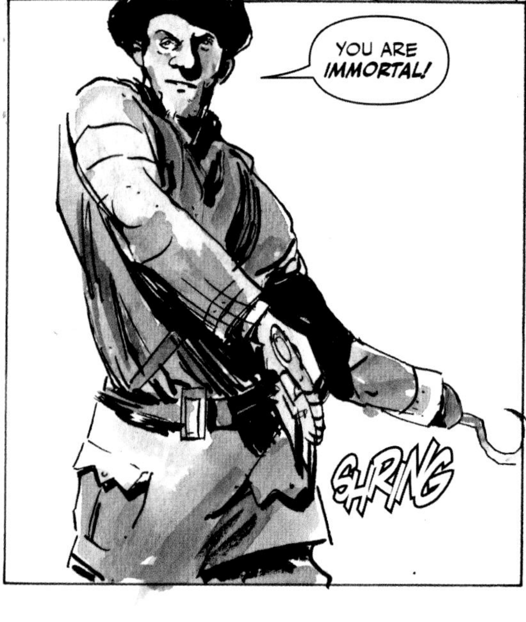
YOU ARE IMMORTAL!
SHRING

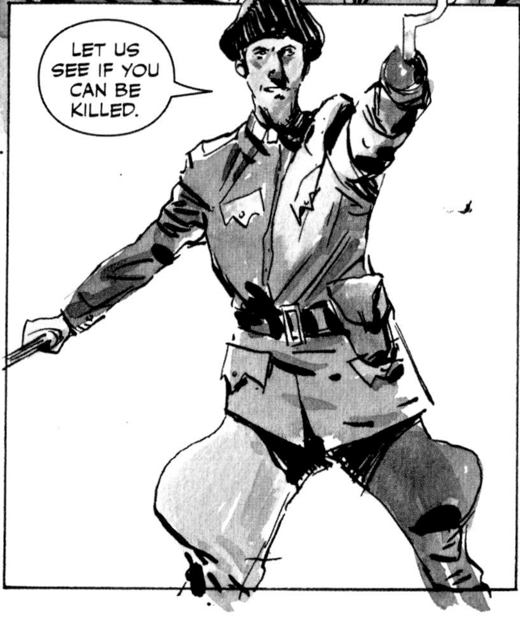
LET US SEE IF YOU CAN BE KILLED.

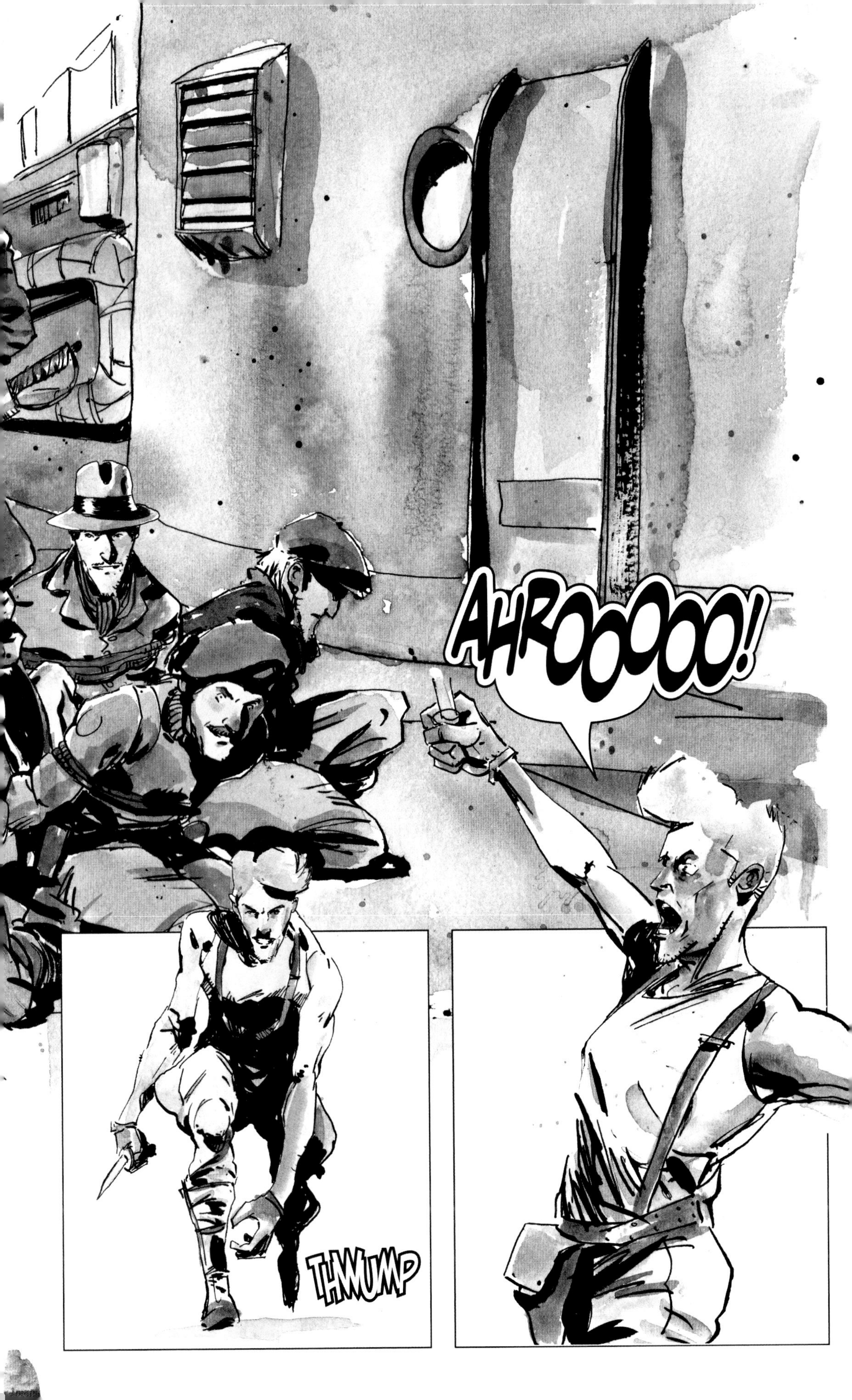
AHROOOOOO!
THWUMP

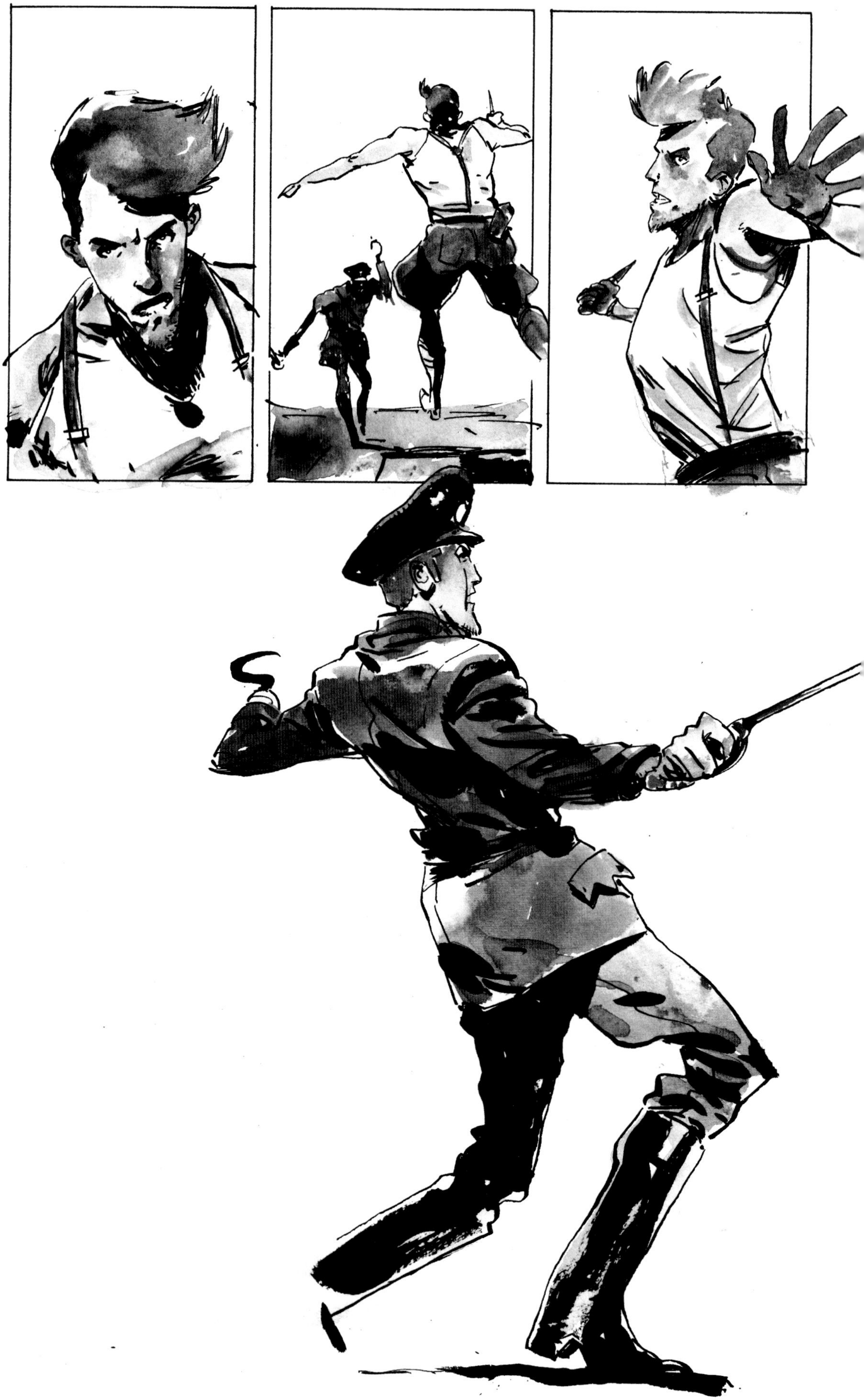

Rejected cover for issue #25

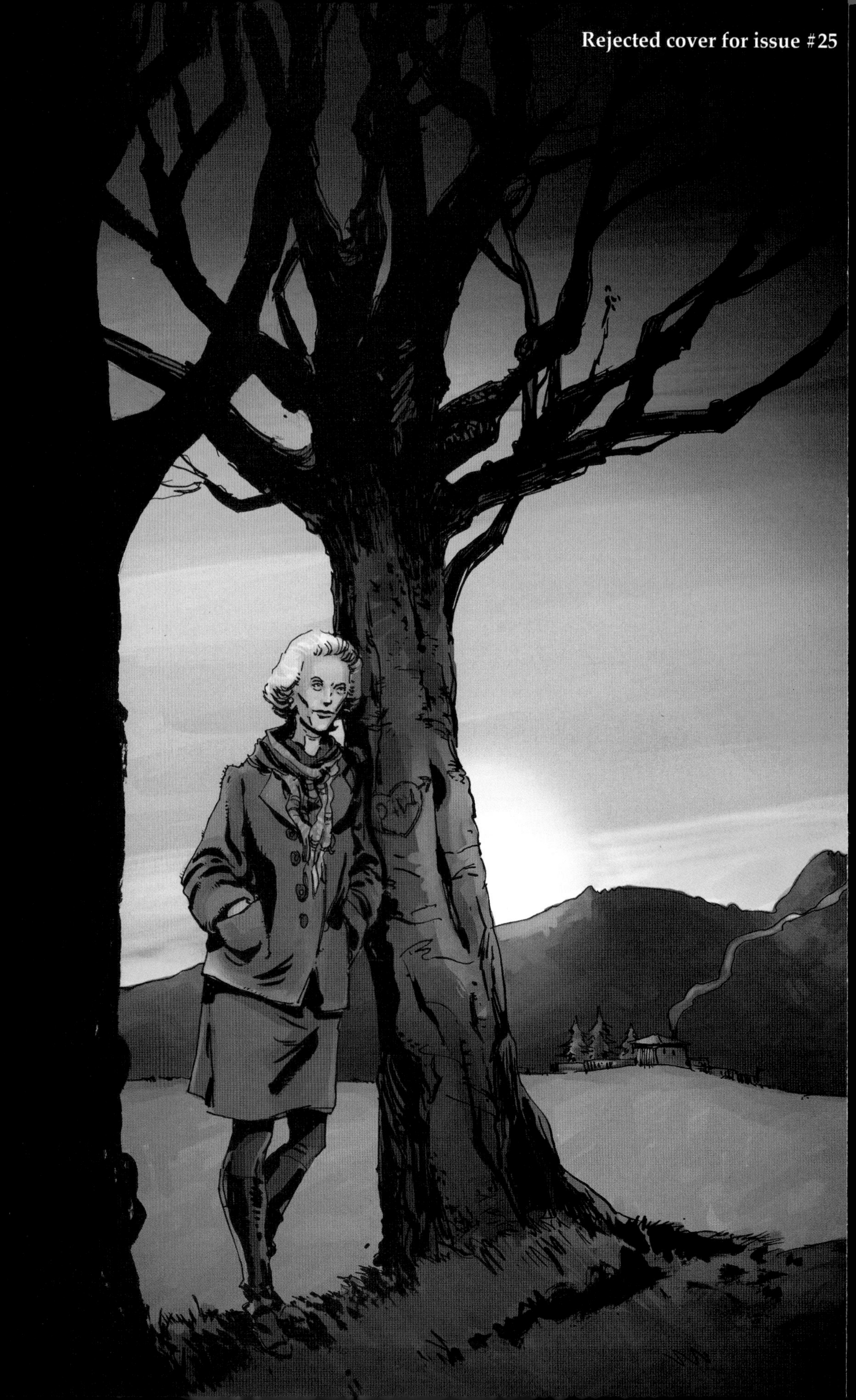

CHAPTER TWENTY-FIVE

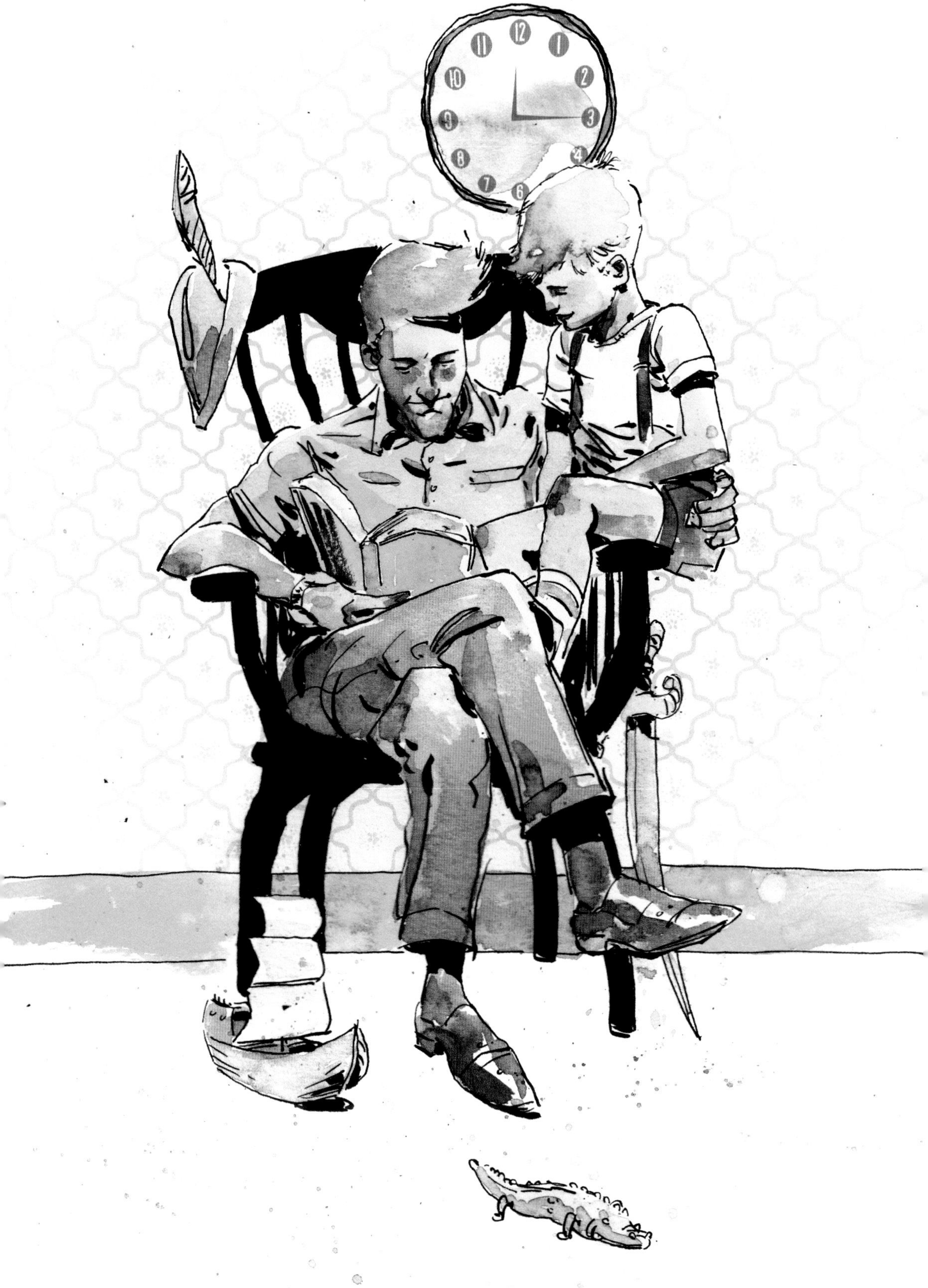

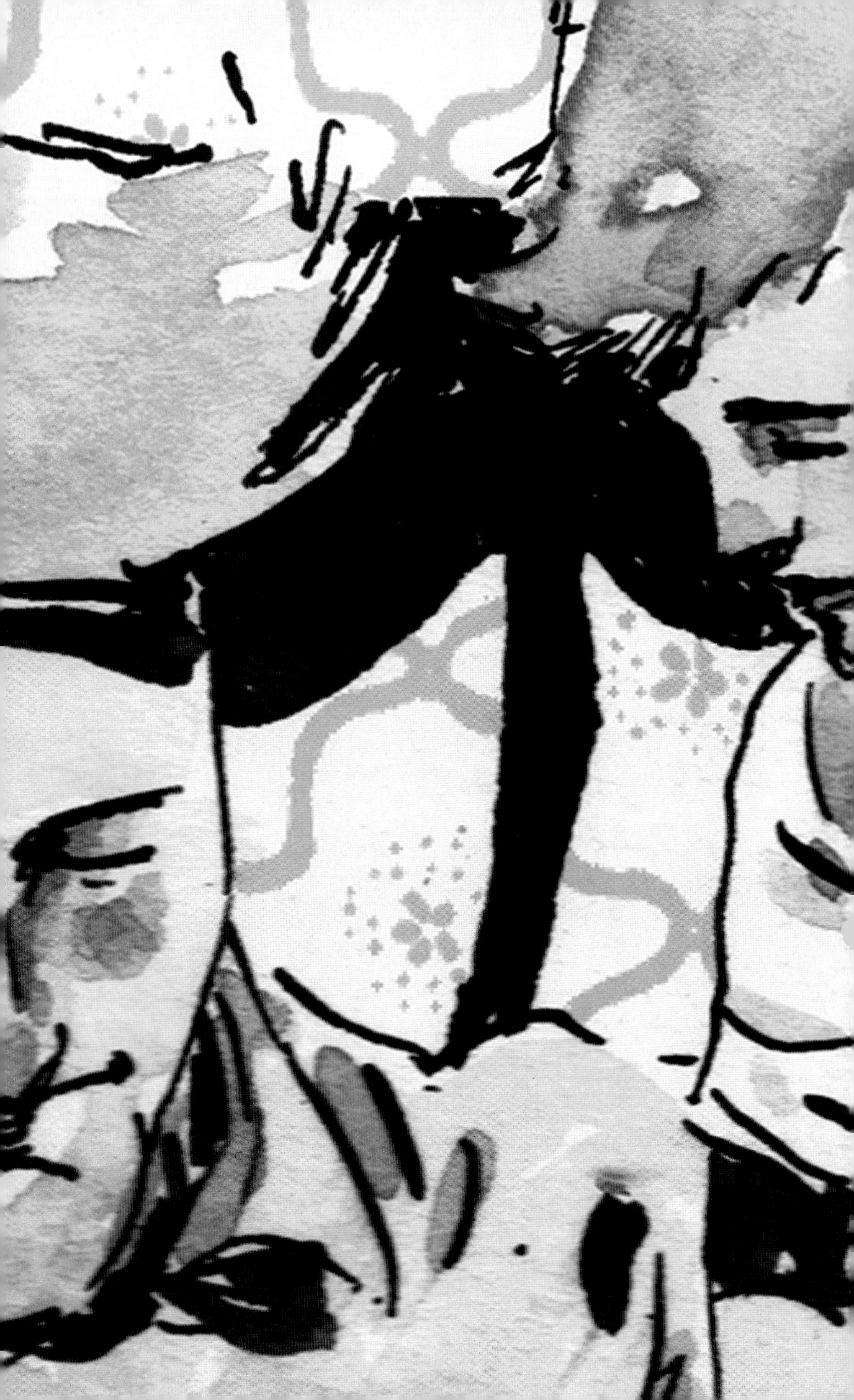

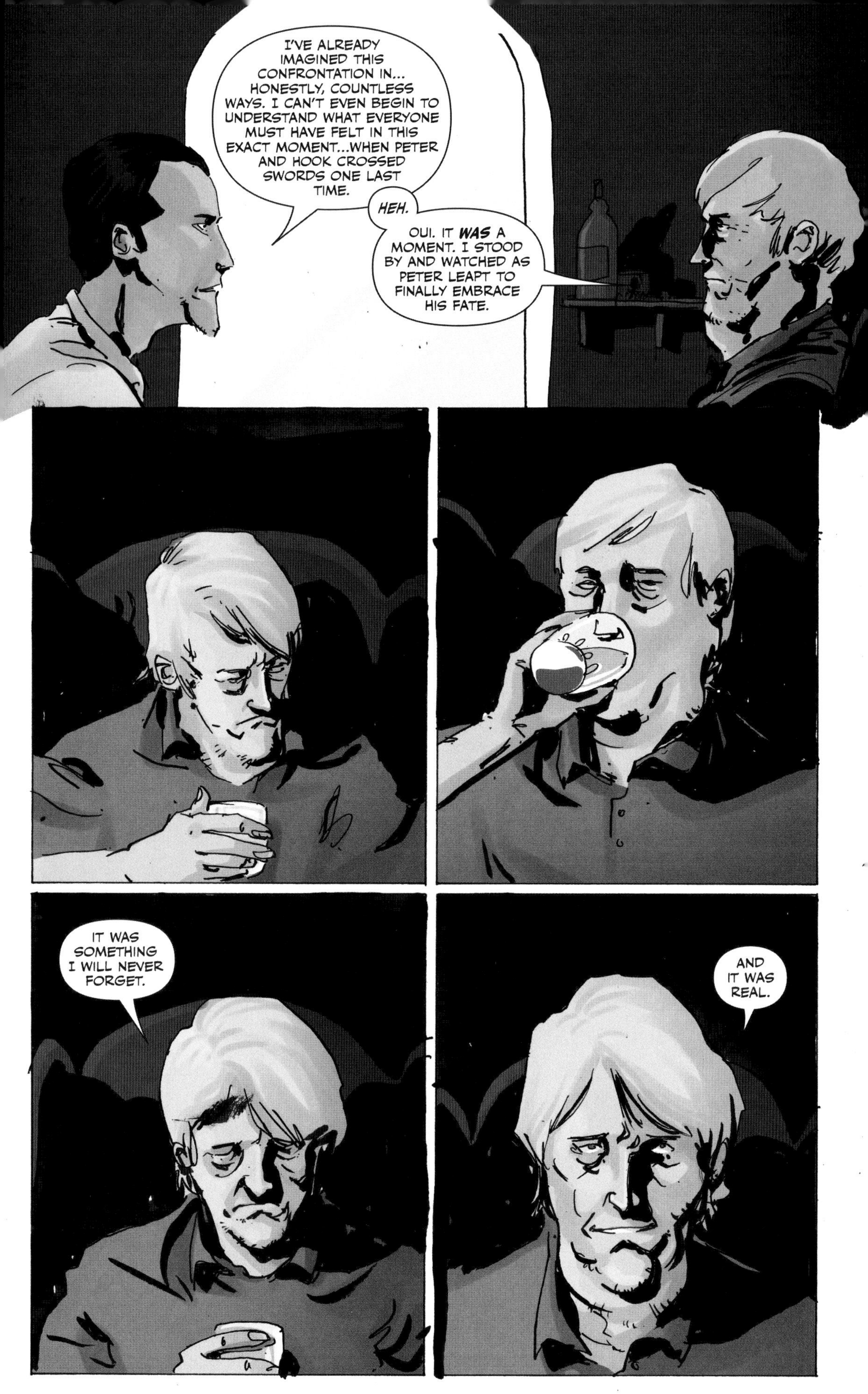
I'VE ALREADY IMAGINED THIS CONFRONTATION IN... HONESTLY, COUNTLESS WAYS. I CAN'T EVEN BEGIN TO UNDERSTAND WHAT EVERYONE MUST HAVE FELT IN THIS EXACT MOMENT...WHEN PETER AND HOOK CROSSED SWORDS ONE LAST TIME.
HEH.
OUI. IT WAS A MOMENT. I STOOD BY AND WATCHED AS PETER LEAPT TO FINALLY EMBRACE HIS FATE.
IT WAS SOMETHING I WILL NEVER FORGET.
AND IT WAS REAL.

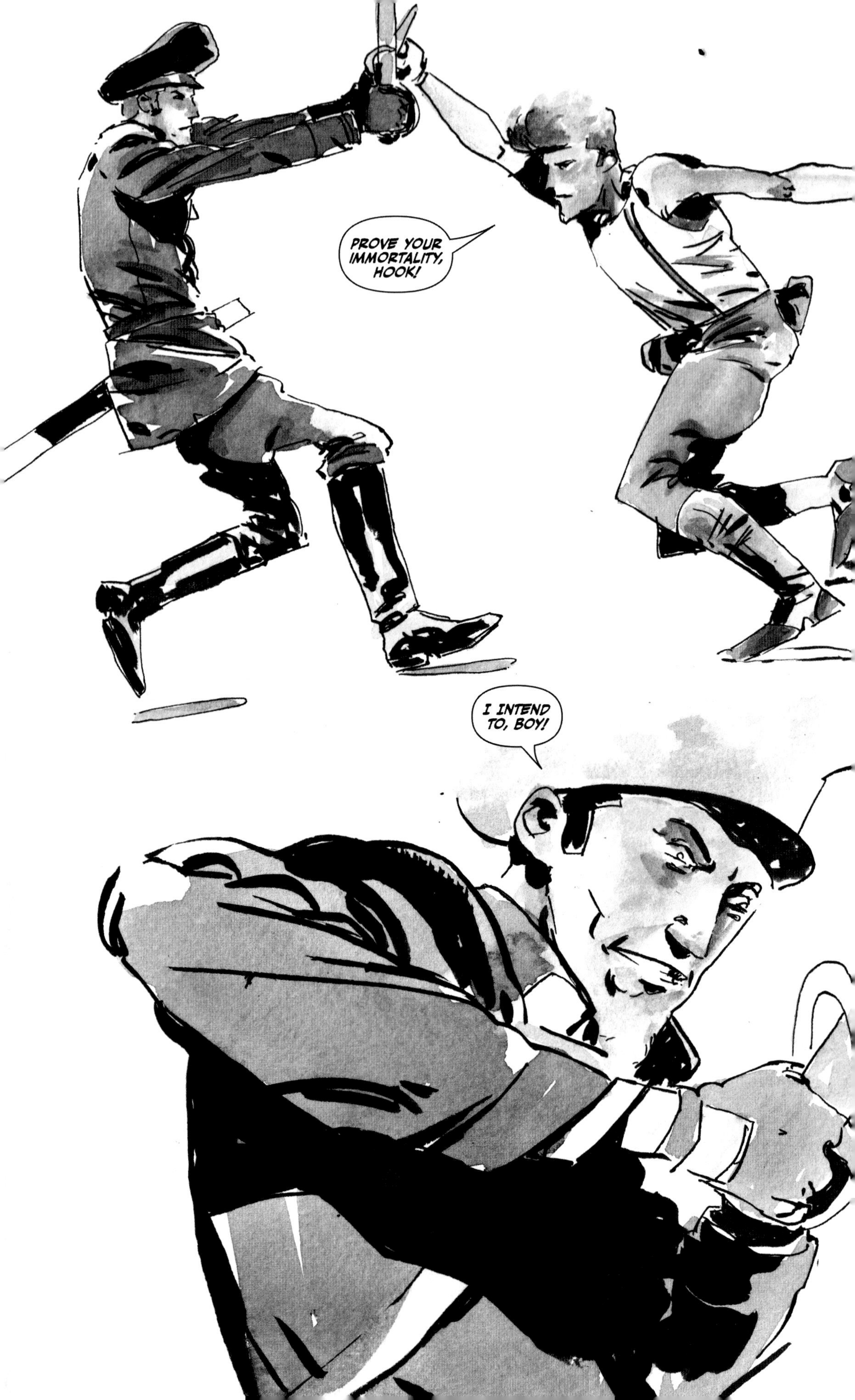
PROVE YOUR IMMORTALITY, HOOK!
I INTEND TO, BOY!

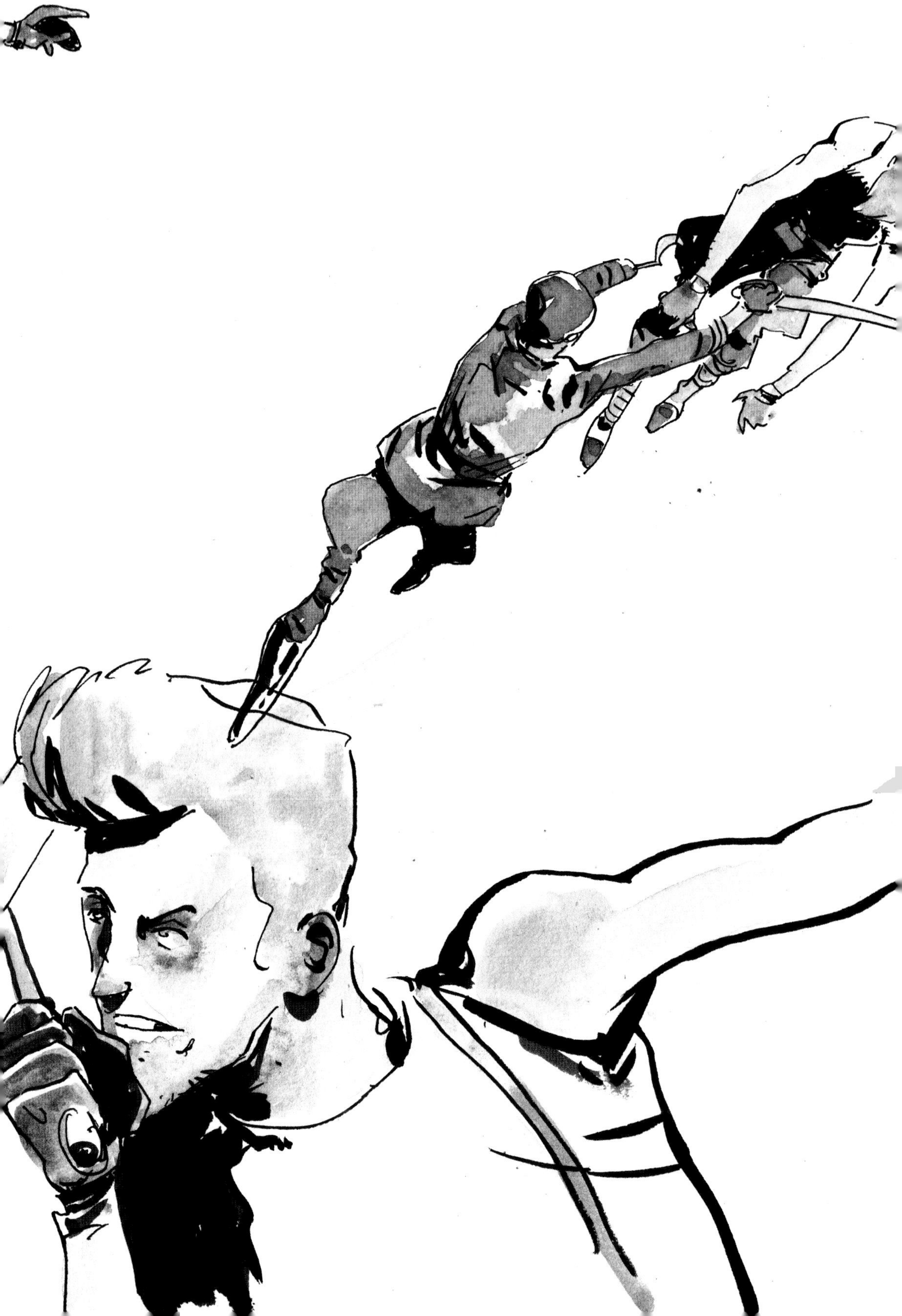

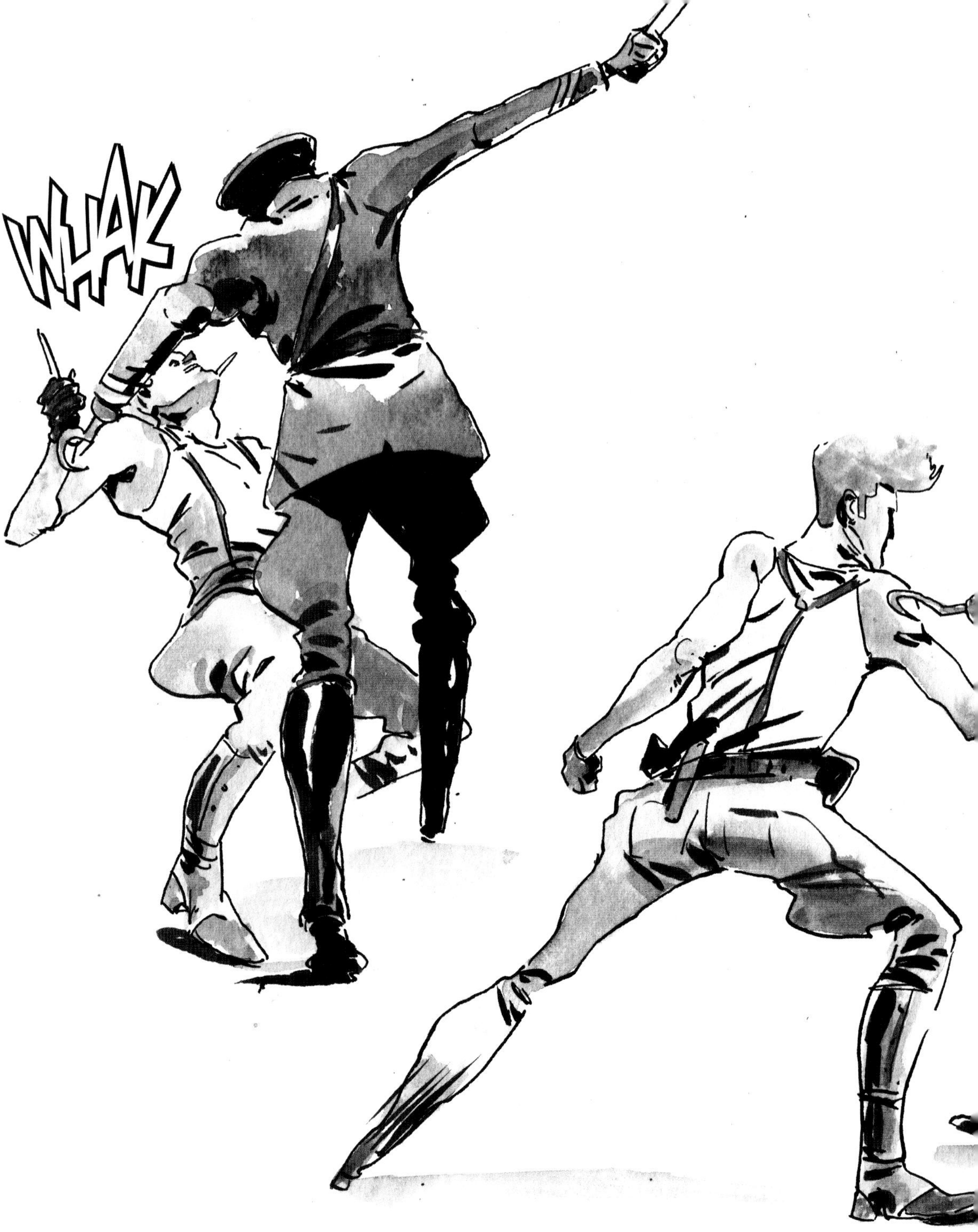
WHAK

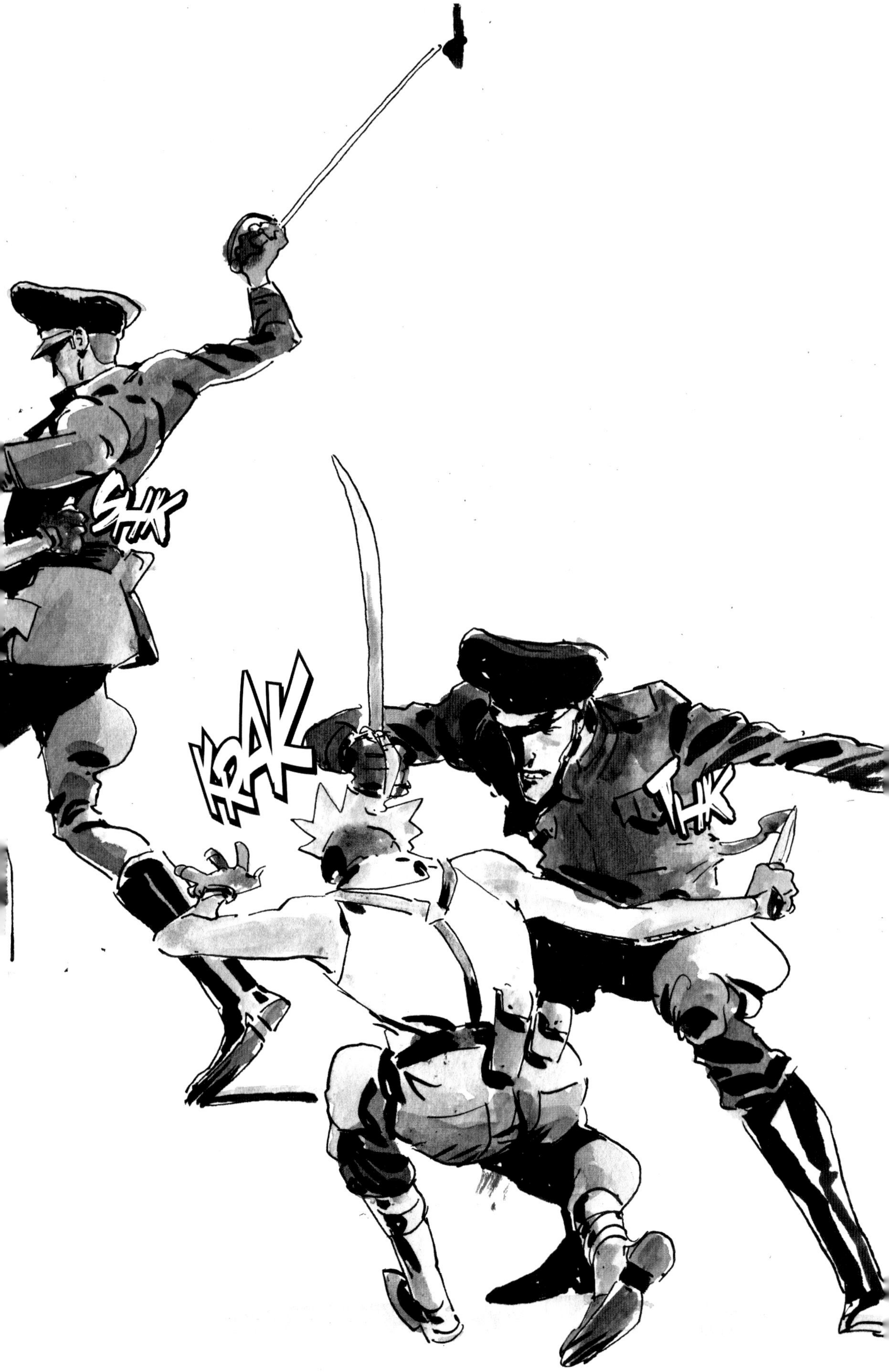
SHK
KRAK
THK

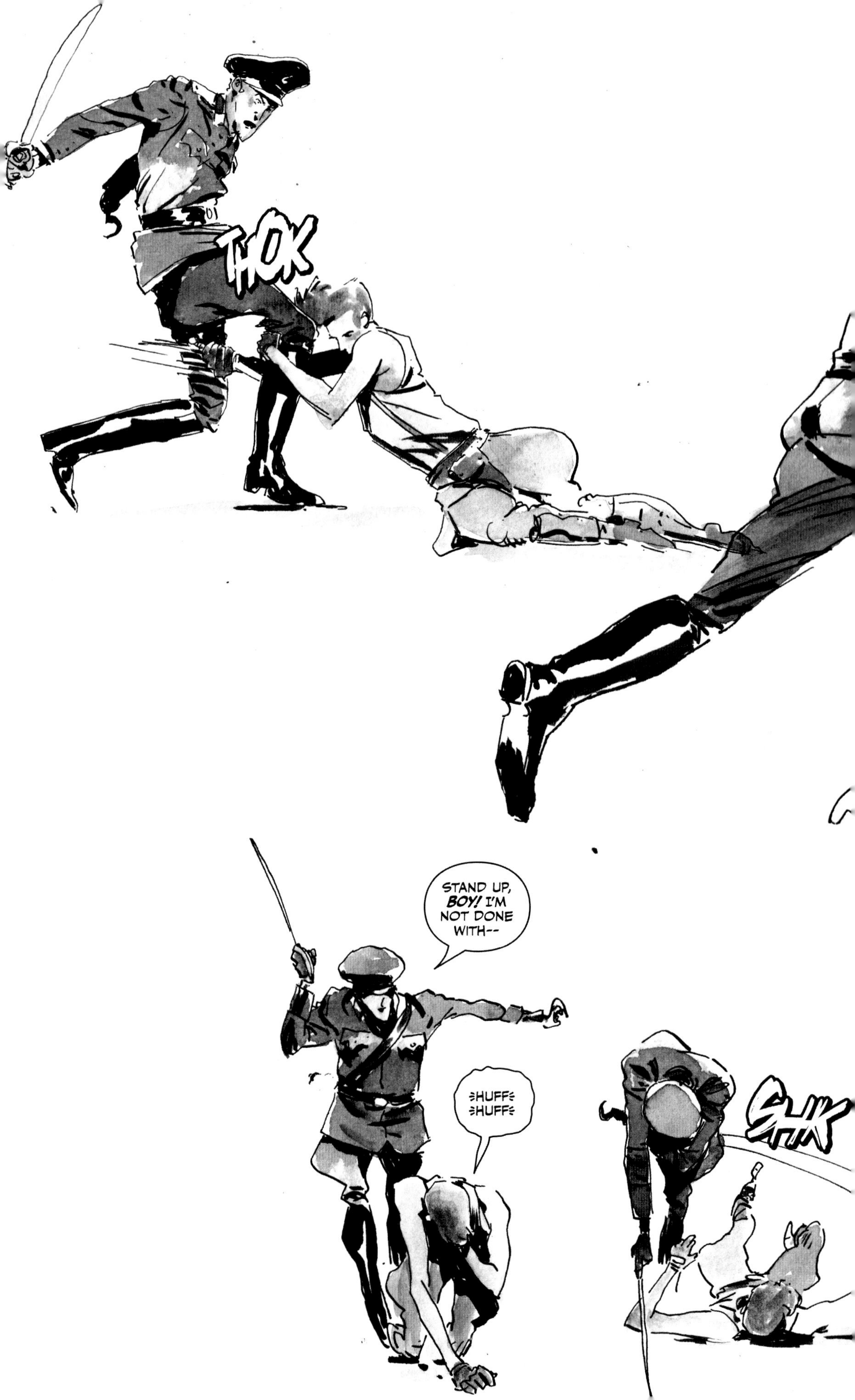
THOK
STAND UP, BOY! I'M NOT DONE WITH--
HUFF HUFF
SHK

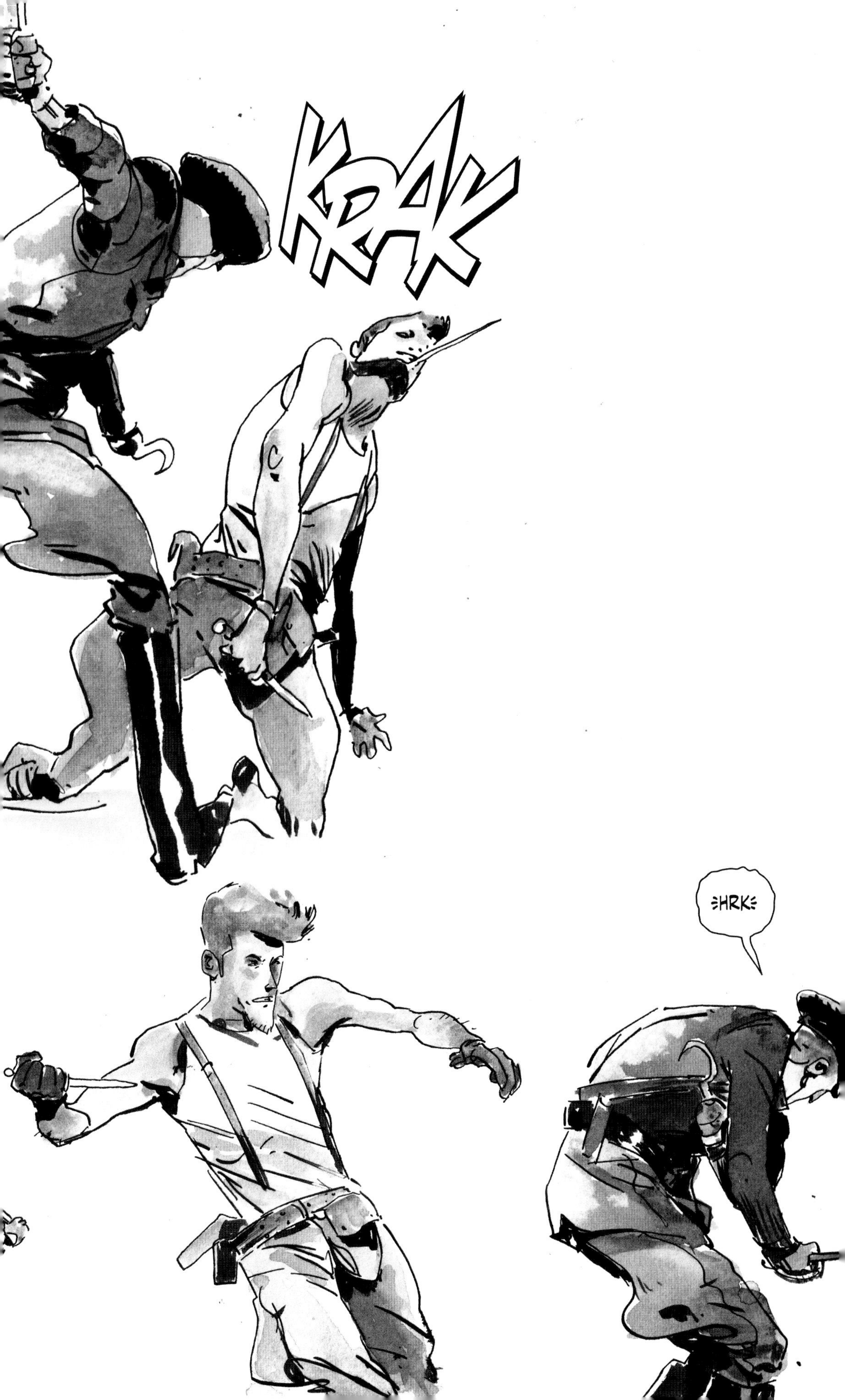
KRAK
HRK

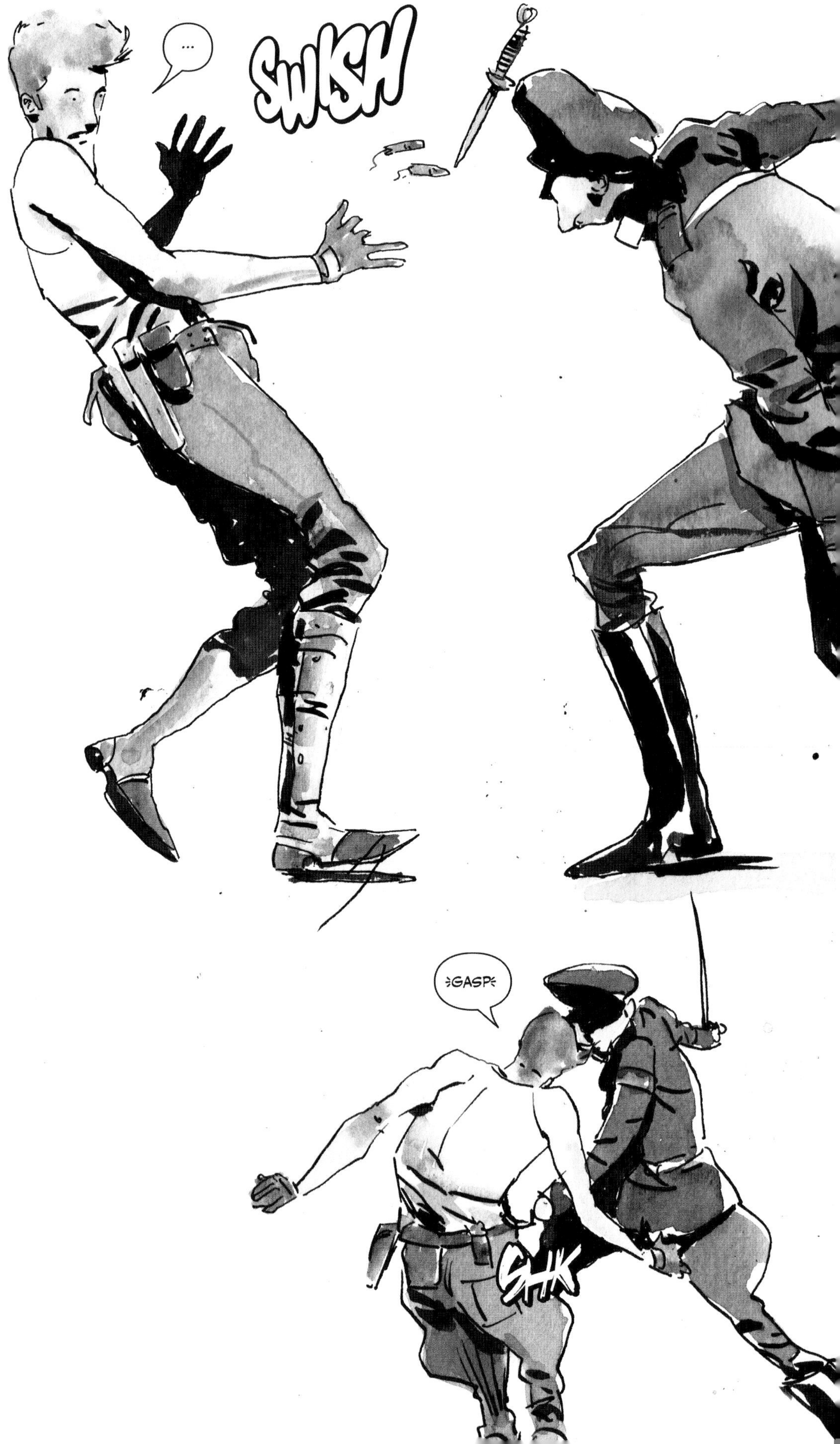
...
SWISH
GASP
SHK

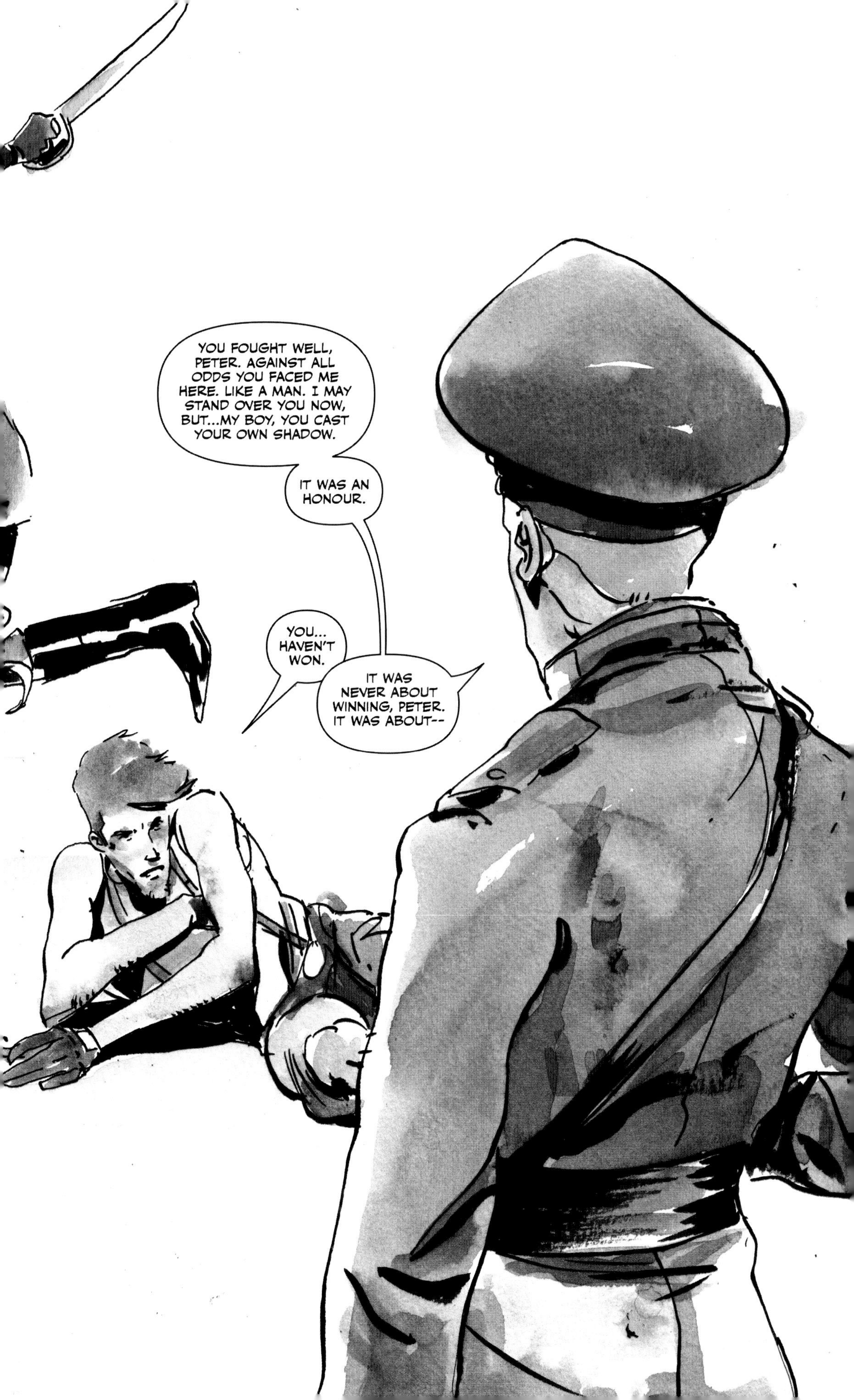
YOU FOUGHT WELL, PETER. AGAINST ALL ODDS YOU FACED ME HERE. LIKE A MAN. I MAY STAND OVER YOU NOW, BUT...MY BOY, YOU CAST YOUR OWN SHADOW.
IT WAS AN HONOUR.
YOU... HAVEN'T WON.
IT WAS NEVER ABOUT WINNING, PETER. IT WAS ABOUT--

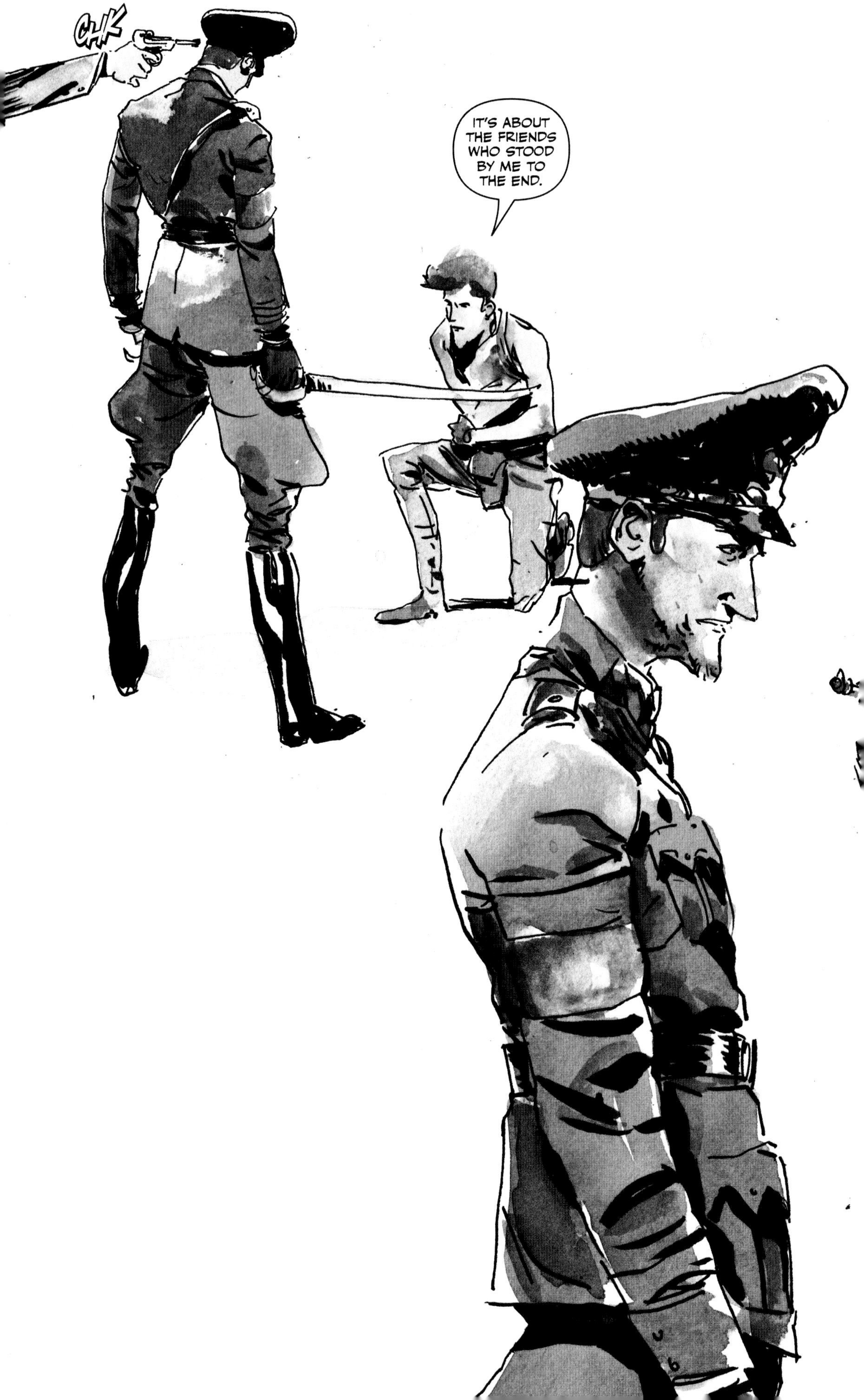
CHK
IT'S ABOUT THE FRIENDS WHO STOOD BY ME TO THE END.

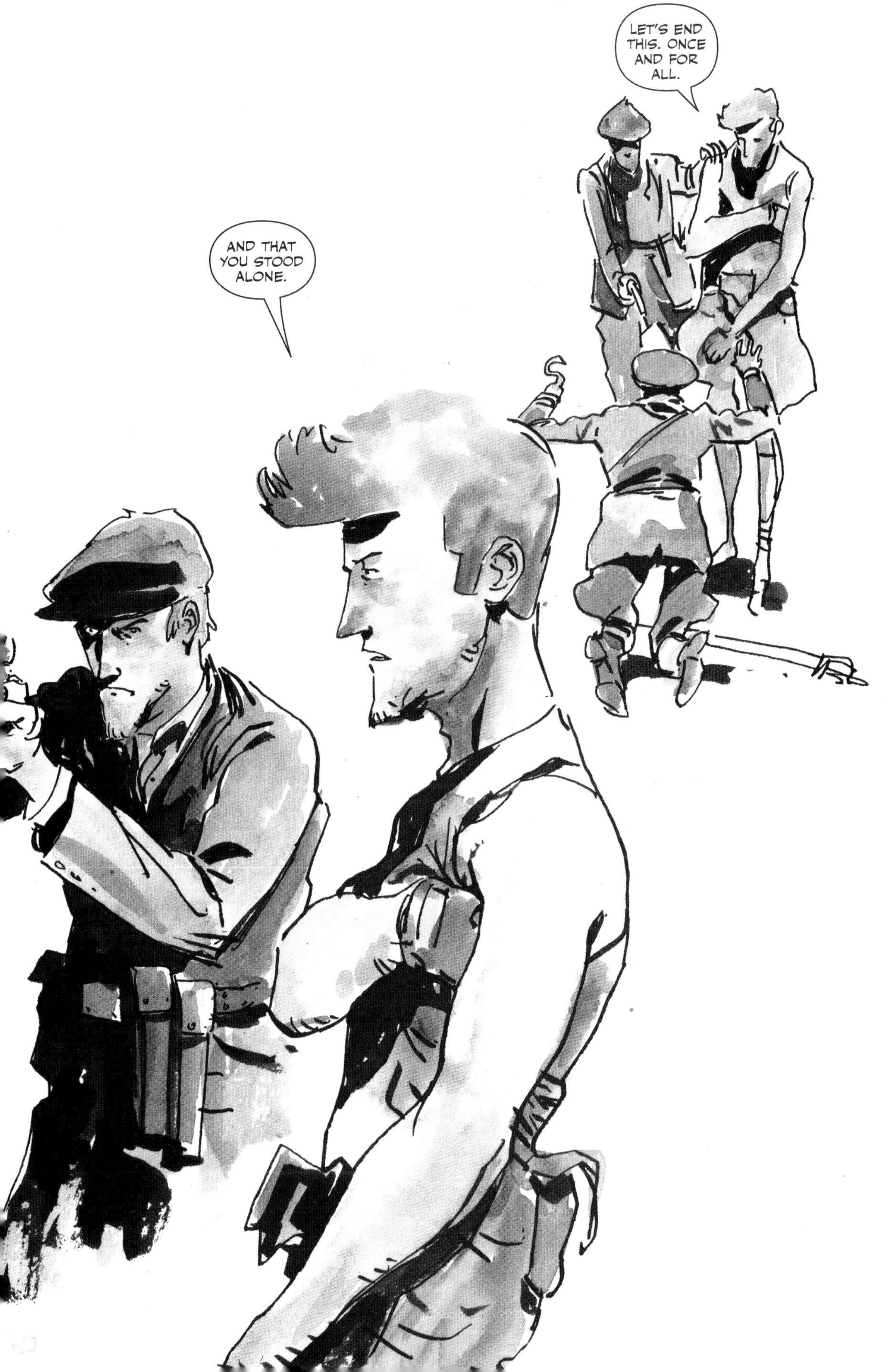
LET'S END THIS. ONCE AND FOR ALL.
AND THAT YOU STOOD ALONE.

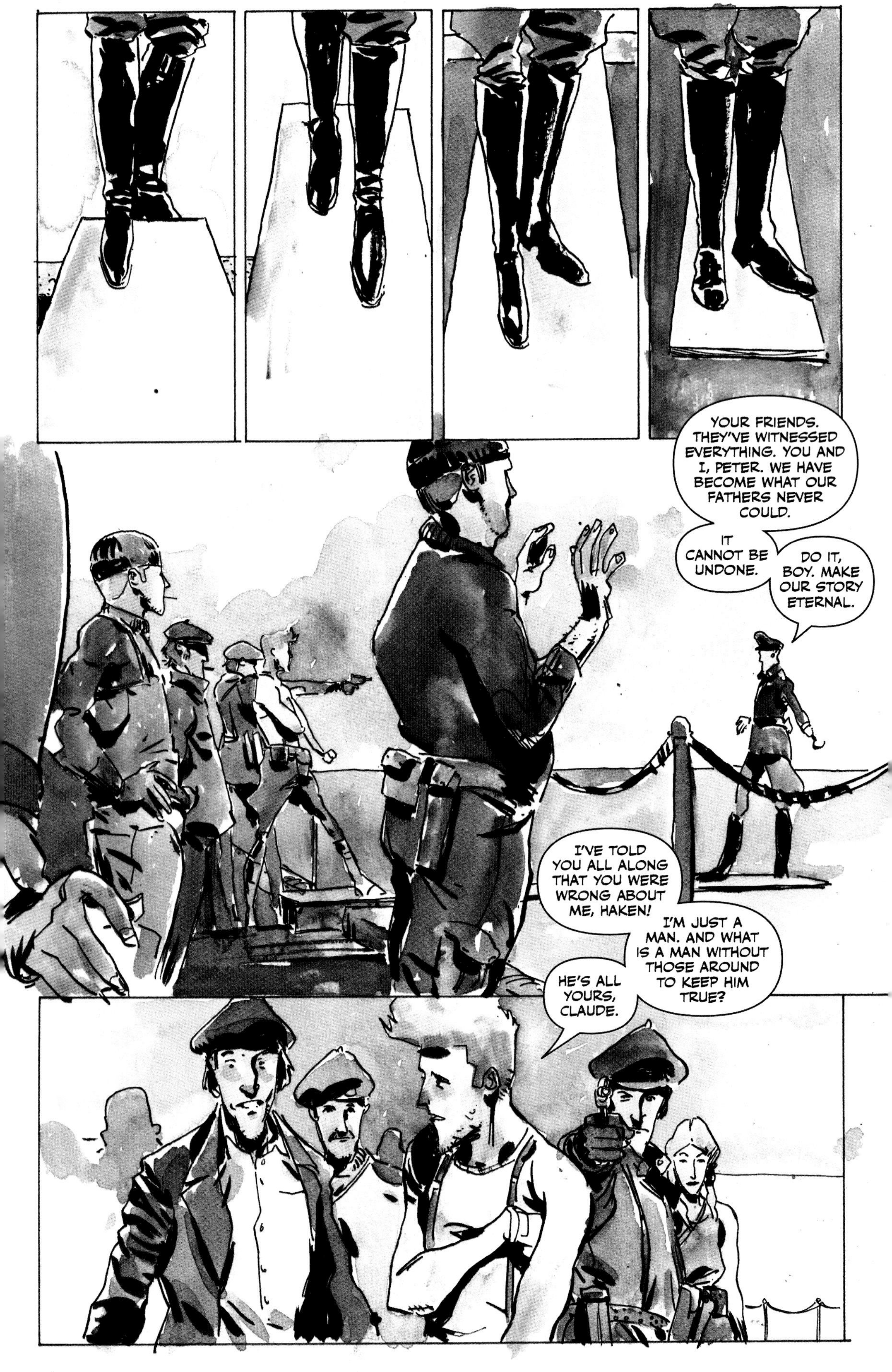
YOUR FRIENDS. THEY'VE WITNESSED EVERYTHING. YOU AND I, PETER. WE HAVE BECOME WHAT OUR FATHERS NEVER COULD.
IT CANNOT BE UNDONE.
DO IT, BOY. MAKE OUR STORY ETERNAL.
I'VE TOLD YOU ALL ALONG THAT YOU WERE WRONG ABOUT ME, HAKEN!
I'M JUST A MAN. AND WHAT IS A MAN WITHOUT THOSE AROUND TO KEEP HIM TRUE?
HE'S ALL YOURS, CLAUDE.

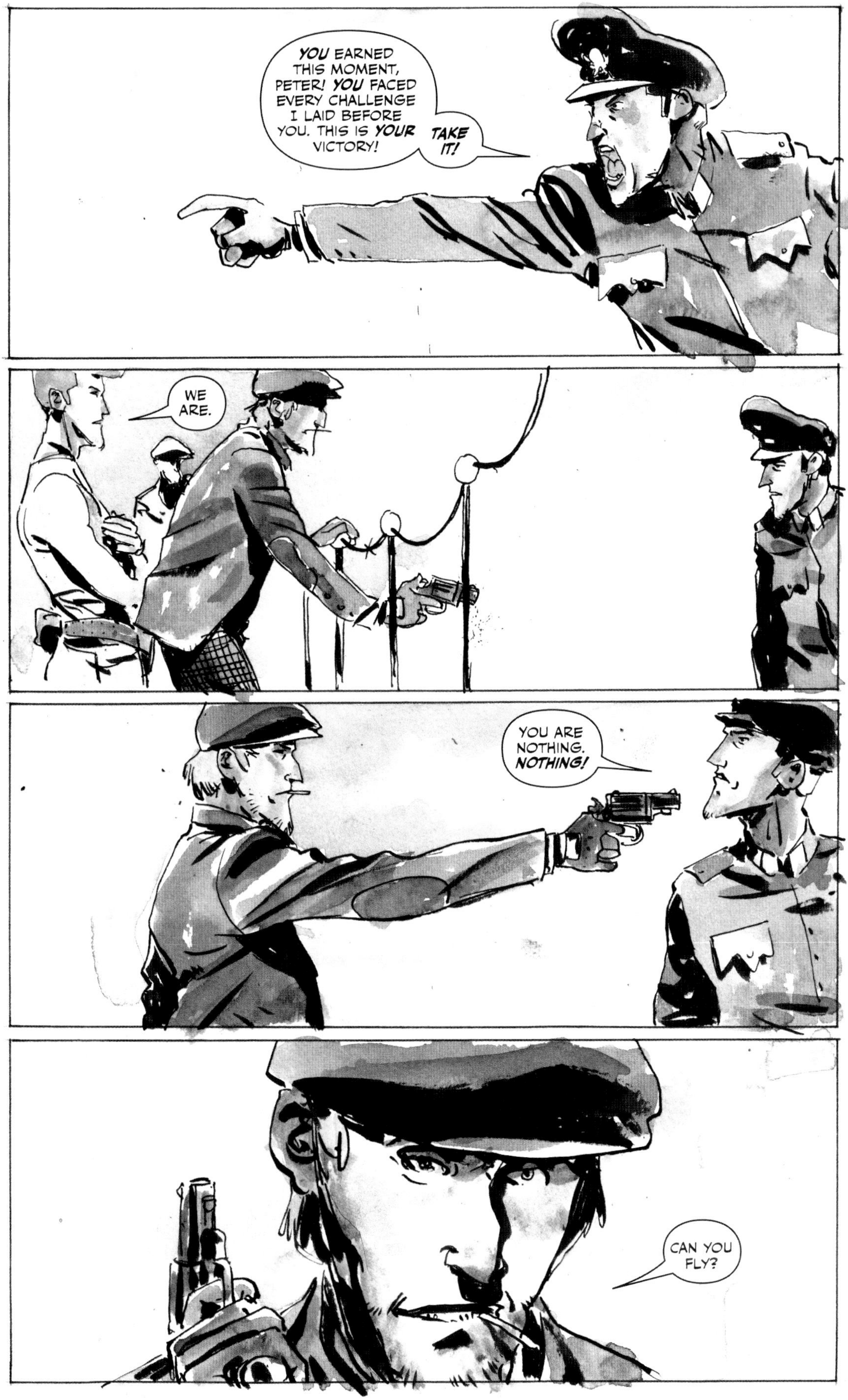
YOU EARNED THIS MOMENT, PETER! YOU FACED EVERY CHALLENGE I LAID BEFORE YOU. THIS IS YOUR VICTORY!
TAKE IT!
WE ARE.
YOU ARE NOTHING. NOTHING!
CAN YOU FLY?

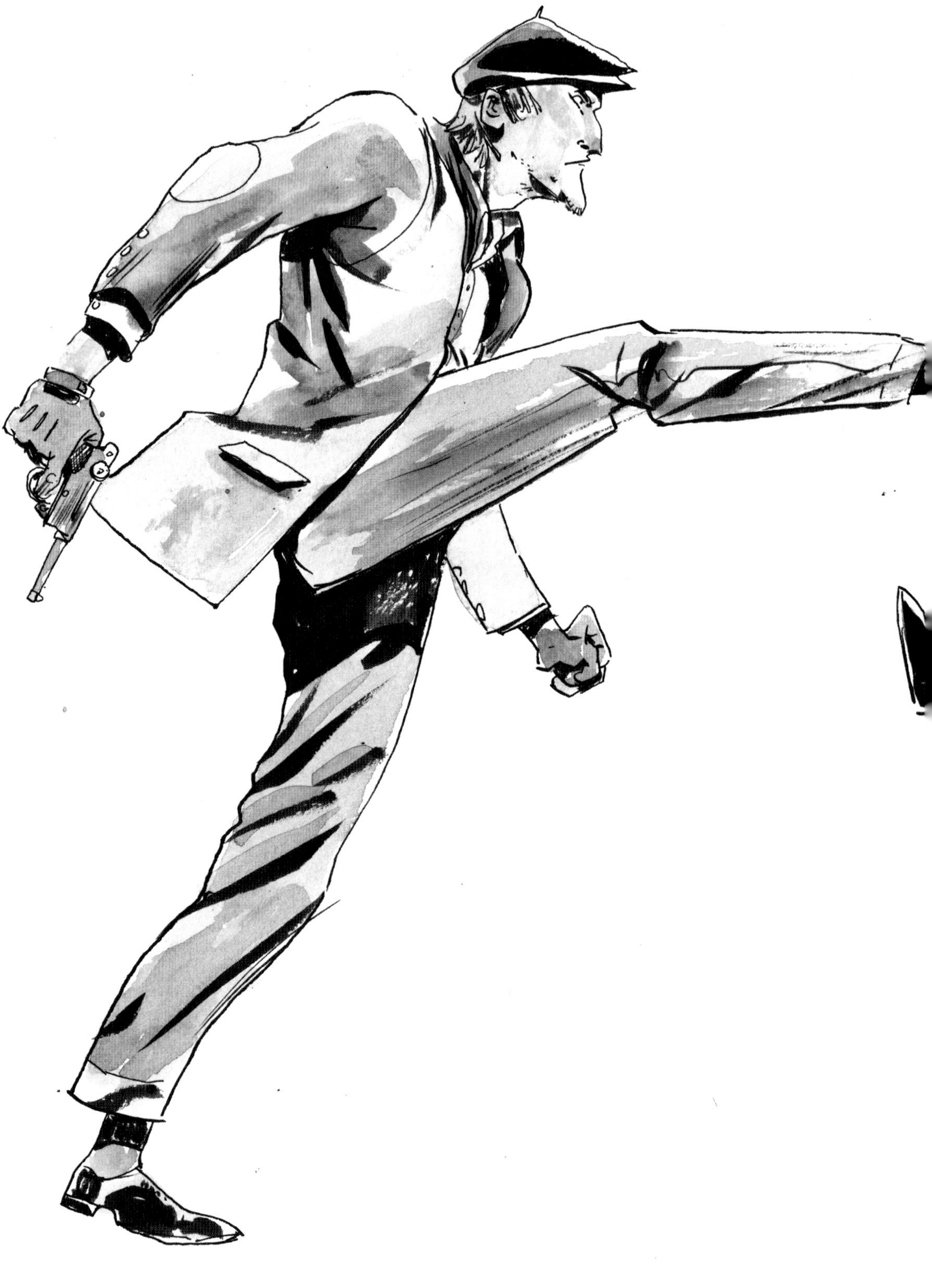

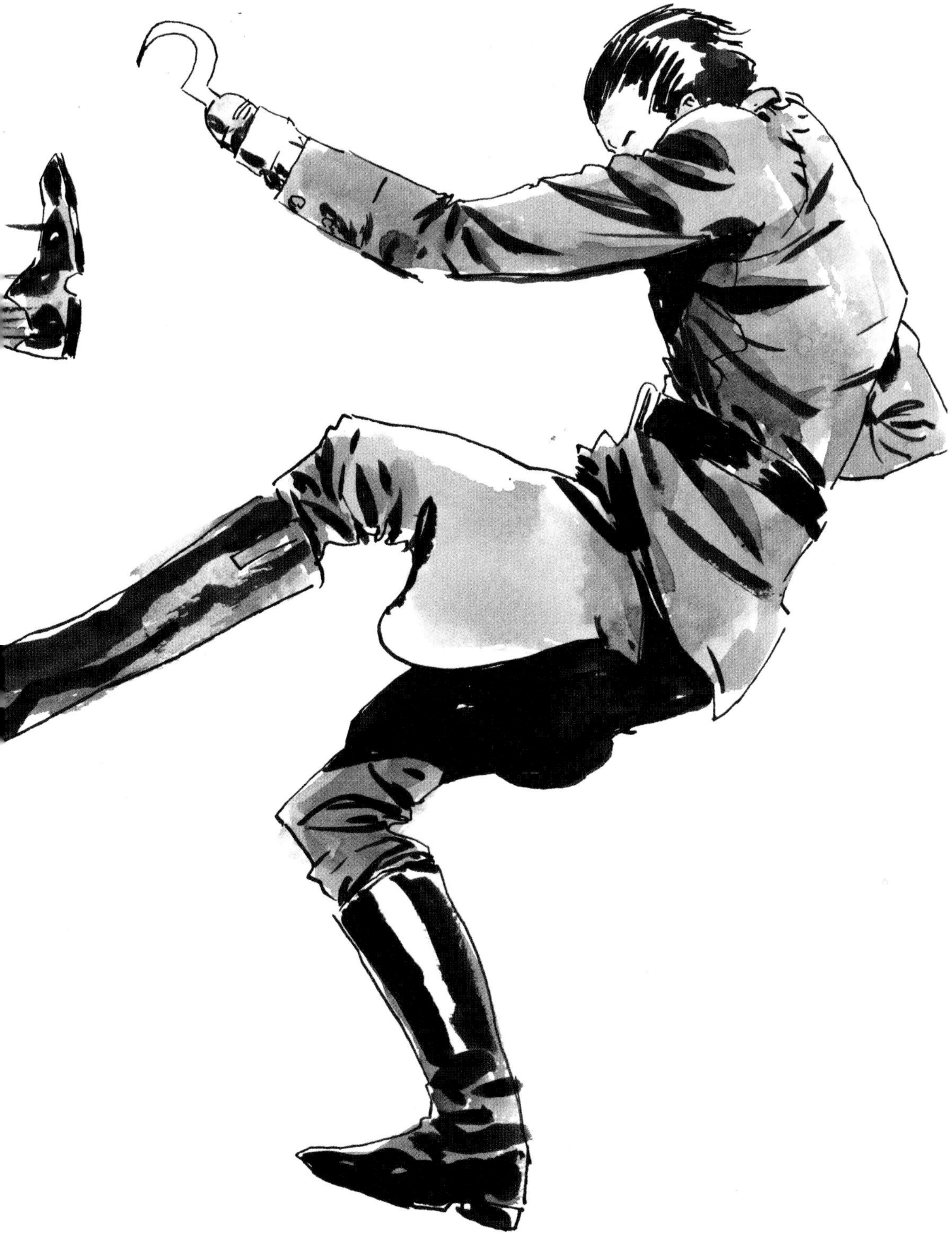

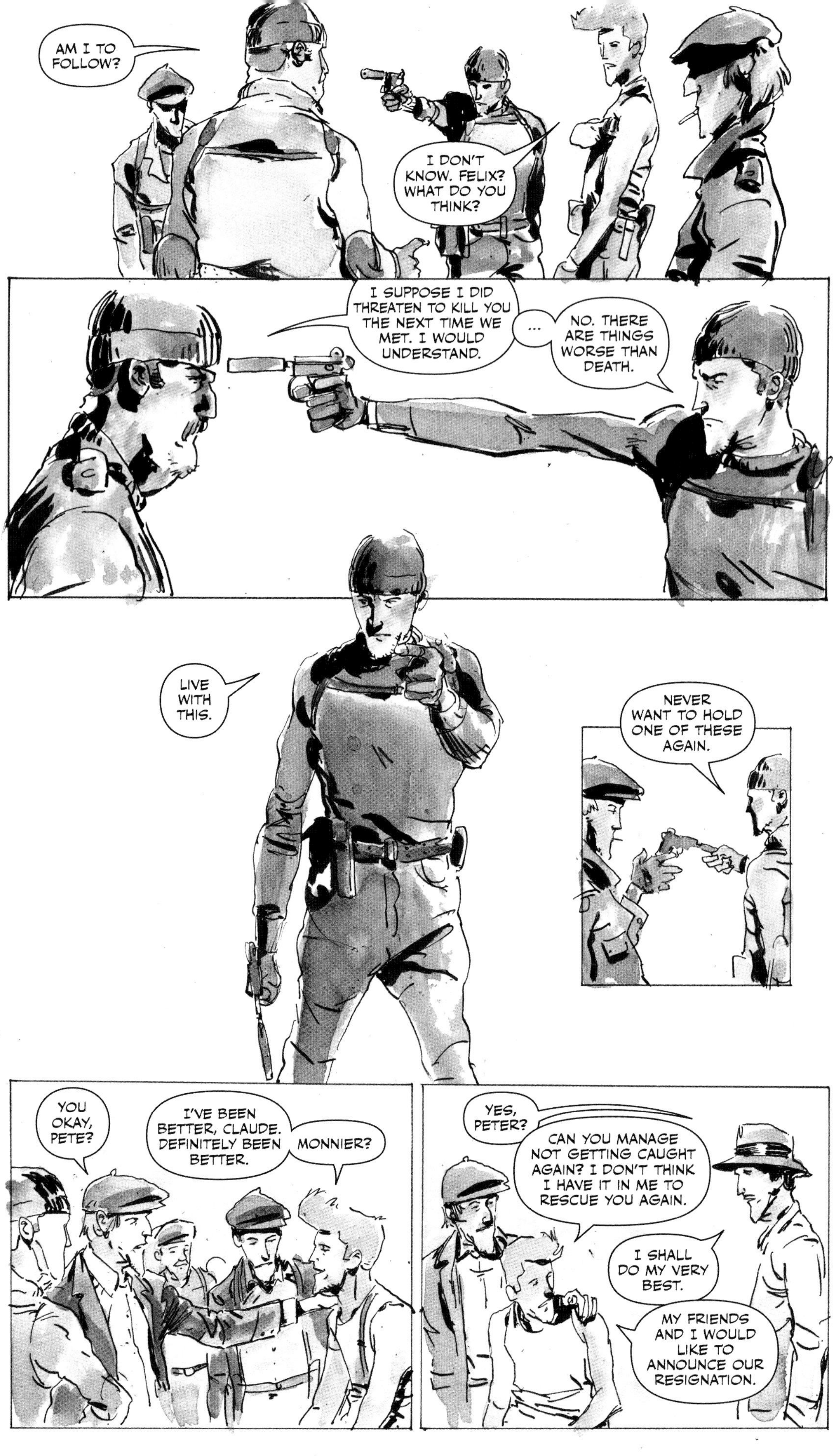
AM I TO FOLLOW?
I DON'T KNOW. FELIX? WHAT DO YOU THINK?
I SUPPOSE I DID THREATEN TO KILL YOU THE NEXT TIME WE MET. I WOULD UNDERSTAND.
...
NO. THERE ARE THINGS WORSE THAN DEATH.
LIVE WITH THIS.
NEVER WANT TO HOLD ONE OF THESE AGAIN.
YOU OKAY, PETE?
I'VE BEEN BETTER, CLAUDE. DEFINITELY BEEN BETTER.
MONNIER?
YES, PETER?
CAN YOU MANAGE NOT GETTING CAUGHT AGAIN? I DON'T THINK I HAVE IT IN ME TO RESCUE YOU AGAIN.
I SHALL DO MY VERY BEST.
MY FRIENDS AND I WOULD LIKE TO ANNOUNCE OUR RESIGNATION.

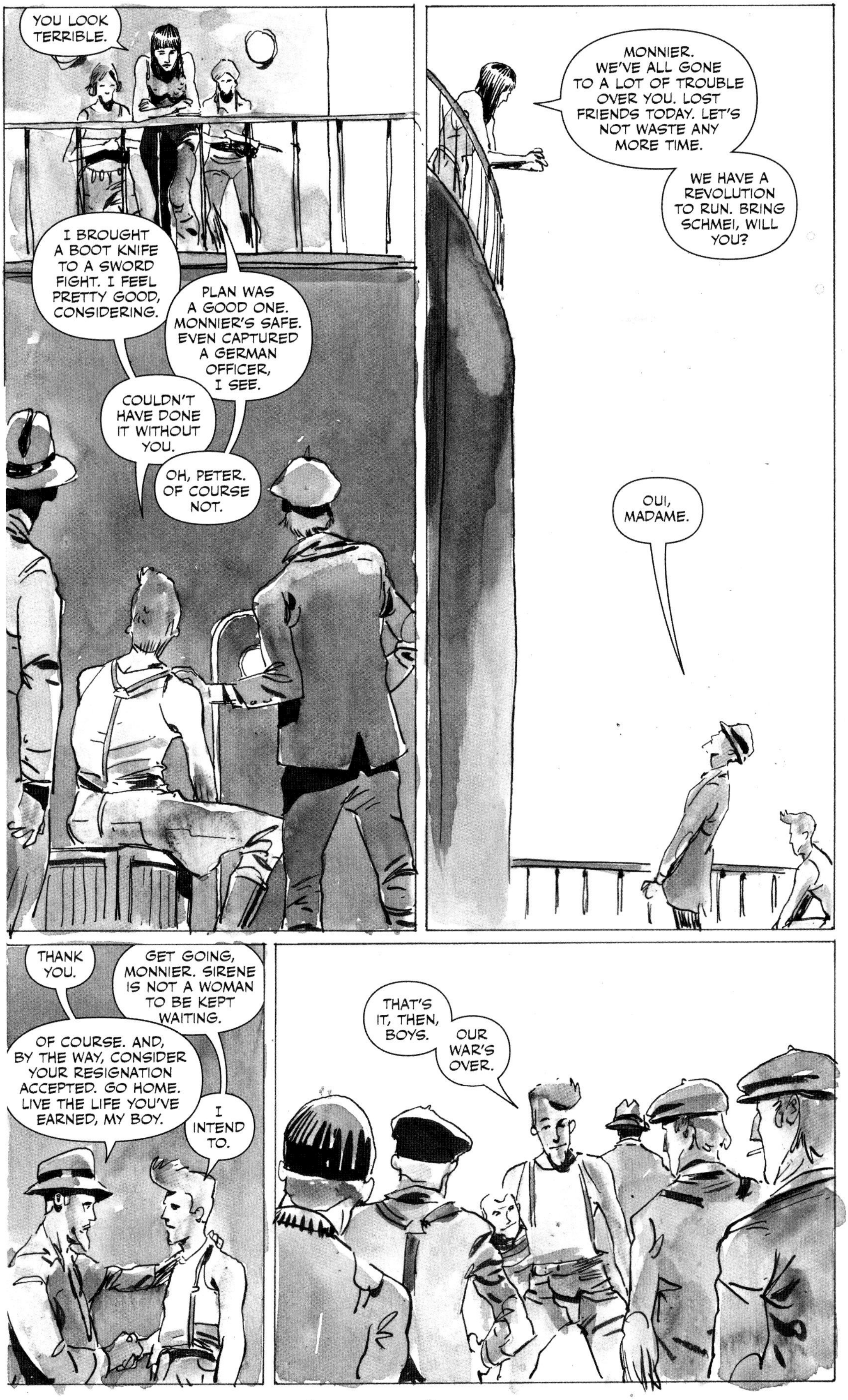
YOU LOOK TERRIBLE.
I BROUGHT A BOOT KNIFE TO A SWORD FIGHT. I FEEL PRETTY GOOD, CONSIDERING.
PLAN WAS A GOOD ONE. MONNIER'S SAFE. EVEN CAPTURED A GERMAN OFFICER, I SEE.
COULDN'T HAVE DONE IT WITHOUT YOU.
OH, PETER. OF COURSE NOT.
MONNIER. WE'VE ALL GONE TO A LOT OF TROUBLE OVER YOU. LOST FRIENDS TODAY. LET'S NOT WASTE ANY MORE TIME.
WE HAVE A REVOLUTION TO RUN. BRING SCHMEI, WILL YOU?
OUI, MADAME.
THANK YOU.
GET GOING, MONNIER. SIRENE IS NOT A WOMAN TO BE KEPT WAITING.
OF COURSE. AND, BY THE WAY, CONSIDER YOUR RESIGNATION ACCEPTED. GO HOME. LIVE THE LIFE YOU'VE EARNED, MY BOY.
I INTEND TO.
THAT'S IT, THEN, BOYS.
OUR WAR'S OVER.

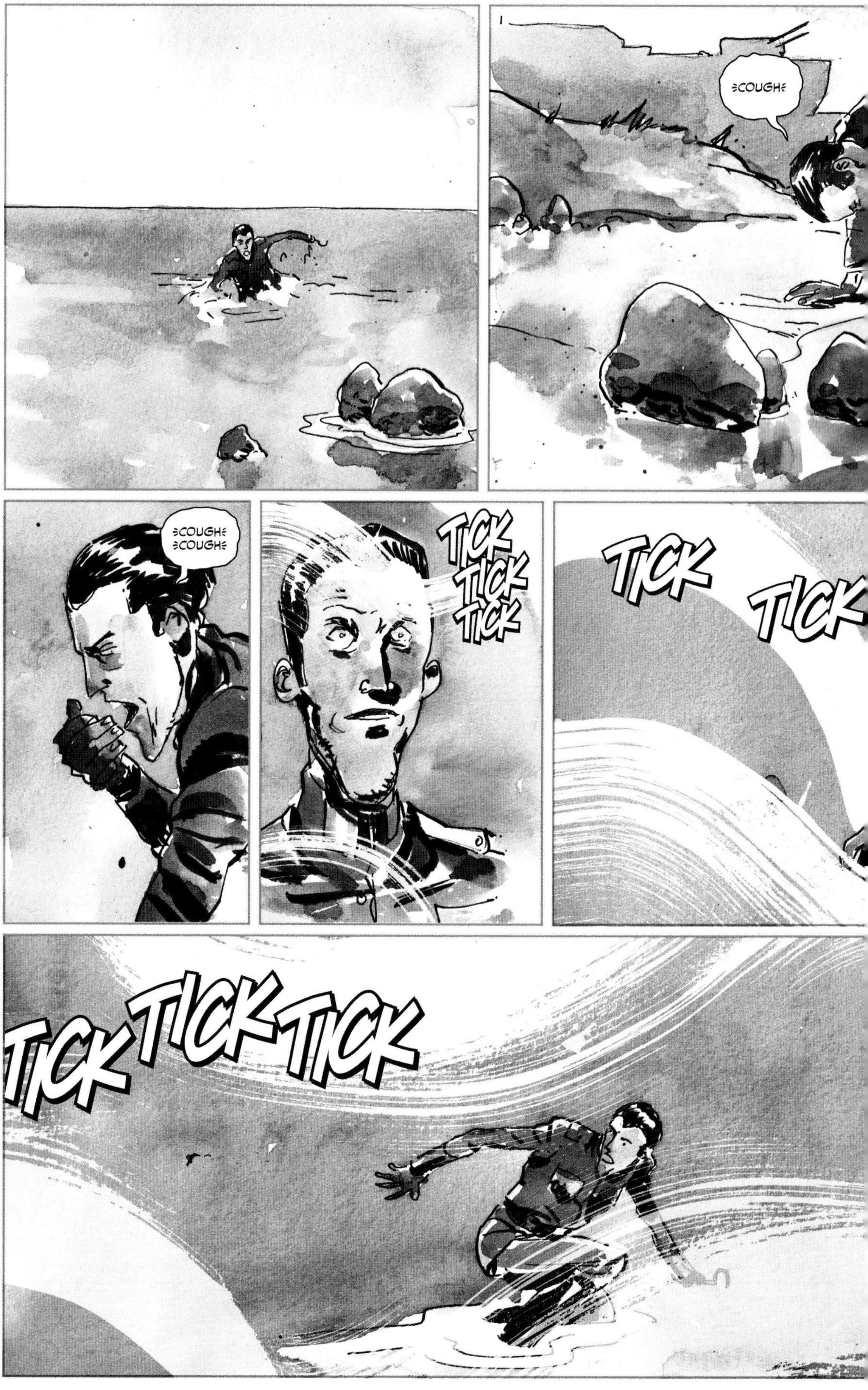
COUGH
COUGH COUGH
TICK TICK TICK
TICK TICK
TICK TICK TICK

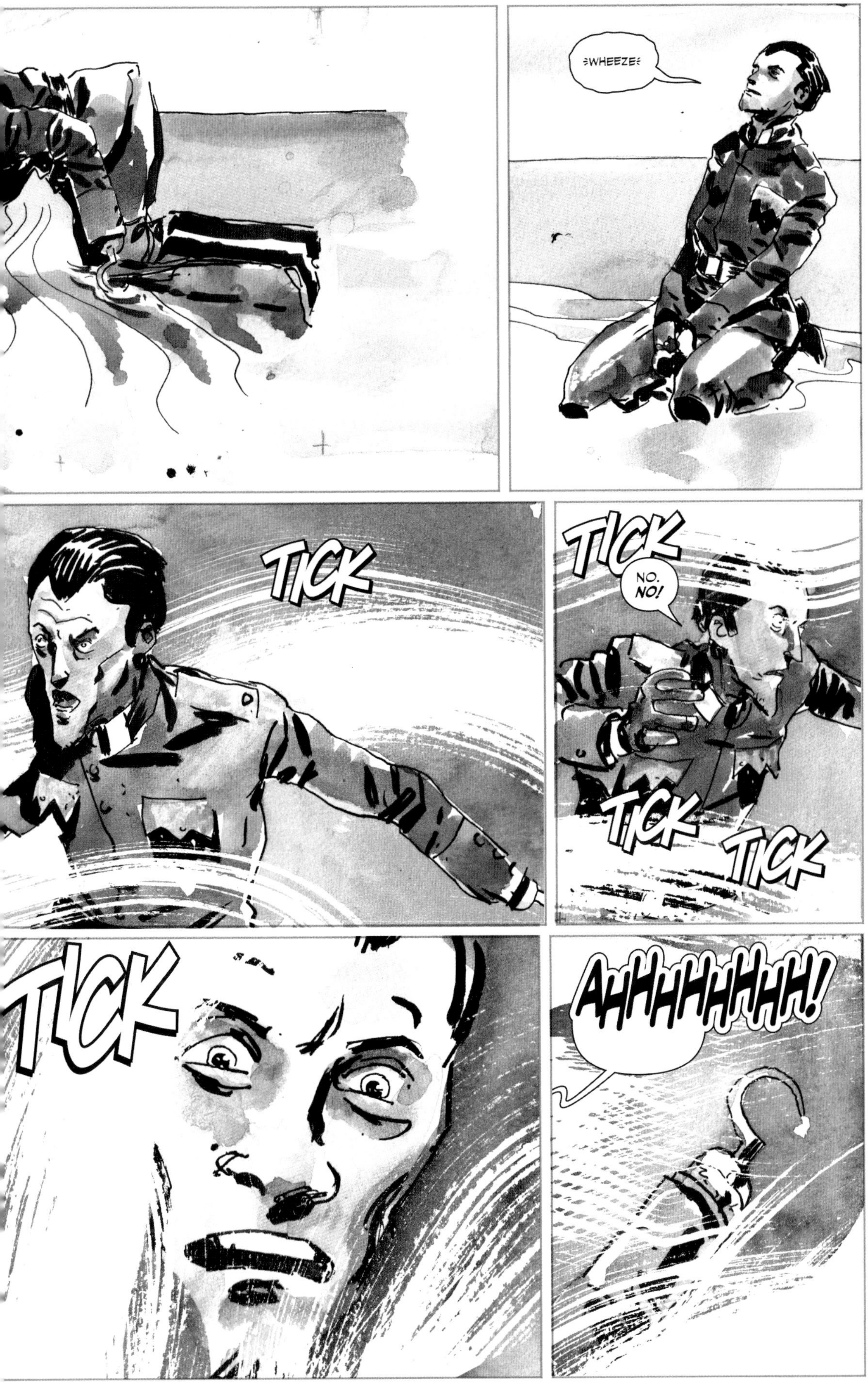

≈WHEEZE≈
TICK
TICK
NO. NO!
TICK
TICK
TICK
AHHHHHHHH!

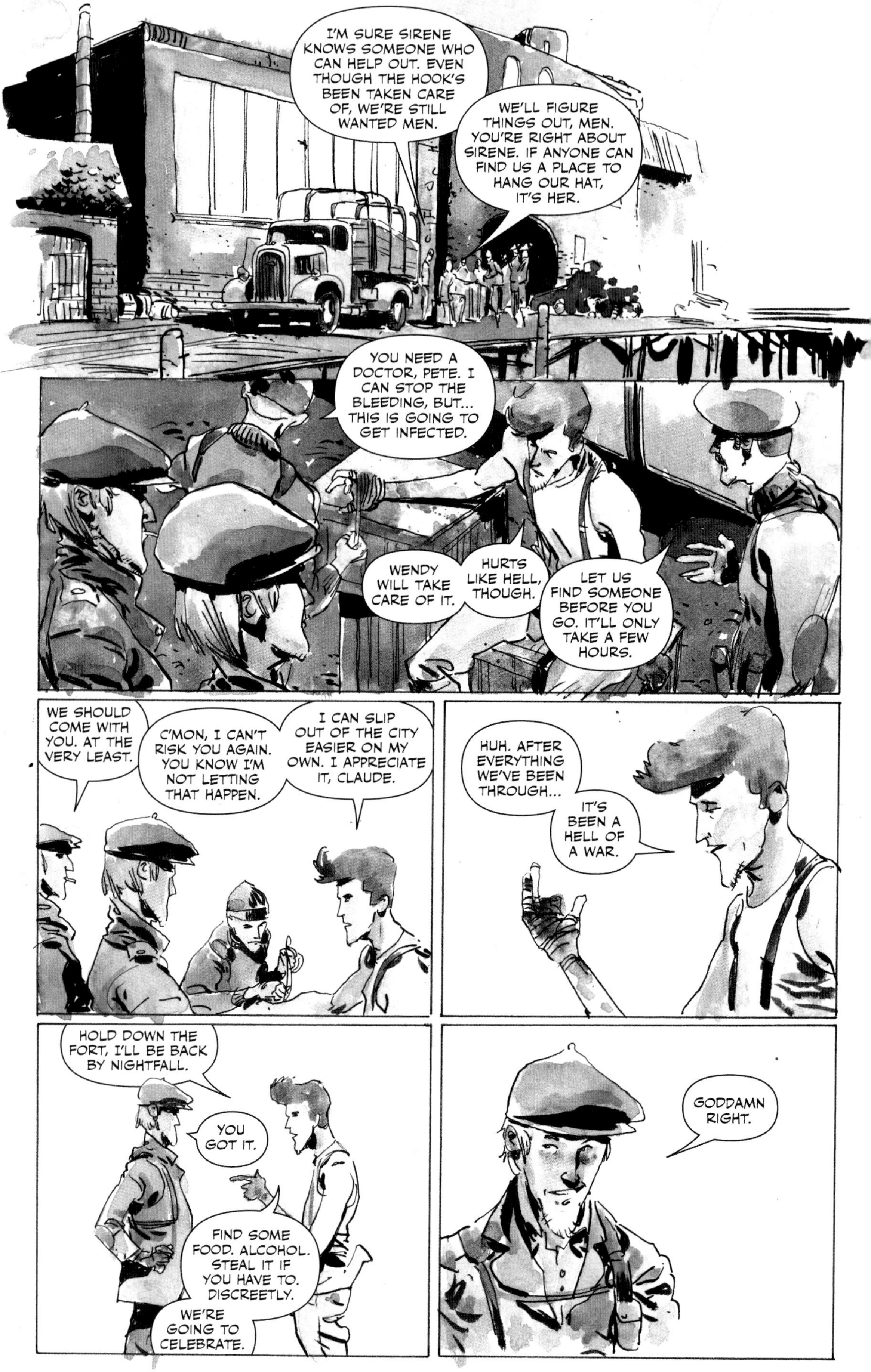
I'M SURE SIRENE KNOWS SOMEONE WHO CAN HELP OUT. EVEN THOUGH THE HOOK'S BEEN TAKEN CARE OF, WE'RE STILL WANTED MEN.
WE'LL FIGURE THINGS OUT, MEN. YOU'RE RIGHT ABOUT SIRENE. IF ANYONE CAN FIND US A PLACE TO HANG OUR HAT, IT'S HER.
YOU NEED A DOCTOR, PETE. I CAN STOP THE BLEEDING, BUT... THIS IS GOING TO GET INFECTED.
WENDY WILL TAKE CARE OF IT.
HURTS LIKE HELL, THOUGH.
LET US FIND SOMEONE BEFORE YOU GO. IT'LL ONLY TAKE A FEW HOURS.
WE SHOULD COME WITH YOU. AT THE VERY LEAST.
C'MON, I CAN'T RISK YOU AGAIN. YOU KNOW I'M NOT LETTING THAT HAPPEN.
I CAN SLIP OUT OF THE CITY EASIER ON MY OWN. I APPRECIATE IT, CLAUDE.
HUH. AFTER EVERYTHING WE'VE BEEN THROUGH...
IT'S BEEN A HELL OF A WAR.
HOLD DOWN THE FORT, I'LL BE BACK BY NIGHTFALL.
YOU GOT IT.
FIND SOME FOOD. ALCOHOL. STEAL IT IF YOU HAVE TO. DISCREETLY.
WE'RE GOING TO CELEBRATE.
GODDAMN RIGHT.

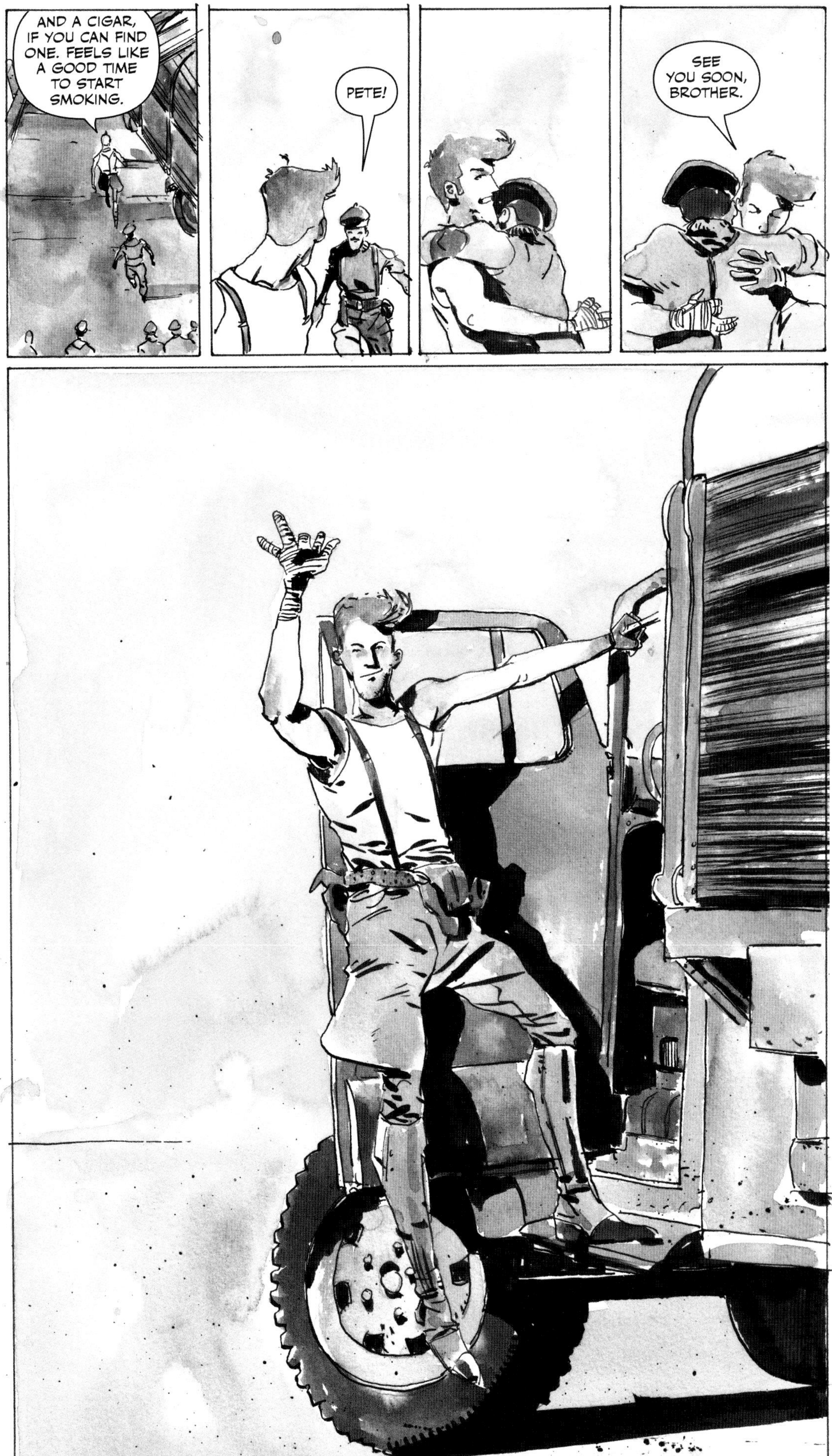
AND A CIGAR, IF YOU CAN FIND ONE. FEELS LIKE A GOOD TIME TO START SMOKING.
PETE!
SEE YOU SOON, BROTHER.

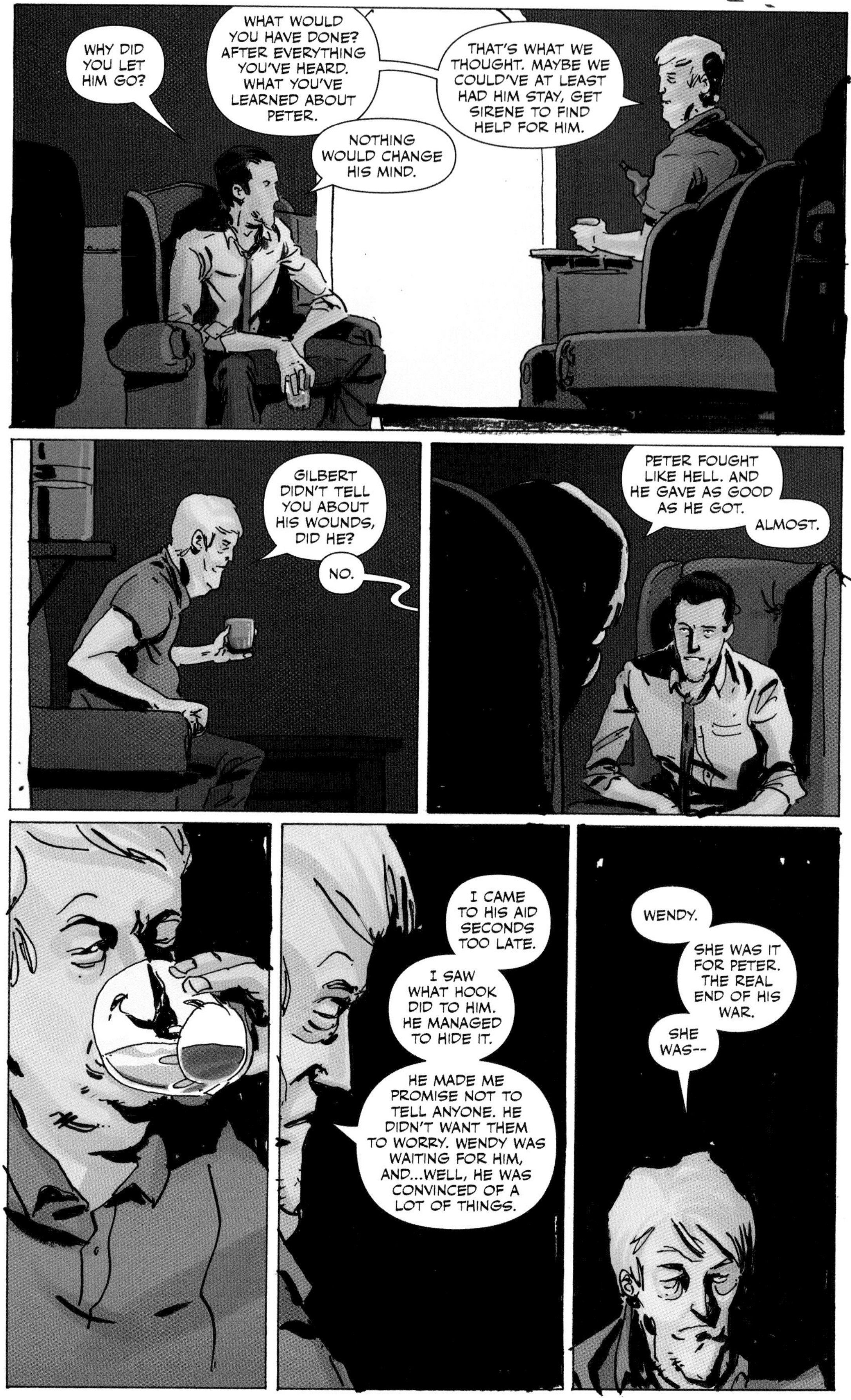
WHY DID YOU LET HIM GO?
WHAT WOULD YOU HAVE DONE? AFTER EVERYTHING YOU'VE HEARD. WHAT YOU'VE LEARNED ABOUT PETER.
NOTHING WOULD CHANGE HIS MIND.
THAT'S WHAT WE THOUGHT. MAYBE WE COULD'VE AT LEAST HAD HIM STAY, GET SIRENE TO FIND HELP FOR HIM.
GILBERT DIDN'T TELL YOU ABOUT HIS WOUNDS, DID HE?
NO.
PETER FOUGHT LIKE HELL. AND HE GAVE AS GOOD AS HE GOT.
ALMOST.
I CAME TO HIS AID SECONDS TOO LATE.
I SAW WHAT HOOK DID TO HIM. HE MANAGED TO HIDE IT.
HE MADE ME PROMISE NOT TO TELL ANYONE. HE DIDN'T WANT THEM TO WORRY. WENDY WAS WAITING FOR HIM, AND...WELL, HE WAS CONVINCED OF A LOT OF THINGS.
WENDY.
SHE WAS IT FOR PETER. THE REAL END OF HIS WAR.
SHE WAS--

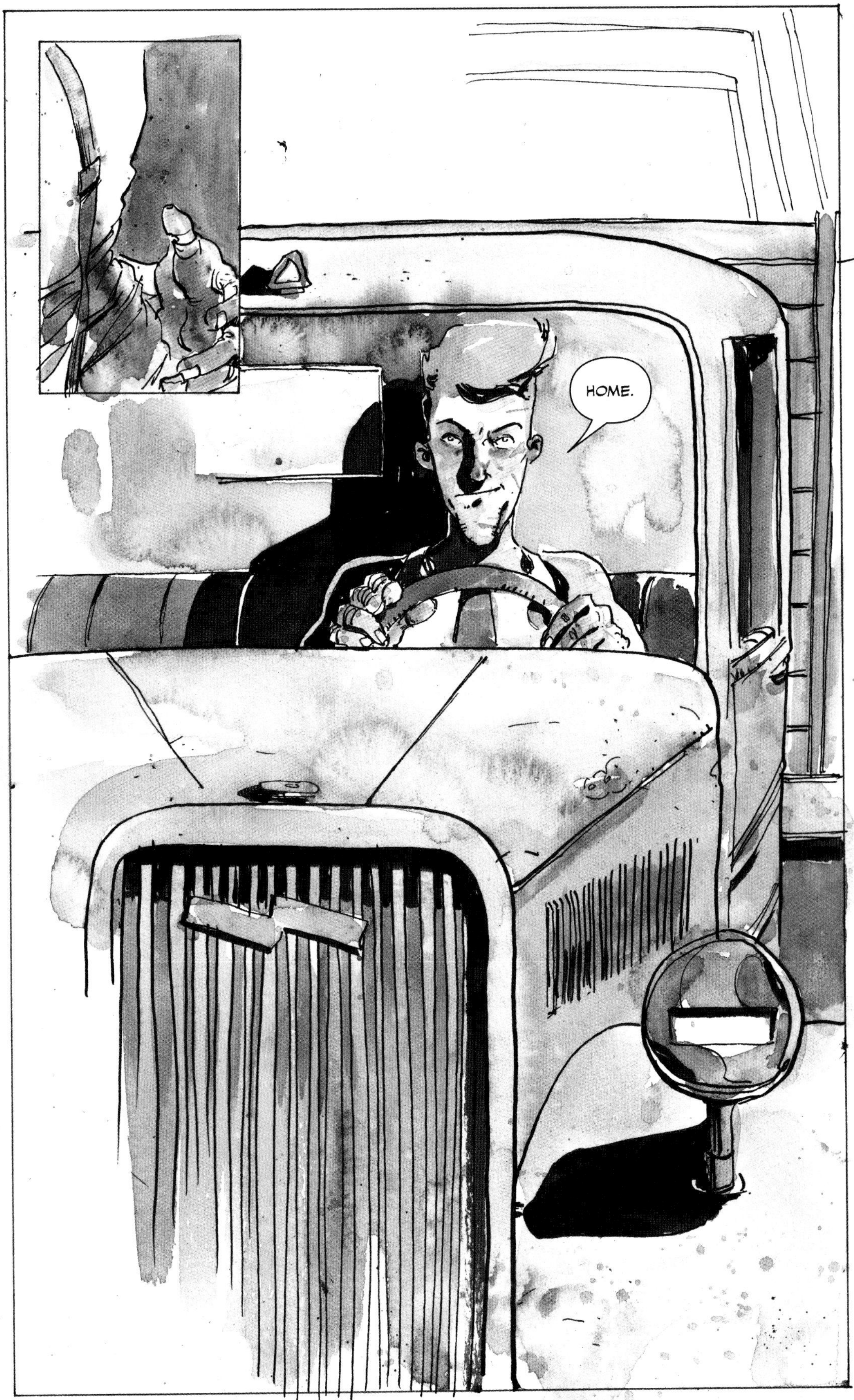
HOME.

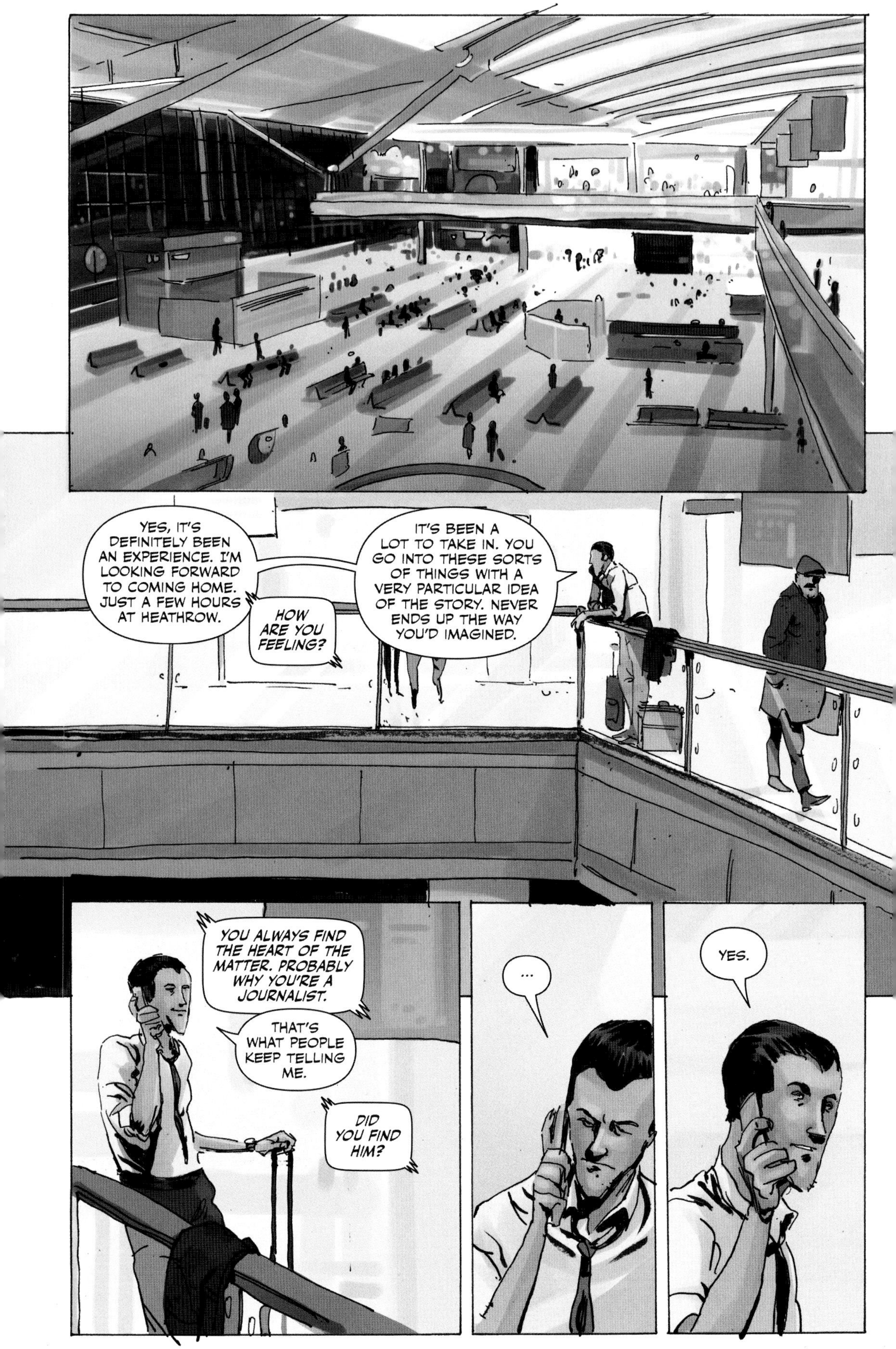
YES, IT'S DEFINITELY BEEN AN EXPERIENCE. I'M LOOKING FORWARD TO COMING HOME. JUST A FEW HOURS AT HEATHROW.
HOW ARE YOU FEELING?
IT'S BEEN A LOT TO TAKE IN. YOU GO INTO THESE SORTS OF THINGS WITH A VERY PARTICULAR IDEA OF THE STORY. NEVER ENDS UP THE WAY YOU'D IMAGINED.
YOU ALWAYS FIND THE HEART OF THE MATTER. PROBABLY WHY YOU'RE A JOURNALIST.
THAT'S WHAT PEOPLE KEEP TELLING ME.
DID YOU FIND HIM?
...
YES.

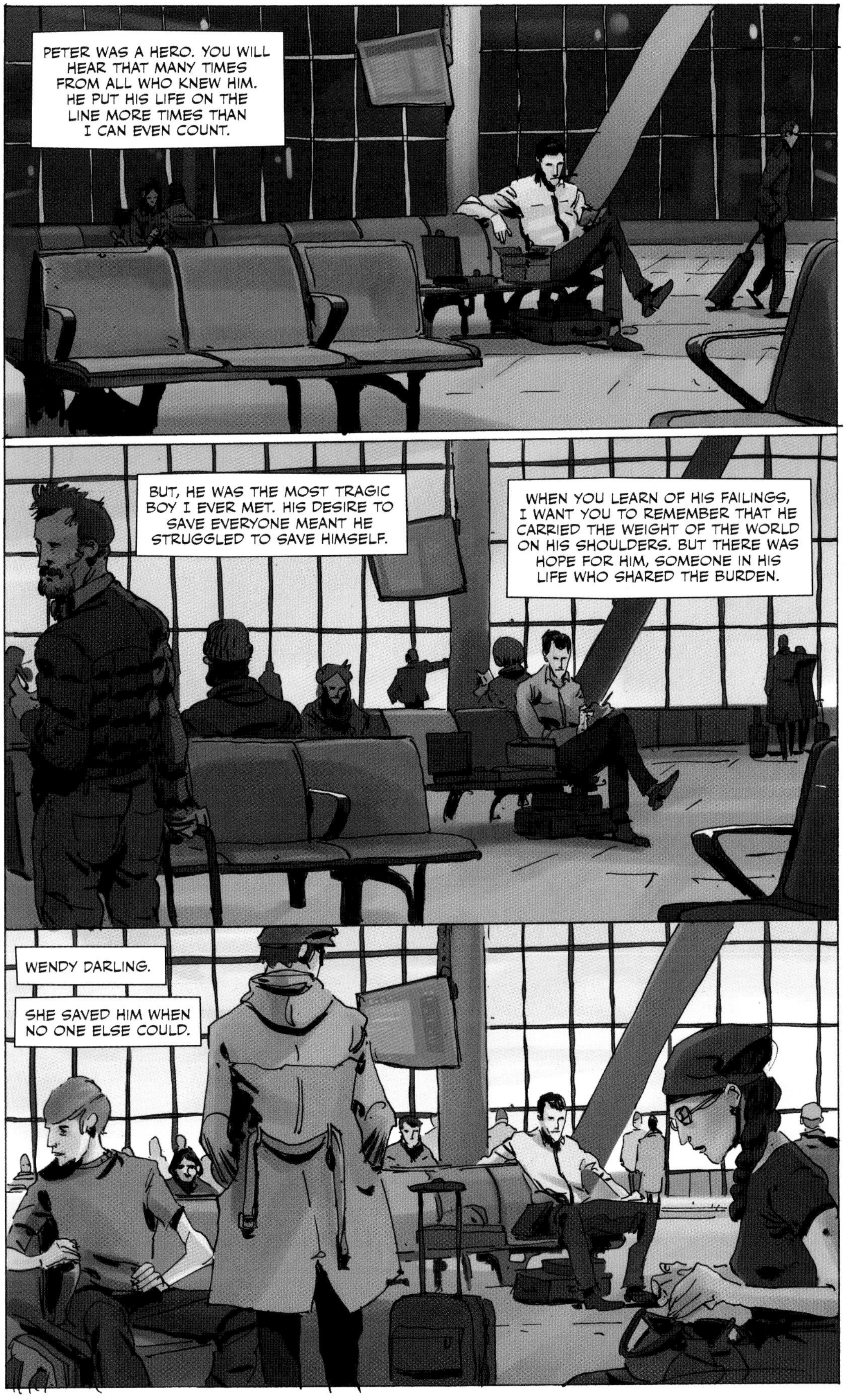
PETER WAS A HERO. YOU WILL HEAR THAT MANY TIMES FROM ALL WHO KNEW HIM. HE PUT HIS LIFE ON THE LINE MORE TIMES THAN I CAN EVEN COUNT.
BUT, HE WAS THE MOST TRAGIC BOY I EVER MET. HIS DESIRE TO SAVE EVERYONE MEANT HE STRUGGLED TO SAVE HIMSELF.
WHEN YOU LEARN OF HIS FAILINGS, I WANT YOU TO REMEMBER THAT HE CARRIED THE WEIGHT OF THE WORLD ON HIS SHOULDERS. BUT THERE WAS HOPE FOR HIM, SOMEONE IN HIS LIFE WHO SHARED THE BURDEN.
WENDY DARLING.
SHE SAVED HIM WHEN NO ONE ELSE COULD.

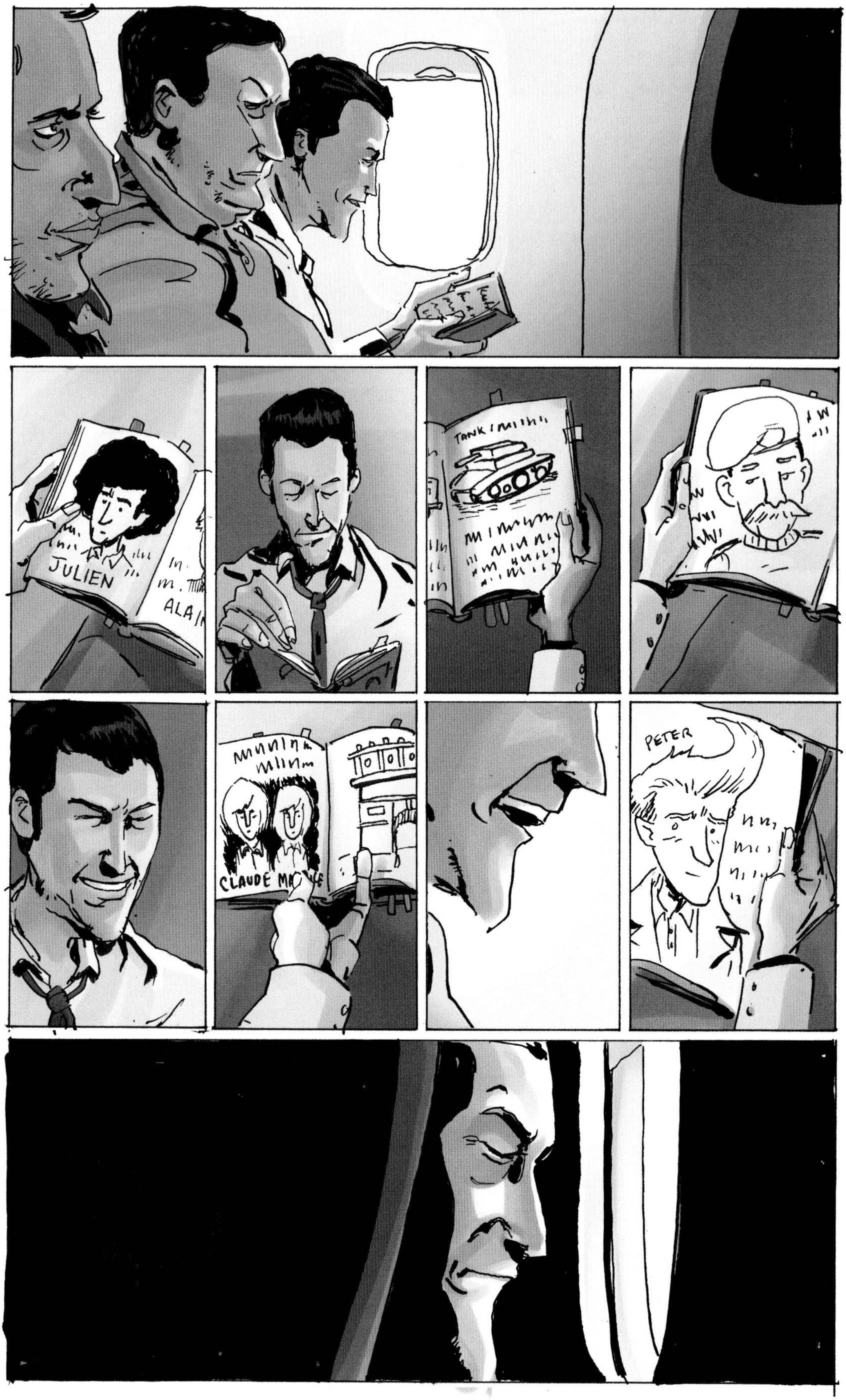
JULIEN
TANK
CLAUDE
PETER

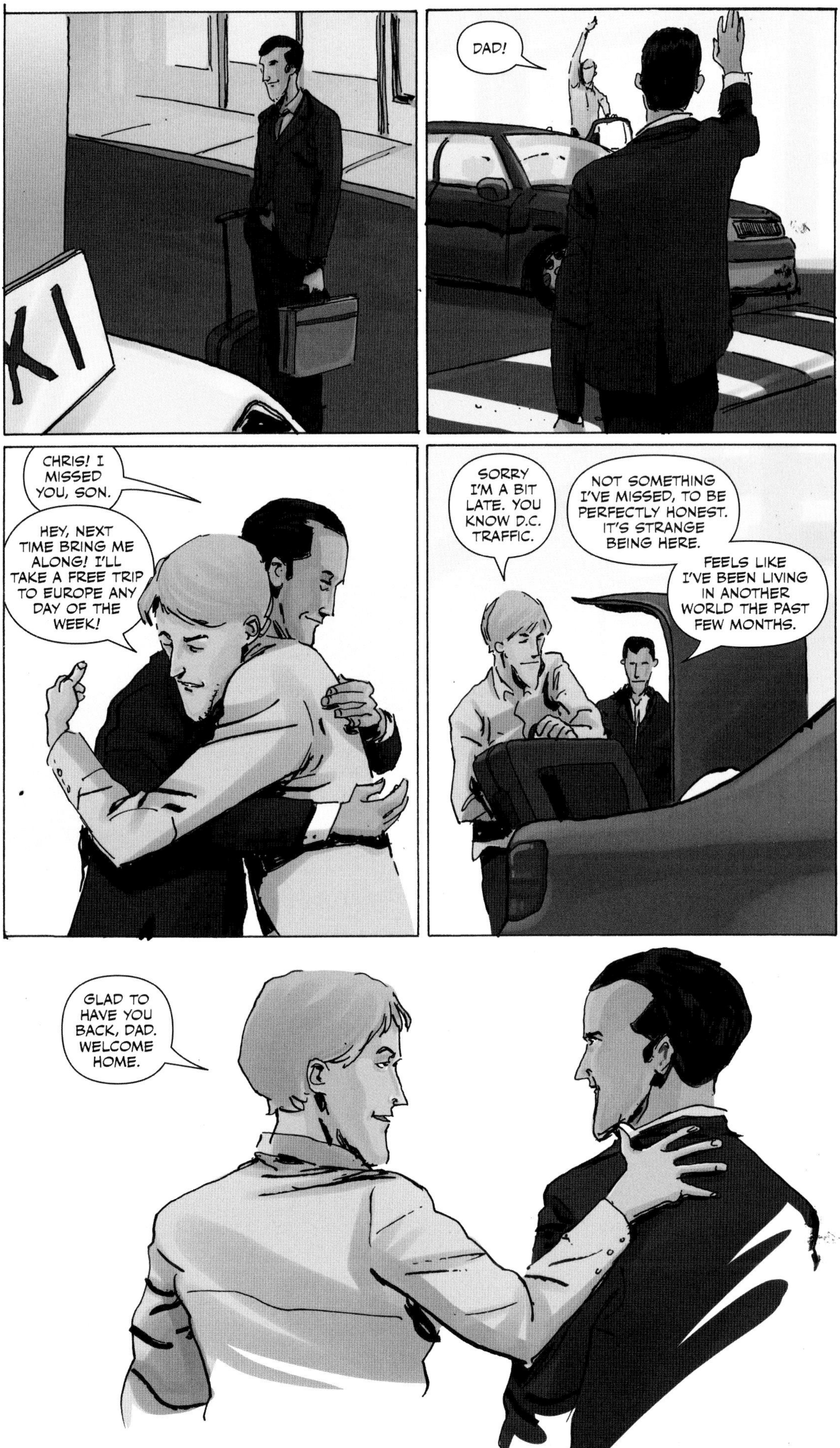
DAD!
CHRIS! I MISSED YOU, SON.
HEY, NEXT TIME BRING ME ALONG! I'LL TAKE A FREE TRIP TO EUROPE ANY DAY OF THE WEEK!
SORRY I'M A BIT LATE. YOU KNOW D.C. TRAFFIC.
NOT SOMETHING I'VE MISSED, TO BE PERFECTLY HONEST. IT'S STRANGE BEING HERE.
FEELS LIKE I'VE BEEN LIVING IN ANOTHER WORLD THE PAST FEW MONTHS.
GLAD TO HAVE YOU BACK, DAD. WELCOME HOME.

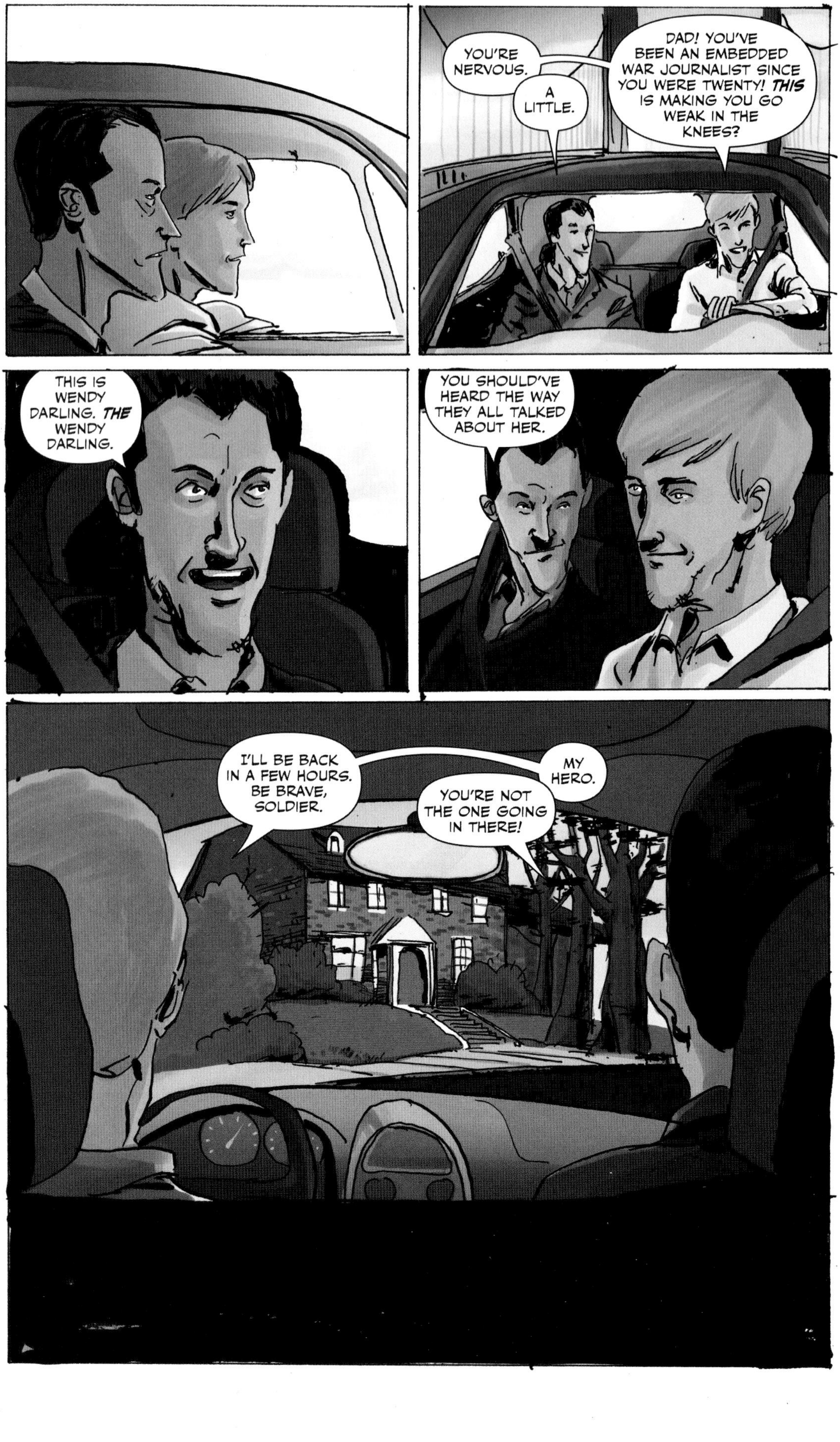
YOU'RE NERVOUS.
A LITTLE.
DAD! YOU'VE BEEN AN EMBEDDED WAR JOURNALIST SINCE YOU WERE TWENTY! *THIS* IS MAKING YOU GO WEAK IN THE KNEES?
THIS IS WENDY DARLING. *THE* WENDY DARLING.
YOU SHOULD'VE HEARD THE WAY THEY ALL TALKED ABOUT HER.
I'LL BE BACK IN A FEW HOURS. BE BRAVE, SOLDIER.
MY HERO.
YOU'RE NOT THE ONE GOING IN THERE!

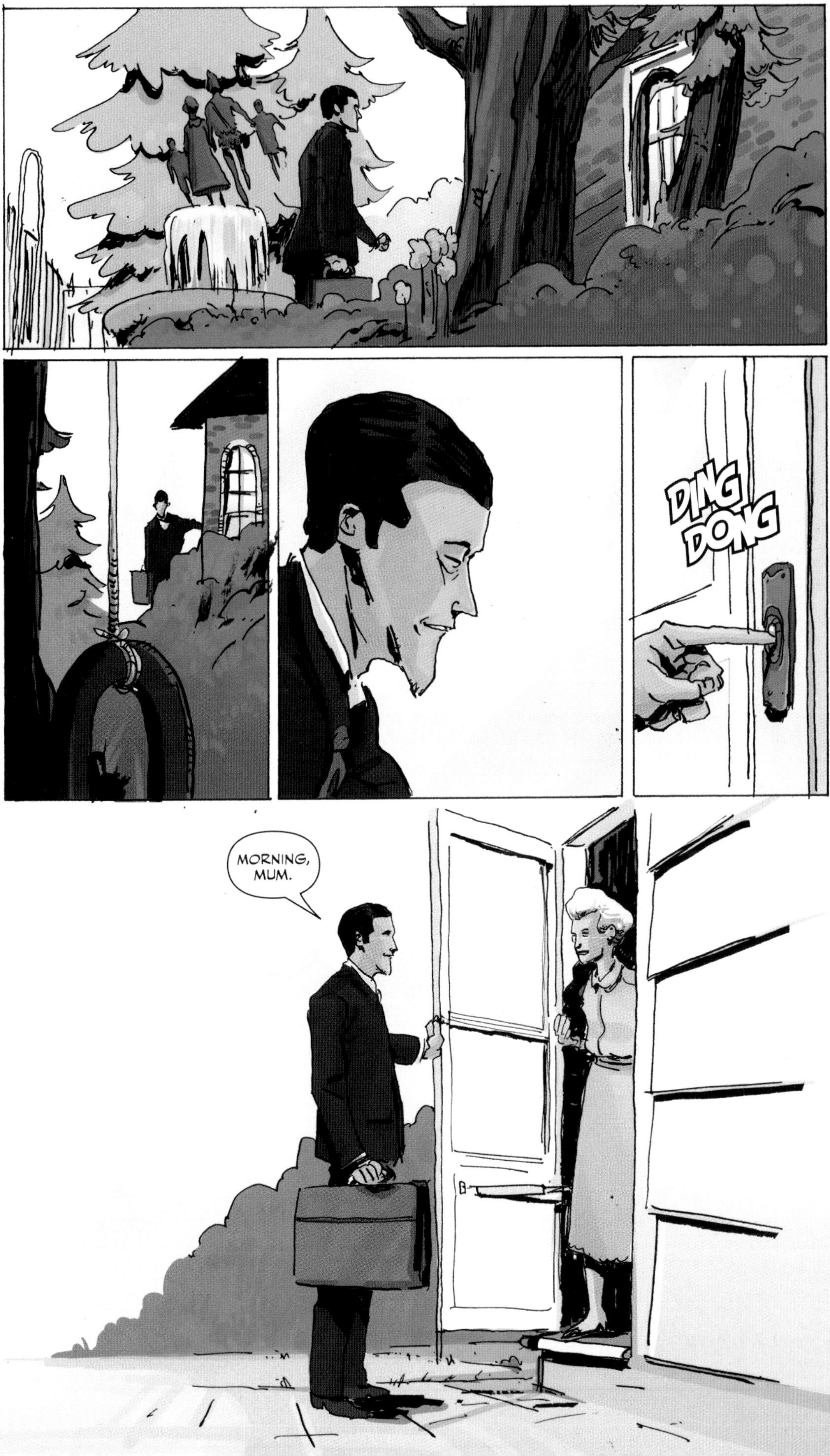
DING DONG
MORNING, MUM.

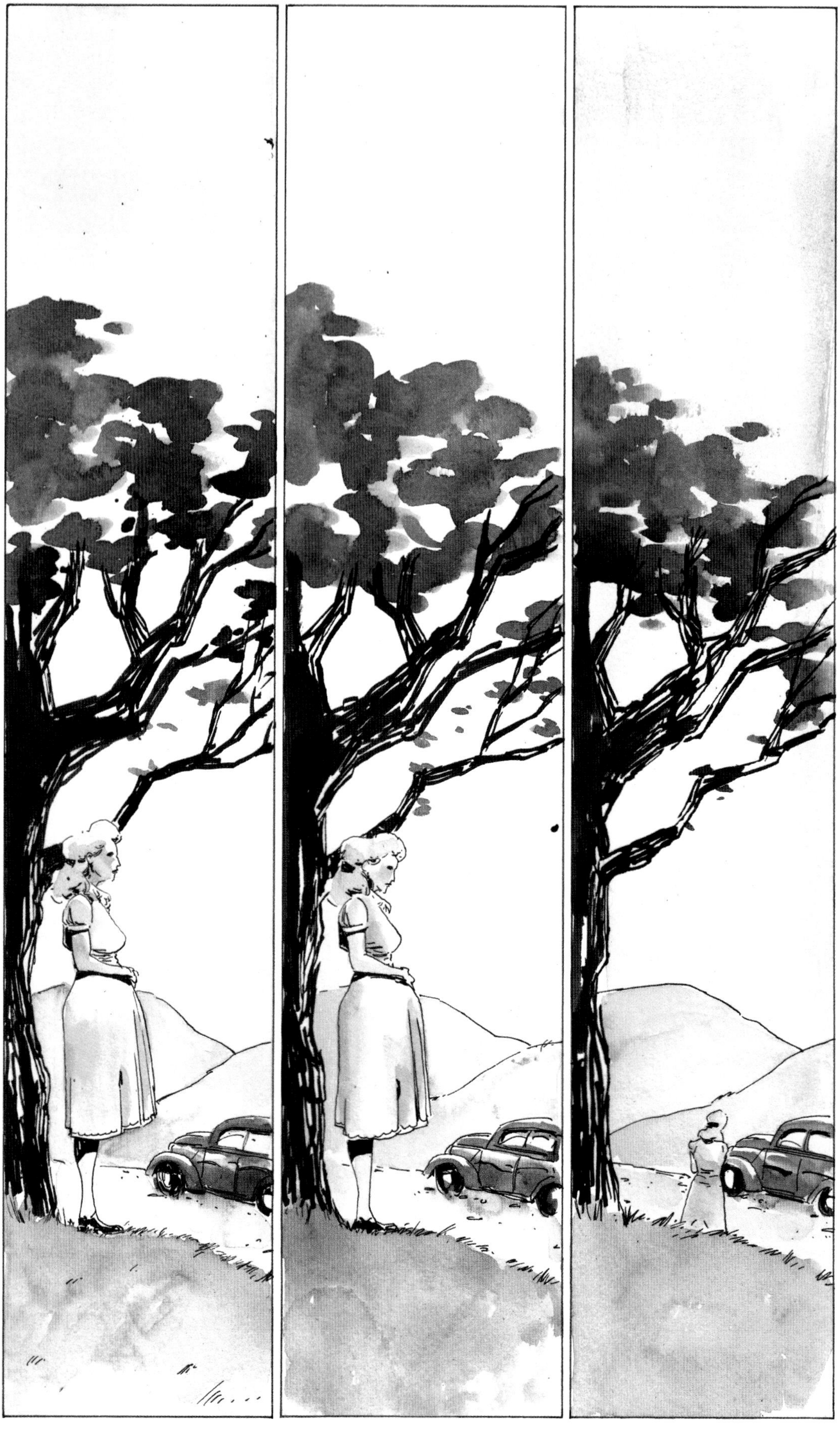

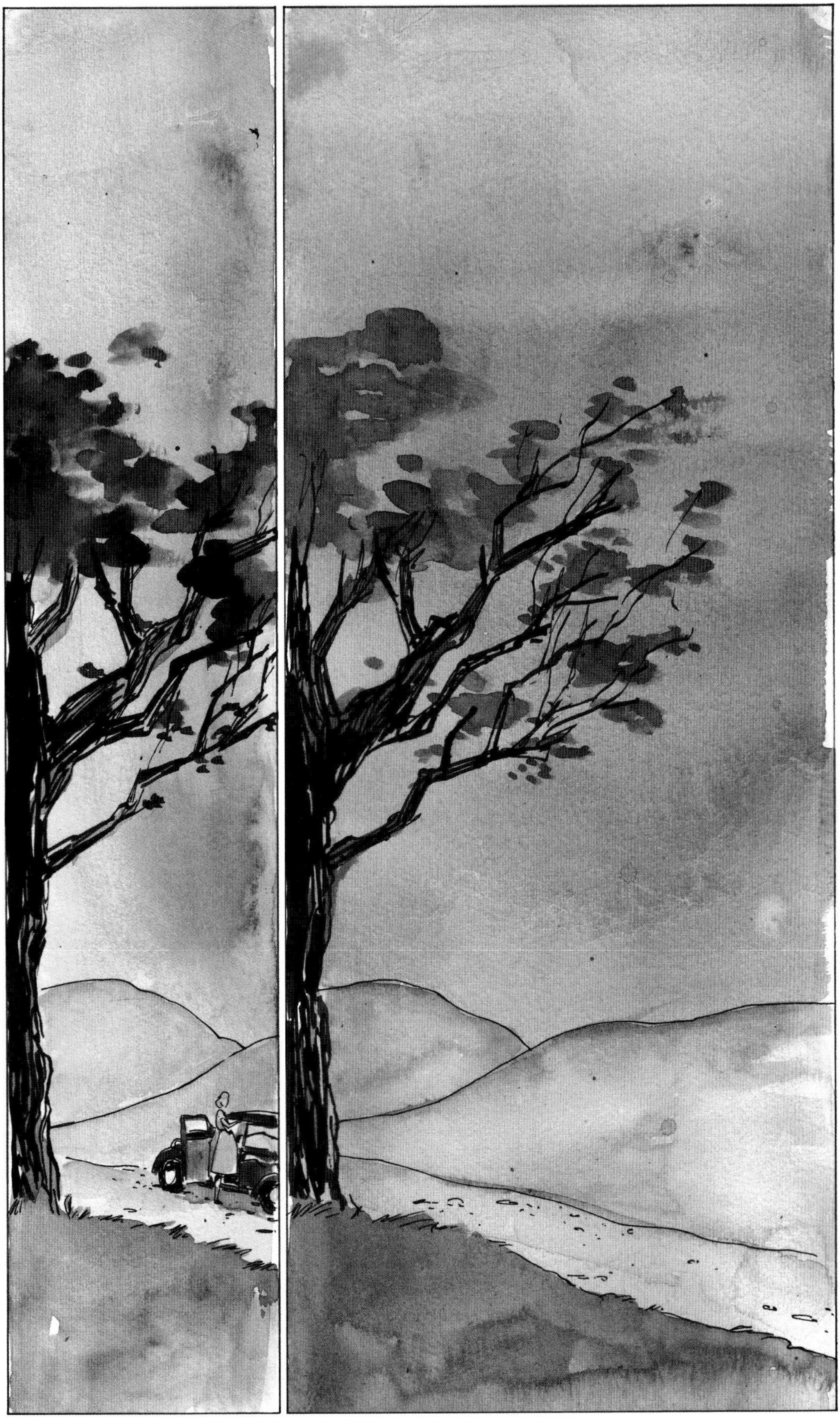

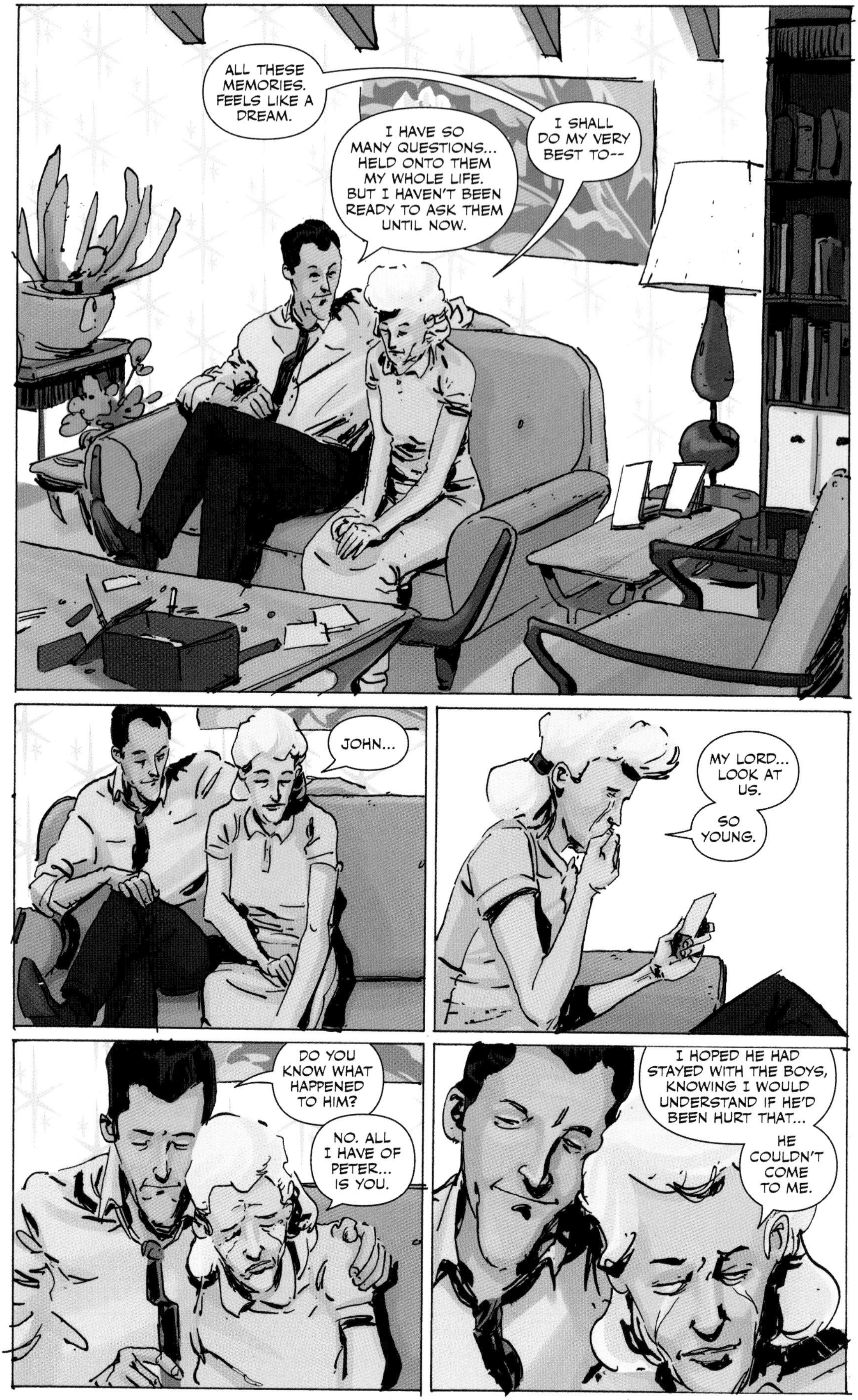
ALL THESE MEMORIES. FEELS LIKE A DREAM.
I HAVE SO MANY QUESTIONS... HELD ONTO THEM MY WHOLE LIFE. BUT I HAVEN'T BEEN READY TO ASK THEM UNTIL NOW.
I SHALL DO MY VERY BEST TO--
JOHN...
MY LORD... LOOK AT US.
SO YOUNG.
DO YOU KNOW WHAT HAPPENED TO HIM?
NO. ALL I HAVE OF PETER... IS YOU.
I HOPED HE HAD STAYED WITH THE BOYS, KNOWING I WOULD UNDERSTAND IF HE'D BEEN HURT THAT...
HE COULDN'T COME TO ME.

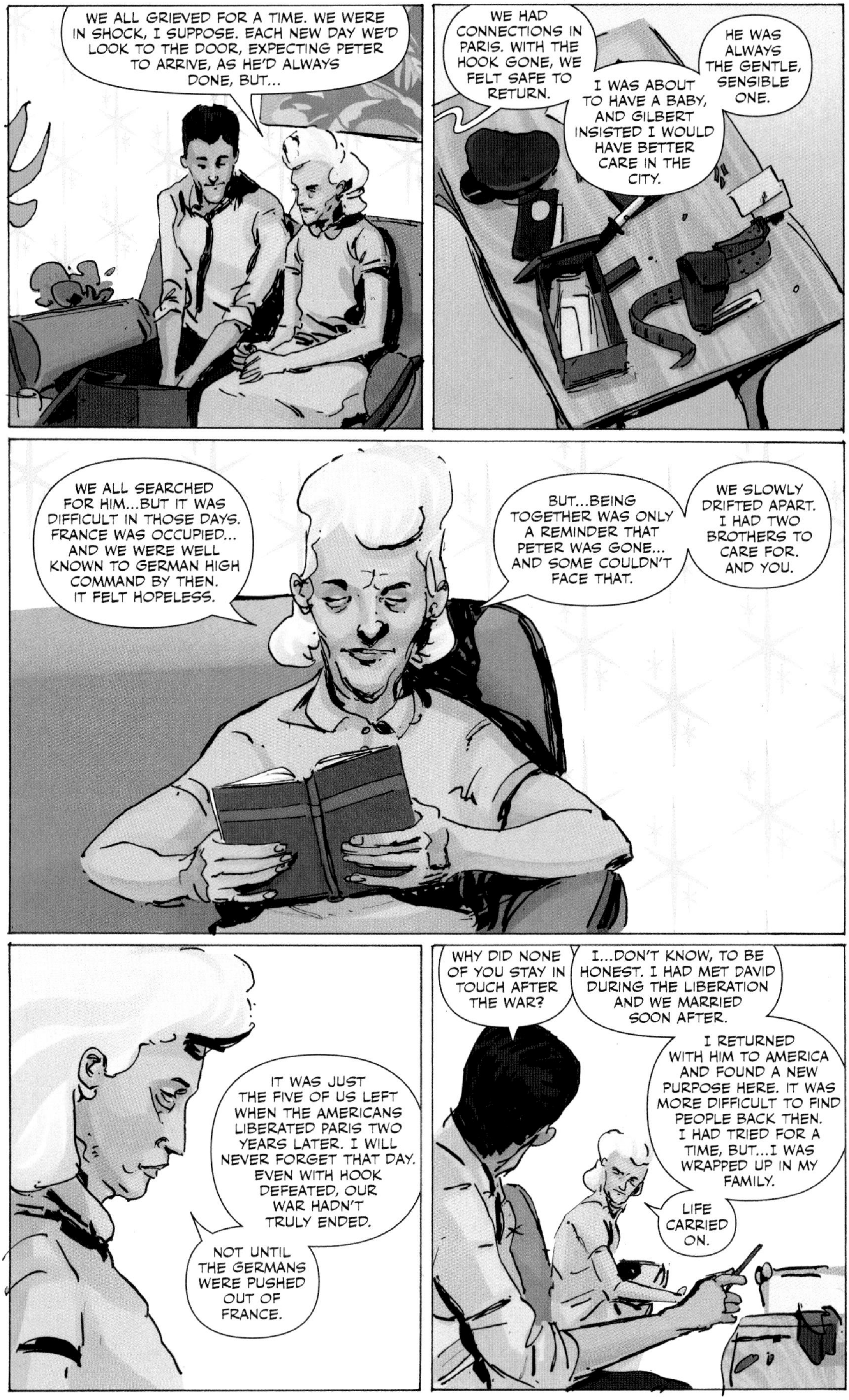
WE ALL GRIEVED FOR A TIME. WE WERE IN SHOCK, I SUPPOSE. EACH NEW DAY WE'D LOOK TO THE DOOR, EXPECTING PETER TO ARRIVE, AS HE'D ALWAYS DONE, BUT...
WE HAD CONNECTIONS IN PARIS. WITH THE HOOK GONE, WE FELT SAFE TO RETURN.
I WAS ABOUT TO HAVE A BABY, AND GILBERT INSISTED I WOULD HAVE BETTER CARE IN THE CITY.
HE WAS ALWAYS THE GENTLE, SENSIBLE ONE.
WE ALL SEARCHED FOR HIM...BUT IT WAS DIFFICULT IN THOSE DAYS. FRANCE WAS OCCUPIED... AND WE WERE WELL KNOWN TO GERMAN HIGH COMMAND BY THEN. IT FELT HOPELESS.
BUT...BEING TOGETHER WAS ONLY A REMINDER THAT PETER WAS GONE... AND SOME COULDN'T FACE THAT.
WE SLOWLY DRIFTED APART. I HAD TWO BROTHERS TO CARE FOR. AND YOU.
IT WAS JUST THE FIVE OF US LEFT WHEN THE AMERICANS LIBERATED PARIS TWO YEARS LATER. I WILL NEVER FORGET THAT DAY. EVEN WITH HOOK DEFEATED, OUR WAR HADN'T TRULY ENDED.
NOT UNTIL THE GERMANS WERE PUSHED OUT OF FRANCE.
WHY DID NONE OF YOU STAY IN TOUCH AFTER THE WAR?
I...DON'T KNOW, TO BE HONEST. I HAD MET DAVID DURING THE LIBERATION AND WE MARRIED SOON AFTER.
I RETURNED WITH HIM TO AMERICA AND FOUND A NEW PURPOSE HERE. IT WAS MORE DIFFICULT TO FIND PEOPLE BACK THEN. I HAD TRIED FOR A TIME, BUT...I WAS WRAPPED UP IN MY FAMILY.
LIFE CARRIED ON.

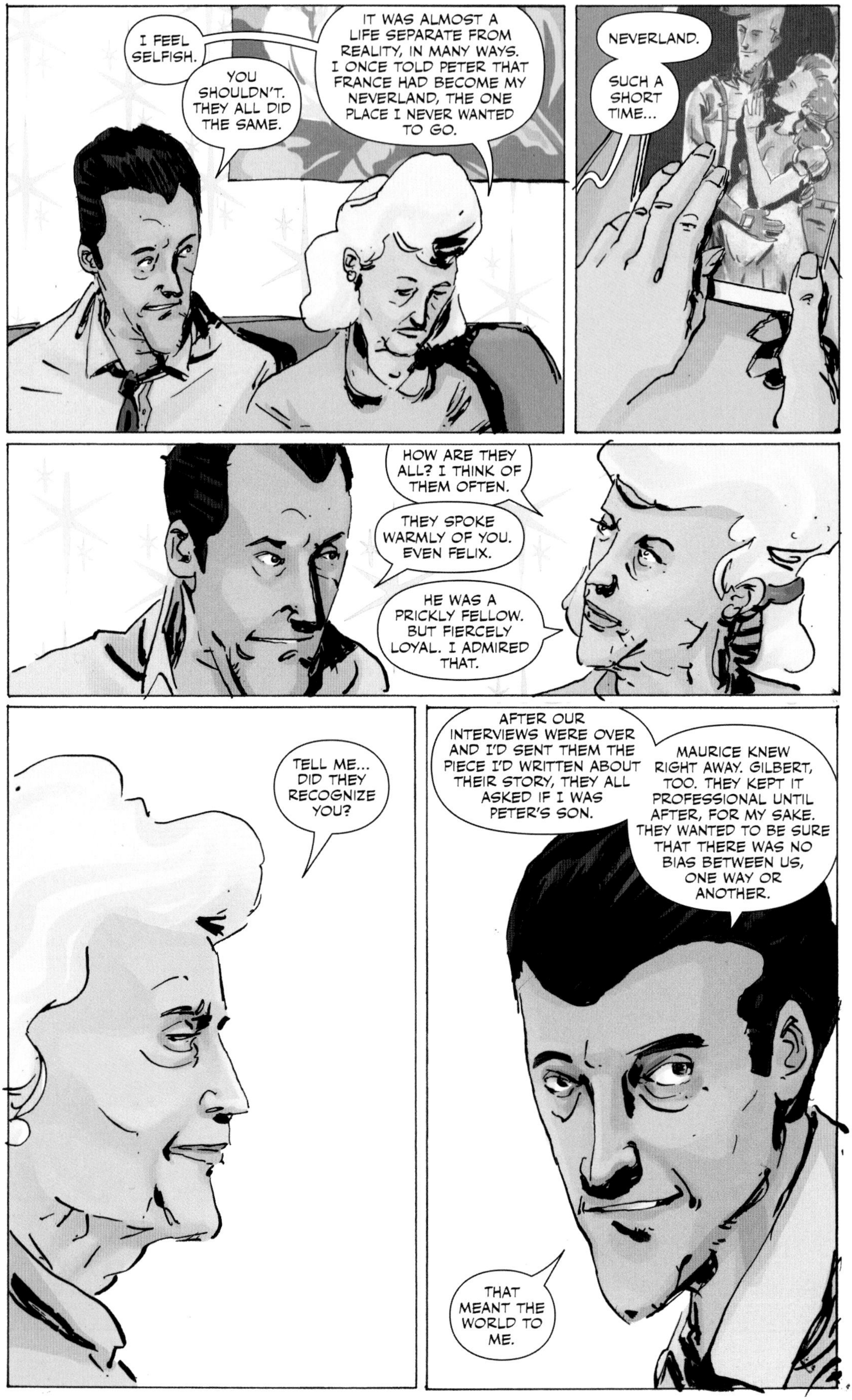
I FEEL SELFISH.
YOU SHOULDN'T. THEY ALL DID THE SAME.
IT WAS ALMOST A LIFE SEPARATE FROM REALITY, IN MANY WAYS. I ONCE TOLD PETER THAT FRANCE HAD BECOME MY NEVERLAND, THE ONE PLACE I NEVER WANTED TO GO.
NEVERLAND.
SUCH A SHORT TIME...
HOW ARE THEY ALL? I THINK OF THEM OFTEN.
THEY SPOKE WARMLY OF YOU. EVEN FELIX.
HE WAS A PRICKLY FELLOW. BUT FIERCELY LOYAL. I ADMIRED THAT.
TELL ME... DID THEY RECOGNIZE YOU?
AFTER OUR INTERVIEWS WERE OVER AND I'D SENT THEM THE PIECE I'D WRITTEN ABOUT THEIR STORY, THEY ALL ASKED IF I WAS PETER'S SON.
MAURICE KNEW RIGHT AWAY. GILBERT, TOO. THEY KEPT IT PROFESSIONAL UNTIL AFTER, FOR MY SAKE. THEY WANTED TO BE SURE THAT THERE WAS NO BIAS BETWEEN US, ONE WAY OR ANOTHER.
THAT MEANT THE WORLD TO ME.

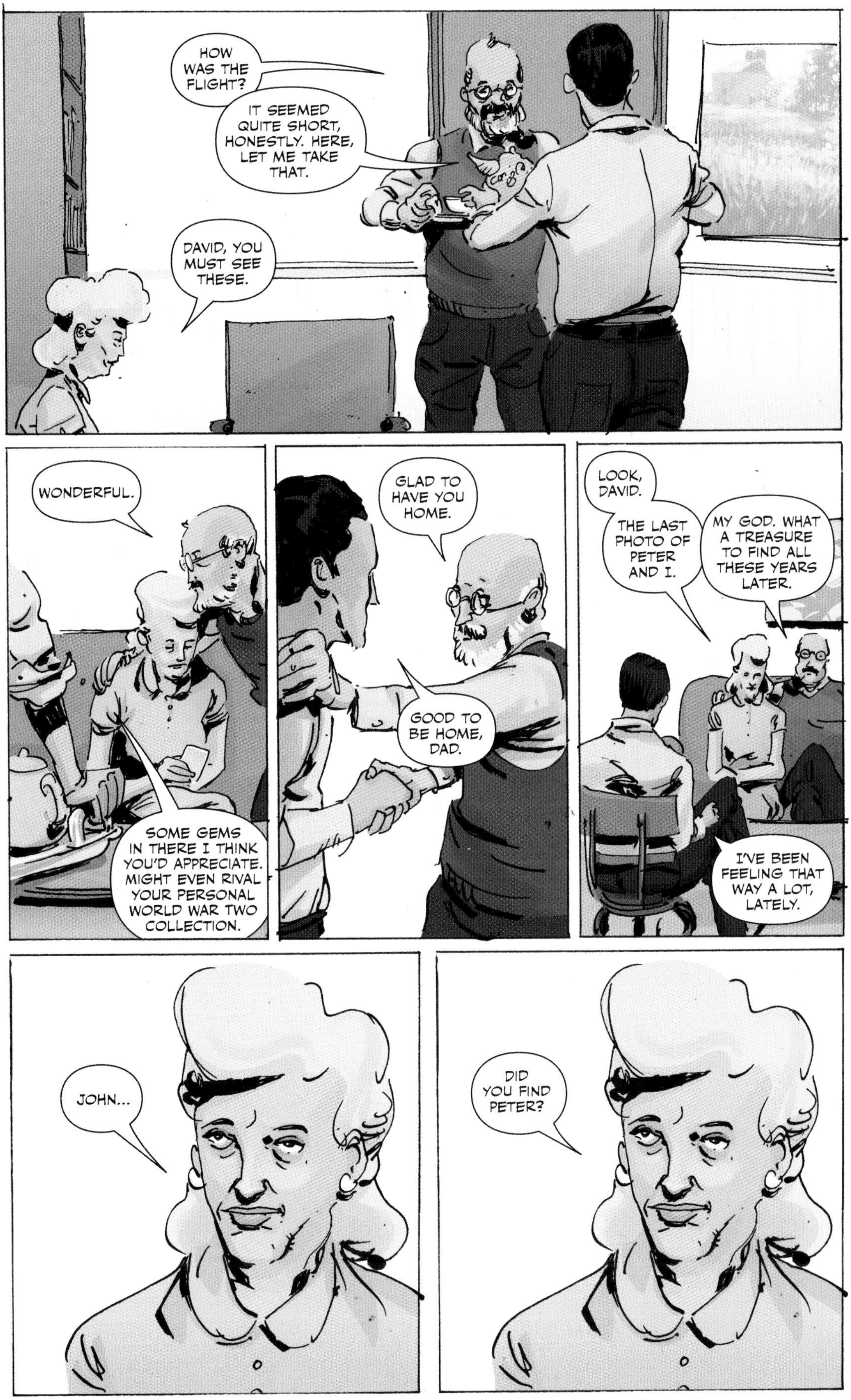
HOW WAS THE FLIGHT?
IT SEEMED QUITE SHORT, HONESTLY. HERE, LET ME TAKE THAT.
DAVID, YOU MUST SEE THESE.
WONDERFUL.
SOME GEMS IN THERE I THINK YOU'D APPRECIATE. MIGHT EVEN RIVAL YOUR PERSONAL WORLD WAR TWO COLLECTION.
GLAD TO HAVE YOU HOME.
GOOD TO BE HOME, DAD.
LOOK, DAVID.
THE LAST PHOTO OF PETER AND I.
MY GOD. WHAT A TREASURE TO FIND ALL THESE YEARS LATER.
I'VE BEEN FEELING THAT WAY A LOT, LATELY.
JOHN...
DID YOU FIND PETER?

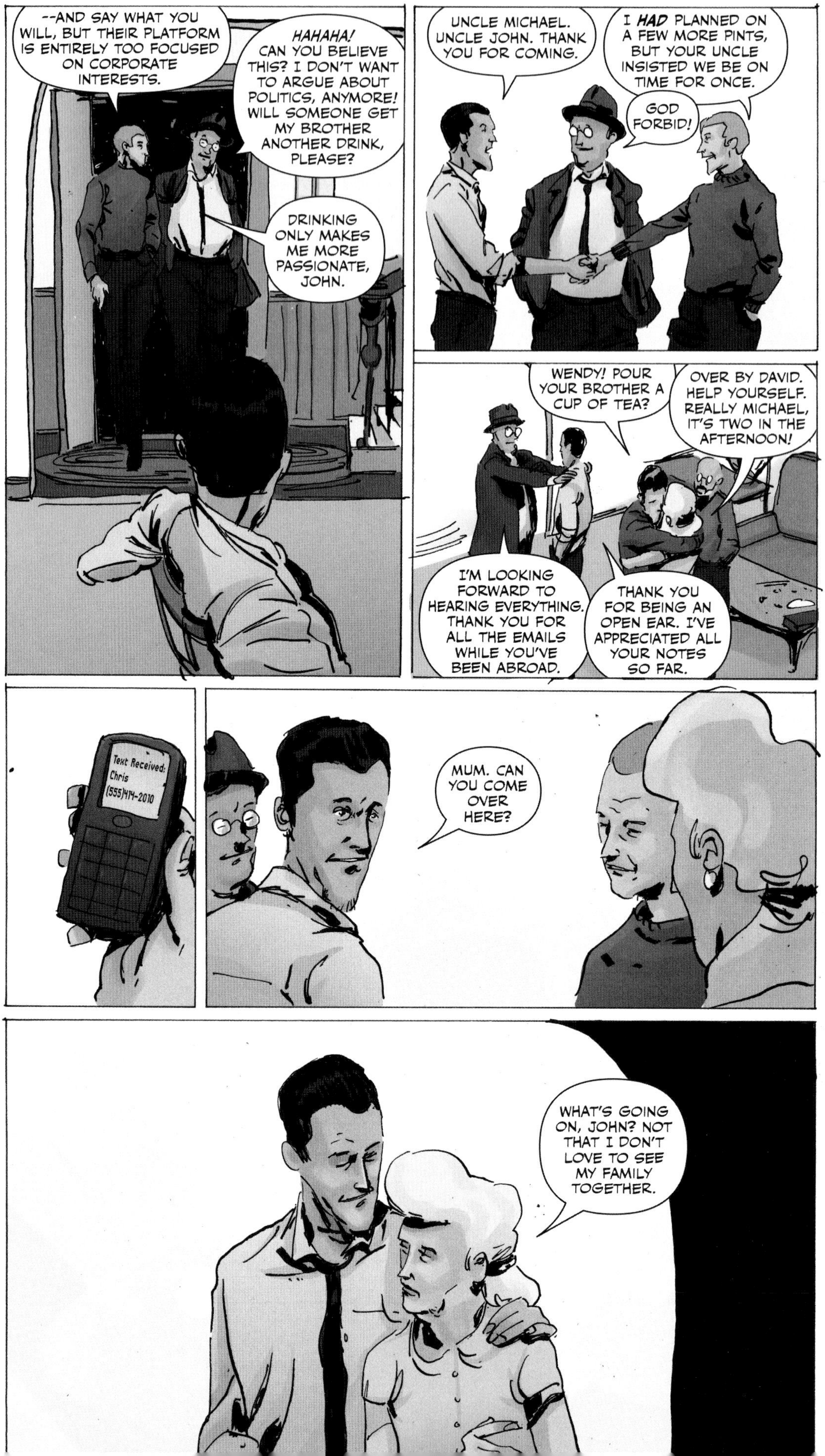
--AND SAY WHAT YOU WILL, BUT THEIR PLATFORM IS ENTIRELY TOO FOCUSED ON CORPORATE INTERESTS.
HAHAHA! CAN YOU BELIEVE THIS? I DON'T WANT TO ARGUE ABOUT POLITICS, ANYMORE! WILL SOMEONE GET MY BROTHER ANOTHER DRINK, PLEASE?
DRINKING ONLY MAKES ME MORE PASSIONATE, JOHN.
UNCLE MICHAEL. UNCLE JOHN. THANK YOU FOR COMING.
I HAD PLANNED ON A FEW MORE PINTS, BUT YOUR UNCLE INSISTED WE BE ON TIME FOR ONCE.
GOD FORBID!
WENDY! POUR YOUR BROTHER A CUP OF TEA?
OVER BY DAVID. HELP YOURSELF. REALLY MICHAEL, IT'S TWO IN THE AFTERNOON!
I'M LOOKING FORWARD TO HEARING EVERYTHING. THANK YOU FOR ALL THE EMAILS WHILE YOU'VE BEEN ABROAD.
THANK YOU FOR BEING AN OPEN EAR. I'VE APPRECIATED ALL YOUR NOTES SO FAR.
Text Received: Chris (555)414-2010
MUM. CAN YOU COME OVER HERE?
WHAT'S GOING ON, JOHN? NOT THAT I DON'T LOVE TO SEE MY FAMILY TOGETHER.

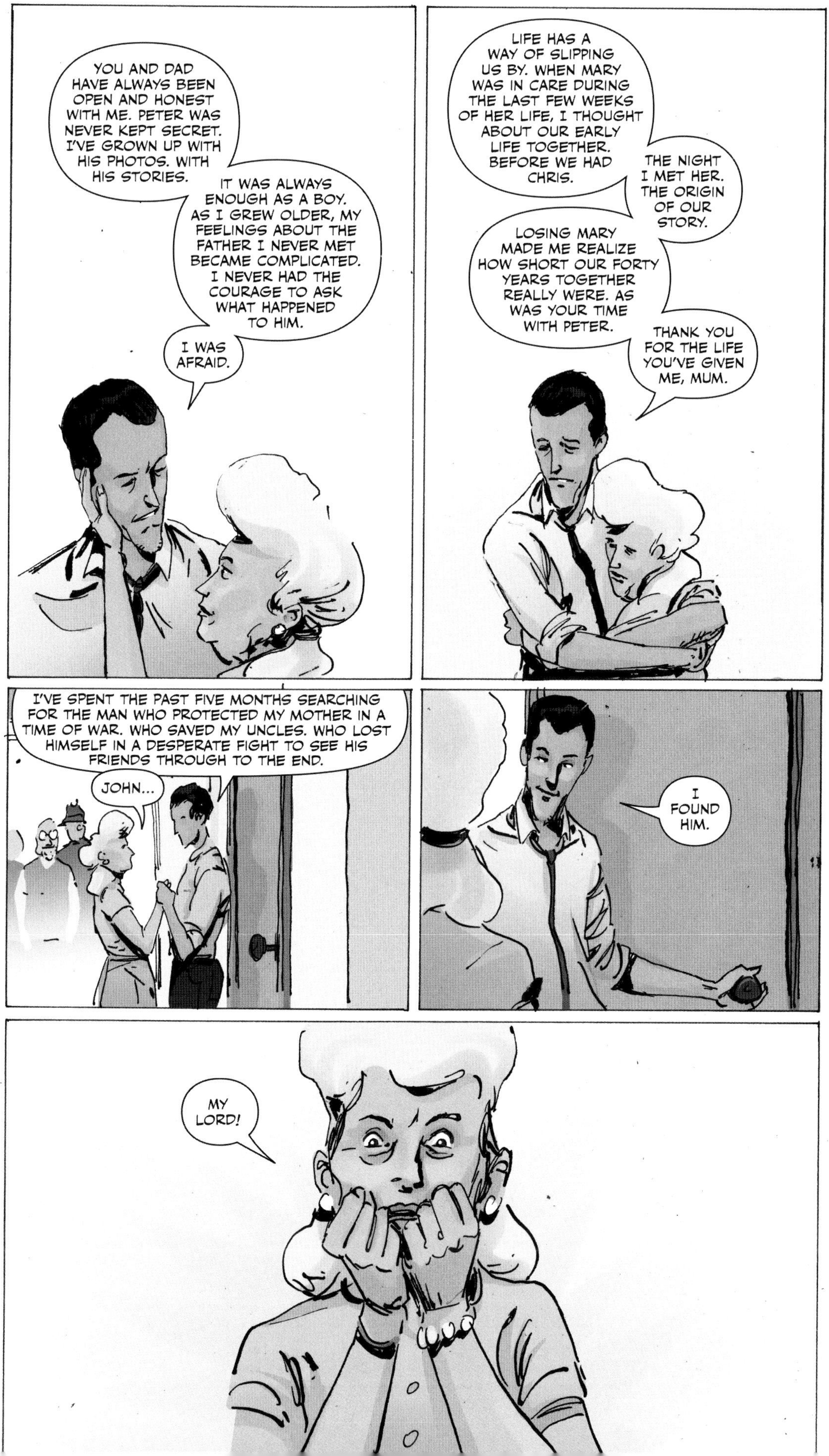
YOU AND DAD HAVE ALWAYS BEEN OPEN AND HONEST WITH ME. PETER WAS NEVER KEPT SECRET. I'VE GROWN UP WITH HIS PHOTOS. WITH HIS STORIES.
IT WAS ALWAYS ENOUGH AS A BOY. AS I GREW OLDER, MY FEELINGS ABOUT THE FATHER I NEVER MET BECAME COMPLICATED. I NEVER HAD THE COURAGE TO ASK WHAT HAPPENED TO HIM.
I WAS AFRAID.
LIFE HAS A WAY OF SLIPPING US BY. WHEN MARY WAS IN CARE DURING THE LAST FEW WEEKS OF HER LIFE, I THOUGHT ABOUT OUR EARLY LIFE TOGETHER. BEFORE WE HAD CHRIS.
THE NIGHT I MET HER. THE ORIGIN OF OUR STORY.
LOSING MARY MADE ME REALIZE HOW SHORT OUR FORTY YEARS TOGETHER REALLY WERE. AS WAS YOUR TIME WITH PETER.
THANK YOU FOR THE LIFE YOU'VE GIVEN ME, MUM.
I'VE SPENT THE PAST FIVE MONTHS SEARCHING FOR THE MAN WHO PROTECTED MY MOTHER IN A TIME OF WAR. WHO SAVED MY UNCLES. WHO LOST HIMSELF IN A DESPERATE FIGHT TO SEE HIS FRIENDS THROUGH TO THE END.
JOHN...
I FOUND HIM.
MY LORD!

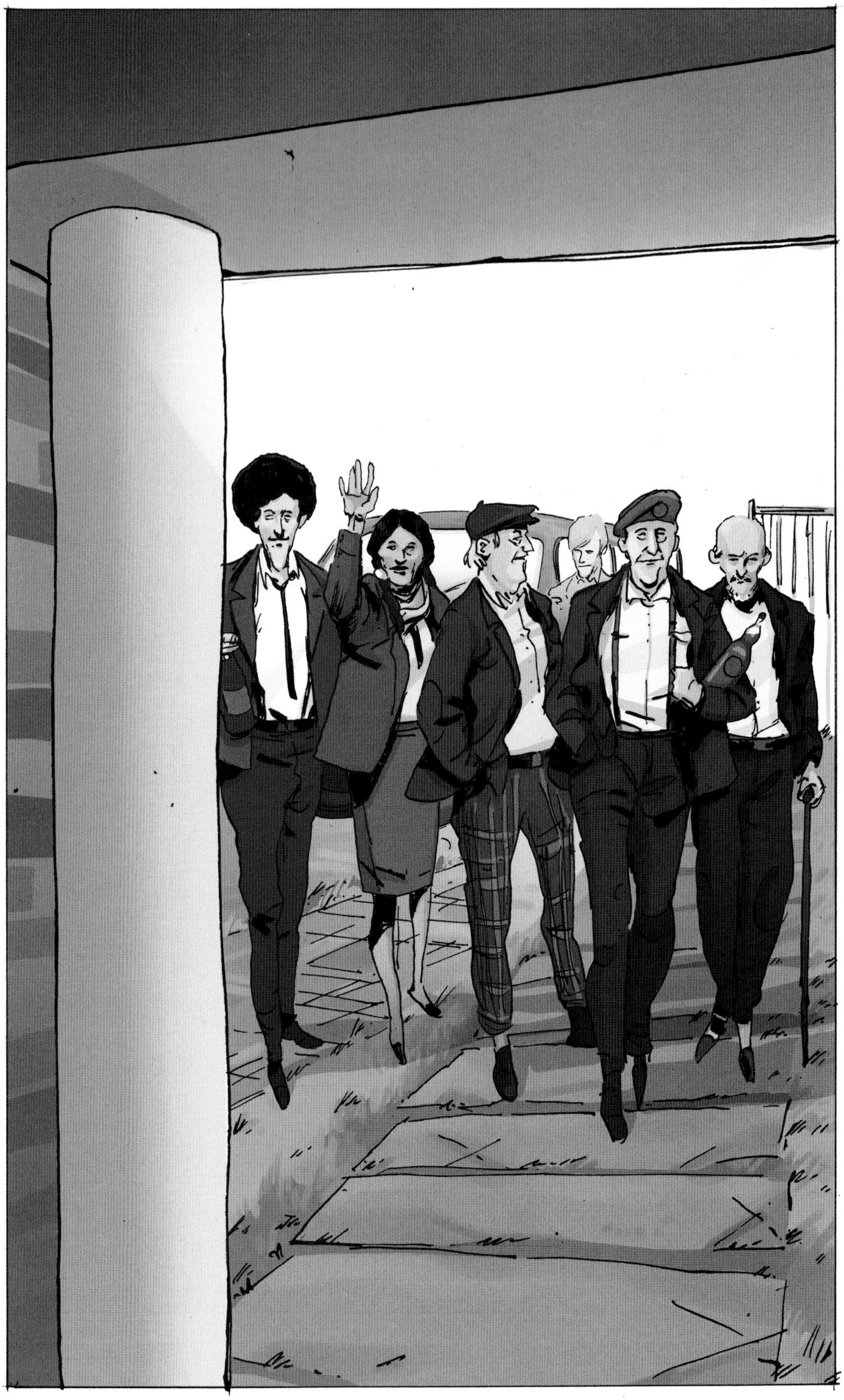

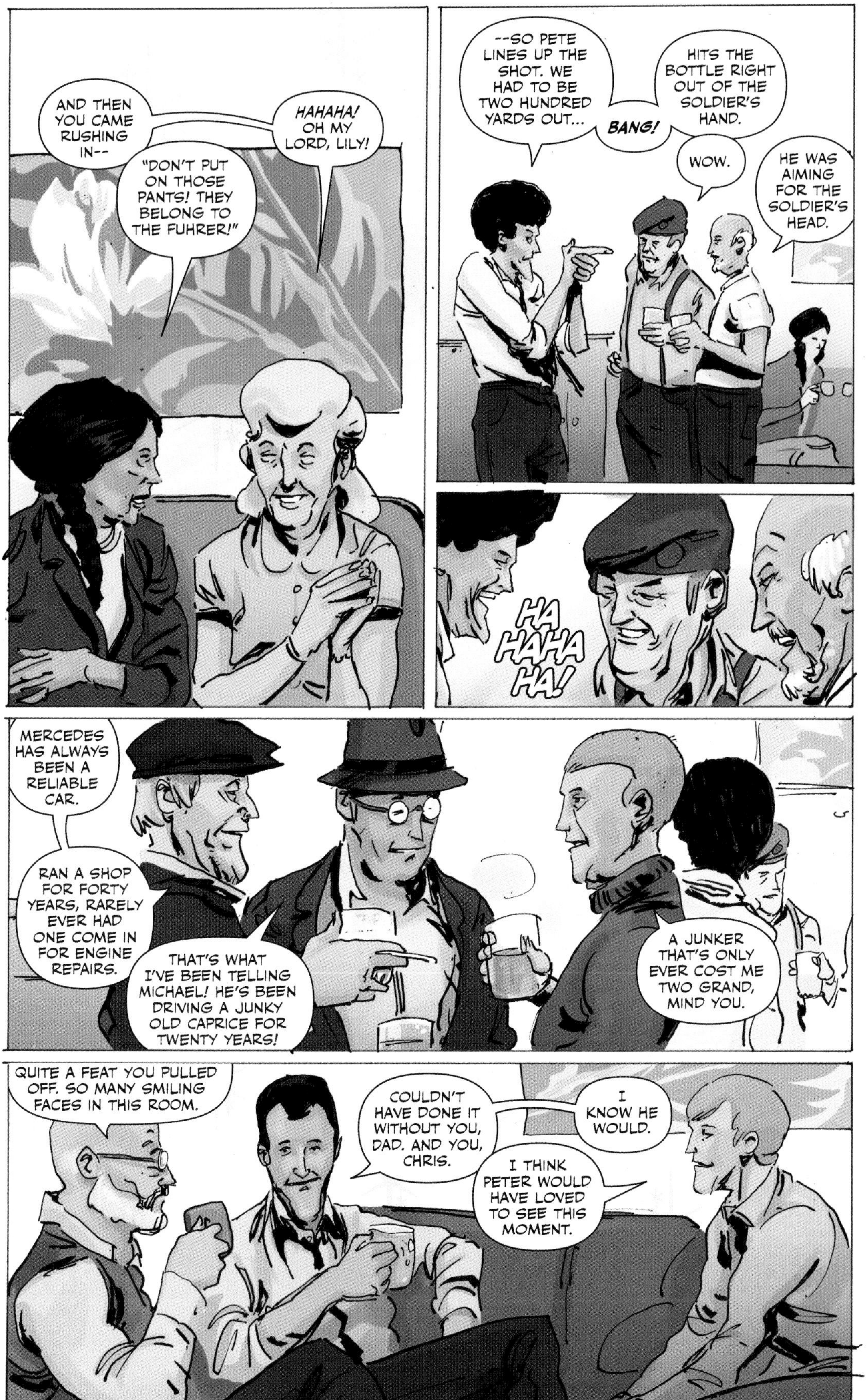
AND THEN YOU CAME RUSHING IN--
"DON'T PUT ON THOSE PANTS! THEY BELONG TO THE FUHRER!"
HAHAHA! OH MY LORD, LILY!
--SO PETE LINES UP THE SHOT. WE HAD TO BE TWO HUNDRED YARDS OUT...
BANG!
HITS THE BOTTLE RIGHT OUT OF THE SOLDIER'S HAND.
WOW.
HE WAS AIMING FOR THE SOLDIER'S HEAD.
HA HAHAHA HA!
MERCEDES HAS ALWAYS BEEN A RELIABLE CAR.
RAN A SHOP FOR FORTY YEARS, RARELY EVER HAD ONE COME IN FOR ENGINE REPAIRS.
THAT'S WHAT I'VE BEEN TELLING MICHAEL! HE'S BEEN DRIVING A JUNKY OLD CAPRICE FOR TWENTY YEARS!
A JUNKER THAT'S ONLY EVER COST ME TWO GRAND, MIND YOU.
QUITE A FEAT YOU PULLED OFF. SO MANY SMILING FACES IN THIS ROOM.
COULDN'T HAVE DONE IT WITHOUT YOU, DAD. AND YOU, CHRIS.
I THINK PETER WOULD HAVE LOVED TO SEE THIS MOMENT.
I KNOW HE WOULD.

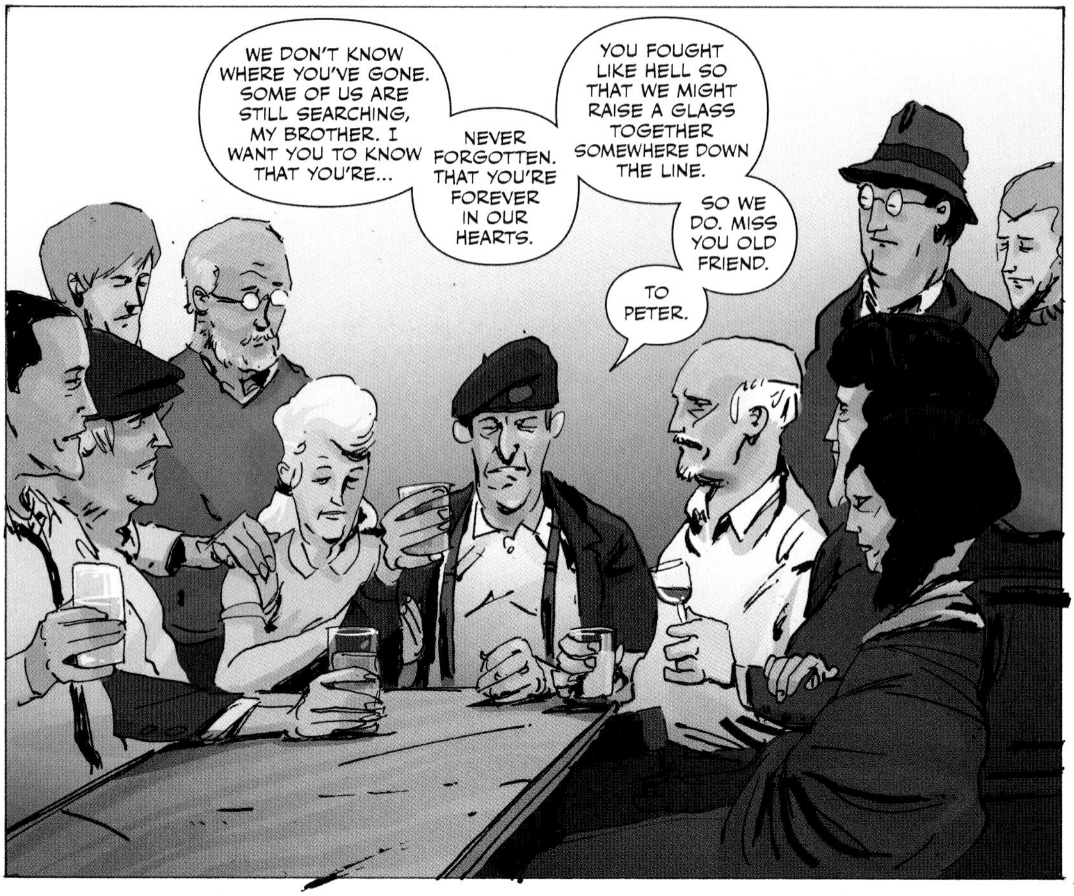
WE DON'T KNOW WHERE YOU'VE GONE. SOME OF US ARE STILL SEARCHING, MY BROTHER. I WANT YOU TO KNOW THAT YOU'RE...
NEVER FORGOTTEN. THAT YOU'RE FOREVER IN OUR HEARTS.
YOU FOUGHT LIKE HELL SO THAT WE MIGHT RAISE A GLASS TOGETHER SOMEWHERE DOWN THE LINE.
SO WE DO. MISS YOU OLD FRIEND.
TO PETER.

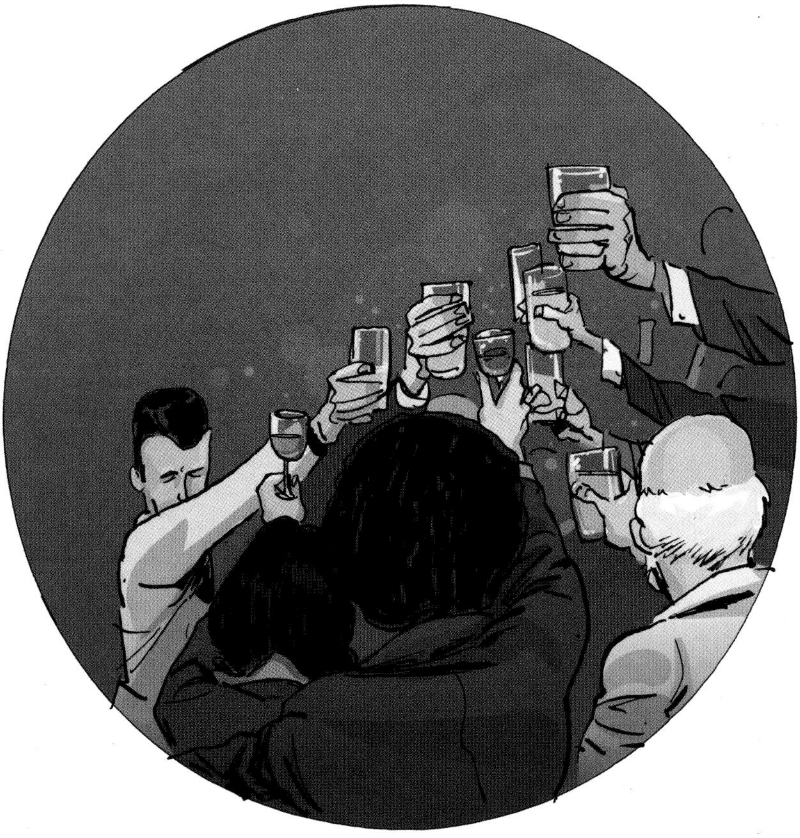

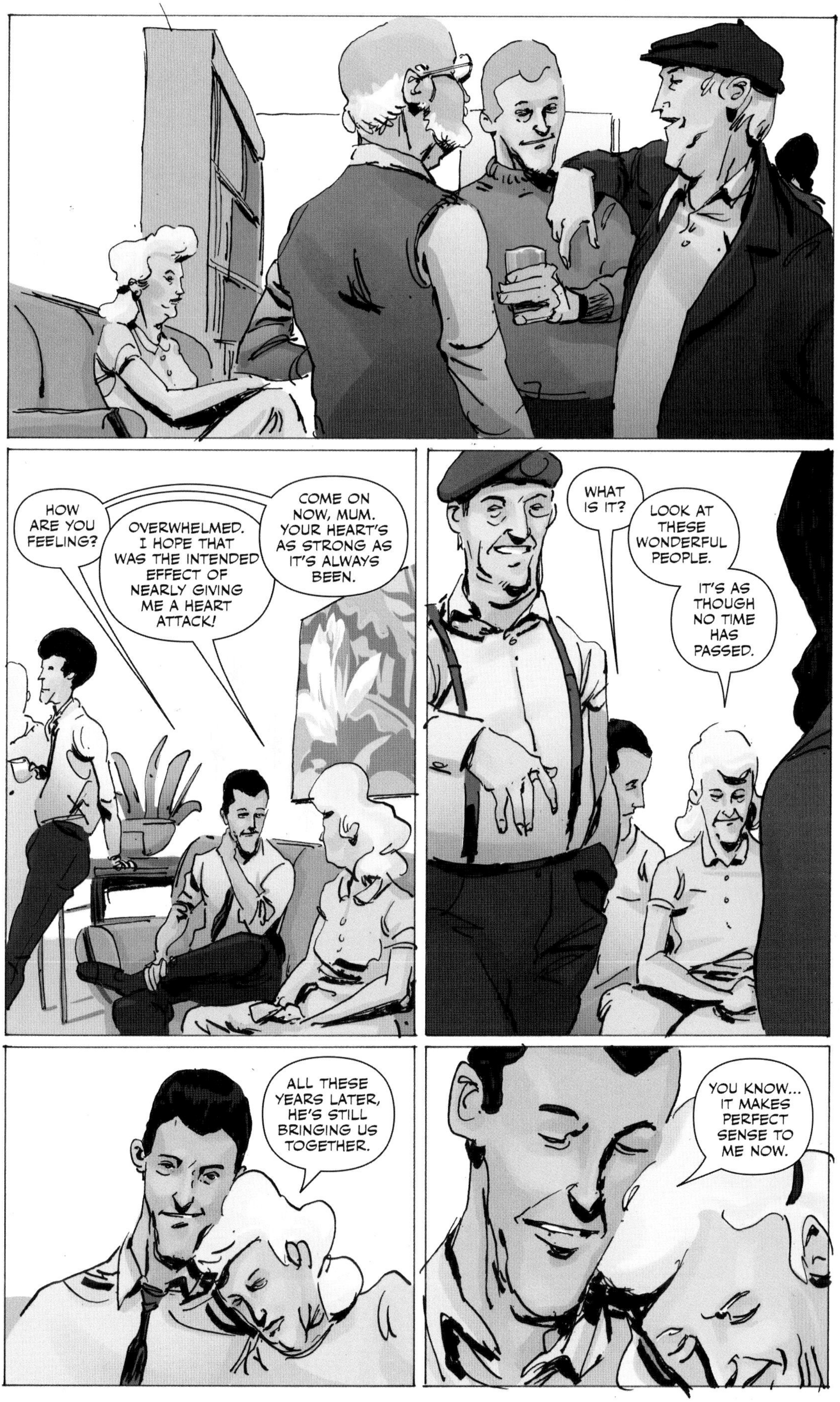
HOW ARE YOU FEELING?
OVERWHELMED. I HOPE THAT WAS THE INTENDED EFFECT OF NEARLY GIVING ME A HEART ATTACK!
COME ON NOW, MUM. YOUR HEART'S AS STRONG AS IT'S ALWAYS BEEN.
WHAT IS IT?
LOOK AT THESE WONDERFUL PEOPLE.
IT'S AS THOUGH NO TIME HAS PASSED.
ALL THESE YEARS LATER, HE'S STILL BRINGING US TOGETHER.
YOU KNOW... IT MAKES PERFECT SENSE TO ME NOW.

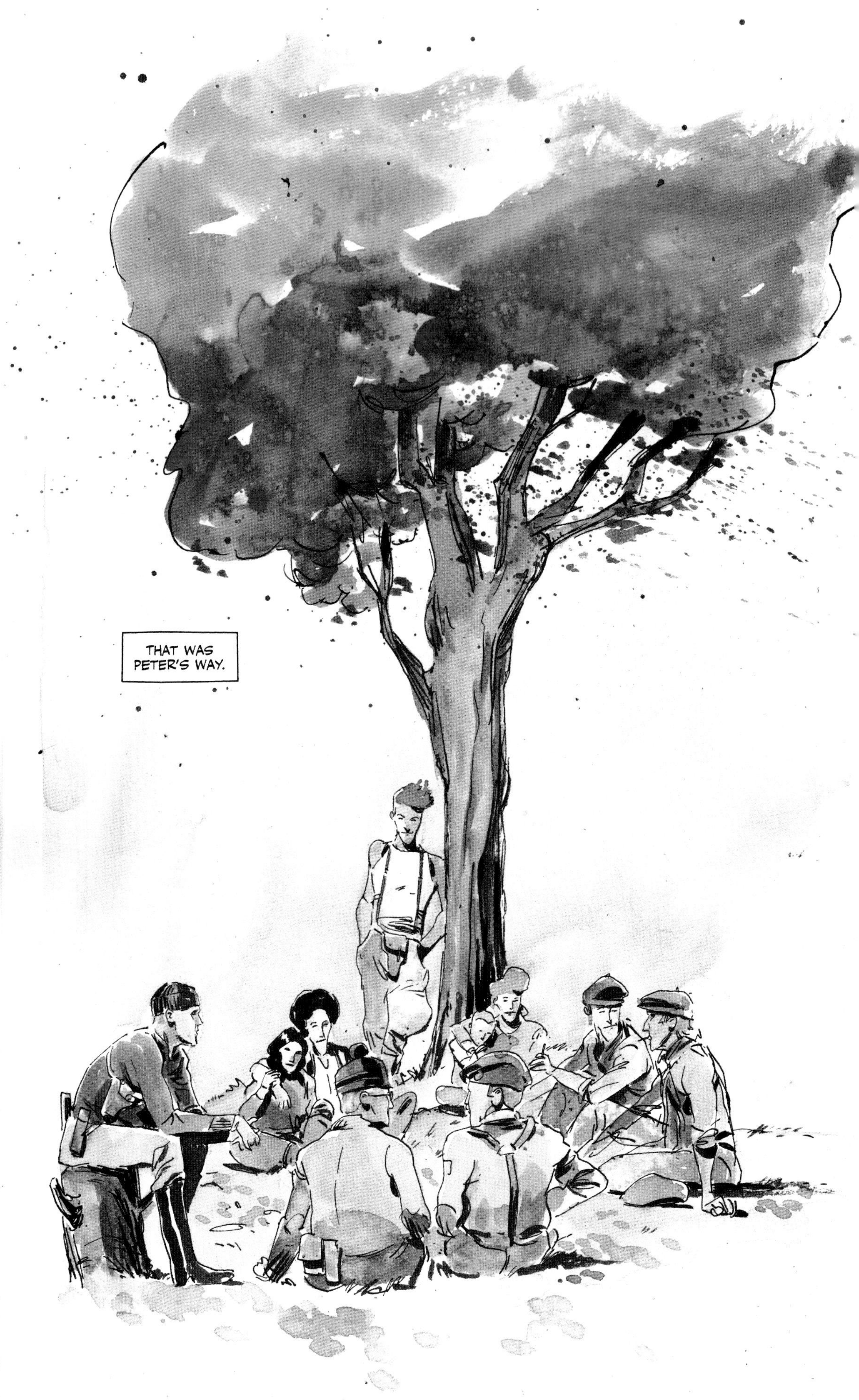
THAT WAS PETER'S WAY.

Get the Whole Story by Kurtis J. Wiebe & Tyler Jenkins

PETER PANZERFAUST
VOLUME ONE:
THE GREAT ESCAPE

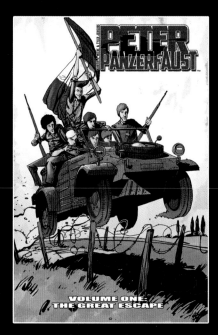

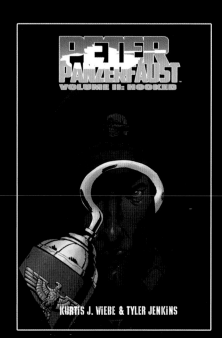

VOLUME ONE:
THE GREAT ESCAPE

Collects issues 1-5 plus
Special features

PETER PANZERFAUST
VOLUME II: HOOKED
KURTIS J. WIEBE & TYLER JENKINS

VOLUME TWO:
HOOKED

Collects issues 6-10 plus
Special features

PETER PANZERFAUST
VOLUME THREE:
CRY OF THE WOLF
KURTIS J. WIEBE & TYLER JENKINS

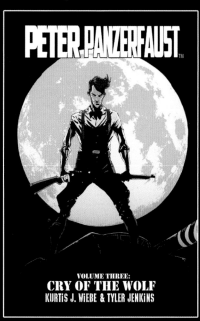

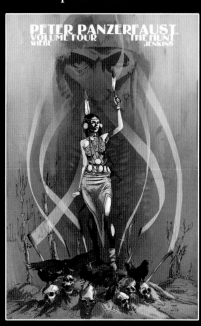

VOLUME THREE:
CRY OF THE WOLF

Collects issues 11-15 plus
Special features

PETER PANZERFAUST
VOLUME FOUR
THE HUNT
WIEBE
JENKINS

VOLUME FOUR:
THE HUNT

Collects issues 16-20 plus
Special features

On sale at finer comics shops everywhere!

only from image Shadowline

A Book For Every Reader...

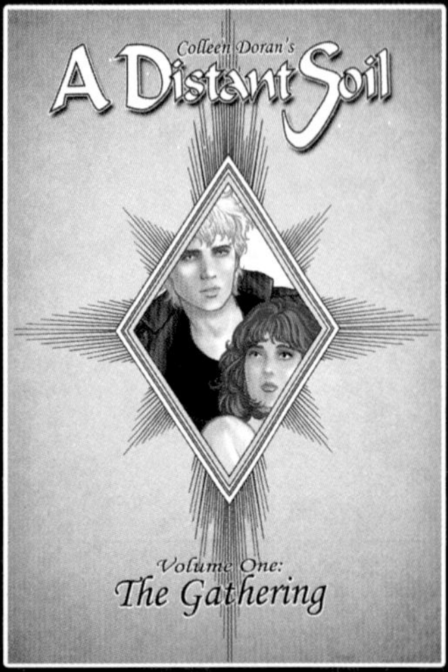
Colleen Doran's
A Distant Soil
Volume One:
The Gathering

COLLEEN DORAN

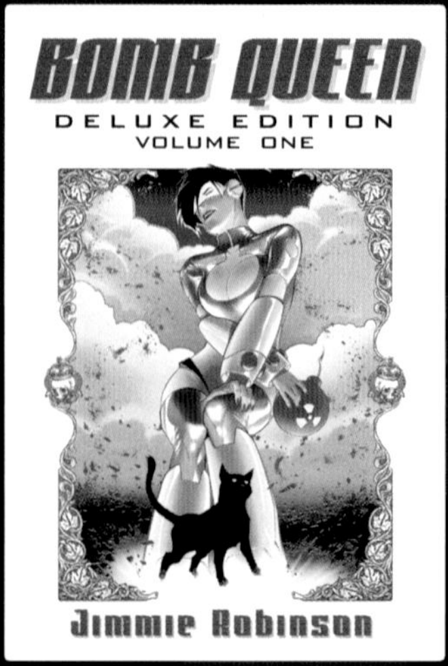
BOMB QUEEN
DELUXE EDITION
VOLUME ONE
Jimmie Robinson

JIMMIE ROBINSON

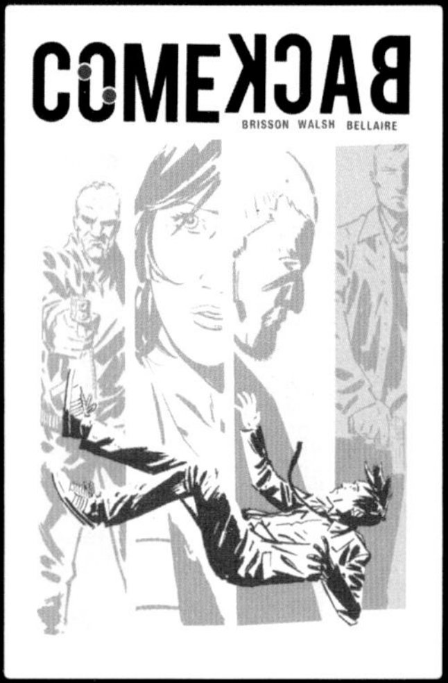
COMEBACK
BRISSON WALSH BELLAIRE

BRISSON/WALSH

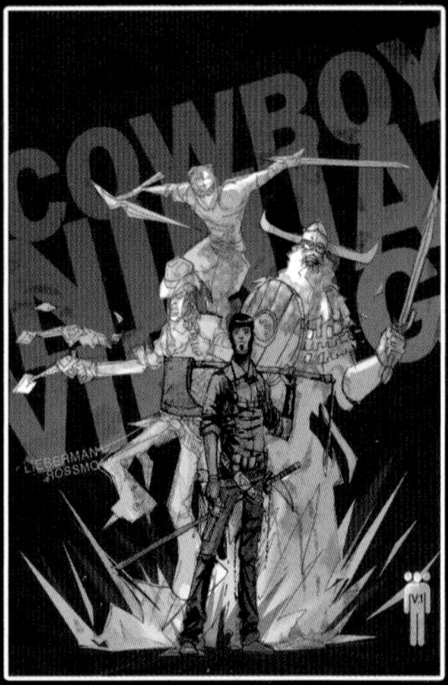
COWBOY
LIEBERMAN
ROSSMO

LIEBERMAN/ROSSMO

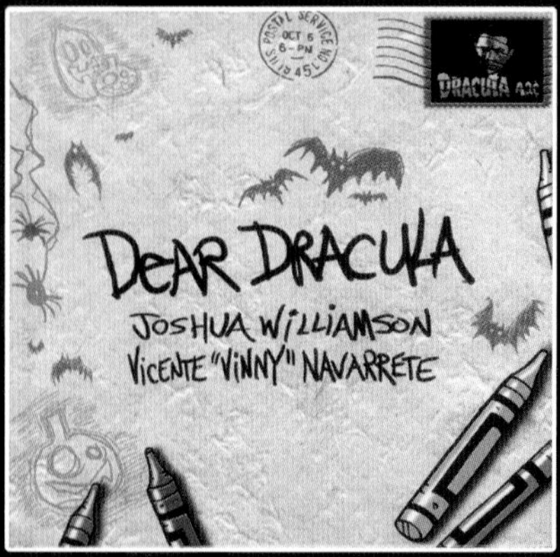
DEAR DRACULA
JOSHUA WILLIAMSON
VICENTE "VINNY" NAVARRETE

WILLIAMSON/NAVARRETE

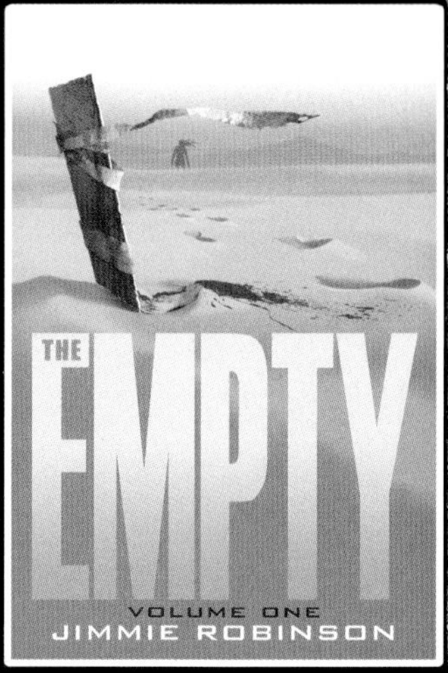
THE
EMPTY
VOLUME ONE
JIMMIE ROBINSON

JIMMIE ROBINSON

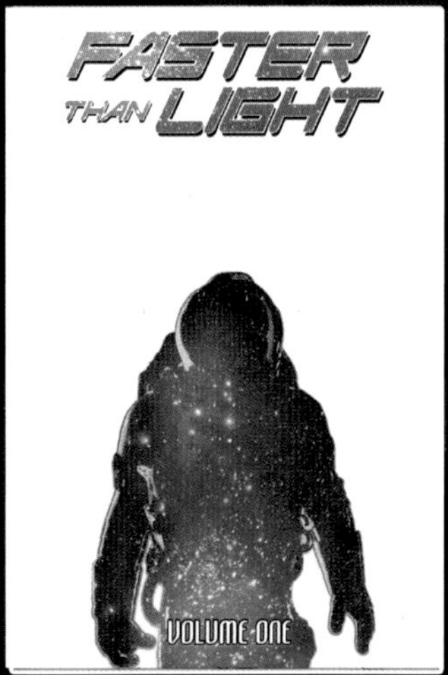
FASTER THAN LIGHT
VOLUME ONE

HABERLIN

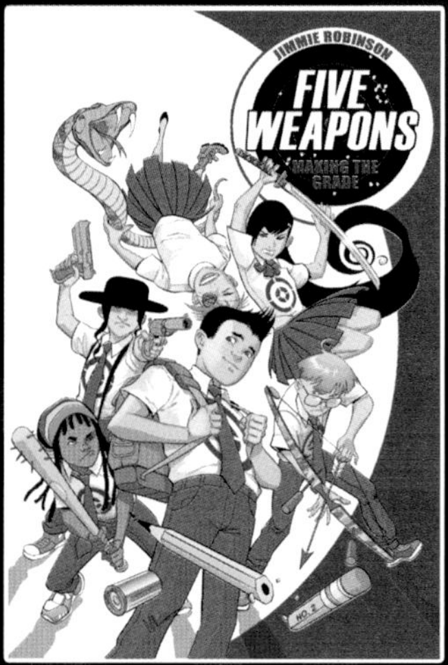
JIMMIE ROBINSON
FIVE WEAPONS
MAKING THE GRADE

JIMMIE ROBINSON

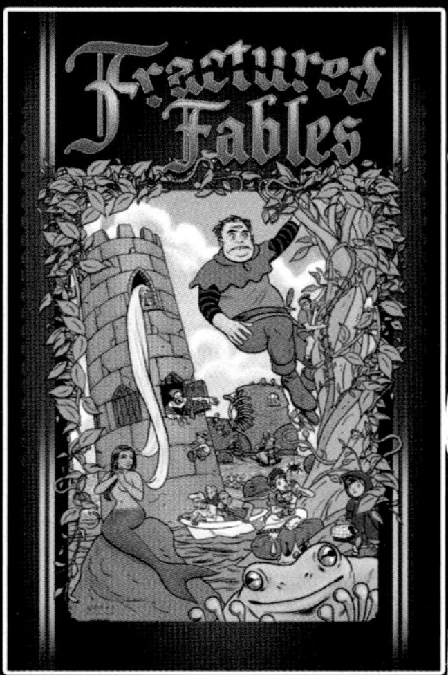
Fractured Fables

VARIOUS ARTISTS

THIS is Diversity... image® Shadowline®